SEVEN MONTHS OF UNRULY SINNERS

Politically-incorrect Crime

SIENNA RIDDLE

CW01659176

Copyright © 2019 Sienna Riddle

ISBN: 979-12-200-4737-1 (ebook)
979-12-200-4738-8 (paperback)

Cover design by Jane Dixon-Smith

Sienna Riddle has asserted her right under the Copyright, Designs and Patents Act, 1988, to be identified as the author of this work. All rights reserved. No part of this publication may be reproduced, stored, or transmitted in any form, or by any means electronic, mechanical or photocopying, recording or otherwise, without the prior permission of the copyright owner.

This is a work of fiction. Resemblance to persons living or dead is purely coincidental. Any long-standing institutions, establishments, organizations, agencies, public offices and countries mentioned, are portrayed in a fictitious manner and the characters involved are wholly imaginary. The opinions expressed are those of the characters and should not be confused with those of the author.

Website: www.siennariddle.com
Twitter: @siennariddle1

For Gianni, Vanessa, Mauro,
Matteo, Sara and Stefano

And of that second Kingdom will I sing
Wherein the human spirit doth purge itself,
And to ascend to heaven becometh worthy

Dante Alighieri
The Divine Comedy: Purgatory. Canto I

MARCH 1986

The seance

4 March

At the Tudor Tea Rooms on Witherington High Street, fifty-year-old funeral director Bertha Goodbody chooses a table for two by the window. The room is warmed by electric radiators and a March sunbeam bursting through the glass. Bertha sits on a chair where a gingham curtain provides shade, leaving florist Marigold Birch with the sun directly in her eyes. Marigold takes off her blue heavy wool jacket and places it on the back of her chair. Underneath she's wearing a long-sleeved white blouse buttoned at the cuffs. If the weather had been nicer, she would have worn a sleeveless blouse to show off her perfectly smooth bare arms. At forty-two years of age she prides herself on her soft unblemished skin and enjoys the compliments heaped upon her for looking less than her age.

Bertha studies the menu. 'Shall we have a pot of Indian Blend tea? Perhaps we should give the scones a miss, seeing as we have to watch the pennies now.'

Marigold nods agreement. The homemade scones with clotted cream and strawberry jam look deliciously tempting, but she's the guest and Bertha is paying the bill.

'Only two deaths this month,' Bertha complains. 'If it

continues like this, we'll both be out of business. However, looking on the bright side, quite a few in the old folks' home are on their way out. And I suppose we can count on a couple of accidents.'

Marigold nods again, used to Bertha's nonchalant and unfeeling chatter about the dead and dying. On the other hand, the deceased keep her in business.

'Luckily there are a few weddings coming up and I've got quite a few orders for flowers,' Marigold says enthusiastically.

'A fat lot of good that is to me.'

The tea arrives. They let it stand in the cups to cool. Bertha takes a teaspoon and stirs it while blowing into the cup. Marigold does the same. The tea room is empty and they don't have to worry about the noise of clinking teaspoons against cups. Both are deep in thought. Marigold notices Bertha is wearing her funeral parlour dress – the one she greets grieving relatives in – much too small, emerald green satin, bursting at the seams. She pictures Bertha's husband Norman straining to zip up his wife's dress every morning and stifles a laugh. Had Bertha been her best friend she might have suggested a bigger size, more flattering for her ample figure, but she kids herself she's losing weight and apparently prefers to subject Norman to the daily zipping routine in the name of vanity. How she wishes she could take her to the hairdressers to sort out her wild bottle-blonde hair and then to the beauty parlour to scrape off dark foundation which seems to have been applied with a trowel. But what Marigold hates most is the shiny blood-red lipstick smeared across her fleshy lips which has found its way into the wrinkles around her mouth. The only item of make-up Marigold can't find fault with is her emerald green metallic eye shadow which matches her dress. If only she *was* her best friend. But she's not. And, given Bertha's short temper, she doesn't want to run the gauntlet of her unwanted opinions stirring up a war of words. She's there to read the tea leaves.

'I think the tea is cool enough now and we can start,' Bertha says, replacing the teaspoon in the saucer. 'I invited you to read the tea leaves because I know you're psychic and we need to know if Cecilia jumped or was pushed. They say she was having an affair with the night watchman, not that it's anything to do with me.'

Marigold smiles. Bertha's curiosity stems from her obsession of poking her nose into everyone's business, including the dead.

They drink the tea down to the dregs. Bertha removes a tea leaf from her tongue. She pushes a newspaper with a grainy image of Cecilia Willows towards Marigold. It's dated 5 January 1986. The headline reads: 'DEAD WOMAN'S FOOT WALKS OFF BY ITSELF'. Then a sub-heading: 'Retired ballerina Cecilia Willows plunges to her death at the Wailing Willows Hotel'. The article goes on to mention bush telegraph and rumours of a local pig called Porkchop, who, according to investigators, could have eaten her foot.

Marigold leans towards Bertha and says quietly, 'They say James murdered her because he wasn't getting enough sex.'

Bertha smiles wickedly, her mouth pursed and tight. Her eyebrows rise knowingly. She waits while Marigold studies both their tea leaves.

'Well, did she fall or was she pushed?' Bertha asks.

Marigold tells her Cecilia's fall from a third-storey window at the family hotel may or may not be murder. The answer doesn't satisfy Bertha.

'You can't tell me it was an accident if her right foot went missing. Can you ask the tea leaves where it is? And if James Willows murdered his wife over her affair and the poison pen letters?'

Marigold tells Bertha there are too many questions all at once for the tea leaves to answer. Bertha agrees, saying they would need quite a few more pots of tea and she can't afford it with business being slack. Her eyebrows knit together in thought.

Bertha says, 'I think we should hold a seance with the cards. We can do it in the viewing room at the funeral parlour. It's perfect for calling up spirits. Constable Ernest Barnstable's lying there in his coffin for viewing, but he won't bother us seeing as he's dead. And my Norman will be out at the pub.'

Marigold replies she's not keen on sitting next to a dead man and Constable Barnstable, had he been alive, would have lectured them about dabbling with the occult.

'We have to search for the truth,' Bertha insists, offering Marigold a drink at the pub afterwards as an incentive.

At 8pm Marigold is at the Goodbody Funeral Home. Having delivered flowers there for thirteen years, she's able to visualise the viewing room with eyes shut – an access door leading to the garden through which relatives of the deceased enter; sombre dark wood panelling; a grey-and-red tree-of-life patterned carpet, probably bought at the flea market and a sideboard upon which stands a water carafe, three drinking glasses, two boxes of tissues and a pot of smelling salts. When grievers enter from the garden, in front of them is the coffin set against the wall, supported by a heavy metal frame. To complete the furnishings, three chairs – gold-painted, intricately carved and high-backed with red velvet upholstery – are positioned around a second-hand circular table – good quality and painted white by Jeppo the odd-job man. Marigold remembers the majestic chairs being the centre of a violent argument between Bertha and Norman. *He* wanted six to make the room more homely but *she* insisted more than three would encourage grievers to hang around and chat. Bertha's calculation was based on three scenarios – one person feeling faint, a relative to administer smelling salts and an extra chair for any further emergency. In the end Bertha triumphed, being an expert at having the last word.

Removing a vase of chrysanthemums from the white table, Bertha writes out cards with letters of the alphabet, plus two for YES and NO, then numbered cards zero to nine. Watched by Marigold, she arranges them in a wide circle and in the middle places a drinking glass turned upside down. While Bertha's organising small candles around the room, Marigold looks into Constable Ernest Barnstable's coffin. He looks at peace and, at fifty-two years old, is still a good-looking man. Seeing as the constable's mother had insisted on him being interred in his police uniform and wanted him to look good for viewing, Norman had camouflaged his paunch by placing his hands and helmet over it. The rest was done with morticians' make-up – a light touch of the brush to slim down his jowls and double chin and a fine dusting of blusher on Ernest's pale plump cheeks. His hair had been combed the way his mother wanted it. She said his greying temples and receding hairline should be left alone as natural grey gave him an aura of authority. The whole effect pleased her.

Marigold whispers, 'Rest in peace, Constable,' and says a prayer for him.

Bertha calls her. She's finished lighting the candles. After turning out the main lights, they find the room a bit too dark and open the door leading to the garden through which a dim light shines from a downstairs window. Sitting at the table, they both place an index finger on the overturned glass.

'Hurry up and get on with it,' Bertha says impatiently.

Marigold asks, 'Is anybody there?' She has to repeat it several times before the glass starts to move.

'Who are you and where are you?' she asks, her heart beating faster.

The glass moves slowly to the letters to spell out, 'Swinging from gallows'.

'Are you pushing the glass, Marigold?' Bertha asks, her nostrils widening and lips tightening.

'Certainly not. It's moving by itself.'

'Ask him again who he is.'

'Who are you?'

The glass slowly spells out 'Headless Hannah's husband'.

Bertha booms, 'That's ridiculous. I don't believe a word.'

Marigold says, 'Don't you remember? There *was* a woman found in a farmhouse outside Witherington in the fifties. Her husband decapitated her with an axe. He was hanged.'

'Vaguely. I can't remember every dead body.'

Marigold shivers. 'Shall we stop the seance? We're talking to a murderer.'

'Nonsense,' Bertha says. 'He's probably having a little joke. Ask him about Cecilia's missing foot.'

Marigold complies. 'Where's Cecilia's foot?'

The cards spell out 'Rattling bones and headless chickens'.

Bertha loses her patience and calls him a bloody liar. Marigold warns her not to insult a spirit but it's too late. A sudden draught whirls around them and blows out a few candles.

Bertha is spooked. 'There's an icy wind and I can smell death.'

'It must be coming from the drains. Or perhaps the coffin,' Marigold says, wanting to believe her own words.

'I can tell the difference between a dead body and a drain smell,' Bertha snaps.

Marigold is reluctant to continue. 'Shall we stop? We shouldn't be calling up the dead. Reverend Pottering says it's against the Church's teachings.'

'Certainly not. We have to investigate. Ask him whose bones they are.'

'Are you still there?' Marigold's voice is shaking.

The glass moves again to spell out, 'Want to roast her alive'.

The spirit manifests himself above Bertha in a red fiery cloud. He's wearing a yellow-and-black checked shirt and a rubber butcher's apron. Burning coals sit in his sparse hair. An axe hangs over Bertha's head.

The temperature in the room starts to rise. Marigold shrieks, 'Look up!' Bertha does as she's told. She sees the axe-man and the axe and the fiery cloud. Her mouth opens. Her finger falls off the glass. She starts to scream that her head is burning. Marigold jumps up and tries to drag Bertha from her chair but she's rigid and heavy. The glass spins around the table of its own accord, out of control. In the vortex, candles flicker and letters of the alphabet fly off the table. The glass picks up speed. Bertha is hit by a candle and tries to get under the table to no avail. She jumps up and heads for the door when Marigold shouts, 'Get out into the garden!' The glass takes off and leaves the table. It flies across the room to shatter against the wall by the door just missing Bertha by inches. Marigold watches helpless, transfixed as headless-Hannah's husband chases Bertha around the room. She cowers at the side of Ernest's coffin, terrified for Bertha, but also for herself.

On her third lap of the carpet, Bertha struggles to breathe. Her bosom heaves. Face red, eyes bulging. Blood pressure rising. Coals on the spirit's head burning brighter. Bertha stumbles and loses a shoe. It's too late to steady herself. She's off balance, arms flailing and still running. Marigold sees her precipitate headlong towards Ernest's coffin. A thud as her head hits the sharp metal corner, like a log of wood being split by an axe. The metal stand rocks and shudders. The spirit fades away. Constable Ernest Barnstable sits up in his coffin and asks, 'What's all the noise about? Can't a body rest in peace?'

All Marigold remembers before sliding into oblivion is the spirit vanishing, leaving her in semi-darkness and a lot of blood oozing from Bertha's skull.

Someone is calling Marigold back to consciousness. The voice says, 'Wake up, Marigold.' She opens her eyes. She's lying on the carpet. Constable Barnstable is sitting next to her.

'I'm sorry to say Bertha's dead. Let it be a lesson to you for messing with the devil,' he admonishes.

Marigold's nerves are shot. Tears prick her eyes and start to fall. She says she's devastated and terribly sorry.

He offers her a box of tissues. 'Dry your eyes and go and tell Norman his wife's dead. You can tell him it was an accident, no need to mention the devil.' He fades away leaving her sobbing and grieving for Bertha.

While Bertha is lying dead in the funeral parlour, her widower stands at the counter of the Bull and Bullocks pub ordering a round of drinks for a group of five men sitting in the bar. It's warm inside and Norman removes his black coat to reveal casual clothing underneath. He's glad to get away from Bertha for a while but he might take a packet of salt and vinegar crisps back for her. He relaxes. The quaint, typically English rural pub offers a warm haven at the end of a long, hard, cold day and a place where people can gossip and slag off their enemies in peace. Pete the landlord considers it a service to the community. He pulls six pints and takes them to Norman's table where the locals are discussing Cecilia Willows' missing foot. Mystery and death keep their minds away from the daily slog and Pete enjoys their banter.

'What's your opinion, Pete? Was it eaten by a wild animal or cut off with a knife?' The question comes from a young farmhand with ruddy complexion. Pete never lets himself get drawn into their arguments. People sometimes get offended and it's bad for business.

'Tell me what *you* think,' he says, passing the ball back.

The farmhand playfully nudges middle-aged farmer Bert Wormsley, sitting on his right. 'I think her husband fed it to Porkchop.'

They see Bert's jaw tighten. He says, 'Mind your mouth, son. My Porkchop doesn't eat human meat. He's no ordinary pig.'

The four of them sense Bert's irritation. They don't blame him. A word too many has ruined more than one business in Witherington. Bert sinks back in his chair and studies a stain on his overalls.

A short silence precedes a debate about whether James Willows might have had good reason to push his wife from the window of the Wailing Willows Hotel, given her various affairs and bad temper. With them is a middle-aged artist – a kind of intellectual hippie-type – who likes to dig dirt with the local farmhands to be able to impart his extensive knowledge of the world and its affairs to the deprived population of a literary backwater. A self-proclaimed reader of cowpats, he's known locally as Artsy-fartsy Weirdo to everyone but himself. Feeding on their superstition, he questions the coincidence of Cecilia dying on her seventieth birthday at almost the same hour she'd been born seventy years before. He suggests they play the lottery using her birthday numbers and then changes his mind mentioning black magic afoot. 'There's evil spirits drifting around the hotel for sure. It's most likely haunted by a couple of James's evil descendants from Tudor or Elizabethan times.' He quotes the willow trees wailing in the wind on the fatal night and the full moon highlighting the dark gothic turrets.

The others guffaw and ask if he'd been drunk that night as the moon had been hidden behind clouds and there were no turrets at the hotel. They question James Willows' sins and the likelihood he's still carrying a flame for Tallulah Millstone, the woman he jilted before marrying Cecilia.

Intellectual Artsy-fartsy Weirdo's flight of fancy can't be stopped. He says, 'Tallulah Millstone is dabbling in anti-Christ, anti-Christian cryonics and the moon's not even aligned with Jupiter or Mars. In my opinion, the old Bluebell Vicarage is haunted by all those chickens she's decapitating.'

The others burst into laughter.

The pub door opens and a few dead leaves blow in. An old man with brown and grey dishevelled hair, dirty faded black trousers and an ancient brown tweed jacket with patches approaches their table.

'What'll you have, Jeppo?' Norman asks.

'The usual whisky, thanks.'

Norman signals to Pete who brings a glass with a couple of measures in it.

Jeppo says, 'You're a good man, Norman, but you have to go home. I smell blood. The devil's at work in the parlour.'

Norman laughs, 'Ha ha, do you mean Bertha? She's a devil all right.'

Jeppo says, 'I hear drip, drip, drip.'

'Is this another of your doomsday predictions? I'm not really in the mood. It's probably a dripping tap.'

Jeppo shakes his head, downs his whisky and thanks Norman. He says he's going home and gets up from his chair. He looks at Norman and says, 'She won't need those crisps tonight.'

Norman is surprised. He doesn't remember telling Jeppo about the crisps. But he's not superstitious and is sure there's a logical explanation behind it.

The debate about Tallulah Millstone and the headless chickens continues for about an hour – which they will all recall later, along with Jeppo's words.

Before 10pm, the pub door opens and a cold wind blows round the room. In rushes a red-eyed Marigold, distraught and calling Norman's name.

The day of Cecilia's death

Two months earlier

Cecilia Willows rummaged impatiently through an old trunk in a first floor room of the Wailing Willows Hotel. It was 3 January, her seventieth birthday.

She pulled out a long white silk and tulle sleeveless ballet dress she'd worn forty years ago in *Swan Lake*. Removing it from the cellophane bag, she quickly stripped off her clothes and slipped into it. The room was cold and there was ice on the outside window ledge but it was of little consequence and she hardly noticed the chill, being overjoyed she could still get into the dress. Admiring herself in the full-length mirror and stretching her arms out like wings, she saw a graceful swan, barely noticing the thin flabby arms of an old woman or her grey hair. Throwing her ballet pumps back in the trunk as they were too tight, she searched for one of her props from a previous ballet performance – her magic wand. It was missing. Rushing barefoot down the stairs, she slipped into the cleaning cupboard and pulled out a long-handled pink feather duster which would suffice to impress James. At the beginning of their marriage, James had paid her a lot of attention. He'd often complimented her on her golden locks and pretty dresses. But now he hardly noticed what she was wearing. This morning he hadn't even mentioned her seventieth birthday. Stewing for most of the day while awaiting compliments and at least a 'Happy Birthday, dear', she decided it was time to jog his memory.

Waving the pink feather duster, she pirouetted into the living room in her bare feet.

'Look at me, James. Am I still beautiful in my ballet dress?'

James, sitting in front of an open fire, looked up from his newspaper and breathed a sigh of annoyance. Cecilia's soft American accent that forty years ago sounded like a siren song had turned into a monotonous drawl. Once upon a time, her conversation was bright and full of laughter, but had since faded away. And the lithe young body that had once led him to paradise was now slack and lifeless in bed.

Cecilia pirouetted around the settee. 'Do you remember how much we were in love? For my thirtieth *birthday* you bought me a lovely pair of diamond earrings? For my fortieth a ring? And for my fiftieth a bracelet.'

He said, 'That was a long time ago. You can't live in the past forever.'

'You used to call me your princess when I was in *Swan Lake*. You said I was beautiful.'

James looked her up and down. 'For God's sake, Cecilia, you're no longer a spring chicken. You look ridiculous in that ballet dress.'

'You once said it was stunning. You said my beauty would be eternal,' she said sharply.

'I don't remember saying such a thing.'

'You've forgotten today's my birthday!'

Cecilia's rage came to a boil. She looked at James's tight mouth, his liver-spotted hands, the soup stain on his tie, then struck him with her furry pink magic wand and pushed him from the chair. He fell head first onto the carpet and seized her ankle in a vice. She hit him with the feather duster until he let go. Screaming and whirling, her bare feet barely touching the carpet, she flew down the corridor and up the stairs to the hotel's third floor. James grabbed the poker and ran after her, stopping to get his breath at the top of the stairs on each landing.

Darting into a room, Cecilia placed a chair under an open window and climbed up onto the windowsill after dusting it with the pink feather duster. She saw the outside window ledge was icy and looked across the fields to the cattle farm. Then her mind went blank. Was she there to clean the windows or just to admire the bucolic view? Someone entered the room and grabbed her ankle. She kicked out at the person behind. The hand let go. She tottered forwards and slipped off the window ledge into an empty space, feet first, arms and legs flailing. No time to scream. In those two seconds she knew she was going to die.

Cecilia remembered no more until she got up, leaving her dead body on the hard path bordering the lawn.

The shock at leaving her body was nothing compared to the mortification she felt looking down at her corpse. Somehow her long tulle ballet dress had flown up over her head revealing skinny legs and yesterday's knickers – white bloomers, yellow with age, which she often wore in bed with James, her red frilly ones being reserved for the night watchman. Her fanny would soon be the talk of the whole of Witherington and it would have been better had she not worn any. She could almost hear her mother turn in her grave and say, 'Make sure you put on clean underwear before you go out, you never know when you might have an accident.' Mother had a thing about someone turning up on the doorstep and saying, 'Your daughter's in hospital with dirty knickers.'

In her state of limbo, Cecilia wandered aimlessly around the garden looking for James and wondering why he wasn't out looking for her. Feeling confused, she sat on the roof picking off damp moss while on the ground a shadow moved towards her lifeless body.

James regained his senses and found himself lying in a cold third floor bedroom against the leg of a chair. Rubbing the back of his head, he found blood on his fingers. Had he had a dizzy turn because of his blood pressure? He looked around for Cecilia. She usually helped him when he wasn't well. Had she gone to call the doctor?

Much later he lay in bed wondering why neither Cecilia nor the doctor had materialised. He asked himself if she'd gone out shopping without giving him a second thought. He dug up past memories about her spending. The money wasted on clothes. The sofa, bought during one of her creative moods, which gave him backache. An ugly black art deco mirror which he hated. In the bedroom, the gold-painted exquisitely carved olive briarwood rococo headboard was majestic, but so high it gave him a crick in the neck when reading. He told her he'd have preferred something less grand and more comfy, as his mother considered luxury-buying was a waste of hard-earned money. Cecilia called them both misers. Because of her spending, he'd been forced to forego some repairs to the hotel. Its decline had been a bitter blow to his idea of living out his last years in his dream palace, where, in its heyday, he'd danced with the rich and famous.

A further waste of money had been the nuclear shelter built in the back garden in the sixties. Cecilia's reasoning was, 'You never know when those crazy Russians are going to blow us into space'. He let her get on with it and when the bomb never happened, they were stuck with living on tinned food for months. Then they discovered the nuclear shelter had increased the rateable value of their property. The only thing he and Cecilia agreed upon was about the government bleeding them dry to cover costs for the emergency services, four-minute warning sirens, upgrading of the War Rooms and the building of nuclear shelters for high-ranking military and government officials.

The lack of agreement between Cecilia and himself was present in many forms. One example was their personal washing line. Cecilia insisted it be erected in the garden somewhere, but James was against it as the guests would be able to see his smalls. Ignoring her tantrums, he decided to place it behind the garden shed, which in any case was not long enough to hide it all and shrubs would need to be planted to hide the sheets. He asked her what type of washing line she wanted. There were two options – a long line between two poles or a compact circular revolving one. She opted for the long one, so that at least one or two pairs of sheets could be hung out at one time. She insisted on a second parallel line so she could hang out his shirts, socks, smalls and nightwear as well. James said he didn't want the garden looking like a Neapolitan street laundry and insisted on two circular rotating ones which could be folded down to take up less space. No, she preferred the Neapolitan street laundry so she could run between the sheets and sniff their perfume. She said she wouldn't be able to run between the sheets on the circular rotating one unless she wanted to hang herself.

In moments of deep despair, James wished he'd married beautiful, sensitive, lively Tallulah instead of Cecilia. For the past forty years he'd regretted leaving Tallulah crying in Paris after the war because he hadn't had the courage to break off his engagement with Cecilia. On the other hand, Tallulah was now sixty-eight years old with a reputation in Witherington of being a sour old lady.

The next morning James awoke to find the bed empty on Cecilia's side. He wandered around the garden listening to the crunch of frost under his slippers and admiring the snowdrops, almost forgetting he was supposed to be searching for his wife. When he stumbled upon Cecilia's corpse, she was lying face down with her ballet dress up over her waist and her right foot had been severed in a messy way.

The constable's passing

2 March

On a cold January morning about two months ago when he was still alive, Constable Ernest Barnstable had driven to the Wailing Willows Hotel following a gabbled call from James Willows about his wife Cecilia being found dead in the garden minus her right foot. Ernest's elation at being involved in helping solve an accident or possible murder was short-lived when, upon returning to the station, he received a formal letter informing him he was being relocated to nearby Rottingham Police Station. Witherington Police Station, his second home for over thirty years and a listed Victorian jewel was being closed down. The letter quoted the merging and modernisation of the police force.

The day of Ernest's death started off badly – historic files in boxes, no closure on Cecilia's death, no recognition of his long service and loyal duty and no consideration for closing down a piece of England.

Ernest shared a semi-detached house with his mother. Situated not far from the town centre, it was his haven at the end of each day. It had a small tidy garden. The neighbours were nice with well-behaved children. The odd dog barked, but not so much as to disturb. And it was only a short bike ride to the police station where he'd been working for as long as he could remember.

Sitting at the breakfast table, Ernest watched his mother take his eggs, bacon, beans and sausages out of the frying pan and place them on his plate.

'Thanks, Mum, it's a good start to a cold day at the station.'

She smiled. 'Only the best for you, dear. The eggs and sausages are fresh from the Wormsleys' farm.' The kettle whistled and she quickly turned it off and poured the water into the teapot. Fussing around him, she made sure not to spill a drop of tea on his saucer. Ernest sipped it and made a mental note to buy her some flowers and a voucher to have her hair done for her birthday next week.

After making sure Ernest was happy, his mother began to steam the creases from his police jacket. 'I'll be down at the station later to give you a hand to pack up the last things,' she said running her hand over a sleeve to make sure it wouldn't crease under the iron. Ernest nodded, grateful she cared so much. He put on his jacket and overcoat and kissed his mother lovingly on the cheek before leaving. He knew she was watching him from the living room window as he mounted his bike and rode down the street towards the police station. Passing a group of young children larking about, Ernest was reminded of when his mother used to take him to Sunday school each week. It was here he learned the Ten Commandments, a few of which had served him through his working life and given him good moral values to share with others. His mother had been instrumental in pushing him in the right direction and sharing his achievements joyfully.

Riding along the High Street, Ernest nodded to passers-by. Having lived in Witherington all his life, he knew the honest, the dishonest and the names of kids to keep an eye on. When they were in trouble, he reasoned and tried to give each one a sense of moral values. He struggled to teach respect. It was an uphill climb. Ernest was often tempted to hand out a clout, but always resisted and a good talking-to often worked. And when it didn't work, he went to talk to their parents. It wasn't like the big city where people soon lost their identity, dignity and sense of community. He knew he'd probably enjoy his new job. He knew the Rottingham police, although it might be a bit embarrassing seeing Babs again more than thirty years after they'd sworn eternal love when they were too young to know better. No doubt since then they'd both changed and put on a bit of weight. She was now a married woman with a grandson, so he'd heard, and he was just a middle-aged single man.

Stepping into the police station, Ernest shivered as the cold air met him. Ignoring the boxes containing umpteen years of police history, he headed for the kitchen to make a cup of tea. He turned on the tap to find a very slow drip. Shortly after, Matt the plumber arrived, clumping up the steps and through the front door.

'You must have read my mind, Matt, nothing's working,' said Ernest.

'Well actually, I just popped in to see how you are and to give you a goodbye present.'

'I'm only going down the road to Rottingham.'

'Yes I know, but I wanted to show my appreciation – since you saved my little Pam's life.'

'A long time ago, Matt. She must have her own family by now.'

'Not yet. She's living in the big city. You know what young people are like, they want to enjoy themselves.'

'I hope she finds a nice man,' Ernest said.

'She should have stayed in Witherington, there's many a nice lad here.'

'You can't stop progress and there's not much of a life for her here, if we're being realistic.'

'I suppose you're right.' Matt handed Ernest a package. 'You can open it now if you want. It's freezing in here.'

Ernest opened it and took out a red, white and green striped hand-knitted hat and scarf. 'Thanks, Matt. I suppose your wife knitted them. It's great to know there are still some decent folks around. I'll miss you all.'

'You're the institutional memory of this place and tomorrow it'll all be history. But we'll all remember you. It's thanks to you we can all sleep soundly in our beds.'

'It'll be hard settling into something new. I'm getting on in years and times have changed. My health isn't what it used to be.'

'You'll soon fit in,' said Matt.

Ernest sat down at his desk, thinking of all the pending cases he'd never wind up. 'It won't be the same. I've been here a lifetime, building up trust in the neighbourhood. It's the personal touch that counts, not someone on the other end of a telephone telling people to call this or that number.'

'Times are changing fast,' Matt replied.

Ernest put his head in his hands and allowed himself a few words that weren't ruled by his loyal duty to keep all emotion under wraps. 'I won't sleep tonight,' was all he said.

Matt put a comforting hand on his shoulder.

Ernest's throat tightened. His head felt light and dizzy. He gasped for air and panic overtook him. A stab of pain shot down his arm. He clutched his chest and slumped forwards in his chair, his face slamming the desk. Matt picked up the phone to call for an ambulance, but the line was dead. He left Ernest and ran across to the council office at the town hall and shouted and hammered on the counter and demanded an ambulance but by the time it arrived it was too late. Ernest had gone.

A crowd gathered. They watched silently as Constable

Barnstable was carried out of the police station on a stretcher covered by a sheet. Everything else seemed trivial in comparison. Ernest's mother screamed the house down upon being told gently of her son's death. She drew all the curtains and took a bad turn. The only thing she could console herself with was that he died in his comfortable wooden chair – the chair he sat in every morning after breakfast in his home from home at the police station.

At Ernest's funeral, Reverend Pontius Pottering lauded Ernest's dedication to duty, his heroism and his untimely demise, while the community demanded to know who was to blame for causing him to go in the prime of his life. The gossips were silent. There was nothing they could slight him for.

A final gesture came from Matt, who insisted the hand-knitted hat and scarf be put in Ernest's coffin. Before it was closed, he whispered, 'To keep you warm in the afterlife. God bless you, Ernest.'

After the funeral, Ernest's mother wandered down to the police station and ran her fingers over his chair, imagining he was still sitting there. It was a chair which had seen history and served her darling courageous son through thick and thin until one week before her seventy-third birthday. No more ironing his police uniform and making him breakfast every morning. Ernest had been caring and good company since his father's death. Although she'd miss him, his presence would be with her every day in every room – in the kitchen looking over her shoulder while she made the tea; in the living room smiling from photos in his police uniform; and in every other place in the house. In time the pain would lessen, but it would never pass completely. Lovey, her blue budgerigar, was good company and she fussed over him and made sure his cage was cleaned every day because Ernest had given him to her on her birthday last year. She talked to Lovey and let him fly round the living room while she watched television. He seemed to like the television too and would settle on her shoulder and nuzzle her cheek and give her a kiss. When Lovey was next to her she felt Ernest's presence.

Mind games

At Bluebell Vicarage, Tallulah Millstone stood in front of her Victorian dressing table mirror and dusted light-coloured powder over her face. She was proud of her skin – an alabaster white with wrinkles she passed off as laughter lines. At sixty-eight years of age, her tall slim frame had begun to put on a tiny bit of weight, but not so much as anyone might notice. Each morning, she applied her make-up and considered the mirror as a picture frame in which she was creating a self-portrait. She experimented with different-coloured lipsticks to see how to make her portrait more beautiful. This morning she ran her finger around a palette of pale blue eyeshadow, remembering she'd been told, since childhood, that her biggest asset was her mesmerising, constantly alert, china-blue eyes. She added a touch of pink lipstick – parsimoniously, so as not to smudge it into the lines around her lips. Her make-up was not so much a vanity thing, but rather to maintain a sense of decorum in the event of unexpected visitors. One never knew when one would be caught out in a state of dishevelled untidiness first thing in the morning by the paperboy or the milkman.

For today, the portrait was complete. She straightened her grey wool skirt, patted her white, wispy hair into place and made sure her white blouse was buttoned to her neck. She looked at the clock. The shops would soon be open and she needed to buy a few groceries – as many as could fit into the front basket of her bike. Today she would wear her green wool overcoat and hat.

A barely perceptible dot on the map, Witherington, Gloucestershire, boasted an entry in the Domesday Book of 1086. At the end of the Second World War, reunited families were finally able to breathe freedom in the fresh country air. Adults trod Neolithic and Roman ruins, while William the Conqueror provided inspiration for children's imagined battles. It was a haven and an escape from post-war hardship. In the 1960s the economy picked up and the council realised it could reap earnings from regular tourism. Witherington was back on the map until budget constraints forced the Tourist Information office to cut its opening hours. This didn't deter the serious-minded tourists who flocked to see the mix of Jacobean, Gothic, Tudor, Elizabethan and Victorian architecture, the occasional thatched cottage, drystone walls and, at weekends, a performance by singing milkmaids. A decline in the tourist business came when the town changed to meet needs. The old market hall might have been a point of interest had it not been turned into an amusement arcade. Likewise, the Victorian-built Witherington Railway Station might have been too, had it not been bulldozed to make way for a supermarket, a housing estate and a cultural heritage path.

Disgruntled visitors complained there was not one souvenir shop, although the tourist leaflet did boast one shop of each category all the way down the High Street – a butchers, bakers, greengrocers, ironmongers, florists, shoe shop, opticians, hairdressers and a corner shop selling sweets. It was little compensation because by the time the tourists had walked the length of the High Street to the town hall, past the local schools, police station, dentists and doctors' surgeries and around the various churches and graveyards, there was not much else to see. Out of desperation for beer, tea or a pit stop, most headed for the Bull and Bullocks pub or the Tudor Tea Rooms in the High Street. For those who accidentally stumbled across the Wailing Willows Hotel, with its tall lattice-leaded windows, it didn't escape them that it could have been promoted as a scary-night ghost-hunting experience given its dark gothic atmosphere.

A little later, Tallulah stepped out of the bakers to come face to face with one of the 'Witherington vipers' holding a wreath.

'Well hello, Tallulah, how nice to see you. I was just talking about you this morning.'

Tallulah's face froze into a smile. She could see the woman was dying to impart information otherwise she would have just walked on by. Instead she was almost blown up with hot air.

'I hear your ex-husband Stanley's in town. Well not exactly in town, he's rented the old farmhouse about five miles down the road towards Rottingham – you know, the dilapidated place that's been on the market since God knows when. The one where they found the headless body of the butcher's wife in the fifties. It's probably overrun with rats now. I don't know how he's going to manage to make it decent.'

Tallulah shuddered, not at the rats or the headless woman, but rather at the thought of her personal life being resurrected at the next Witherington funeral.

The woman stopped to recover her breath and Tallulah quickly stepped in with, 'Thank you, my dear, I won't keep you, just in case your flowers start wilting.'

'Yes, we can't have that, can we? I'm in a bit of a hurry.' She scuttled away leaving Tallulah thinking she wasn't in such a hurry that she couldn't stop and impart a bit of gossip. On the other hand, the woman had given her information about Stanley Butterworth, who she still hadn't managed to throw off, even after a divorce, so many years ago she couldn't remember. Their marriage had come to a bitter end because of his boozing nights at the old boys' club when he was supposed to be at home with her. The secret service had instilled in him camaraderie and loyalty, of a kind which he'd never shared with her. For a while they maintained a dignified friendship until he found another woman, after which she retrieved her maiden name of Millstone, not wanting her married name to remind her of Stanley bloody Butterworth ever again. Some hope – he had a habit of popping up now and then just to annoy her.

The phone rang in the afternoon as she was walking past the hall table.

'Bluebell Vicarage. Yes?'

'Tally?'

'Yes, Stanley? To what do I owe the pleasure?'

'Just thought I'd give you a ring. I've rented a farmhouse. Witherington was the only place I could find cheap accommodation for my new project.'

'What project?'

'I'll tell you later.'

He never gave her a straight answer. She said sharply, 'What happened to my Military Cross medal?'

'It wasn't our fault. Everything except rebuilding the country after the war was on the back burner. I've told you before, Tally, it's just a matter of time.'

'How much time has to pass? I risked my life jumping out of a plane with a radio set on my back. All my bones could have been shattered.'

But she knew he wasn't interested in bones. He'd been too obsessed saving his little corner of England from foreign spies, left-wing agitators and too busy blackmailing homosexuals to be bothered with her gripes. She knew him well from years of plans of action, priorities and deadlines and bloody-mindedness. She remembered him at security meetings with wet perspiration patches under his armpits and his fleshy lips getting a stroke of the tongue when he was under pressure. And many years later after retirement, his blatant lies to boost his ego when he didn't feel so important.

'You promised to bring my case to Churchill's attention.'

'He's dead now.'

It was pointless to go on. She said, 'What do you do all day?'

'I'm debriefing communist infiltrators. I have to do something to keep myself busy after spending fifty years working to keep our country safe.'

'A kind of personal crusade for yourself?'

'Not just for myself but for our country. I'm re-educating the dregs of society for a better world. The leftists, in other words.'

She remembered the notorious MK-Ultra programme of the post-war years and the use of chemicals, hypnosis and LSD to bend the minds of the wayward, the meek and the idealists who wanted a better world. 'Does it mean you're brainwashing and drugging them? Isn't it against the law?'

He changed the subject. 'By the way, I hear Scarlett's editor-in-chief at *Agriculture and Business Monthly*, Serge Gallo, is screwing a Russian spy and that her other journalist Roland Wheeler is ranting against the establishment at Hyde Park Corner.'

'Leave my niece out of it. She isn't responsible for her staff.'

'They could be passing information to the Russians. Witherington seems to be a hotbed of reds.'

'Don't be ridiculous. It's a rural backwater.'

'Most journalists have leftist tendencies and are a risk to national security.'

'You're paranoid,' she replied snappily.

'We want you to find out.' Stanley always hid behind the 'we'.

'Get a life. I'm retired, remember? I have a deadline today. I'm working on my cryonics project.'

'That should be fun, floating in liquid nitrogen for eternity.'

'Well I don't want to find myself six feet under when I die.'

'Sounds ridiculous to me. Never mind. I called you for something else. It's my sixty-sixth birthday and I want to invite you to lunch tomorrow. Can you come?'

'It's a bit short notice.'

'Tally, I remember you as a young girl when you'd be up and out on a job to faraway places with just a couple of hours' notice.'

Stanley didn't offer to pick her up in his car. In the office he'd been known as 'the sinker', being an expert at pulling the plug on plain sailing without any consideration for others. She scribbled his vague instruction on a notepad as how to get to his place, 'After four miles as the crow flies from Bluebell Wood in the direction of Rottingham, take a right turn and then half a mile down the road turn left onto a dirt track and keep going until you see the farm.'

She reckoned on four miles to the farmhouse and four back, perhaps in the rain, taking into account Murphy's Law and wind and showers being as unpredictable as the weather forecast in March. It was a problem what to wear for cycling long distances. Her long green wool coat would be a hindrance. In the end she decided to wear a wool sweater beneath a light raincoat. Her skirt was tight around the hips but it had a few pleats at the bottom so she could move her legs. She packed a waterproof hat and an umbrella into the rear basket of the bike for any eventuality, hoping there wouldn't be a tempest to blow the umbrella inside out or knock her off the bike. In March it could be sunny in the morning and windy in the afternoon. Discounting a pair of court shoes in case of mud at the farm, she wore a pair of brown brogues – not very elegant for a birthday celebration, but practical.

Passing through Witherington High Street, Tallulah called in on Marigold the florist. Although she was tempted to buy a gift-wrapped bouquet of poisonous hemlock and belladonna, she opted for a terracotta plant pot of gentian violets.

Stanley's directions proved accurate and in just over half an hour she took a right turn off the main Rottingham road and, after calculating half a mile, swerved left onto a dirt track flanked on either side by wild hedgerows. Cycling around a bend, the untidy green mass gave way to tidy low stone walls. When the farmhouse came into view, she guessed it had been built in the last century. The stonework was grey with black mould patches. Ivy almost obscured a side window and she assumed the faded 'For Sale' sign had probably been there since the headless woman's husband had been hanged. At a wide wooden gate, Tallulah dismounted and rang the bell. Stanley appeared dressed casually smart in a green Fair Isle sweater and jeans, his pate gleaming. There wasn't much left of his hair – a thinning grey halo stretching around the back of his head from ear to ear. Embracing her, he took her bike and wheeled it into the yard. She gave him the gentian violets and wished him a happy birthday.

'Thank you, Tally, a lovely gesture. Glad you got here all right.'

'You could have come and picked me up. I was terrified it might rain.'

'The weather forecast predicted fine weather.'

That was typical of Stanley. No consideration for her age or her little legs pedalling four miles there and four miles back.

'It's a bit run down,' he said, gesturing around the yard which was flanked on one side by empty cow sheds and on the other by outhouses. 'I'm renting until the owners can find someone to buy it. I think it's unlikely as it's been on the market for decades. No one wants to buy a place that needs total renovation and where a woman was decapitated. Most of the sheds are full of rusty farm machinery and some roofs leak, but luckily the house is liveable apart from a bit of mould in the downstairs bathroom.'

He led the way through the front door and set the violets down on a side table.

'I threw out all the old furniture and painted the walls white,' he said proudly.

Tallulah admired the pale blue velvet settee and modern, heavy floral curtains. A brand-new teak table had been set for lunch for two people. The stone floor gleamed. A fire burned in the ancient grate, warming the room and a smell of roast chicken came from the kitchen.

'I didn't know you could cook. You never cooked when we were married.'

Stanley smiled sheepishly.

'Well actually I don't. I have two cooks.'

'Two? What do you need two for? Isn't one enough?'

'It's a bit complicated.'

'Don't tell me, let me guess – both were very beautiful and you didn't know which one to choose so you kept them both.'

'Not exactly.'

'For God's sake, Stanley, stop being so secretive; you're retired now.'

'Very well. You might as well know the truth. Do you remember the MK-Ultra mind-control experiments?'

'Of course I do. They were in operation in 1953, if I remember rightly, with six per cent of CIA funds.'

'The Soviets had been experimenting with the truth drug and in those days it was a rush to see who could do things first, like the rush to get a man on the moon before the seventies. We beat them to it in 1969.'

'I know all that. So what's it got to do with your cooks?'

'One of my cooks is here on a cultural visit to write a cookery book and I use the other to run a mind-control programme to re-educate communists. We pick them up at various protest meetings and invite them here using LSD as bait. When they're high, we inject them with the truth drug. We use hypnosis to get them to forget the experience afterwards. Santeros, my Cuban cook and helper, is a former voodoo priest and hypnosis expert. He's also an expert at culling chickens humanely. He's not here right now. He said he had a few knives and an axe to sharpen at the ironmongers, but you can meet him later if you want. Mr Kim is a North Korean. He's thirty-seven and the son of a UN diplomat. While his father's in New York, Mr Kim is taking a year to study British cultural habits and is writing a cookery book of our traditional recipes to see if he can take any ideas back to his country. Don't laugh but it's called *Glorious Revolutionary Recipes of the British People*.'

Tallulah said it all sounded a bit far-fetched seeing as foreigners usually turned up their noses at the British cuisine. She asked him how come he had a Stalinist in his house.

His answer was, 'I've been asked to keep an eye on him and I'm all for cultural exchanges.'

When Tallulah gave a sarcastic laugh, he said, 'Let's eat.'

Stanley disappeared into the kitchen and came back with a young, slim foreign man with almond-shaped eyes and short black hair. He was dressed in black trousers and a white shirt.

'Meet Mr Kim from North Korea,' said Stanley, as the man placed a white tureen on the table next to a small pot.

Mr Kim gave a short bow and said, 'Welcome to my delicious national dish,' and returned to the kitchen. Stanley removed the lid of the white tureen and lifted a forkful of what looked to Tallulah like white spaghetti and placed it on her plate.

'I'm not keen on foreign food,' she said, 'and there's no sauce on the spaghetti.'

'It's not spaghetti, it's a Korean delicacy. Mr Kim will be offended if you don't eat it.'

'What is it?'

'Cold noodles.'

Tallulah's mouth turned down in an expression of disgust.

'And in the small pot?'

'Kimchi – fermented cabbage spiced with hot chillies. It has nothing to do with Mr Kim's name, just in case you're about to ask me if it was his invention and named after him. It's a national dish. When the cabbages are ready to be cut, the whole country takes time off to pick them. The cabbage takes a year to ferment in a pot under the ground, so I've been told. But don't worry, this was bought at a South Korean restaurant in London.'

'I thought the northerners and the southerners hated each other's guts?'

'Kimchi breaks down borders,' Stanley said dramatically as though imparting an important philosophical pearl. 'Just think of the War of the Roses. I'm sure the Lancastrians didn't turn up their noses at Yorkshire pudding.'

Tallulah struggled through the cold noodles, helped down by the kimchi, which she liked even though it was sprinkled with hot chilli peppers. The chilled white wine helped.

Stanley said, 'He's a nice guy. I want to ask you if you can give him a few cookery lessons so he has recipes to add to his book. It'll keep him busy and out of mischief.'

'I'll think about it and let you know.'

Stanley disappeared into the kitchen and returned with a large platter of chicken and black beans that he said Santeros had prepared before his trip to the ironmongers. There followed a celebration of Stanley's birthday whereby he pulled out two crystal flutes from the sideboard and a bottle of champagne from the fridge along with a cream cake with one candle on it. He lit the candle and Tallulah wished him a happy birthday. When her glass was half empty he poured more champagne into it.

'We must finish the bottle,' he said.

'I'm not drinking any more. I have to ride my bike home.'

'You can stay the night if you want,' he added, mentioning the good times they'd had in the sack when married.

Tallulah shuddered at the thought of a night with Stanley. She used the excuse of needing to get back home because tomorrow morning she had a life or death decision to make for her cryonics project.

'I'll introduce you to Santeros so you can learn how to cull humanely,' he said.

'Thanks. It could be useful,' she replied.

At the end of the lunch, Stanley led her to the outhouse where Santeros lived, and kissed her on the cheek and said, 'I'll say goodbye now. When you've finished, you'll find your bike propped against the gate.' He turned away and trundled back to the house. She wasn't surprised. It wasn't the first time he'd abandoned her on the street because she'd refused him sex.

She knocked on the door and waited. Her thoughts were interrupted when she heard a key rattle in the lock on the other side and the door opened.

Tallulah's head tilted backwards as she looked up at Santeros. His head almost touched the top of the door frame and a white, tent-like caftan left no doubt as to his heavy physique. Straight black hair at chin level. Skin the colour of milk chocolate. Softly lined face. About fifty years old. Thick, purple-tinged lips. Penetrative eyes. He stared at her in a most intrusive way and seemed to be looking into her mind. She felt like a wild animal in front of a predator. He blinked and so did she and the moment was gone. Perhaps it had just been her imagination.

Holding out his hand, as people do when they first meet, she felt obliged to shake it. She managed a tight smile and said, 'Pleased to meet you, Mr Santeros.' He said he was pleased to meet her too. His firm handshake, according to popular belief, meant she could trust the man.

'Please come in, Mrs Tallulah, I believe you are interested in seeing how to sacrifice chickens humanely for your cryonics project.'

She nodded. He stood back, allowing her into the dark hall. The door closed behind her and the key rattled in the lock. He led her along the hallway, down some stairs, along a dark corridor and into a whitewashed room with a long shiny metal table. In front of the far wall, a white sheet with hand-painted Caribbean figures and blobs of red hung from the ceiling. Upon walking closer, she saw each figure holding a hen by the neck, blood spurting from a knife cut. In a corner, a low oblong table had been adorned with candles, pictures of saints and smooth white bleached bones. She noticed a sweet smell of herbal tobacco which could only be marijuana. Her attention was drawn to neatly arranged knives and an axe on a rough wooden butcher's table. In a corner of the room a chicken lay huddled in a cage.

'I will bring you the chicken so you can practise,' he said.

'I'd rather have a demonstration from yourself, if you don't mind,' she replied, not having an apron with her and worried about getting blood on her clothes.

'My pleasure.' Santeros picked up a shiny knife with a blunt tip and ran his finger up and down the blade. 'First of all the blade must be sharp so as not to cause any pain.'

Santeros advanced on her with the knife. Startled, she tottered back until she was almost against the wall. His left hand reached out and grabbed her around her throat before she could fall. Then she felt the blade against her jugular. She'd been through a war and dodged bullets. But she'd never been so close to death before. Adrenalin pricked the backs of her hands but she kept still, as Stanley had taught her to do in a situation of extreme danger.

'This is how you must hold the chicken,' he said, slightly squeezing her throat with his wide stubby fingers.

Tallulah saw him go slightly out of focus with the rest of the room.

'This is how the culling is done,' he said, tracing an imaginary line from one of her ears to the other.

The demonstration consisted of Santeros symbolically slicing Tallulah down the breastbone, removing her wishbone, heart, bladder and intestines and cutting off her drumsticks before chopping her into small pieces. As soon as he mentioned soup, Tallulah lost her nerve and ran screaming from the room. She stumbled down the dark corridor, up the stairs, unlocked the front door and raced out. Fumbling with the gate and frantically retrieving her bike, she pedalled away at full speed.

Upon reaching home in record time, Tallulah picked up the phone, her hands trembling. Stanley said he was on his second bottle of champagne.

'I've just nearly had my throat cut by your mad cook,' she blurted out.

Stanley laughed. 'He's harmless,' he slurred.

'He wanted to chop me into small pieces and make soup out of me.'

'Did he do it?'

'Of course not, otherwise I wouldn't be calling you, would I?'

'Then what's the problem?'

'The man's crazy, dangerous and you may not live to see your next birthday.'

Stanley thanked her for her concern and said he was feeling on top of the world and nothing could spoil his day. He wished her 'nighty-night, sleep tight tonight' and put down the phone.

That night she didn't sleep tight but kept thinking of what might have happened had she not fled. She fell into a nightmare. She was a chicken on a slab and Santeros was advancing on her with a sharp knife and a soup pan.

Fred's murder

Today it was back to bloody business when all Tallulah wanted was a quiet life in Witherington where nothing was supposed to happen. Last night she'd decided on a deadline of 9am for the killing and put some rags and plastic sheeting in a bag. After setting her alarm clock, she'd recited her prayers and said a prayer for Fred, who was trussed up in the shed and didn't know it was his last night on Earth.

This morning Scarlett, her twenty-four-year-old niece, left for work shortly after 8am. Tallulah washed the breakfast dishes, watered the living room plants and stood at the kitchen sink staring across the fields.

She didn't feel like doing it this morning, but couldn't put off the job any longer. Her fingers hovered between knife, meat cleaver and axe, thinking of Fred, who wouldn't last another night in the cold. Her hand stopped over the meat cleaver. A bluebottle buzzed over her head. She eyed it suspiciously and shuddered. Flies were something to take account of. They were a dead giveaway.

To bide time, she drifted around the living room tidying cushions, then opened her writing desk, took out a copy of the advert she'd posted a week ago to both the *Witherington News* and *Rottingham Times* and read it again.

Are you interested in cryonics? Do you want to cheat death and preserve your brain? Former intelligence operative looking for cryonics manager with emergency experience and possible partner to share canister and costs. Interesting conversation. No pets. Please reply to Box 78.

T. M.

She hoped it wasn't too vague. Her cryonics project would be explained in more detail when someone showed an interest and as soon as she had the information she badly needed. Fred was going to help her find the timeframe between life and death.

At 8.20am she put on her transparent plastic raincoat and flicked away a stray wisp of grey hair. She removed her slippers and slid into her rubber boots. She was still torn between the meat cleaver and the knife, seeing as Santeros had given her an idea how to slit a throat humanely. But she briefly lost her nerve, remembering the terror she felt when the knife rested on her neck. Grabbing the meat cleaver, which was probably quicker, she decided: in the name of science, Fred's hour had come.

Yesterday Fred had felt groggy after drinking something sweet. Someone had done a good job trussing him up. The last thing he remembered was keeling over on his perch in the chicken-run between two hens and the old lady grabbing his legs. He'd squawked in terror. His black feathers and red crest had stood on end. The four chickens squawked like crazy. Then he'd passed out.

This morning he awoke on a freezing cold marble-top table. The shed door opened. The old lady marched in carrying a weapon and a stopwatch. His heart was racing and he felt faint. This person, who had nurtured him since he was a chick, now looked at him with eyes as cold as his rear end.

As the meat cleaver came down slicing Fred's head from his body he saw a light above him. The old woman shouted, 'Take that, Stanley, you bloody bastard,' and he wondered who the hell Stanley was.

Fred's head remained on the table while his body flapped onto the floor. One of the hens from the chicken-run screeched, 'Fred's lost his head.' Another replied, 'There wasn't much in there anyway.'

His torso staggered blindly around the table four times leaving bloodied footprints in his wake before dropping dead. Two seconds later, a wisp of ectoplasm left Fred's head and floated gently upwards to meet his ghostly body on the ceiling.

From on high, he saw the old woman look at her stop-watch and mutter her displeasure.

'Timeframe between life and death only forty seconds. Not enough time. I need four minutes.'

Half an hour before Fred's death, Scarlett Carrick had closed the front door on Bluebell Vicarage, slid into her Morris Minor and driven into Witherington, wondering why Aunt Tallulah hadn't lit the fire this morning. It was part of her daily routine like dinner on the stove at night and breakfast on the table in the morning. The house always had a homely smell of hotpots, stews or cottage pies and fresh flowers of the season, but this morning the homely smell was absent. There had been no eggs for breakfast, just toast and marmalade with a cup of tea. On the other hand, her aunt was sometimes unpredictable and could be prickly at times. Scarlett asked herself if she'd done the right thing moving back to Witherington from London. Perhaps if her parents hadn't both passed away within weeks of each other, she might not have returned. And if they hadn't made her promise to look after

Tallulah and discovered Tallulah didn't need much looking after, she might have gone back to London.

From the roundabout, after the Witherington Pig and Cattle Farm, she took a left turn into the High Street and parked the car. Mist hung over the town. She shivered and pulled her white wool hat further down over her shoulder-length, naturally red hair. When she walked into the newsagents, Sam looked up from an open newspaper laid out on top of a gathering of magazines while his wife busied herself stocking up the sweets jars. He asked Scarlett how business was faring.

'Not so good, Sam. We need another journalist to fire some passion into it. People are tired of reading about fields of cows and such.'

He nodded. 'I suppose people nowadays want a bit more excitement. The *News of the World* sells because it has sex in it. I suppose you want copies of today's newspaper?'

'Just one, thanks.'

'Don't you want an extra copy for your aunt? She's a real character.' He opened a copy of the local daily newspaper and handed it to her. Scarlett's hand flew to her mouth when she saw a familiar face looking at her from the second page. The caption below Tallulah's photo was: 'CRYONICS WOMAN WANTS TO CHEAT DEATH'.

Sam's wife said, 'Does it mean she'll be sharing a canister in the nude with a strange man? Keep us informed. A bit of sex sells newspapers. But she's sure to be excommunicated from the Church.'

Scarlett glared at her, paid Sam for the two newspapers, snatched them from the counter and left without saying goodbye. Getting into the car, she opened one of the newspapers and read the article.

Many citizens are choosing an alternative to burial through cryonics. Before brain death occurs, the client will be packed on ice and taken to a facility in Brighton to be encapsulated in a canister full of liquid nitrogen until science finds a way of bringing the person back to life. Clients may choose between a full body freeze or head freeze only. Local woman Tallulah Millstone is seeking a cryonics manager to build an emergency siren to alert her of her impending death. When asked about the timeframe between life and death she said, "I'll let you know. I'm doing some experiments with chickens".

The article questioned legal and moral issues such as: will the Church excommunicate cryonics participants who aren't going to Heaven? Can a relative inherit property if the person isn't technically dead? And, can someone be prosecuted by law for carrying out experiments on chickens when they are being legally slaughtered en masse every day?

Scarlett threw the newspapers into the back of the car and made for home. Any deadlines or emergencies at the office could wait. She fought her growing rage, knowing the futility of tackling Tallulah before calming down a bit. When faced with confrontation, Tallulah would shut down like a nuclear reactor, cutting off any channels of communication. Scarlett had learned, over time, to prepare a little psychological speech beforehand. Tallulah had, throughout her working life, used diplomacy to deal with thorny challenges rather than meet problems head on. The best approach, Scarlett decided, was to tell her aunt she understood perfectly how easy it is to get carried away with a new idea and forget to inform everyone else and that she was disappointed not to have been informed about the cryonics and advert and Tallulah being nude in a cryonics canister with a strange man. The thorny question would be: 'Which chickens are you experimenting with and what are you doing with them?' She hoped Tallulah wasn't harming Fred, Ethel, Virgin, Ms Prim or even nasty Gottfried, not wanting to have to contact the RSPCA to report her for cruelty to animals.

Parking outside the house, she switched off the engine and tucked the newspapers under her arm. What was needed now was to put aside her fears and start with reasoning based on the facts. As her Irish father had once told her, 'There are always two sides to a coin.'

She expected to see smoke coming from the chimney but the fire still hadn't been lit. Following the path around to the back garden into the orchard, she noticed the hens were squawking and Fred was missing. Her heart missed a beat. They were supposed to take him to the Blessing of the Beasts church service soon.

A light in the shed told her Tallulah must be inside.

Her fist pounded the door. 'Anybody there?'

She heard Tallulah shout, 'I thought you were at work.'

'Can you open the door? I have to talk to you about your photo plastered all over Witherington.'

The bolt slid back. Scarlett stepped inside the shed. She didn't notice the blood on the floor at first but she did see splatters of it on the tabletop and on Tallulah's plastic raincoat. Tallulah was holding Fred's head and looking into his eyes. She talked to him. 'Fred, can you hear me? Speak to me. Tell me – is your brain still working?' There was no reply. 'Fred, blink twice if you're still alive.' But Fred didn't blink.

Scarlett screamed so hard she passed out. She woke up on the couch with Tallulah standing over her. Her head pounded in time to the clock, her legs seemed absent and her brain was stuffed with cotton wool and moving in slow motion. Sunshine coming through the window seemed to bathe the living room in a hazy fog. She could hear birds singing in the distance. Her throat felt like gravel.

Tallulah said, 'I've given you a sedative, dear, so don't worry if you feel a bit groggy. I'll help you upstairs to bed.'

She was too tired to argue and let herself be led. Her arms were heavy. As soon as her head touched the pillow, Scarlett fell into a deep sleep. She found herself on the roof sitting next to Fred. He hopped onto her left shoulder and nuzzled her cheek, pecking her ear softly, playfully. Then he was sitting in her lap. She took him in her arms and rocked him. 'I love you, Fred,' she whispered, caressing his red crest. Fred gazed at her affectionately, his eyes like twinkling stars. He seemed happy and calm. She sat him gently back on the tiles. 'I'll never forget you.' She said it with sadness, knowing she had to let him go. Fred's black plumage began to turn white and he started to fade into a cloud-like fog.

She kissed his beak and said, 'Goodbye, Fred, I know you're going to a better place.'

The Pearly Gates Express

Fred sat on the roof of Bluebell Vicarage thinking he'd miss Scarlett and wondering why his black plumage had turned white. He was confused and angry. The old hag had cut off his head and separated him from his loved ones. Staring over the fields, he saw a woman in the distance sitting on a roof belonging to the Wailing Willows Hotel. She looked very old and was wearing a long white ballet dress and holding a pink feather duster in her hand. He badly needed to talk to someone about the afterlife but thought it best to keep away from troublesome old ladies. Suddenly she was sitting beside him, her legs dangling over the guttering. He noticed there was a stump at the end of her leg where her foot should be. Startled and afraid, he began to squawk.

The very old lady spoke with a strange accent he hadn't heard before. 'For gawd's sake, stop that goddamn awful noise. Squawking gives me a headache. I've never had chickens for such a reason. Their clucking gets right up my nose.' She pronounced 'right up my nose' as 'ride up my nose'.

Fred said, 'First of all, I'm not a chicken. I'm a cockerel. I'm a Jersey Giant and I have a very long lineage. My ancestors came over from the United States in the nineteenth century.'

The old lady picked moss off the roof and threw it into the garden. 'Jersey Giants are usually black and you're white,' she said.

He didn't like her sing-song way of speaking and was sure she was putting it on. 'Does it matter whether I'm black or white?'

'Not to me it don't, but it could do to some.'

'I didn't choose to be white. It happened after I died. I want to be black again.'

'If you've turned white it means you're privileged. It means you're a ghost and you can do what you like – for example, scare people out of their wits. All black things turn white in Heaven. Have you ever seen an angel in a black coat? Or a black angel sculpture in church? No, they're always white.'

'It seems to me the church is inventing all the rules,' said Fred.

'Stop talking blasphemy, you mangy, ungrateful bird.'

Fred said, 'I hate old ladies.'

She stated she was not used to being spoken to in such a way. 'I'm not old, I'm only seventy. That's not old in my book. Inside my head I'm still seventeen.'

There followed a long silence as Fred tried to consolidate the information.

He said, 'Can we introduce ourselves?'

'Why?'

'Well, I suppose we're going to be sitting together for a long while.'

She stuck out her chin. 'I didn't invite you to sit with me. We haven't yet been introduced.'

Fred thought she was being absurd. He introduced himself. 'I'm Fred.'

The old lady looked him up and down. 'I'm Cecilia, though polite people call me Mrs Willows.'

Fred said he was tired of being polite and asked her if she thought she'd go to Heaven or Hell.

'Of course I'll go to goddamn Heaven, you silly bird. Where d'ya think I'm going? I just have to work out how to get there.'

He said, 'You have to wait for the Pearly Gates Express train. It's fast but never on time.'

'Well, I'm a lady and prefer to take a cruise. I want to arrive at the Pearly Gates on the same boat upon which Cleopatra swanned up the Tiber to Rome. And while I'm in Rome I want to visit the Holy Father to see if I can take my washing machine to Heaven.'

'Maybe I can come with you?' Fred asked.

She looked at him as if he'd just asked her to eat worms.

'Absolutely not. I don't remember it being written in the scriptures about chickens being allowed into Heaven. Have you ever heard of a chicken mentioned in the Bible?'

'I remember some people riding horses in the Bible and something about "The fowl of the Earth".'

'If all animals were toilet-trained it might be different. Can you imagine – the clouds will be raining excrement and fleas and there won't be even standing room for the rest of us.'

Fred had to admit it sounded rather crowded, but contested the fleas saying he'd been fumigated on several occasions. 'Maybe you could come to animal Heaven, then, if there is one. Perhaps it's divided into two floors – one for humans and one for animals. There's sure to be a lift between the two.'

Cecilia's eyes softened. She stroked his head. 'Look, Fred, we eventually have to part ways. I can't come with you because I can't cluck.'

'I could give you a two-week training course?'

'I've no intention of sitting among hens. I'd look ridiculous. And in any case, I'm not sure there are two separate heavens.'

Fred wasn't sure either. 'If there's no separate heaven for animals, I'll have to come with you,' Fred said.

Cecilia stiffened and mentioned the fleas again. 'And you can't come to my heaven because your eggs might give people salmonella.'

'I'm a cockerel and I don't lay eggs.'

'Well, that's another good reason. You'd be a liability.

What are people going to have for breakfast if you can't give them eggs?'

Fred said she was just looking for excuses.

Cecilia changed the subject. 'What do you intend to do in your heaven, Fred?'

'Well, if there is one and we can choose our roles, I want to be an entertainer. I can sing and dance. My partner Ethel and I used to dance. She was Ginger Rogers and I was Fred Astaire. We did tap-dancing.'

'Was she a big black Jersey Giant too?'

'No, she was a California White. Big, white and beautiful. She was born here but always said she wanted to go back to her roots and maybe to Hollywood.'

Cecilia began to wail. 'I always dreamed of dancing in Las Vegas, but now I'll never dance again.' She held up her stump.

Fred quickly took her mind off it by asking her where she was born.

'Chicago.'

'Is it near Chiswick?'

She chuckled. 'It's in the United States. I can tell you haven't been very far in life.'

She told him she'd been a ballet dancer and had danced in Chicago and New York for the Ballet Caravan Company. 'I danced in the 1938 premiere of *Billy the Kid*, and I want to dance in the afterlife if I can find my missing foot. The rest of my country is very big, much bigger than your little island. We have billionaires, Las Vegas and the Statue of Liberty.'

'We have royalty,' said Fred, stretching his neck proudly.

Cecilia acknowledged royalty was an asset to a little island. The royal family was rich, internationally famous, travelled on free holidays and were always in the papers, magazines and on television.

'When I go to Heaven, I want to be Queen. I just can't

abide the thought of washing my own clothes. I don't want my hands to get wrinkled.'

Fred said nothing. She said she was hungry and wanted to go and look for something to eat.

'Can I bring you anything, Fred?'

Fred thought how kind and caring she was. 'Just a few worms and snails, please.'

Cecilia didn't bat an eyelid. Tottering to one side because of her stump, she smoothed down her white ballet dress. 'OK, no problem. But you'll have to wait a bit. There's always a goddamn queue in the fast food restaurant.'

Fred asked, 'So what are you going to have, Cecilia?'

Cecilia grinned mischievously. 'Aw, just a leg of Kentucky Fried Chicken.'

That was when Fred keeled over and slid towards the guttering. Cecilia tried to catch him, but he went over the edge. Fred, paralysed with fear, felt the air ruffling his feathers.

Cecilia shouted, 'Sorry, Fred, I didn't mean it. I was only joking. Open your wings and fly, you goddamn stupid bird.'

He did as he was told and found he could fly quite well, better than he'd been able to do when alive.

When Fred was back on the roof, Cecilia put her arm around him and kissed him on the beak. 'Let's be friends,' she said.

In the distance a black-and-white blob flew towards them.

'Here comes Ernest,' she said.

'Ernest?'

'Yes, Constable Ernest Barnstable. Maybe you've never met him. He's the one who dropped dead when he found he was being transferred to Rottingham Police Station. Mind what you say, he's a tough nut.'

Fred shuddered.

As the black-and-white blob came closer and alighted on

the roof, Fred found himself looking at a man in a police uniform.

Cecilia spoke first. 'Constable Ernest Barnstable, may I introduce you to Fred, my friend – he's waiting for the Pearly Gates Express train with me.'

Ernest looked down at Fred. 'Make sure you get in the right carriage – the one for animals,' he said brusquely.

'I'm not an animal, I'm a cockerel.'

Cecilia said, 'Fred and I have just been discussing the problem and I say he will travel in the same carriage as us.'

Ernest opened his mouth to speak and shut it again, thinking better of starting an argument with a pernicious woman he'd met while they were still alive.

'Fred and I are going to pick wild flowers for my grave. You can come with us if you want,' she said.

'Why not. There's not much else to do now we're dead, is there?'

Cecilia told Ernest she was sorry to hear he'd had a heart attack after the shock of the police station being closed down, while Ernest with his usual *savoir faire* said, 'Too bad about your accident.'

Her lips tightened. 'It was no accident, I was murdered. James, my husband, pushed me from a window.'

Ernest drew himself up to his full height and beamed. 'Well, thank the heavens for small mercies. I was wondering what I should do all day long. We need to investigate,' he said enthusiastically.

Ernest's eagerness was catching. Fred declared he wanted to work as an informer because he was good at flying around poking his nose into everyone's business.

'Count yourself hired. You can be my right-hand man and start by helping me write a project. I'll give you a quick briefing: I wrote a letter to Saint Peter applying for the forthcoming vacancy as Security Officer at the Pearly Gates and *ad interim* Gatekeeper of Purgatory. I received a letter back saying that the seven hellish terraces of Wrath, Lust, Envy, Sloth, Gluttony, Greed and Pride are presently overflowing and therefore the Pearly Gates Express won't depart until September. In the meantime, I've been requested to submit a new project to redesign the terraces and punishments for sins which, after a few centuries, are out of date and no longer working. You can both put your heads together and come up with something.'

Cecilia replied she'd no intention of working and quoted her missing foot and reduced mobility. Fred said he'd try to help given his limited experience of the matter.

Ernest said, 'All you have to do is go to the library in Rottingham and read up on Dante's *Divine Comedy* and come up with a modern version of the seven terraces.' Fred said it seemed a tall order and likely to need more than one night.

'Do you want the job or not? If you don't, I'll have to find someone else. In any case it's cold and damp here on the roof so you might as well be in the library.' Ernest cut the conversation by saying, 'I'm going back to the graveyard. If you can deliver, I'll see you at my graveside tomorrow morning.'

Cecilia said, 'I'm going to visit James, he's probably missing and grieving for me.'

Ernest and Fred looked at each other and rolled their eyes.

James lay in his bed at the Wailing Willows Hotel, thinking of young Clara the cleaning lady. Twice a week for the past three years he'd secretly watched her through a crack in the door, smoothing his pale green satin bedspread with the tenderness of a woman caressing a man's body. But today she'd given in her notice. It was a sad ending to the pleasure of seeing her bend over, showing her shapely legs. He tried not to brood over her decision to leave him now she was getting married, especially as he would have to find someone else and it wasn't easy.

It was a mistake to think dark thoughts at bedtime. His night terrors and sleep paralysis advanced on him after midnight. He'd try to read a book, but at seventy years of age, sleep crept up quickly.

Tonight he tried to fight it, but the book dropped from his hands and he fell into the void. He found himself in a deep pit with no steps to the surface. A bee buzzed in his head. Panic-stricken, he struggled to climb up towards the light. His mind was awake but his body asleep and paralysed. He struggled up out of the pit. Everything in the room was the same as before – except he couldn't move. All he could do was to wait for *her* to arrive.

The quilt glided across the bed onto the floor. Something slid inside, between the sheets and he felt an icy cold body climb on top of him. He tried to scream but no sound left his lips.

A familiar voice said, 'There's no point screaming, James. No one can hear you and in any case I thought you'd be glad to see me back home.' Cecilia sat on his chest in her long white ballet dress.

'Well, I'm not! You're supposed to be dead.'

'I've just popped in to do a bit of dusting,' she said tickling his nose with a pink feather duster. James tried to shake her off but she dug her nails into his side and put her nose within an inch of his. He began to sneeze. 'Get off my chest and stop waving that filthy feather duster.'

'It's clean. I washed it in the river only yesterday.'

'There are no rivers near here.'

'Then it must have been a pond or a drain.'

'Which explains the disgusting smell.'

She ignored his comment and flicked her duster across the bedside table.

'Stop that. You know I'm allergic to dust.'

He tried to shake her off his chest.

'You're pushing me off the bed like you pushed me from the window,' she said hanging on tightly.

'No I didn't.'

The truth was, neither of them remembered much about the last minutes of Cecilia's life. Their conversation came to a halt when she jumped off him, plugged in the Hoover and started to vacuum the carpet.

James shouted above the din, 'I hated you because you were always driving me mad with the housework.'

'Someone had to do it.'

'You didn't have to dust everything again after the cleaning lady had just done it. And you were always heaping my clothes on the chair and I could never find anything.'

'You should have been tidier.'

Cecilia turned off the vacuum cleaner and bent over him. 'You drove me nuts with your nagging.'

'I didn't know I was doing it.'

'But you did.'

'I want to turn the clock back and make amends,' James whined.

'Well, it's too late now – I'm dead. You should have been nicer to me when I was alive.'

'Get out of here and leave me alone!'

Cecilia finished cleaning his bedroom and headed for the bathroom. She flushed the toilet four times and then screamed, 'Did you push me from the window because you were still in love with Tallulah?'

James shouted back, 'I should have married her instead of you, you old hag.'

Cecilia came back into the bedroom and whirled round the room, stirring up the dust.

A night in the library

Fred spent all night in Rottingham Library flicking through Dante Alighieri's *Divine Comedy*, which he found full of blood, guts, torture and severed limbs. Hell and Purgatory seemed to be overrun with evil nobles, wayward popes and ambitious hierarchy of the Roman Catholic Church of Rome. But what had happened to the dead warriors of the rest of the world? Genghis Khan and the roving hordes? Great Britain's decapitated nobles or ancient warriors, slashed limb from limb on medieval battlefields? Had Dante mentioned them? Further reading enlightened Fred about Peter's Gate, guarded by an angel who branded sinners on their foreheads with a 'P' for entry to Purgatory. How was that for a complimentary dose of pain? At the top of Mount Purgatory stood the entrance to Earthly Paradise – and here Fred became confused because Earth had been no paradise – at least not in the henhouse. Earthly Paradise referred to the Garden of Eden before Adam and Eve sinned, consumed by lust. The nice part was being accompanied up the mountain to Heaven by angels singing and a tourist guide lecturing them on their deficiencies all the way up to the top. By which time they were indeed relieved to meet God.

Fred's reading of the *Divine Comedy*, superficial though it was given the short time available, made him wonder whether the Witherington dead, or the rest of the British Isles, really needed to pass through Hell, the 'Inferno', considering the New Testament preached forgiveness and that the Church absolved people of their sins before they kicked the bucket.

Fred asked himself if Dante Alighieri had studied international history, given that all his time seemed to have been taken up reporting on bloodthirsty, unruly Italy and its many regional wars.

As the night drew on, Fred set about designing the new terraces. He likened it to a building so that Cecilia and Bertha could understand.

Basement: Hell, the Inferno.

Floors 1–7: Purgatory.

Floor 8: The mountainous climb towards salvation.

Floor 9 Penthouse: The Garden of Eden.

Writing furiously to meet the deadline, Fred had his report written before cock-crow. Exhausted, he returned to the graveyard and handed it to Ernest, then slumped to the ground and fell into a deep sleep. Ernest began reading Fred's notes. He was pleased because they had a modern twist, even though there was no rhyme or reason to any of them.

The Seven Terraces of Purgatory
Pride: Valley of odd shoes and lost socks.
Envy: Swamp of bile-green boiled cabbages.
Wrath: Cliff of Scottish Whirling Dervishes.
Sloth: Stream of snapping turtles under treadmills.
Greed: Coal mine of fools gold.
Gluttony: Cesspit of fermented prunes.
Lust: Field of raw garlic and onions.

While waiting for Fred to wake up, Ernest sat on his grave writing a few notes to start his investigation into Cecilia's death, hoping former funeral director Bertha Goodbody would stay away at least until he'd finished. Her family tomb was nearby and she was probably lurking around reading inscriptions on headstones just to know who her neighbours were. The night in the viewing room when she'd met her death against his coffin was still fresh in his mind.

It wasn't long before she arrived, wearing an Irish tartan dressing gown over her heavy frame and a pair of matching slippers. The funeral home hadn't done a good job on her face and hair seeing as her emerald green eyeshadow and red lipstick were smudged and her curly blonde hair stood up at the front. Sitting alongside Ernest, she peered at his notepad, while he covered it with his hand and kept on writing.

'What are you writing, Ernest?'

'The names of those who love the Lord,' he said, quoting a poem he'd read somewhere.

'I hope you've got my name down or I shall be a bit miffed.'

He smiled. 'Of course. By the way, when are you due to pass on?'

'I haven't been called yet. I'm waiting for the Pearly Gates Express train. I hear you'll be the Gatekeeper of Purgatory *ad interim*, so I hope you'll put in a good word for me seeing as we're neighbours.'

'Of course. Which of the seven terraces do you want to go to? Pride, Envy, Wrath, Sloth, Greed, Gluttony or Lust?'

Bertha shook her head. 'I'm pure of heart and haven't sinned.'

Ernest coughed politely. 'If I remember rightly, madam, you were forever losing your temper with your husband, the tradesmen and the clerks at the town hall.'

'Of course I did. They were all incompetent and their services didn't match my requirements or standards. And my Norman was a lousy lazy womanising bastard.'

'Anything else?'

'Yes, he was a drunken layabout and said he'd like to see me six foot under.'

'I believe you were rather controlling?'

'What rubbish. I just stood up for myself.'

'I seem to remember I was called to the funeral home when you launched a metal urn and hit your husband above the eye.'

'It was just a tiff.'

'I'll put you down for the Terrace of Wrath – the cliff of Scottish Whirling Dervishes,' said Ernest.

'I told you I'm not going anywhere. I'm going straight to Paradise, you horrible man.'

Bertha flew at him and he felt her hand whip his face. His face stung and he was furious about her lack of respect. He grabbed her wrist then let it go.

'My name is Constable Ernest Barnstable, so don't address me as a horrible man ever again.'

She swore at him and called him a nitwit, then whirled towards the family tomb. He should have throttled her, but he was a gentleman. No wonder her husband Norman had showed no emotion at her funeral.

Fred's head

Tallulah wrenched open the front door at the insistent ringing of the bell. Before her stood a familiar gangly young man whose hair reached the lapels of his long black coat. His boots, caked with dry mud, had shed a few lumps of it on the welcome mat. She noticed his face was flushed, he was breathing heavily and his bike was propped against the bay window, squashing her rose bushes. Tallulah took a deep breath and her lips tightened as she forced herself not to make a disparaging comment. At twenty one years of age Roland Wheeler still hadn't learned respect, so what was the point in wasting her breath?

'Roland, get your finger off the bell. I heard you the first time.'

'Sorry, but I thought you hadn't.'

'I was busy washing blood from my hands.'

'Sorry.' Roland's stomach lurched.

'Come in and take your boots off, I don't want mud all over the carpet. You can talk to me while I'm stuffing Fred,' she said, inviting him to step into the hall. He was rather reluctant to remove his black calf-length boots to show his bright yellow fluorescent socks. Embarrassed, he tugged the legs of his tight cinder-coloured trousers down as far as they would go to hide them. Placing his boots neatly by the door, he followed Tallulah into the kitchen. Fred's innards and carcass were sitting on the draining board next to a glass bowl of sage and onion stuffing. A few sodden plucked feathers were clinging to the sink. He regretted calling in on Tallulah unannounced and remembered Scarlett saying Tallulah was a stickler for protocol.

'Sorry to disturb you, Mrs Millstone, I should have rung you first. I had to pick up some proofs for the magazine for Scarlett. It was on the way and she doesn't know I'm here.'

'That's all right. You're here now. How about a cup of tea?'

Without waiting for him to answer, she invited him to sit at the kitchen table and said, 'Are you working in Scarlett's office?'

'Yes, I run errands, but I'm hoping to get a better job eventually,' replied Roland, feeling his face redden.

Tallulah filled the kettle. Reaching into one of the cabinets, she brought out two cups and saucers reserved for guests – white porcelain decorated with red and pink roses. She placed a sugar bowl, a milk jug and a matching teapot on the table. Roland waited in silence for the kettle to boil. He felt naked and vulnerable without his boots. He hid his socks from view under the table. Tallulah scalded the teapot and threw the boiling water into the sink.

'What kind of tea? Earl Grey? English Breakfast tea, Darjeeling, camomile, cinnamon, Bangkok jasmine or Singapore dried ginger?'

'Just plain English tea, please.'

Tallulah reached for the air-tight tin and heaped a tablespoonful into the teapot. 'I take it you've never been abroad, then?'

'No, just as far as London.'

'Strong, weak, milk, sugar?'

'Weak please, no milk or sugar.'

'It has to stand for a few minutes.'

Roland knew the tea ritual. 'No problem, my mum always stews it.'

'Would you like a biscuit?'

'Yes please.'

'Plain digestive? Milk chocolate digestive? Dark chocolate digestive? Chocolate fingers? Lemon creams? Rich tea? Cream crackers with butter?'

'The last ones, thanks.'

'I see you're not fond of chocolate.'

He was, but afraid to ask her to repeat it all again. 'Not much,' he lied.

A few minutes later, Tallulah poured pale tea from the spout into Roland's cup and let the pot stand another few minutes before filling her own. Roland stared at the teacup's handle, which was curved and delicate and wondered how he was going to get a finger through. He picked up a buttered cream cracker.

Tallulah broke the silence. 'I suppose you've come about my niece?'

'Yes.'

She said, 'Perhaps it wasn't a good idea for Scarlett to come and live with me. I didn't get on well with her mother when she was alive – my sister was too sensitive. Scarlett takes after her mother. I have a problem with sensitive people.'

Tallulah's ice-blue eyes bored into Roland's and sweat threatened to break out on his brow. He was sure she was reading his sensitive mind. He fidgeted in his chair and studied the fine cup handle, finally grasping it between forefinger and thumb while avoiding eye contact.

'Scarlett doesn't seem to be at all sensitive,' replied Roland, not wishing to contradict Tallulah directly, while remembering how Scarlett could ride slipshod over the best of them where deadlines were concerned.

'Oh, so you know her well, do you?' He detected a note of concern in her voice.

'Not so well. We just work together.'

'I see.'

'I came to tell you Scarlett's not coming home tonight.' He expected her to be surprised, even upset, with maybe a few hysterics, but her expression didn't change.

'I'm not surprised. You'd think she was being murdered the way she was screaming and carrying on. And all over the death of a silly cockerel. Fred would have gone into the pot eventually.'

Scarlett had been right about her aunt being insensitive. He said, 'Scarlett watched him hatch. She said he was her baby.'

Tallulah's lips tightened. 'She should be thinking of settling down instead of being surrogate mother to the whole chicken coop.'

'She was upset because you were both going to take Fred to the Blessing of the Beasts church service.'

'We can take Ethel instead.'

'I don't think Scarlett would be too happy about that.'

'Where's she staying?' Tallulah said abruptly.

'Both of us lodge at the Wailing Willows Hotel. We live on the ground floor and have our office on the second floor – the floor below where Cecilia Willows was pushed from a window on the third floor.'

'We don't know she was pushed. And I'm not interested where you have your office. I hope Scarlett isn't staying in your room.'

Roland felt the urge to pee. 'I wouldn't do such a thing. I respect Scarlett too much.'

Tallulah's nostrils flared. 'Well, you didn't respect your father's position as councillor when you were prancing around outside the town hall dressed as a tree.'

'I was protesting about the decision to build council houses in a green area.'

'Roland, if you don't respect your father, how can I be sure you'll respect my niece?'

'Mrs Millstone, Scarlett and I are just colleagues. I came here to let you know she's not coming home so you won't worry or call the police when she doesn't turn up.'

'She could have picked up the phone and called me.'

'She doesn't want to speak to you.'

A vein on Tallulah's neck began to expand. 'For heaven's sake! You wouldn't think she was a grown woman. When I was twenty four, I was in Europe seeing people being shot during the war. We had more important things to think about than dead animals. I once had to eat a French cat to survive.'

Roland, confused, began to feel out of his depth. He didn't know enough about wars to commit to an opinion. His feet were getting cold. 'I have to go. We have a few deadlines.'

'Don't you want to finish your tea?'

He got up from the table without waiting for her to get up first. 'No thanks.'

Tallulah put her hand on his arm. 'Roland, I apologise if I offended you, but please talk some sense into Scarlett. She has to come home.'

'She's upset. She said you murdered Fred in cold blood.'

'Scarlett will have to get over such nonsense. Hens and cocks have a short lifespan anyway.'

'It's not much fun losing a pet,' said Roland, chickening out of telling her his mother had never killed one of his furry friends. He clamped his lips together, being tempted to swear.

Tallulah reached inside the fridge. 'Here are two eggs for your breakfast. Ethel laid them a week ago but they're still fresh.'

'Thanks a lot, Mrs Millstone.'

'Ethel's ovaries are packing up. As soon as she stops laying, she'll be going into the pot.'

He imagined Scarlett passing out upon hearing Ethel was being served up for lunch but didn't have the courage to make a comment. He bit his tongue again and tried diplomacy. 'I thought you said you were taking her to the Blessing of the Beasts church service in place of Fred?'

'There's always Gottfried to fall back on.'

Roland paled. Scarlett was likely to commit murder if Ethel got the chop or if Gottfried got to go to church – he was aggressive and she didn't trust him.

'Please tell Scarlett that Fred had a painless death.' Tallulah took Fred's head from the fridge and waved it in front of his nose. Fred's neck skin had been snipped and his trachea was showing. His eyes and beak were open and he smelt a bit off.

Scarlett's baby had been brutally murdered.

Roland felt the cream crackers rise from his stomach to his diaphragm.

Tallulah went on, 'There, you see, he didn't suffer because I brought the meat cleaver straight down on his neck. It was a clean cut. Just like a guillotine.'

Roland turned, put his head in the sink and retched. Tallulah nimbly grabbed the bowl of sage and onion and placed it safely on the kitchen table. Then she removed Fred's carcass and innards from the line of fire. When Roland had finished bringing up his tea and biscuits, Tallulah made him a cup of camomile. She said, 'What a waste of tea and biscuits!'

'Sorry, but his head just reminded me of a film I saw last week.'

'I didn't know they showed cock decapitations at the cinema.'

Roland felt a panic attack coming. He clutched his crotch and said, 'No, just headless people.'

Tallulah's face twitched. 'Good heavens, what's the world coming to?' She changed the subject as her mind filled with images of war. 'What a good thing I didn't give you teacakes or you could have blocked the sink.'

Roland, who never judged people on gossip and who prided himself on being a pacifist and co-listener for the tormented, had to agree with Scarlett – her aunt 'had no feelings or consideration for others'. He made for the front door and retrieved his boots. He didn't care whether she saw his socks or not. And he was glad she didn't ask him why he was staying at the hotel otherwise he would have to tell her about his dad kicking him out of the house and Scarlett rescuing him by offering him a job.

'Thank you for coming, Roland. At least I know where Scarlett is. By the way, get your long hair cut, it's untidy and makes you look like a lost child. In my day—'

Without waiting to hear Tallulah's history, Roland jumped on his bike and pedalled towards the gate. He regretted his good deed for the day – saving an old lady from heartbreak and the police from combing the countryside looking for a young woman who was safe in the room next to his at the Wailing Willows Hotel. Then he asked himself why he continued doing old people a good turn when they didn't deserve it.

Tallulah shouted after him, 'Roland, take care your coat doesn't catch in the back wheel – and put your lights on, it's getting dark.'

Footnotes

The next morning, following a short conversation with Stanley, Tallulah opened the front door to find Mr Kim smartly dressed in a white shirt and black suit and tie. He made a short bow from the waist, his coal-black hair smooth and shining under the hall light. Before leading him to the kitchen, she suggested he remove his jacket and put on an apron, which he declined stating, in a dead-pan voice, that only women wore aprons in North Korea. To avoid creating a diplomatic incident, she suggested he roll up his sleeves and sit down at the table and read the recipes from her own cookery book. Mr Kim reminded her he was writing *Glorious Revolutionary Recipes of the British People* and would appreciate her suggesting traditional British recipes he could modify to the Korean palate.

His first question was, 'Why is there only one recipe each from Wales and Ireland – do they not eat English food?'

'Yes, they also eat English food,' she replied.

'Why is shepherd's pie called so when the word shepherd suggests a sheep-herder? Are sheep herded in Great Britain?'

'Not as far as I know. They might do in France but here they live in flocks.'

'But they are not birds.'

'No, but the English language is full of words foreigners don't understand.'

Mr Kim went on to query toad-in-the-hole as he said Koreans ate dogs but not toads. She explained it was simply a Yorkshire pudding with a sausage in it.

'And why is it called Yorkshire pudding when there is no sugar in it?'

Tallulah suggested a footnote. When she placed a simple recipe in front of him – liver and onions – he enthusiastically translated it into liver and garlic and added a second footnote as his countrymen preferred garlic. He liked the idea of stuffed cabbage leaves as they had tons of cabbages in North Korea with which to make kimchi. Spotted dick was out as he didn't like the sound of it. In the end, Mr Kim decided he'd like to learn to make Lancashire hotpot, with one small difference.

'I would like to replace neck of lamb with dog.'

At this point he inserted a third footnote renaming the dish *Lancashire dogpot.*

To please Mr Kim, Tallulah decided upon a practical demonstration of shepherd's pie, which would be a communal activity in keeping with his communist beliefs. She thereby thrust a paring knife into his hand and told him to get on with peeling the potatoes and cutting up onions.

During the lesson, Mr Kim spoke about something that had been puzzling him greatly since his arrival in the glorious British Isles.

'I do not find it at all funny the self-deprecating comments the British make about their own shortcomings. In my country, people are not so mad as to announce they are stupid. They would be sent to a mental institution. I think the British must be quite mad as I have heard a song, "Mad Dogs and Englishmen", which seems to confirm my suspicions but I am surprised that also the dogs are mad.'

Tallulah wasn't sure how to answer the question in a way he might understand. 'We are poles apart,' she said, quickly changing the subject before he could ask her about poles. 'Tell me something about yourself and your country.'

'Perhaps I will reveal to you something about myself and my country the next time I come.'

Mr Kim left the old woman's house not sure that he wanted to reveal anything about himself. Mrs Tallulah wouldn't understand the communist way even if she lived to be five hundred years old. He was reluctant to tell her about his childhood and youth: summer holidays spent planting rice in the mosquito-infested fields; digging ditches for latrines or hammering smoothed rocks into the dirt to make roads. Mrs Tallulah wouldn't understand about the young heroic people of the shock brigades, building roads encouraged by prizes to see who could carry the most rocks on their backs – the girls trying to outdo the boys and laughing all the way as they waved red banners with patriotic and revolutionary slogans to encourage the others. Then, growing into adults, running beside the tractors waving the red flags as the earth was turned. It was customary to rise very early and their alarm clocks were vans with loud speakers booming revolutionary music as a start to the day. There was much snow and flooding. As a soldier of the People's Army, he remembered when the temperature dropped to more than thirty degrees below zero and often being hungry, but never complaining because his country needed his patriotic loyalty. He was ready to die for his country. The fatherly State did its best to feed them satisfactorily as it considered the army should be looked after before everything else. In hierarchical order from top down, the Party and the army came first, then the family.

He was tempted, but he wouldn't tell Mrs Tallulah about the political indoctrination sessions and the fear of speaking out, save to denounce a traitor or about the power cuts or the broken electricity pylons in the countryside. Nor would he put her in the picture about the air-raid shelters in Pyongyang which were built because the people believed, ever since the amnesty at the end of the Korean War in 1953, that they were still at war with the United States and rogue countries like her own. If he told her all these things he'd feel a traitor. It was best to keep Westerners ignorant of what was going on in his strong country, so they wouldn't find any weaknesses to exploit. In Pyongyang it would be difficult for a foreigner to snoop around as there were no street names written in any Western language. Only the Russian military advisers and the United Nations knew the city was a showcase to conceal the poverty and hide starvation in the countryside, which was out of bounds except to selected foreigners, who in any case would be taken to fancy hotels and kept watch over. The Russians were often busy lying on the small beach in Nampo drinking beer and vodka and eating caviar imported from Russia to maintain their elite habits. As for official visitors from other countries – after a week in Pyongyang they thought were experts on North Korea. Foreign politicians, dignitaries and businessmen would be picked up by official minders who would monitor their every move and report back. Sometimes the foreigners would be filmed and these films would be screened, without their knowledge, on State television. His comrades enjoyed playing games with the businessmen. The fun part was inviting them to dinner and plying them with gallons of drink to eliminate any resistance when it came to clinching business deals.

Although he liked her, Mrs Tallulah was in any case an enemy of the North Korean State and he could not reveal all these secrets. So he would tell her a little bit about their history. She might be shocked to learn about the pretty young comfort women kidnapped during the Japanese invasion for the sexual pleasures of the military and the cultural assimilation policy when Koreans were forbidden, on pain of death, to speak or write their own language. All this was deeply rooted in their hatred against the Japanese and he wished to share it with her. He sat on his bed at the farmhouse and started to sing, with fervour, 'Song of the Anti-Japanese War'.

Birth of a man called Veronica

Scarlett ate a frugal breakfast in her room at the Wailing Willows Hotel. Teabags and crackers were all she had in the cupboard. Her thoughts went to Tallulah and her sumptuous breakfasts; the garden and the front door needing a touch of green paint; the ivy creeping up the grey stone exterior towards the slate roof. And in summer, the orchard filled with wild flowers, strawberries and thyme. She remembered Fred, and the hens searching for grubs in the vegetable patch and her beautifully furnished Laura Ashley bedroom. Her thoughts went to her parents and the obstacles they'd put in her way by cutting off her university allowance just because she'd been on a couple of anti-nuclear protests. They never tired of saying, 'If you'd finished your studies at university, you'd be earning a lot of money by now.' She questioned if they'd ever considered her hurt feelings and why, rather than support her while they were still alive, they'd left a substantial inheritance which she could have done with some years ago. At least the money had enabled her to start the business and she was grateful for that, even though she harboured strong feelings against them for not being sensitive enough to foresee her eventual achievements and success.

Roland was stapling documents for the morning meeting when Scarlett arrived at the office.

'Where's Serge?' she asked sharply.

Roland shrugged his shoulders. 'He's late every day so

why should he be early this morning just because we have a meeting?'

'Can we sit at my desk?'

Roland nodded.

Scarlett said, 'I'm planning to revolutionise *Agriculture and Business Monthly* by inserting a few extra pages, perhaps a centrepiece. You'll be supervised by Serge. The new insert will promote equality and feminism in the community. I want you to write an agony aunt column under a pen name. I was thinking of "Trudy"?'

'A man answering questions about women's problems?'

'You'll be able to give a different perspective. This is a unisex magazine and it doesn't matter what sex you are.'

'Well, it does to me.'

'OK, Roland, so what about the pen name Trudy?'

'No, it reminds me of being stood up by Trudy Simmons.'

'What about Suzanne?'

'She was the one I sat next to in school. She had BO.'

'Cynthia?'

'Snogged all and sundry in the locker rooms.'

'Jane?'

'Strip show in the showers.'

'For heaven's sake, Roland, what kind of a school did you go to?'

'Secondary Mod.'

'OK, so why don't *you* choose a name?'

'Veronica. I like Veronica.' Roland's eyes took on a dream-like quality.

'I suppose Veronica went the whole hog?'

'Certainly not. Not the first time anyway.'

'Roland, can we get back to business? Is the pen name Veronica acceptable?'

'Too right it is.'

Serge Gallo arrived at ten, looking as if he'd slept in his green corduroy jacket and dark brown trousers. Scarlett thought he could have been a Marcello Mastroianni look-alike if it hadn't been for his limp mouth which, first thing in the morning, puffed and pouted in annoyance for nothing in particular except for dramas going on in his head. This morning, the mop of mousy brown hair over his forehead, had barely been touched by a comb. Scarlett watched as he slumped into his high-backed chair. His whole body language said, 'I'm knackered.'

'I woke up with a terrible headache—' He accentuated 'terrible' and deliberately left the sentence unfinished as he usually did when he didn't want to justify his lateness.

Scarlett said, 'You're late. We were supposed to have a meeting at 9am. Now you're here, we can get down to business. Pull up your chairs. We need to employ an in-house journalist and an external graphic artist.'

Serge raised one eyebrow. 'Since when?'

'Since I'm responsible for staff. I've decided to launch an insert for the magazine to help women and men work better together; advise them on sex; help harmony in the family; and deal with conflicts in the kitchen and bedroom.'

'What for?'

'Because there's a need for one.'

'I can't see men buying it. You'll come up against a lot of opposition. Witherington's not exactly Fleet Street.'

'Yes I know, Serge, but it's time people started to get with it and realise they have choices. In other words, if many women in the city burnt their bras in the sixties, in the countryside it was a rare phenomenon and not many women wanted to walk around with bouncing breasts in a predominantly man's world.'

She saw Serge squint again.

'Sounds dangerous to me.'

Roland said, 'All the better if it's controversial.'

'We can't make it too controversial. We don't want to rock the boat,' Serge replied sourly.

'That's exactly what I intend to do. Serge, you'll continue being responsible for agricultural and farm issues as well as business and our finances. I intend employing another journalist to write an agony aunt column to answer readers' letters and be in charge of advertising, public relations and general office work.'

Serge said, 'Agony aunt? I hope you're not employing an old lady. I wouldn't mind working with a young female, even though it seems you're making all the decisions. I thought we're supposed to be partners. On a par.'

Scarlett retorted, 'Someone has to lead unless we want complete anarchy.'

Serge continued muttering about lack of democracy and his regret at not having returned to his roots on the Isle of Wight where at least he could get out and walk along the beach instead of tramping fields of cow shit. She imagined him going berserk over her next initiative – there would be no female journalist and Roland would have priority in the selection process and work as a trainee under him.

When Scarlett explained Roland's role, Serge became red in the face and started to sweat. He said belligerently, 'I don't want to work with someone who spends half his time at Speakers' Corner defending the rainforests and the downtrodden. We need someone dedicated.' Serge's definition of dedication was having a young, pretty, well-endowed twenty-three-year-old playing with him. The last thing Serge wanted was long-haired Roland with his leftist ideas.

Scarlett smiled at Roland and said, 'It's nice to know someone cares about what's going on in the world. And I'm sure Roland won't be spending time at Speakers' Corner if we have an urgent Sunday deadline, will you, Roland?'

Roland wasn't keen on having Sunday deadlines. 'Of course not,' he lied.

'Serge, you can interview our female vet about challenges in a predominantly male world in the countryside. Have you spoken to her about artificial insemination of horses for next month's issue?'

'No. The vet said she'd rather do worms in rabbits.'

Roland scowled. 'But I've already come up with a photo of a horse.'

'Then I suggest you come up with a photo of a rabbit instead,' Serge said, storming out of the office.

Arriving home, Serge called Anushka at her Mayfair flat and told her he was furious with his colleagues and was coming to see her. She said she'd help him control his anger and put his favourite poetry book by the bed. One hour later he tore down the motorway going south. He swerved to avoid a car travelling slowly and screamed obscenities at the driver. Two hours later, he was in London.

She opened the door wearing a black satin bodice, seamed stockings held up by a suspender belt and a long red wig over her short blonde hair. In preparation for Serge, she'd smeared her lips with shiny red lipstick and applied black eyeshadow and thick black lines along her lower lids.

Serge hoped she wouldn't start whining today about being twenty-three years of age and needing to find a husband.

Serge drummed his fingers on the kitchen table while she sat and watched.

'Serge, stop worrying about work. You are here for relax. Do you need to release tension? Do you want a fantasy?'

'No thanks.'

'You can be a knight on horse and I waiting to be ravished. I can take my make-up off to look like a fair maiden.'

He gazed at a spider running up the curtain. 'Scarlett more or less told me I could look for another job and I'm thinking to myself why do I have to write about women's problems when I have enough of my own?'

Anushka pouted. 'The last time you pretended to ride me to Serengeti and we made love under lion's tree.'

'For God's sake, Anushka, can't you see I'm in the middle of a crisis?'

'You could pretend I'm Scarlett and ride me to big crater where I totter on the edge?'

'I wouldn't touch her with a barge pole.'

'Would you like a special job?'

'I might take a day off tomorrow just to annoy her. We have a deadline so Roland will have to do my bit as well. He'll be in a sweat. He's not used to deadlines. Scarlett wants me to write a piece about women's challenges. I mean, how should I damn well know?'

She pulled down one of the straps of her black satin bodice. 'Serge, why don't you forget about office and come to bed?'

'Before long Roland will have us singing "Keep the Red Flag Flying".'

She pulled down the other strap. 'What is wrong with glorious red flag?'

'We don't want it here.'

'Do you want to see my titties?'

'Not today.'

She pulled down the bodice and let her breasts sit on the table.

Serge looked at them. 'Which reminds me, it's my mother's birthday soon.'

Anushka screamed, 'Damn your mother,' and ran into the

bedroom. Serge followed and watched her strip off her clothes to sit naked against a pale blue velvet padded headboard.

'I can look at them now, if you want?' He ducked as she threw his favourite poetry book at him.

'Can I make you a cup of tea?' he asked to pacify her.

Anushka scowled. 'Vodka better. Vodka makes man strong. Tea makes too much piss.'

Serge went into the kitchen and made them both a cup of tea. He handed her a tray with tea and biscuits and sat on the edge of the bed drinking his. He cheered her up by telling her a joke which she didn't understand.

She said, 'You British are always pissing and laughing. In my country, such people are sent to a lunatic hospital.'

'Ha! That's communism for you. Nothing to laugh about. No freedom of speech,' he scoffed.

'In Russia, our revolutionaries fight for the glorious red cause.'

'Yeah and your jails are full of those who can't say what they like.'

'People are not allowed to criticise our glorious government like in Speakers' Corner.'

'Yeah, I know, you send them to the gulag.'

'They are traitors. Police must arrest them. The police should arrest Roland.'

She had a point there. Serge's ideas about democracy were on the wane. He watched her finish drinking her tea and placed their cups on the bedside table. Then she undressed him and pulled him under the satin sheets, massaging his shoulders. He relaxed. She whispered in his ear, 'I like capitalist state because state police are not lurking around every corner.'

He murmured, 'I thought you said you didn't like them?'

'I do. I want to marry a British man so I can stay in England and be a good wife.'

Serge started to sweat at the thought of being trapped in a relationship. 'I think Roland would make the ideal husband for you. He's into fervour and banner-waving. You could take him back to Russia with you.'

'I don't want to go back to Russia. My mother and father paid a lot of money to Boris to get me to London. He set me up in this flat. Boris is a beast and I like you better.'

Serge said, 'I can't stand children.'

'We could have two dogs instead?'

'Can't stand dogs,' he said, mentioning ringworm, hookworm, heartworm, rabies, fleas and ticks.

'Cats?'

'Cat scratch disease, leptospirosis, mange, roundworm, hookworm, toxoplasmosis.'

'Birds?'

'Psittacosis, cryptococcosis, histoplasmosis, mites and West Nile disease.'

'Babies?'

'Scarlet fever, meningitis, influenza, chickenpox, measles and whooping cough.'

'Do you never want to have a family?'

'Maybe one day. But you might want to marry Roland first. He loves dogs, cats, birds and anything that moves. You'd be very happy with him. He goes to Speakers' Corner in Hyde Park. Go and see him one Sunday.'

She smiled. 'Yes I will. Perhaps I can study the Bible and have a white wedding in the Holy City. In Russia we are not allowed to believe in religion. Many people are punished for having Christian meetings. Now I feel free for the first time.'

Serge said he was happy to hear it and that she should continue feeling free.

Anushka beamed. 'So now do you want a fantasy? We could have one where you spray me with vodka.'

'I prefer water. How about if I'm the romantic poet Percy Bysshe Shelley in a water-filled boat before he drowns near Livorno? There's something poetic about water. We can skip the bit about him being cremated on the beach near Viareggio.'

'I prefer vodka and I do not like water unless it is lapping a beach in the Caribbean.'

'I could ride you up to the lake in the Andes?'

Anushka frowned. 'But the Andes is very far, I will be tired bucking all night. Why don't you look in your poetry book for a better fantasy?'

'How about the Haystack in the Floods by William Morris? Getting wet is a turn-on.'

'There is no haystack in here.'

'Just pretend there is one.'

'The hay will be wet.'

'For heaven's sake, Anushka, stop being pedantic. I can pretend it's wet and you can pretend it's dry.'

He got as far as reading '*Along the dripping leafless woods; The stirrup touching either shoe; She rode astride as troopers do; With kirtle kilted to her knee; To which the mud splash'd wretchedly*' before she asked what a kirtle was and why there was mud on it.

He groaned. 'It's an archaic petticoat and you just have to *pretend* to have mud on it.'

'So you will not be rubbing mud on me?'

'Not unless you want it mixed with horse shit.'

Betrayed

The letter for Tallulah arrived with the postman on Friday morning. A woman on the radio was saying: "A Russian double agent has passed to the British government, documents of a cover-up of nuclear testing in Semipalatinsk in Kazakhstan in 1956 when thousands suffered acute radiation sickness—"

Tallulah turned off the radio and read the letter.

From: James Willows, Wailing Willows Hotel, Witherington.

Dear Tallulah,

I'm writing to you about your advertisement in the paper for a cryonics manager. I saw the insert and although your full name was not at the bottom, I knew it was you (your reference to intelligence). I would like to apply for the job. Since Cecilia passed away I've been trying to get my life back on track. By the way, I didn't kill my wife and your life won't be in danger with me. I would never dream of letting you die. I think I would be perfect for the job as I've already seen you in the nude – unless you want the butcher, baker or undertaker to see you. Maybe you haven't forgiven me yet for abandoning you in Paris all those years ago. I realise it was a mistake. I would ask you to be understanding and give me another chance. Can we meet and discuss it?

Yours,

James

Should she reply to his letter or ignore it? She needed to reflect. On the other hand, she didn't want to put her naked body into the hands of just anyone.

Tallulah ran the bath until it was half full. Upon her return from World War II, bath night had been once a week and for the days in between it was 'top and tails'. On Sundays, a bath of water washed the whole family.

Water steamed from the tap. She threw in bubble bath and stirred the water. When the temperature was just right, she slipped off her robe and slid down into the silky foam to reflect on whether James Willows was sincere or hell-bent on further deception after deserting her forty years before when he'd left her sobbing in the lobby of a Paris hotel to marry Cecilia Willows. She remembered the concierge saying, 'Mademoiselle, the men, you know, they like to have some fun. If the man has left you, such a beautiful woman, then maybe he has another beautiful woman to go to?'

She'd missed the signs – James's thin mean mouth and his tight purse. A pair of silk stockings would have been nice. She'd put him on a pedestal and then spent the night crying when he told her he was already engaged and would marry Cecilia.

On Saturday morning, at around 9am, Tallulah walked across the fields and rang James's bell a few times before he opened the door. She was surprised to find him unshaven and still in his pyjamas. Forty years ago in Paris he'd been well turned out in his soldier's uniform and she couldn't help making a comparison with how he looked now. His skin had aged and his fair hair had become fine and wispy, the way it is when men lose their hair. But what could she expect, he was seventy years old.

He apologised and said, 'It takes a while to walk down the

corridor from my quarters.' He took her hand and kissed it. 'You're looking good, Tallulah. You haven't changed a bit.'

'Thank you, James, and neither have you.'

It was something people with short memories said after not seeing each other for some time.

'I'll just shave if you don't mind waiting. Please make yourself at home. Have a wander around the garden or read the newspaper. I'll be as quick as I can.'

Tallulah's nose registered the smell of mildew. Underfoot, the red plush carpet where the rich had once trod was now flat, worn and faded. By the time she'd read the newspaper, James returned, smartly dressed, holding a tray of tea and biscuits.

'I'm sorry to hear you've had to close a few rooms and let some staff go,' she said as James handed her a cup of tea.

James grunted. 'This country's going to the dogs thanks to the new bypass and the damned council. When I was young, the world was a better place. Now we have idiots for politicians. What we need is a New World Order. Get the United Nations in to shake it all up.'

Tallulah laughed. 'James, can you imagine being governed by a gaggle of incompetent international bureaucrats? We could be in a full blown nuclear war while they're writing their recommendations.' She put down her cup. 'Can we talk about my cryonics project?'

'Of course. I sent you a letter—'

'Your job will be to set up a four-minute early warning siren between my house and yours. When I push the button you have to rush to me and put me on ice before my brain deteriorates and then drive me to a cryonics facility in Brighton. We'll have to do a dummy run but we can talk about it later. You've seven months to get it together.'

'Plenty of time,' replied James.

'Good. You've got the job. Can I have another cup of tea?'

'How about a late breakfast? Eggs and bacon with a glass of bubbly? We might as well celebrate.'

'Thank you, James, but no thank you. I have to go and speak to Scarlett. I know she's staying here. Roland told me.'

'She's down the corridor in room forty-three.'

Tallulah rapped on Scarlett's door and waited for her to open it. It was obvious her niece wasn't expecting anyone judging by the untidy state of her room. Tallulah walked straight in, threw her handbag on a chair, looked around the room and said, 'You should put the safety chain on when you're in your bedroom.'

Scarlett tossed her red hair and slammed the door behind her. 'This is my home now and I'll do what I want.'

Tallulah looked around the room. 'How drab. It's no place for a young woman—'

'I'm not coming home.'

Tallulah sighed. 'It's my birthday tomorrow.'

'You don't need to remind me. I've never forgotten one of your birthdays.'

'I know you're angry but I need to explain about Fred.'

'There's nothing to explain. You murdered him in cold blood,' Scarlett said, picking up a stray sock from the floor and throwing it in a corner.

'I had to do it to find the timeframe between life and death. Cryonics is helping people like me live on until we can be brought back to life.' She didn't say it meant nothing to her killing in cold blood as she'd done it before.

'Do you know anyone who's been brought back to life recently?'

'No, but it's just a matter of time. By the way, you might have to drive me to Brighton to the cryonics place if James gets sick.'

'Forget it.'

'If you don't get me to Brighton, I'll be buried six feet under and suffer claustrophobia if I'm not altogether dead. I might have narcolepsy. I don't want my orifices stuffed with God knows what and my brain with its institutional secrets has to be preserved for eternity, just in case there's another war on the horizon.'

'If there's another war, we'll be blown away in a thousand-degree fireball and you can kiss goodbye to your brain. By the way, what happened about reincarnation? I mean, you were on about it for months.'

'Well, I've changed my mind. I don't want to come back as an insect. I want to be preserved until science finds a way to bring me back to life.'

'So you can come back as an old lady?'

Tallulah turned away huffily and fiddled with the curtains. 'Did I tell you it's my birthday tomorrow?'

'Yes you did and I already know. There's no need to keep reminding me.'

'I'd like you to come home.'

'So we can have Fred for lunch?'

'I'm not *that* insensitive.'

'I'll see.'

Scarlett cried after Tallulah had gone. She wasn't sure if it was because she felt alone in her room or because she missed Bluebell Vicarage and poor Fred. For sure, she missed the hens.

Minefields

Towards evening, Scarlett decided she'd cried enough. She called Tallulah to tell her she would arrive tomorrow, then washed her face, reapplied her make-up to camouflage puffy eyes and decided to start planning the new insert, including the agony aunt column. Sitting at her writing table under the window in her room, she jotted down a few lines.

Dear readers,

Witherington's heritage is steeped in history. Its rural origins go back to a time when people hoed the land, built their own houses and milked cattle by hand. Rural practices were passed down from father to son. Mothers taught their daughters good housekeeping. Eventually women woke up and demanded more independence. Some found jobs in the community. However, there are still pockets of resistance to change in Witherington. Inside Agriculture and Business Monthly, there will be an insert to address inequality in the community by providing a forum to express concerns or suggestions as to how women and men can work better together.

We have employed an agony aunt to assist you.

Yours sincerely,

Scarlett Carrick, Director

After reading it several times, she tore it up and threw it into the waste bin. It sounded pompous and patronising. Writing it in a lousy mood had not been a good idea. She thought

Roland could make a better job of it and she wanted to put him to the test.

Roland opened the door to his room wearing a painter's overall on top of his jeans and T-shirt. A smell of paint hit Scarlett's nostrils.

His eyes lit up when he saw her. 'Come in. I'm just doing a bit of decorating,' he said, stepping aside. She walked in to find three of the four walls painted green. The only trace of the ugly grapes and vines wallpaper was under the window. The room was bare apart from the bed, bedside table and wardrobe which were covered in plastic sheeting.

'Sorry I can't offer you a chair as they're stacked in the bath under my stuff. If you want you can sit on the bed.' He pulled off the plastic sheeting and she sat down on the edge.

'Won't James mind you decorating?' she asked.

'I couldn't take another day of looking at that wallpaper.'

A short silence followed.

'Would you like some coffee? I've only got instant and powdered milk,' he asked.

'No, but thanks anyway.'

Scarlett's eyes were drawn to a tall theatrical tree propped next to the window.

'I like your tree,' she said.

'I made it myself from rubber, cardboard, crêpe paper and papier mâché.'

She got up off the bed and walked over and touched it. Butterflies, bats and swooping parrots hung from the branches.

'It's supposed to represent the Amazon jungle being destroyed by the multinationals. I like to lie in bed and imagine I can smell the rainforest.'

'It's amazing but I'm not sure about the bats. Are they bloodsuckers?'

'Yes, vampire bats,' he said with wicked smile.

She shuddered in mock fear.

'It's my protest outfit. It's hollow inside. It has holes in the trunk for my arms. I wore it outside the town hall to protest about a supermarket being built in a green area. Dad was furious and kicked me out of the house. He's a councillor.'

'Well, no wonder. It must have been really embarrassing to have his son traipsing around dressed as a tree. If you feel so strongly about the environment, how come you decided to work for my magazine?'

'I didn't want to spend the rest of my life clearing people's gardens in all weathers.'

'It's a big change going from the garden into a stuffy office.'

'I don't find it stuffy at all. I like the magazine. When I was younger, I wanted to be a newspaper reporter but my parents got in the way.'

'I know what you mean,' she replied, remembering the arguments with her own parents.

A sudden question, which had nothing to do with what they'd been talking about, took her by surprise. Roland asked bluntly, 'How come you don't like Serge?'

'Does it show?'

'Yes.'

'I'd prefer not to say. I don't like criticising colleagues. It's not professional.'

She hoped he'd get the message but he followed with another question.

'Why did you come back here when you had a good job in London?'

She was sure he'd continue asking personal questions unless she answered at least one.

'My parents left me an inheritance and I used it to set up the magazine. They made me promise to take care of

Aunt Tallulah, who, by the way, doesn't deserve it after murdering Fred.'

Roland said, 'Some people are a bit insensitive when it comes to animals, they don't see them as having a soul. If I were you I'd go home and give her a hug, seeing as she's an old lady.'

Scarlett looked at Roland from beneath hostile eyebrows. The last thing she needed was half-baked advice.

She said stiffly, 'I appreciate your peace-loving approach, but I'm not a tree- or bunny-hugger and I don't think I can do that after she killed Fred. How would you feel if one of your relatives slit your pet's throat?'

Roland backed away, picked up the paintbrush and wiped it across the ugly wallpaper beneath the window.

Scarlett said, 'I have to go now. Can you write a short letter to inform our readers about the new insert to *Agriculture and Business Monthly* and your role? You can sign it under my name. See you in the office tomorrow.'

She left and the door slammed behind her.

Roland finished slapping paint on the remaining wallpaper under the window and washed his hands. He wanted to take a bath but the chairs and stuff he'd cleared from the bedroom filled it. He took off his overalls, opened the windows to let out the smell of paint and slid fully clothed into bed. He lay back looking at the ceiling, which he thought could also do with a coat of paint but too late now. His thoughts drifted to Scarlett and the way a nice friendly situation had degenerated because of his inane curiosity. Had he offended her by asking her about Serge and offering advice she didn't want? Had she slammed the door deliberately? Would there be an atmosphere in the office tomorrow?

He thumped his pillow, cursing himself for being too

familiar with his boss. He should have stayed away from the minefield of personal issues. In retrospect, she hadn't helped matters either by heaping extra work on top of his deadlines. He muttered, 'You could have written the bloody letter yourself seeing as it's from you.' Then he slid into an uneasy sleep. He was on the run from Scarlett. Racing through a minefield somewhere in the Amazon rainforest. Parrots screeching. Vampire bats biting his neck. Big beetles nibbling his toes. He was alone, afraid, perspiring and wishing he was somewhere else as long as it wasn't the office.

The necklace

The next day after lunch, Scarlett packed an overnight bag and wrapped the present she had bought a short while ago for Tallulah.

At reception, James Willows, immersed in the local newspaper, greeted her and began pouring out his woes.

'Did you see this? The council's at it again. They've increased the water rates. I've got hundreds of baths and toilets to fill several times a day.'

'They've been talking about it for months,' Scarlett replied with a smile.

Turning to the middle page, James said, 'I've just read my stars for this week. It doesn't look good. "*Libra: Beware of plumbing problems this week. A woman you are fond of will desert you*".' James's face clouded over. 'Clara the cleaner has given in her notice,' he said gravely.

Scarlett sympathised. 'Before she leaves, can you please ask her to vacuum under my bed to remove the rolls of fluff and the dust? It certainly couldn't have accumulated in the short time I've been here.'

James grimaced. 'Sorry, she used to be good when she first started. I'm looking for another cleaner, if you know anyone?'

Scarlett shook her head. 'And you might want to do something about the stiff towels and the mould around the bath and the smell of mildew and the broken curtain cord.' She could have reeled off a few other things but she stopped there.

'I'll have to do it all myself soon,' said James dejectedly.

'Hope you find someone else.' Scarlett told him she'd be

back early Monday morning as she was going to stay the night with Tallulah and left James Willows to his sorrows.

Getting out of her car at Bluebell Vicarage, Scarlett looked around. Across the field behind the cowsheds a tractor spluttered into action. Smoke curled from the chimney and she could smell soup and freshly baked cakes. She imagined Ethel, Gottfried and the hens would be sitting on their perches, if they weren't in the freezer. Tallulah opened the door before she'd time to ring. 'I heard the car. Welcome home, dear.'

Scarlett broke the stiff silence with a forced, 'Happy birthday.'

'Thank you, dear.'

'I'll go up and unpack.'

'Your slippers are by your bed and dinner's in an hour.'

Scarlett had been away only a few days but she noticed the difference. The bedroom she had slept in since she was a child, now seemed luxurious. It had beautiful wallpaper and coordinated furnishings and didn't smell of mildew.

Coming down the stairs, Scarlett could smell Lancashire hotpot with dumplings. Tallulah was flapping between sink and table. 'I made you a chocolate cake as well. I know it's your favourite.'

Scarlett noticed her aunt was wearing the pink cardigan she gave her last birthday and an apron she'd bought her in Harrods. Putting her arm around Tallulah's shoulder, she kissed her on the cheek and handed her a small gift-wrapped package with pink ribbon.

'Happy birthday, Auntie.'

Tallulah turned the present around in her hands and shook it gently. 'I knew you would come. I prepared your room this morning. I'm psychic you know.'

'We always spend your birthday together.'

'I'll open it when we're ready for chocolate cake and champagne. I like to leave the best things till last.'

'I know,' replied Scarlett, happy her aunt had set the table near the open fire, which blazed fiercely and was reflected in the crystal glasses. After a prawn cocktail, Tallulah served the Lancashire hotpot with dumplings. Between mouthfuls, they talked about things in the past they used to laugh about. Neither of them mentioned Fred.

'How are the boys getting on?'

'Roland's still learning and Serge is always causing trouble.'

Tallulah said she'd no time for timewasters. 'Get rid of him. In my day we'd have sent him to Turkmenistan. Just give him a month's notice.'

'You make everything sound so simple.'

'There's nothing simpler than putting words to paper. A flourish of the pen has put a stop to wars.'

Tallulah served the chocolate cake with two glasses of champagne. Scarlett raised hers and wished her aunt a happy birthday. Tallulah tore at her present and opened a pale grey satin jewellery box. Inside lay a tiny stainless steel cylinder with gold ends attached to a chain.

'It's hollow so you can put your name inside,' said Scarlett.

'It's exquisite. I've never seen a necklace like it. Thank you, dear.'

Scarlett said, 'It's a miniature cryonics canister.'

Tears began to fall down Tallulah's cheeks. 'It's the best and most beautiful present I've ever had.'

'Well, it's better than a miniature coffin. They were selling those too.'

The next morning at the office, Scarlett found Serge fumbling to get his key in the lock when she arrived at the office. He looked as if he'd had a bad night and was stewing over something.

'Scarlett, I'm not working with Roland, repeat, not working with Roland and that's final.'

'Serge, we need another journalist. He's a good worker and very creative.'

'He's like his father – arrogant and stubborn.'

'He was kicked out of the house. He's not at all like his father.'

Serge said, 'What normal son would protest outside the town hall where his father's a councillor? Or dress up as a tree with parrots, bats and a bloody vulture hanging from it?'

'He was protesting against Bluebell Wood being destroyed in the name of progress. He made the tree himself from rubber and papier mâché. It was his rainforest. The vulture symbolises the multinationals destroying the forests. The bats symbolise the dark dealings going on and the parrots—'

'I'm getting confused.'

'Serge, it's about love of the environment. The parrots symbolise the beauty being destroyed.'

'So they're dead parrots?'

'For heaven's sake, Serge, try not to see everything as a negative. He made the rainforest himself. He's creative. He did a good job designing the front cover of the last magazine and he's a good writer.'

Serge couldn't see the wood for the trees. He put his hands over his ears and shook his head. Then he hammered the desk.

'Over my dead body.'

'Don't tempt me. I make the decisions and I'm going to give him a trial whether you like it or not.'

Scarlett watched him out of the corner of her eye tearing a sheet of A4 paper into tiny pieces. Someone rapped on the office door and she opened it to a plump medium-height woman in her late forties, who introduced herself as Gladys Wheeler, wife of Councillor Wheeler, Roland's mother.

Mousy, wavy hair cut below the ears gave her a no-nonsense look. Mrs Wheeler's dress sense was surprisingly plain for a councillor's wife. Scarlett had expected someone brighter and more elegant. The woman seemed to have a penchant for boring colours. Her wool overcoat, skirt and sensible thick-heeled court shoes were all various shades of brown. The only respite was a hand-knitted yellow cardigan and a maroon clutch bag which didn't seem to go with the rest, as if she'd grabbed it blindfold from the wardrobe.

'I'm Gladys Wheeler, Roland's mother, and I'd like to speak to Mr Gallo,' she announced.

Scarlett saw Serge scribble something illegible on a piece of paper and knew he was biding his time. Keeping people waiting was one of his tactics to show who was in command.

'Mrs Wheeler. I'm afraid I can give you only five minutes. I have a deadline,' Serge lied, picking up a pen and twirling it around his fingers. Gladys sat down on a chair in front of his desk and folded her arms over her handbag. A loud heaving breath let them both know she wasn't there to waste time. Scarlett realised why colourful creative Roland had left home. It was like the rainforest meeting the desert.

'I hear you're looking for a journalist. My son is creative and needs a steady job.' Her voice, direct and bereft of emotion, left no doubt she'd have walked over hot coals for her offspring.

Serge, unmoved, had his elbows on the desk and hands clasped together to prop up his chin. Scarlett stifled a laugh. It was a position he took when he wanted to look as if he was weighing up words ready to make a big decision – what a great actor! He got up from his chair, hands clasped behind his back and walked to the window. A long illuminating pause followed as he studied something on the horizon before turning and addressing Mrs Wheeler.

'Does Roland know you're here?'

'Of course not. I'm doing it in his own interest.'

'Has he ever worked as a journalist before?'

'No, but he was always a good writer, even as a child.'

'As an alternative, what other job do you foresee for him?'

'Well, as a last resort, as a bookkeeper. He studied bookkeeping at college before he dropped out.'

'Maybe if he hadn't dropped out he might now have a job as a bookkeeper.'

'Yes, but he's a good boy and eager to learn.'

'If he'd been eager to learn, he'd have asked me about bettering himself, don't you think?'

Gladys took offence and shot up out of her seat. Before slamming the door behind her, she retorted, 'I hate to think what my husband, Councillor Wheeler, will say about all this.'

It sounded to Scarlett like a threat but the woman was probably bluffing.

Honour thy awful parents

Gladys picked up the phone at the third ring. Roland's voice was slightly breathless.

'Mum, I've got a job. I'm a journalist now. I've been promoted by Scarlett.'

'I'm sure your father will be delighted. He'll be over the moon. It means you can come home.'

Roland shuddered. Nagging and complaining loomed on the horizon.

'You will come home, won't you?'

'Mum, I've got my own life. If you remember, Dad gave me half an hour to pack my things and go. He called me a coward just because I didn't agree with him.'

'You know what he's like. It's his pride. You dropped out of business school. We made sacrifices to send you there.'

'I didn't want to go there in the first place. I wanted to go to art school.'

The doorbell rang.

'That's probably your dad. He forgot his key this morning as usual. I have to ring off now.'

Gladys hung up and sighed as her husband rang the doorbell a second time. She found him looking through the letter box as she opened the door. Almost knocking her over, he headed for the living room and placed his briefcase on the settee.

'I saw you on the phone. It was Roland, wasn't it?'

'I'll make you a cup of tea; by the way, he's got a job.'

'What's he doing this time – cleaning drains?'

'No, he's got a job as a journalist. You *are* pleased, aren't you? Can he can come home now?'

'Over my dead body.'

'Don't be hard on him, Ignatius, he's doing his best.'

Ignatius got up from the settee and stormed upstairs swearing.

Gladys shouted, 'Iggy, the tea's nearly ready.'

'I'm going to the pub.'

'But I've made you some stew.'

'Stick it in the fridge.'

Ignatius was glad to get out of the house. He hadn't intended going to the pub but the minute she mentioned *his* name he'd decided it was time for a drink. At this hour the Bull and Bullocks was almost empty. Ignatius ordered a pint. He sat at a side table thinking about his son, who, many years ago, had said, 'When I grow up I want to be like my dad.' It seemed natural to take him out and about. They had enjoyed quality time together. The first sign of the worm turning was when Roland had had his thirteenth birthday and refused to go anywhere with his father. Quite normal, assured Ignatius' colleagues who were quick to point out the young lad would emerge from being a chrysalis into a butterfly. Except he didn't. He turned into a layabout.

Ignatius ordered another pint. The bile rose as he thought of Roland dropping out of business school, the long hair, the weird clothes and the purple-painted fingernails, so foreign to his own generation. The son he'd longed to hang out with now hung around with people of dubious sexuality. By the third pint he was convinced it was all Gladys's fault for wishing for a girl when she was pregnant. The drink fuelled thoughts about his own rebellious streak and his father's belt, raised to chastise him. At the time, Ignatius had sworn he'd never treat any kid of his in such a way. He'd hit his wife but never his son – even though Roland had tried his patience many more times than she.

After a few pints, he stumbled back home and shouted through the letter box, 'I never took my belt to Roland but I should have.'

Honey trap

On Sunday morning Anushka set off purposefully towards Speakers' Corner, her breath short with excitement. On the very spot she imagined Marx and Lenin might have stood, she came across a gangly young Englishman with long black hair standing on an orange box.

Trained to observe every detail, she noticed his face was so white with cold it was almost blue. He wore a black overcoat buttoned up to his neck which was circled by a red wool scarf. His hair, pulled back into an elastic band, showed red ears. After blowing hot breath onto his hands, he shouted fitfully and angrily about social and political injustice in his home town of Witherington. And he spat out his words as if they had a bad taste. She liked his passion. Roland was a good communist husband in the making.

Anushka decided to approach him after his speech and chat amiably, tell him how interesting his opinions were and then lean closer to sniff him. If he had a clean smell, Phase Two, the seduction. Or, if he smelt bad – the man on the next orange box might tickle her fancy. Roland was unlikely to be a pushover. She admired his passionate speech about the class struggle and corruption and the way he controlled his fury to use it to his advantage and how his blue eyes burned intensely. Here was a man who could bring her slowly to the boil to give her some pleasure.

A small crowd had gathered, which quickly dispersed when he started talking about the downtrodden natives of the rainforests. She waited until all of them had gone and approached him.

'I liked your speech about the poor people and the rainforests. I like parrots and bats,' she said, remembering what Serge had told her about Roland's interests. He stepped off his orange box, smiled and rubbed his hands together and blew hot breath onto them. She touched his hands.

She said, 'They are freezing. Perhaps they would warm up around a cup of hot coffee.'

She held his gaze for a few seconds. She had him hooked.

'That would be nice,' Roland replied.

They made small talk all the way across Hyde Park. She steered him towards Marble Arch Tube Station. He didn't ask her where they were going as he was too busy telling her about the rainforests. Inside the train, she made sure they stood near the door so that each time the train came to an abrupt halt or swayed, she would be thrown up against him. He put his hand around her waist to steady her and she nuzzled his shoulder. Arriving at their destination, she took his hand and led him out of the station. He suddenly caught her by the arm and pushed her against a wall and kissed her neck and then her lips. He smelt clean and manly.

They ran up the stairs to her second floor flat. Anushka fumbled to get her key out while Roland started unbuttoning her coat. Once inside he took it off and dropped it to the floor, taking off his own and throwing it on top of hers. She saw the bulge in his trousers and knew he was ready.

Between the sheets she barely had time to feel his freezing feet before he began kissing her from head to toe. They rolled around a bit until he was on top of her. She heaved and moaned as she thought was expected of her. It was soon over.

'I forgot the condom,' he said apologising.

'Don't worry, I'm on the pill,' she replied, although she couldn't remember if she'd taken it last night or not.

It was now time for the baptism of fire. She brought a bottle of vodka from the kitchen and poured a couple of tots into two glasses and drank hers down in one go. Roland wasn't prepared for it to be so strong. He coughed, gasped and complained his throat was on fire.

'I'm not used to vodka,' he said with a grimace. She encouraged him to drink a little at a time.

'In Russia we drink it often, especially at weddings. You can stay here tonight if you want and I will tell you about life in Russia.'

'Sorry, but I have to go to work tomorrow.'

She snuggled against him and they kissed for a while. Untangling herself from his arms, she poured some more vodka, drinking a tot in one go and encouraging Roland to do the same. They did it several times until Roland started to feel ill.

'The room's going round. I feel sick.'

She pulled him from the bed and dragged him to the bathroom.

'Sorry,' he said after he'd emptied the contents of his stomach, mostly through his nose, into the toilet bowl. At that point her interest in him began to flag. 'Not to worry, I will take you to the train station,' she said.

'I want to stay here. I'm still feeling sick.'

Anushka said, 'Tomorrow is Monday and you must go to work. We will take a taxi to the station now.'

As soon as Roland was dressed, she hurried him outside and hailed a taxi. She didn't speak to him as he boarded the train to Witherington. How could she introduce him to her father if he didn't like vodka?

Roland spent the rest of Sunday in bed. On Monday morning at dawn, he awoke, not sure where he was. Sliding his hand to explore the other side of his bed, he found it empty. Where was beautiful, soft, perfumed Anushka? His head felt fuzzy and his mouth dry. He urgently needed a pee. He found himself in his own bed at the Wailing Willows Hotel with a hangover. A shaft of light shone through the curtains. A woman in a white ballet dress stood at the bottom of his bed, emanating mothballs.

'Get up,' she said, 'or you'll be late for work.' She smiled and faded away.

Roland lay back on his pillow and slept until 9am. Shortly after, he splashed cold water on his face and shaved. He secured his lank hair with an elastic band and scrambled into his clothes. One concession by James had been to allow long-term guests to have a fridge in the room. But today it was almost empty. No milk. A loaf of bread was breeding mould.

By the time Roland arrived at the office, it was 10am. Dragging himself to his desk and desperately longing for a coffee, he said, 'Mornin' all, sorry I'm late. I woke up with a terrible headache.'

Serge lifted his head. 'Morning, Roland. You've already used that excuse. Go back to your room – no one will notice you're not here.'

Scarlett didn't have time for male backbiting. 'Stop bickering, you two. We've a lot of work to get through today. Roland, try to be punctual tomorrow.'

Climbing into bed at around 11pm, Roland wondered why Anushka had seduced him and then pushed him hurriedly onto the train as if she never wanted to see him again.

Upon the side on which the little valley
No barrier hath, a serpent was; perchance
The same which gave to Eve the bitter food

Dante Alighieri
The Divine Comedy: Purgatory. Canto VIII

APRIL 1986

Cecilia's interrogation

Cecilia removed the dead daisies from her grave pot and replaced them with dandelions. She gave a few short snorts while her eyelids batted up and down like the wings of a bird ready to take off.

She turned on Ernest. 'Constable Barnstable, how are you getting on with the investigation into my death and missing foot?' she demanded.

Ernest rolled his eyes, glancing at Fred with a look that said, 'here she goes again' and took pad and pen from his pocket.

'Perhaps I could ask you a few questions,' he said.

'It's good to know you're not procrastinating.'

'I never procrastinate,' replied Ernest.

Fred nudged him and said, 'Keep cool.'

'Now, Cecilia, you told me James pushed you from the window. You said he grabbed you by the ankles but there were no red marks or bruises on the skin to prove it.'

'I probably had broken bones in my neck.'

'Your neck wasn't broken.'

'We had a terrible argument. James chased me up the stairs with a poker. He pushed me from the window and then severed my foot.'

'Why would he do that?'

'He was jealous of my dancing and he was an expert with a knife – an expert at dissecting chickens.'

Fred shuddered and hid his head under his wing.

'And what do you suppose he did with your foot?' Ernest asked.

'That's up to you to find out,' Cecilia replied sourly.

'One question – why were you standing on the windowsill?'

'I was doing a bit of dusting.'

Ernest wrote *Cecilia Willows was dusting the windowsill when the incident happened.*

'You mean after a violent row with your husband you decided to dust the windowsill, knowing he was chasing you up the stairs with a poker?'

Cecilia started to feel hot just at the thought of running up the stairs with her heart thumping.

'Well, what's wrong with it? Everyone knows I'm house-proud. I can't put my bare feet onto filth.'

'The police found the poker lying on the landing, which suggests your husband dropped it when he saw you climb onto the sill. Don't you think he might have wanted to save you?'

'No, he wanted me dead. James's face was red with anger.'

Ernest leaned towards Cecilia and whispered, 'Is it possible you jumped? Your husband said you were depressed just before your death and you no longer had intimate relations.'

'That's none of your business,' she whispered back.

Fred said he didn't like people whispering behind his back.

'There are things you don't need to know, Fred, this is a confidential interrogation,' Ernest said.

Cecilia added, 'Yes, it's my business and you're too young to understand certain things, being a chicken.'

Fred's crest stood on end and his nostrils narrowed. 'Just for the record, I'm a cockerel not a chicken.' He plucked a daisy from the pot, threw it on the ground and stamped on it.

Ernest said, 'Fred, unless you want to go to Purgatory you'd better calm down.' He continued interrogating Cecilia.

'Were you upset because James wouldn't give you any more money?'

'He was controlling. He often said he could kill me.'

'People say things in the heat of the moment. Were you milking him of all his money?'

Cecilia's ears turned a dark shade of pink. Fred said, 'Look, Cecilia, what Ernest says makes sense.'

'Shut up, Fred, it's none of your business,' she snapped.

Ernest reminded him he'd be in contempt of court if he poked his nose in again.

Fred ignored the threats. 'I heard her dress was up over her head when she did a dive from the window and her bloomers were the talk of the whole of Witherington.'

Cecilia flew into a rage. A foggy mist swirled around her as she waved her arms and screeched, 'Did James tell you to say that?'

The mist coiled around Fred's neck and held him in a vice until he couldn't breathe. Luckily Ernest intervened. 'Cecilia, let Fred go before you choke him to death.'

She stopped swirling and the mist receded.

'He's already dead and can't die twice,' she said huffily as she flew off to sit on someone else's grave. Ernest wrote on his pad: *Cecilia and Fred both qualify for the Terrace of the Scottish Whirling Dervishes*.

Parental rights and male bonding

The first thing Scarlett said when Roland arrived at the office was, 'After all the advertising about the agony aunt column, we've only received two letters so far.'

He said, 'It takes time and nothing's been published yet. You'll see letters rolling in after the first issue. She handed him the two letters. One was from a frustrated woman and another from a frustrated man. The first letter read:

Dear Editor/Director,

My husband says our son is a layabout and needs a good thrashing but I don't agree. I feel like a buffer between them. They treat me like a doormat. I want to be liberated. What are my rights?

Yours faithfully,

Desperate Witherington housewife

The second letter was from a desperate Witherington father.

Dear Veronica,

My son is a layabout and a compulsive liar. I wanted him to follow in my footsteps but he has a mind of his own. I would like to give him a good thrashing but my wife says it's against the law. How can I rein him in?

Yours sincerely,

Desperate Witherington father

Roland said both letters looked suspiciously like his mother's handwriting. Scarlett told him not to be ridiculous and impressed upon him the importance of fostering harmony in the community.

She said, 'Just imagine I'm a reader who loves our magazine but I'm exasperated and I, as a parent, want to know if parents have any rights. In other words, I suggest you get down to the park and do some interviews with the kids and parents to see what points of view they have on this. Then reply to the letters.'

'You've got to be kidding. Parents don't have any rights – mine walked all over me – they just have duties.'

'Roland, you're in a time warp. You need to get out there and speak to the public and get the facts.'

Roland groaned.

'And come back with something constructive.'

In the park adjoining Bluebell Wood, two boys wearing faded jeans and windcheaters kicked at a ball. The taller of the two, around fourteen years old, had his hands in his pockets. The other boy, shorter and perhaps twelve years old, was wearing gloves and a cap. Roland wrote on his pad: *About to interview two boys aged around fourteen and twelve.*

He shouted, 'Hey, you two.'

They stopped playing and the taller of the two swaggered over. 'Waddya want?'

'Would you like to be interviewed for a local magazine?'

'Yeah.'

'Your names?' He jotted down Ronnie Smith and Shorty Brown, explaining he wanted to talk to them about their parents and parents' rights.

Ronnie, the tallest, puffed out his chest. 'As far as I'm concerned they're dead. Mum ran off with Dad's best friend and Dad's always in the boozer.'

Shorty said, 'I live with Gran.'

Roland asked them both, 'Should parents have rights?'

Ronnie cocked his head to one side. 'What for?'

Roland sighed. 'Supposing you're a mother and you work all day and come back home dead tired and have to cook and clean, don't you think the kids should help out?'

Ronnie wiped his nose on his sleeve. 'We don't have time for domestic stuff. We have to do our homework.'

'So who does the domestic stuff?'

'My sis.'

Shorty said, 'I help Gran with the shopping.'

Roland wrote their comments on his pad.

'Great. Thanks a lot. Your comments were really helpful.' He waited until they had resumed their game and wrote: '*First interview – kids thought parents shouldn't have any rights. No rights for sisters but some for grannies*'.

Feeling pleased with his first interview, Roland glanced around the park looking for any girls to get a different perspective. Two young girls held a squashed-face pug on a leash. The dog growled as Roland approached. The eldest girl said, 'Goliath doesn't like men in long coats.'

The younger girl added, 'He usually bites them.'

After they'd explained why, Roland wrote on his pad: '*A while ago two young girls about twelve and thirteen years old were chased by pervert in a long beige raincoat who exposed himself. The man also kicked the dog*'.

'I'm not a dirty old man,' insisted Roland. 'I'm a journalist. I write for *Agriculture and Business Monthly* magazine.'

'That's OK, then,' said the eldest who told him her name was Lizzie and was thirteen years old.

He asked her if she helped her parents.

'I make my own bed.'

And what do you do for your dad?'

'I tell the dog to bring him his slippers.'

Maggie, who said she was twelve, added, 'And I help Dad weed the garden.'

Roland asked the burning question – should parents have rights?

Lizzie shook her head. 'Definitely not. My mother's always snooping in my room and reads my secret diary.'

Maggie didn't have much of interest to say either. 'No, because she forces me to do the housework during school holidays and my brother doesn't have to do anything.'

'And what about your dad? Does he have rights?'

Lizzie spoke for them both. 'I don't mind if Dad has rights because he never shouts and screams like she does. My dad should have the right to smash Ronnie Smith's face in when he annoys me.'

'How old is Ronnie Smith?'

'Fourteen.'

'And your dad?'

'Thirty-nine.'

Roland's pencil hovered over his pad as a woman with untidy blonde hair and wearing what looked like an inflated pink nylon jacket, approached wielding a rolled-up umbrella.

'Hey, you. What do you think you're doing? I want to see what you've got on under your coat,' she shouted.

Roland, feeling intimidated, couldn't remember whether he was wearing the trousers with the tear or the shirt without a button.

He said, 'No, I'm not going to show you.'

The woman shouted over her shoulder, 'Sam! That flasher's come back.' A heavyweight muscular man ran towards them.

Lizzie said, 'That's my dad. He wants to smash Ronnie Smith's face in.'

Roland took to his heels. The woman unleashed Goliath.

He heard her say to the girls, 'I've told you so many times not to speak to strange men. You know what happened the last time.'

Her husband ran after Roland, shouting, 'You bloody pervert,' while the dog, running on his little legs, tried to overtake Roland, who, helped by his adrenalin, ran like the wind into the ladies' toilets and locked himself inside a cubicle.

The man shouted, 'I'll be waiting for you when you come out.' Then all was silent as it usually was in films when the baddy was psychologically scaring the shit out of his victim.

Roland spent half an hour swatting Goliath with his notepad to keep him from sliding under the cubicle door. He was rescued by police who'd been notified about a pervert in the ladies' toilets. When they arrived, Goliath was retrieved by his owner who attempted to punch Roland as the police escorted him out. Scarlett, alerted by the police, rushed to the 'scene of the crime' to justify Roland's presence in the park and why he was chatting up underage girls. When the police were satisfied Roland was not a threat to public decency, a stern-looking policeman released and warned him.

'This time you're lucky. The next time you might want to get parental permission first.'

Later Roland wrote on his pad: '*Parents who keep vicious dogs shouldn't have any rights. An innocent citizen who was just doing his job almost had his face smashed in by a parent and spent an hour in the ladies' toilets*'.

A day later, after a ticking-off from Scarlett, Roland gave her his piece. When he read it through, he realised he was speaking from his heart to the awful parents of the world, including his own.

Dear desperate Witherington housewife,

As a parent, forget you have an identity or rights. If you have read the UN Convention on the Rights of the Child, you will realise there will never be one on rights of the parent. Your parental duties consist of feeding, nurturing and paying bills. When he/she lies in bed all Saturday because his/her world is coming to an end but is well enough to go to the evening disco, you might want to learn teen-speak to communicate better. Resist the idea of buying him/her a vacuum cleaner for Christmas or sending him/her to India to bake bricks, as this is considered child cruelty and exploitation by the UN Convention on the Rights of the Child.

Best regards,
Veronica

Dear desperate Witherington father

If your son didn't follow in your footsteps it's because he has a mind of his own. He was wrong to lie and if you have never lied, you have every reason to throw the first (made in India) brick. I see a breakdown in communication typical of the older generation who are reluctant to accept change. You must now accept that he's a grown man with dreams and projects of his own. You can try male bonding. It usually starts in several places: on the football field, the fishing lake, the shooting range or campsite. These are all activities men and boys can practise to show their superior skills – which come in useful when the car breaks down and you have to live off the land because someone forgot the ice box with the sausages. To avoid starvation, nip to the supermarket and buy a chicken. Go back to your tent and cook it. When the women arrive, tell them how you caught, skinned and cooked a chicken that you found in the woods while they were away.

Regards,
Veronica.

Scarlett thanked him and told him to get it to the printers in time to be published at the end of April for the May issue.

Four-minute warning

Tallulah picked up the phone at 8am and called James to see if he'd made progress on her cryonics project. She wasted no time on preliminaries and launched straight into a request for him to get planning permission for a *Four-minute Early-warning Siren* to be erected in his garden and connected to her house, two minutes away by car.

'It'll warn you when I'm about to die. You can ask Roland to get the forms.'

James grunted. He said it was too early in the morning and he'd a plumbing problem in one of the rooms. 'Roland can't stand his father,' he said.

'He can speak to Mrs Horsefield.'

'The one with the horsey teeth?'

'You know damn well she has.'

'What happens if the electricity goes off?'

'It means I die, James. Find a solution. Get a bloody generator.'

He could imagine what she was thinking just by the tone of her voice – how she was surrounded by idiots and if Britain had won the war, it was only thanks to the secret service and her contribution, because the average man like himself and the average woman like Scarlett, hadn't the foggiest idea how to solve simple challenges.

The disastrous implications of a power cut worried Tallulah. After breakfast, she walked across the Wormsleys' muddy fields to the Wailing Willows Hotel, arriving just after nine.

At the third ring, James answered the door. 'Just popped by to see you.'

He grunted and said he was expecting the plumber.

'Are you going to invite me in, or do I have to stand here all day?'

He stood back and let her past. 'Would you like a cup of tea?'

'Thanks. How far are you along with the siren?'

'I still have to ask Roland to help get planning permission, give me time!'

'Then hurry up. I could be dead and buried before it's approved.'

James led her to the sitting room and headed for the kitchen to put the kettle on. Before disappearing to make a cup of tea, he said, 'Do you think you'll ring the emergency bell during the day or night?'

James immediately regretted his question, blurted out without thinking, when Tallulah's nostrils widened and her voice rose a tone.

'How should I know when I'm bloody-well about to die?'

The next morning, James rang Roland at 6.30am. Roland picked up the phone sounding as if he was in a coma. James couldn't have cared less. He'd bigger problems than lack of sleep.

'Roland, would you mind coming over before you go to work. I need to speak to you about planning permission for a project.'

'It's the middle of the night,' he mumbled.

'The birds are singing and you're missing the best part of the day. It's urgent. A matter of life and death and you're only down the corridor.'

There was silence on the other end of the line before it went dead.

An hour and a half went by before Roland turned up. He sat on James's settee, his knees almost touching his chin.

'Sorry, Roland, it's a bit low but Cecilia chose the settee. We didn't have much in common when it came to furniture. She preferred art deco and I liked something classier, but we compromised and bought a bit of both. Thanks for coming, old boy. I appreciate you odd-job men have a busy life what with cleaning stables and chicken-runs and the like.'

'I'm not an odd-job man. I'm a full-time journalist.'

'Glad to hear it—' He broke off and looked at a painting above the door. 'Well, I do believe I've forgotten why I asked you to come here.' James gave an embarrassed cough and tried quickly to retrieve his brain.

'Was it about the planning permission?' Roland asked.

'Oh yes. Can you pick up some forms for me? I need them for an important project, a matter of life and death – a four-minute warning siren for Tallulah Millstone's project. You can ask Scarlett for a couple of hours off and get your father to sign them seeing as he's an expert at everything.'

Roland said he hated his father but would pick up the forms. 'Scarlett will go berserk. We have deadlines.'

James's answer was, 'Don't take any notice, all women are like that.'

Pandemonium

Roland pulled up the collar of his overcoat to protect his ears from the wind and pedalled towards the town hall. In the High Street, at a curve in the road, two men in white overalls were taking down the sign 'Witherington Police Station'. He dropped his bike and ran towards them.

'Hey! What are you two doing?'

'Just following orders, mate. The building's being demolished.'

Roland froze in his tracks. The police station was a noted Victorian jewel; fully operational as a police station not long after the Rural Constabulary Act of 1839. How could they destroy one of the first police stations in the United Kingdom?

'You can't demolish a historic building!' he shouted.

'We were told to.'

'Constable Barnstable's not long dead. He'll be turning in his grave.'

'Just following orders, mate.'

'It should be turned into a museum,' Roland insisted.

The men ignored him. The sign came sliding down on two ropes and clattered to the ground. Witherington Police Station was history.

Roland ran to the town hall, strode past a queue of people and banged his fist on the counter. People murmured and someone said, 'Get to the back of the bloody queue.'

Mrs Horsefield, Councillor Wheeler's forty-year-old assistant, was flicking through a pile of documents with a rubber thimble on her index finger.

Roland interrupted her. 'Excuse me.'

He watched her blonde bushy eyebrows rise and nostrils flare. A red dress signalled danger. Her crimson nails were ready to slash and dismember.

Mrs Horsefield rolled her eyes. 'What's it this time, Roland?'

He leaned over the counter and raised his voice. 'You can't demolish the police station, it's a historic building.'

'Roland, I'm not deaf. How come you're not protesting dressed as a tree today? Lost your parrots?'

An elderly man mumbled, 'Aye, 'e's lost more than 'is parrots.'

Roland turned savagely. 'Some of us have to worry about the destruction of the rainforests and what the council's doing.'

A woman in her mid-fifties stood in the queue holding her sister's hand. The younger woman tried to pull her hand away. 'I didn't know there was a rainforest in Witherington,' she said, speaking like a child.

'There isn't, dear, the rainforest is in Brazil where the nuts come from,' her sister replied.

'Was Roland dressed as a tree to hide from the nuts?'

'For heaven's sake, Mabel, shut up.'

But Mabel refused to be gagged. 'I wish *we* had a rainforest in Witherington.'

Mrs Horsefield called for an end to the chattering about rainforests and announced for all to hear, 'The police station was in such a bad state it couldn't be renovated.'

'No wonder poor old Barnstable kicked the bucket,' Roland said.

Mrs Horsefield said she didn't intend justifying council business and added, 'The new police station is in Rottingham. The bus goes there directly. Now please stand aside, Roland, people are getting fidgety.'

Roland thumped the counter for the second time. 'The archives alone have antique value. If anything should be demolished, it should be this place.'

Mrs Horsefield interrupted, again asking Roland to step aside.

'I want to speak to my father,' he demanded.

'Sorry, Roland, but Councillor Wheeler is on holiday. He's gone to the Caribbean for a few days.'

An elderly fellow in the queue said, 'I 'ope not paid by our taxes.'

This started a debate and the queue dissolved into a crowd around Mrs Horsefield's counter. Questions were fired at her all at once – did the councillor's absence mean they wouldn't get their planning permission signed? Why hadn't she told them when they came in? Was it possible the councillor was dead as there had been a hurricane in the Caribbean somewhere near Hawaii? Was he in Hawaii or the Caribbean? Or was his disappearance connected to Constable Barnstable's death?

'They're both as dead as two dead parrots,' Mabel announced loudly to everyone.

Roland shouted over the commotion, 'I need some planning permission forms.' Added to the din, was the tip-tap clatter of Mrs Horsefield's heels as she ran and locked herself in Councillor Wheeler's office.

James's eyes scanned the planning permission forms Roland had picked up. *Part 1 Your details. Part 2 Information about proposed work. Part 3 Plans and work in relation to existing dwelling. Part 4 Plan view with measurements.* Attached were four pages with explanations, drawings and exclusions. James threw them on the table. 'I can't make head nor tail of them. Never was good at forms. Cecilia always did the paperwork.'

Roland reluctantly offered to help. 'I'll fill them in if you give me all the details.'

James said, 'Tallulah Millstone, Scarlett's aunt, advertised for a cryonics manager. Well I'm her manager and she's asked me to set up a four-minute early-warning siren in my backyard. When she presses the button I have to get to her within four minutes and put her on ice before she dies. Then I have to drive her to a cryonics facility in Brighton where they'll put her in a canister in liquid nitrogen for the next ninety years.'

Roland laughed. 'It sounds like the Cold War when the British government was making plans for an eventual nuclear bomb arriving. What a charade. Imagine you're watching a football match in the pub and the four-minute-warning siren goes off and you have to run for cover and batten down the hatches within four minutes. Supposing your pet dog is at home half an hour away—'

James ignored the implications. 'When you put in the dimensions for the siren remember it has to be the height of two telegraph poles as I can't have it on a level with my bedroom window. I don't want to be blown away on the sound barrier if it goes off in the middle of the night.'

'You'll have to keep your windows closed. The council will throw out the request. It's too high.'

'I'll die in the summer heat.'

'And so will the old lady if you don't get to her.'

When Roland had filled in the forms, James reminded him to keep quiet about the project.

Roland nodded. 'OK, but it's obvious Dad will know if he signs the planning permission.'

'That's alright. Your father has a sense of responsibility. He's hardly likely to spread it around Witherington.'

Panic stations

Following three days of feeble attempts to extract an agreement from Scarlett to give him a couple of hours off just before his lunch break, Roland managed to convince her that her aunt's planning permission was important. And that his father should be back from the Caribbean by now to sign the forms.

Leaving his bike propped against a wall near the council office, he strode past a long queue, ignoring murmurs of discontent as he walked to the counter. He noticed Mrs Horsefield still had the rubber thing on her index finger and she was wearing the red dress he'd seen her in when he went to complain about the demolition of the police station.

She rolled her eyes. From between her equine teeth came a resigned hiss of recognition.

'Yesssss. What's it this time, Roland?'

'Is Dad back from the Caribbean? I want to see him.'

She gave him a disdainful look before disappearing into Councillor Wheeler's office. When she emerged, her blonde bushy eyebrows knit together in annoyance. 'You're lucky, your father's in a good mood. Just make sure he stays that way.'

The wind of change had blown through Councillor Wheeler's office. For as long as Roland could remember, his father had worn black, grey or navy suits with a white shirt underneath. But today he wore beige trousers and jacket with a brightly coloured floral shirt underneath. As was his habit, his father launched straight into conversation with no preliminaries.

'What are *you* doing here? Come to cause trouble as usual?'

Roland placed the buff folder with the request for planning permission in front of him.

'I'm on an errand for James Willows.'

'I thought you were too busy saving the world?'

Roland felt a surge of hate run through him for all the times his father had humiliated him.

'Well I might be when you see this'. Roland pushed the envelope with the planning request towards his father.

'Whatever's in there can wait another day. The world's not about to come to an end.'

'Wouldn't count on it. A lot's been happening while you've been away. The Russians are on alert,' Roland said, as gravely as he could, even though he didn't know if it was true or not. He thought he saw a flicker of fear cross his father's face. His father wouldn't be able to resist opening the envelope.

Roland sat down at the chair in front of his father's desk. 'Remember Tallulah Millstone, the ex-MI6 spy? She wants to set up a four-minute early-warning siren on James Willows' land. Do you think she knows something we don't? I mean, she could be communicating with Fylingdales.' Roland didn't know where it was but it sounded important.

He saw his father's face pale and twitch as he opened the envelope and read the details. *Utmost Urgency. Request to set up four-minute Early-warning Siren. Justification: to save lives.*

His father looked at him quizzically. 'Does it mean—?'

'Yeah, the Russians are filling their missiles with crap as we speak.'

'I never heard anything when I was on holiday!'

'That's because the Americans control communications. Remember the Cuban Missile Crisis of 1962? The Russians had a hundred tactical nuclear weapons and long-range missiles deployed in Cuba that none of us knew about. They could have caused the deaths of a hundred million people on either side. It was the equivalent to one hundred Hiroshima bombs. We could have been blown off the face of the earth in our sleep. That's why you have to sign the forms. It's all about forewarning and being one step ahead. Everyone's got a right to defend themselves.'

A barely perceptible 'Holy shit!' escaped his father's lips. 'I hope this isn't another of your lies, Roland.'

'I wouldn't lie to you, Dad.'

'You did before.'

'I'm different now.'

Roland had clocked up another lie.

His father nodded and pressed a buzzer on his desk and held it down until Mrs Horsefield strode in. She looked at Roland, the bearer of evil. 'Is there something wrong, Councillor Wheeler?' Her eyebrows said she suspected there was something dreadfully wrong.

'Mrs Horsefield, get rid of all those people and call a council meeting immediately.'

She threw Roland a contemptuous look. 'For tomorrow or the day after?'

Councillor Wheeler banged his fist on the desk. 'I said immediately. We could all be dead by tomorrow. Get the other councillors here at once.'

'Right away, sir.'

If his father had been nicer to him, he would have told him the real reason for the siren. But now he wasn't going to tell him there wasn't going to be a nuclear war. Let him stew the night. Roland knew his panic-stricken father, always on alert for conspiracies, would waive correct procedures and sign and stamp the document to make it look acceptable to someone under pressure in an emergency. And so it was.

'Get the siren built straight away, we don't have time to lose.' Then he waved Roland out of the office and started drafting the agenda for the council meeting. He started to write *Urgent security alert...*

Roland rode away from the town hall having second thoughts about his joke in bad taste and the consequences on the community. Pangs of conscience bothered him. He'd set off a chain of events due to go down in Witherington's history as a cog in the wheel of folly. He pictured people hammering nails into boards across windows; heaving sandbags against the walls of houses; searching for sewage buckets. He visualised cast-out animals wandering the countryside with nothing to eat. He'd never been particularly religious but now he needed a place to confess his sins before Witherington's fauna was condemned to a horrifying death.

Entering the Church of Local Martyrs, Roland walked past a striking marble statue of a woman in her forties. Although sculpted in grey marble, Roland visualised blonde wavy hair and a white nightdress that, honestly, left little to the imagination. Her nipples, straining against her nightdress, were clearly visible from the back of the church. The inscription read *Here lies Penelope Warren the Witherington Virgin*. It was a stroke of luck for tourism when Mrs Warren had been blessed with a virgin pregnancy, not having been impregnated by her husband who was absent at sea at the time. Folklore claimed the miracle egg had descended, like a holy ghost, from her ovaries and attached itself to her uterus. According to the Tourist Information leaflet there followed a virgin birth and her death a few days after her husband's ship docked in Southampton. To commemorate the miracle, a statue was commissioned. When it was unveiled, parishioners noticed Mrs Warren's breasts were three sizes bigger than they had been in her lifetime. They talked about calling her Madonna of the Milk, hoping it wasn't blasphemous, convinced her bosom was symbolically engorged with milk for the child she'd left behind, until someone mentioned the sculptor had a fetish about breasts, hence the straining nipples.

Roland tried not to focus on the dead woman's breasts but they had a way of drawing his eyes back to them. They reminded him of Anushka and he desperately wanted her to comfort him. He made his way to the front pew and sat down exhausted with his hands together in prayer.

Seeing movement out of the corner of his eye, he turned his head and saw two people sitting next to him. Perhaps it was the sun shining in through the stained glass window above, but they looked as if they were sitting in a fog. The man was wearing a red, white and green striped hat and scarf and a constable's uniform and the woman was smoothing down a long white ballet dress which emanated mothballs, the back part of which was over her head. She looked like the woman he'd seen at the bottom of his bed at the Wailing Willows telling him to get to work after having been dumped by Anushka.

Roland murmured, 'Holy mother of God!'

The woman replied, 'I'm not his mother. My name is Cecilia.'

He looked the man up and down.

'Jeez, you're wearing a hat in church.'

The man said, 'I'm not Jesus.'

Roland, perplexed, asked who they were.

The man in the hat was the first to reply. 'You should recognise me, you young scallywag. You were called to the police station enough times. Remember me? I gave you a warning for prancing around Bluebell Wood dressed like a tree.'

'Constable Barnstable? But you're—'

'Dead? Yes of course I'm dead, thanks to the police station being closed. Your father had something to do with it and I suspect you're here because of him.'

'Sort of.'

'You always were a little liar. I always said you'd be in trouble one day because of it.' He paced up and down, his hands behind his back.

'I'm not a liar. It's other people's interpretation of what I say. They always get it wrong.'

'May I suggest you now confess your sins in front of us?'

'If you confess you'll feel better,' added Cecilia.

'No, I don't want to confess to two people who pass themselves off as Jesus and the mother of God.'

'We never passed ourselves off as anyone. It was your interpretation. My name is Cecilia Willows and I was murdered by my husband and this is former Constable Ernest Barnstable, the future Security Officer of the Pearly Gates and Gatekeeper of Purgatory *ad interim*, who dropped dead in his office. And who never said he was Jesus.'

'She wasn't murdered, she committed suicide or maybe she jumped,' the constable said.

Roland thought both of them were talking a lot of rubbish. 'Jesus never wore a striped hat and the mother of God never wore a ballet dress,' he said.

Constable Barnstable's voice took on an officious tone as the absurd conversation continued. 'So you admit you lied and led us to believe we were Jesus and the mother of God, therefore we didn't lead you to believe we were such.' He turned to Cecilia. 'There, I told you he was a little liar.'

'Hush, Ernest, we're in the house of the Lord. It's time you forgave him for the past. You said you were looking for a medium through which to channel your investigation. Roland's the ideal person.'

'Poppycock! He's a born liar.' Ernest began to recite, in a lilting voice, 'Childe Roland to the dark Tower Came'. It was obvious to Cecilia he had it in for Roland.

My first thought was he lied in every word,
That hoary cripple, with malicious eye,
Askance to watch the working of his lie,
On mine, and mouth scarce able to afford
Suppression of the glee that pursed and scored
Its edge at one more victim gained thereby.

Cecilia scowled. 'I think you're coming down a bit hard on him. I'm sure Robert Browning didn't write it with Roland in mind.'

Ernest insisted on explaining the symbolic reasoning behind the dark tower and Childe Roland's steed.

'Roland rode his bike, symbolising Childe Roland's steed, to the town hall, which symbolises the dark tower.'

Cecilia became confused and didn't see the connection between the bike, the steed and the hoary cripple. She was relieved when Ernest made for the door shouting, 'Over my dead body! I don't need a medium.'

Roland turned to Cecilia. 'I'm worried about animals being thrown out on the street after the bomb hits Witherington.'

'You know there's no bomb coming. You have to go to your father and confess your lie.'

'Over my dead body,' said Roland, echoing Ernest.

Roland stayed sitting on the pew. He dreamt he pedalled through Witherington looking for dogs, cats, rabbits, cows, sheep, pigs and anything moving on the ground. He had to save them from a giant mushroom before it was too late.

Upon awakening, he left the church wondering what kind of a weird dream he'd had.

Nuclear madness

Gladys was about to sit down for a cup of tea when she received a telephone call from her husband's assistant Mrs Horsefield.

'Good morning, Mrs Wheeler, I'm putting you through to Councillor Wheeler.'

The line clicked and she heard Ignatius say, 'Gladys, I'm in the middle of a national security emergency. Stock up the nuclear shelter and get in some groceries in preparation for a nuclear attack.'

Gladys tried to contain her excitement. Finally, after all these years there was going to be an emergency and perhaps in the confusion Ignatius would agree to Roland coming home. She remembered how thrilling it had been to attend Civil Defence courses in 1964 in preparation for the nuclear bomb and the role she'd play in helping survivors. That was when the whole of the nation had pulled together and communities had never been so close. There'd been a lot of government propaganda and films to warn the population what to do as soon as the British government got wind of a Russian nuclear bomb whizzing towards England's green and pleasant land. They all felt safe knowing the government would activate the 'Four-minute Warning' siren which would give them four minutes to run home and batten down the hatches before they were blown off the face of the earth, although they never explained how to get to the children in four minutes if they weren't in the garden. She remembered the grave voice of a Civil Defence representative telling people to *board up windows with wood or sandbags to keep out nuclear dust and put sandbags against the walls*. She remembered they all felt safe in their 'fall-out' rooms, because the British government told them to wash their boots before entering the house after coming back from doing the shopping. She slept soundly at night knowing the government and armed forces were well prepared with ambulances, fire trucks and useful information emergency advice like *In the event of burns from nuclear fall-out, take two aspirins six times a day*. And the Americans had their films too on what to do when the nuclear bomb was on its way. It was comforting to know that on the other side of the Atlantic, American kids having a picnic could be protected by ducking under a tablecloth or a newspaper, so the authorities said, although she did wonder what they had learned from Hiroshima. Gladys mostly worried about finding a multitude of neighbours outside her door trying to get into the shelter and how Ignatius would survive for fourteen days with noisy children, pets and birds and only one bucket-toilet.

Taking out a small green book from her uppermost cupboard, Gladys consulted it:

Civil Defence Instructors' Course, Sat Dec 5 1964

Aim:

To prepare for nuclear war. Health, education, welfare, information, supply, food, transport, fuel, stores, equipment. Operational Plan, co-ordination of effort; accommodation, cooking, billeting, public health.

Welfare duties:

Dispersal priority classes, children and expectant mothers.

Homeless:

Rest centres. Clearance of damaged areas. Restore morale.

Dispersal Clearance Centre:

Private homes; billeting centre.

Improvised rest centre:

Sports stadium? Parks? Registration.

Rest centre equipment:

First aid, blankets, water source, sanitary equipment, kitchen, feeding equipment, furniture and bedding, lighting, heating, clothing, forms, records, fire-fighting equipment, transistor radios.

Damaged areas:

Serious casualties: assurance, warm drink.

Clearance zones:

Radiation sickness. Vomiting, diarrhoea, fatigue, blood spots, susceptibility to disease. Antiemetic, morphia. Fluid. Saline. Recommended: pre-first aid lectures.

Emergency feeding:

Food rationing introduced – at least one hot meal per person. Ten galls water – boil for 35 minutes with 5lbs coal and 4lbs wood. Drop a piece of wood in water to collect dirt and grime. She stopped where it came to the part about disposal of waste.

It was noon by the time Gladys finished making notes and a list of groceries. Twenty minutes later she was on her way to the local grocery shop to speak to Antonio.

Antonio's olive skin belied his Sicilian origins. He wasn't so young but women young and old found his thick moustache and black hair attractive. They secretly drooled over his tanned, muscled forearms when the sleeves of his white shirt were rolled up to his elbows. And they whispered and giggled, wondering what baggage he might have beneath the counter and in bed. Antonio oozed charm from every pore. The only person standing between the women of Witherington and Antonio was his jealous Sicilian wife. Antonio's shirts were the talk of the town. The community had never seen shirts washed so white and he never tired of telling them what a good wife she was and how proud *he* was she didn't need to work because he earned enough for her not to. In his country only poor women worked. His good Sicilian wife had been a virgin on their wedding day. The morning after, the sheet with her blood on it was hung out on the balcony for all the neighbours to see.

Gladys imagined Antonio putting his arms around his wife, her hands in the dishwater, being dragged laughing into the bedroom. It was a long time since Ignatius had done such a thing. She stood at the counter and greeted him warmly.

'Ah, Mrs Wheeler, so beautiful and elegant today.'

Gladys didn't have time for compliments and handed him her list. As he read it she saw his hairline begin to recede like the tide.

Tuna: 200 tins. Baked beans: 300 tins. Sugar: 100 lbs. Flour: 300 lbs. Tinned tomatoes: 200 tins. Peas, lentils, cling peaches, mandarin oranges: 300 tins of each. Bottles of Scottish Highland spring water: 600. Toothpaste: 30 tubes. Toothbrushes: 50. Ditto for cakes of soap; boxes of Persil, toilet paper, serviettes, paper bags and matches.

She realised Antonio had never seen such a big order in the twenty years he'd been there. He began to sweat and his crisp white starched shirt began to wilt from the humidity emanating from his body. His hairy arms glistened. He exclaimed, '*Mamma mia, questa roba e' per un'esercito!*'. Gladys knew enough Italian to be able to make out he'd just said there was enough food for an army.

'I not have so many foods.'

Antonio's command of English would have been more coherent had someone corrected his mistakes over the years, but obviously no one had.

'Then order them. I want them delivered to my house immediately.'

Antonio's eyes widened and he looked flustered. 'I not have van big enough.'

'Then hire one. My husband, Councillor Wheeler, will be angry if he doesn't see the stuff immediately.'

'Mrs Wheeler, I speak to your husband first?'

'No, not speak to my husband first. In England, woman makes decision. This not Sicily.'

'But he usually pay the bill.'

He had a point there. 'Oh very well, just tell him how much it's going to cost and ask him to give you a cheque.'

After Mrs Wheeler had gone, Antonio shut down the shop and hung a sign on the door *Closed for family death*. He was sweating as he'd never sweated before because he'd never ever asked the councillor for a cheque. It had always been cash on delivery. Antonio made the sign of the cross and kissed the heavy gold crucifix around his neck, praying it would protect him from Councillor Wheeler – the British Godfather who had contacts with the strong, important Masons – a kind of UK secret mafia who did good work instead of killing people. He hoped his wife wouldn't call her father in Sicily or the result would be a contract out on Councillor Wheeler. Antonio wasn't happy at all. He'd come to Witherington for a quiet life. And now he was forced to do business with a woman. The British Godfather's wife was poison, for while she was bringing good business, she was putting him under undue pressure. In Sicily life was never like this. You bought one tin at a time and you didn't order the shopkeeper around as if he was a slave unless you wanted to disappear into a barrel-full of cement. Life in Sicily was good and women knew their place.

Ever since coming to Witherington he'd suffered the rain, snow and the awful British food. He wanted to go back to Sicily to sing, dance and eat decent spaghetti which wasn't from a tin and didn't resemble worms. He picked up the phone to call his supplier and groaned aloud – life was looking like shit on this pissing little island.

Russian missile crisis

Councillor Wheeler paced up and down in front of Mrs Horsefield who was making notes on her pad and asking too many questions. 'Mrs Horsefield, just do what I say otherwise there'll be complete panic in Witherington. If the word gets out—'

She wrote on her notepad '*Russians will be raping and pillaging etc*'.

She said, 'It could be a hoax. Do you remember last year when you put the whole area on alert about a column of army ants marching on Witherington, when it was really about a march-past of the Territorial Army?'

Councillor Wheeler silenced her with a look *mention it again and you're fired.*

The phone rang. Councillor Wheeler put up his hand to stop further questions.

'I'll take it. It's probably about our emergency meeting.'

He picked up the phone. 'Yes!'

He heard a foreign accent say, 'Councillor, your wife, she order hundreds of tins, she say I tell you the price.'

Councillor Wheeler had a mental block for anything foreign. 'For Pete's sake, man, I'm in the middle of an international crisis. I don't have time to discuss tins.'

The foreign accent became desperate. 'But I already order more than one thousand pieces between baked beans and Persil. Mrs Wheeler, is she buying for a wedding?'

Councillor Wheeler couldn't see what a wedding and Persil had to do with a nuclear attack.

'I not have wedding. I have big fucking emergency and I not want tins,' he said imitating Antonio's voice. Mrs Horsefield cringed, shocked at his language. She couldn't hear what Antonio was saying on the other end but whatever it was her boss's voice rose to a crescendo as if he'd been stung. 'But that's more than half of my bloody salary!'

She put her hands over her ears as the altercation continued and retired to her office.

Her phone buzzed insistently. Councillor Wheeler breathed heavily down the phone, 'Type up an agenda and tell the other councillors to get here this afternoon as a matter of urgency.'

She told him the councillors were not used to urgent emergencies. 'Councillors Reed and Smythe are taken up with junior football matches and the rest of them are out.'

What she didn't tell him was they would laugh themselves silly after last year's fiasco over the army ants.

Councillor Wheeler swore some more, this time about lack of social conscience.

'Call them again and hurry up with the agenda.'

She snapped, 'I can't do two things at once.'

STRICTLY CONFIDENTIAL AGENDA

1. Russian missile crisis: How far can you run in four minutes?

2. Getting to the children in record time.

3. Avoiding a secondary emergency (i.e. unplug iron to avoid starting a fire).

4. Medical emergency – stocking up on aspirin for radiation burns.

After finishing the agenda, Mrs Horsefield picked up the phone and dialled Councillor Bacon's number. He answered at the third ring. 'This is Councillor Bacon, how can I help you?'

'Good morning, Councillor Bacon, this is Mrs Horsefield, could you please come to an urgent council meeting?'

'Sorry, but I have to take my wife to Bridge this afternoon.'

'Sir, it's very urgent. It's about an impending Russian attack.'

'She's sprained her ankle. My wife will kill me if she doesn't get to her weekly Bridge game.'

'Councillor Bacon, I foresee Councillor Wheeler killing you first if you don't come to the meeting.'

'Then I have to weigh up my priorities and options.'

'What do you mean?'

'What I mean is, I have to weigh up whether the Russian missile crisis is more important than my wife's Bridge and whether I prefer to be killed by my wife, the Russians or Councillor Wheeler.'

Councillor Wheeler in denial

James noticed Roland's red face and perspiration. 'What is it? Did your father reject the planning permission?'

'No, he signed it.'

'Good boy.'

'I have a confession to make. I let my dad think the four-minute warning siren was for an impending nuclear attack.'

'Good God, Roland! Why on earth did you do it?'

'It started off being a joke.'

'A joke? A fine joke it is. Do you know what that means? It means people will be boarding up windows and turning out animals onto the streets. They'll be hoarding food and digging latrines. Your father will be a laughing stock once again.'

'Nobody is going to believe him after the territorial army ants.'

James looked about to pop a vein. 'Is it your revenge because he kicked you out of the house?'

'Your dead wife Cecilia said I have to tell you the truth.'

James said slowly, 'Cecilia?'

'Yes. I saw her in church.'

'First of all Cecilia never went to church. You're lying.'

'I don't tell lies. It's how other people interpret what I say.'

James had heard enough. 'I would say you're a compulsive liar.'

James wasn't looking forward to calling Councillor Wheeler about his lying wayward son. The thought of being a buffer between the two irritated him and he didn't see why it should fall on him to sort out Roland's mess. In the end he dialled the town hall. A familiar voice answered. 'Witherington Town Hall, how can I help you?'

James doubted Mrs Horsefield, or anyone else, could help him right now. In fact he was sure the lady herself would need help after bearing the brunt of Councillor Wheeler's rage upon learning his son was a liar.

'This is James Willows, please connect me immediately to Councillor Wheeler. It's a matter of life and death.'

She gasped at the word 'death' and asked when the Russians would be on the rampage. He told her she'd got her films mixed up. 'My dear lady, if there's a nuclear blast, which there won't be, there'll be no Russians left. Please just tell Councillor Wheeler it's about his son.'

He heard a sigh of relief. 'He'll hit the roof,' she said, then the line clicked and Councillor Wheeler was breathing heavily as if he'd just climbed stairs.

'What is it, James? What's going on?'

James came straight to the point. 'Ignatius, it's about your son. I know Roland came to see you and I just want to explain why. There was a huge misunderstanding about the four-minute warning siren. It's for Tallulah Millstone's cryonics project and there's not going to be any nuclear attack. Your son Roland lied—'

Councillor Wheeler interrupted. 'Look, James, I'm not easily misled. I know my son. He might be a good-for-nothing drop-out but he's not a liar.'

The man was in denial and bent on defending his flesh and blood. Wasn't it just typical of people in places of power? Always trying to cover up major personal embarrassments. It was obvious Roland had inherited his lying genes from his father.

The councillor sparred him further. 'I'll have you up for slander if you insult my family one more time. And if you don't mind, James, I have more important things on my plate than Roland. There could be a missile heading this way as we speak.'

'There's been nothing on the news or in the papers about an attack.'

Councillor Wheeler bellowed down the phone, 'I know what a four-minute warning is. I don't need the papers to tell me about it. I know the Russians are on alert.'

James thought it a waste of time to try and explain any further. The man was having a panic attack and his brain seemed to be on shut-down.

'There's nothing on the news about an attack,' James repeated.

'You know what the government's like. They hide everything in secrecy.'

'Roland wants to apologise for leading you up the garden path. I think you should give him a chance to explain—'

Councillor Wheeler showed his interest by clicking the phone and transferring him back to his assistant who said, 'I told you he'd hit the roof.'

'So you were listening?'

'Of course I was. I need to know when the Russians are going to push the button.'

James lost his patience and roared, 'Mrs Horsefield. The Russians are only on alert. At the moment they don't have any buttons to push.'

Her voice became threatening. He could tell it was the voice she used with difficult pensioners who didn't understand why their planning permission had been turned down.

She said, 'If I were you I'd get myself a good solicitor because you'll need one when you receive Councillor Wheeler's letter for slander.'

James went on the defensive. 'I doubt he'll have time to write it. There's a missile about to hit Witherington.'

He laughed quietly at his own joke as Mrs Horsefield gabbled, 'Oh my God, must get to the twins,' and rang off in a hurry.

After James had rested his bones, his conscience told him to call the councillor's wife Gladys. At least *she* had some sense. He reckoned she must have been hovering over the phone as she picked it up after the first ring.

'Mrs Wheeler, there's been a misunderstanding about the nuclear attack. I have to tell you there isn't going to be one.'

She could hardly speak. Her nerves were on edge. 'My husband called me and said there is.'

James said, 'Roland lied.'

'He's only a boy.'

'He's a grown man and a bloody liar.'

'Don't you call my son a liar. It may just have been a little prank.'

'Mrs Wheeler, Roland's little prank could cost the British government millions of pounds, not to mention all the disruption and panic around the British Isles. The four-minute warning is for Tallulah Millstone's cryonics project. Therefore, I suggest you call your husband urgently and put him right about Roland's lie.'

Her nerves were too shattered to know what urgency was. 'I don't have time. I'm refurbishing our nuclear fallout shelter. I've ordered hundreds of tins of food and drawn up a contingency plan for the Civil Defence. Which reminds me, I forgot to add dog, cat and goldfish food to the list. Just a moment while I write it on my pad. Wouldn't want to be stuck in the shelter with starving animals.'

James shouted down the phone, 'MRS WHEELER, THE RUSSIANS ARE ONLY ON ALERT.'

Gladys replied, 'I can't handle this. I'm in a state of stress with all the horror going on. Talk to my husband about it.' Then she hung up.

Gladys was shaking when she faced her husband in the hall. 'I had a call from James Willows. He said our son's a liar.'

Ignatius threw his briefcase on the settee. 'I object to other people poking their noses into our business.'

Gladys started to cry. 'It's your fault, Ignatius. He was a good boy until you started on him.'

'He wouldn't do as he was told.'

'You wanted him to be like you and now look what's happened. He's not like you, he's more like me. He's sensitive and caring,' she said, disappearing into the kitchen to put the kettle on before her husband could reply.

Upon returning to the sitting room with a tray of tea and biscuits, she found him reading *Agriculture and Business Monthly*. She wanted him to feel proud of their son. 'He's a journalist there now.'

'It's a lot of rubbish.'

'Then why are you reading it?'

'Just out of curiosity.'

Ignatius had never given her clear answers. She'd shouted so many times 'Talk to me!' but he never had. And she couldn't remember the last time they'd had sex. After the last argument he'd taken off somewhere for a week. She'd been glad to get rid of him.

Gladys poured the tea. 'Where did you go when you left me that time?'

'I went somewhere to get away from it all.'

There he was again, not being clear about where he'd been. 'Did you go with another woman? Is it why you never have sex with me?' She asked the question because she felt pinched and unattractive.

'Of course I didn't. I've had enough of women.'

'Did you go with a man?'

He told her to stop being so insulting about his sexuality.

Hot meditation

Roland was meditating on his bed before going to work when James called him about Tallulah's project.

'Can you help me to get the siren together on Friday?' James asked.

'Scarlett will go bananas. I have deadlines.'

'I'll call her and tell her you're doing it for her aunt's project.'

'To be truthful, I don't feel like it.'

'Scarlett will think you don't care about her aunt.'

'Well I don't.'

'You're a selfish bastard, Roland.'

'You can do it yourself, what's the problem?'

'You have to help me get a telegraph pole, some electric wire, a foghorn, some rope, a hammer and saw. It's all in a good cause. Remember, an old lady's life is at stake. You can't kid me. I know you're soft hearted.'

Roland asked James where he wanted him to put the siren, apart from up his ass. James got furious and said he wasn't used to hearing such bad language seeing as he was from a noble family.

James said, 'Put it as far away from my bedroom window as you can – by the boundary fence.'

A bit later James decided to tackle Scarlett at the office about Roland's time off. And as Roland had predicted, she went bananas.

'Bloody hell, we have deadlines. How am I going to get this magazine on the road if everyone keeps taking days off?'

James said, 'Perhaps half a day on Friday would suffice. What's going to happen if there's no siren and your aunt is about the die?'

In the end, Scarlett agreed to Roland taking time off if he worked on Sunday.

'He goes to Hyde Park on Sundays,' said James.

'Too damned bad! I can't do everyone's work.'

When James told him the news, Roland felt his world falling apart. Gone was his chance of seeing Anushka again. In the past, he'd been criticised by his parents for laying the blame for his disappointments at their door and now he was laying it at James's door. It was *his* fault he wouldn't get to see the beautiful woman he'd fallen for. There would be no erotic sex at the weekend and washing his underwear in anticipation had been a waste of time. He knew it was something to do with destiny.

The next morning Roland called Scarlett and told her he wouldn't be coming into the office today.

She screamed down the phone, 'This magazine is going to the dogs what with Serge being absent.'

Roland then clocked up another lie. 'I'm too ill to get out of bed,' he said, not feeling any pang of conscience, seeing as she'd suggested he work on Sunday. The truth was, he needed to retreat into his rainforest and reflect on his ambiguous feelings and work out whether he was in love with Anushka, who'd temporarily dumped him, or Scarlett who'd squashed him underfoot. On the other hand, was he in love at all? Or could it be he was just a bugger for punishment or a masochist?

Roland decided to meditate on the true meaning of life and retreat into his tree. He stripped off his clothes, seeing as the last time, with his clothes on, he'd sweated like a pig and it had taken two people to get him out after the protest outside the town hall. Even without clothes the tree was a tight fit. He managed to slide in through the bottom end of the trunk and put his arms through the two holes. Having his arms free meant he wouldn't land on his face if he fell over.

Once inside the tree, he talked to the parrots about the screeching arguments with his parents and to the bats about wanting to hang Serge and James upside down from a branch. The meditation was going well until the phone rang. Waddling over he picked it up and heard his mother's voice say, 'Hello, Roland.'

Before she could speak further he said, 'I'm busy right now, Mum.'

'I rang the office and Scarlett said you weren't well. What's wrong, do you have a temperature?'

'Yes. I'm feeling sick,' he lied.

'Your father and I are extremely angry with you about all your lying.'

'I've got a fever, Mum.'

Gladys said, 'Shall I bring you some lemon tea?'

'No thanks I'll survive. I just need to sleep.' Roland's temperature was now rising inside the tree. He had to get out.

'I'll call you tomorrow, Roland, to see how you are.'

'Thanks, Mum.'

He was pleased she'd rung but delighted when she rang off. Her call had stimulated the urge to pee. He tried to extricate himself from the tree but the inside trunk seemed to be stuck to his sweaty body and as much as he tried to wriggle free the tree clung to him. With difficulty he rang the reception. James Willow answered.

'What is it this time, Roland?'

'I need help.'

'Then come down to reception.'

'I'm stuck and can't get through the door. I need to get to

the bloody bathroom. Can you come here immediately? This is an emergency.'

James put down his newspaper and made for Roland's room with a set of keys wondering what the trouble was. He thought he'd seen everything until he saw Roland inside a tree. He was panting heavily. 'I can't get out. I'm going to die. I'm sweating like a pig.'

James had been used to emergencies in the trenches but not in hotel rooms. 'Stay right where you are. I'll get reinforcements.' He made for the reception with Roland shouting, 'Don't call my parents.'

Running up to the office on the second floor, James told Scarlett that Roland was about to die and was sweating like a pig. She dropped what she was doing and rushed to the first aid cabinet to get something to bring down his temperature. 'I didn't realise he was so ill. Shall I call an ambulance?'

James replied, 'Just wait and come and see him first.'

Roland, exhausted, tottered and fell to the floor on his back. When Scarlett entered his room she saw Roland's tree almost blocking the door.

'Where is he?' she asked James.

'He's inside the tree.'

She dropped the first aid box on the bed.

Roland shouted, 'Get me out of here, I have to pee.'

Scarlett ordered James to get a knife.

'I have a knife for cutting linoleum.'

'That'll do.'

Roland shouted, 'Don't slice my tree. It took me six months to make it.'

Scarlett shouted back, 'Shut up, Roland, or we'll leave you in there.'

The linoleum slicer did its trick and Roland was out within ten minutes. He tried to cover his nakedness with his hands. 'My bladder's bursting,' was the first thing he said.

Scarlett looked at him stonily. 'You've got some explaining to do.'

Roland said, 'I've got a fever.'

Scarlett didn't want to know. 'There's a first aid box with some codeine in it on the bed,' she said before stomping out of the room.

That night Roland fell into a deep sleep. It was probably early morning when he awoke and found the lady in the white ballet dress standing at the bottom of his bed. He heard her say, 'Roland, I know you don't want to go to the office today because you feel embarrassed about the tree but you have to have courage and face up to your challenges and not be a wimp. You have to get up now or you'll be late.'

Then he drifted into sleep again.

Scarlett was already at her desk by the time he arrived in the office.

'Sorry I'm late,' he said sheepishly. 'I had to go to the doctors. I've got a terrible headache.'

Scarlett threw him a glance of disbelief and continued reading. Serge was reading an article on the number of working days lost through menstruation. He said, 'Morning, Roland. Feeling dehydrated? Been on the booze? You look like shit.'

Roland waited for Scarlett to mention the tree but she said nothing.

Unemployed spy

Anushka found the letter under the door of her flat when she returned from a friend's house at 9pm. She'd had no forewarning and read it twice to make sure she'd got it right. *You are fraudulently wasting funds and your party card is revoked by the Communist Revolutionary Committee. You are ordered back to your country. You should report to Boris Ustinov at the Russian Embassy.*

The letter went on to give instructions of what she was to expect. The first thing she did was to take out a bottle of vodka from the sideboard and slug a few shots.

The doorbell rang at 10pm. Boris Ustinov, KGB, stood on the doormat wearing a black suit. His heavy frame and mocking smile didn't bode well. A sharp quiver shook her body. 'I didn't expect you tonight. Why are you wearing black? You look as if you are going to a funeral.'

'Yes. I am going to yours.'

As she opened her mouth to scream, he grabbed her and covered her mouth with his hand. 'When I remove my hand, you will not scream or I'll break your neck.' He dragged her into the living room and threw her on the settee face down. Anushka screamed into one of the cushions as he pulled off her trousers. 'Do you prefer gulag or rehabilitation at embassy?'

Rehabilitation meant she'd never step outside the embassy

again and Boris would have carte blanche to do what he wanted with her. He enjoyed humiliating women and thought nothing of inflicting pain. She kept still, terrified, while he unzipped his trousers and took off his belt. He said he expected her to enjoy the lashing as much as he would.

After Boris had left, Anushka screamed under the bedclothes until she was exhausted. Her backside stung and she had no painkillers. At midnight she called Serge and told him she'd been kicked out of her flat but he said he was in no mood to talk after a tiring day walking around sodden fields.

'Look, Anushka, I'm exhausted. Can we speak tomorrow?'

'Please, please help me. I'm going to die if you don't.'

Serge rang off and she cried intermittently until morning – furious she'd been made redundant, terrified Boris would come back and enraged that Serge had turned his back on her.

The next morning Serge received a phone call in the office from Anushka. He came out in a sweat, foreseeing a challenge to his orderly day. 'What do you want, Anushka? There's a limit as to how I can help you.'

'Can I come and stay with you?'

'No, absolutely not. I have people coming and going all the time at my place.' It was a lie.

Preparing himself for a tearful answer, he waited for her to sob down the phone with a flourish of drama. She sniffed, hiccupped and sobbed. 'Please, Serge. I want to come to Witherington. I can get the train.'

'I have to go interview a farmer for an article on recycling manure and I don't have time to worry about other people's problems.' His head was bursting and it was only 9.30am.

'I'm going to get killed today,' she whimpered.

'OK, but just for a few days. You'll have to stay in a hotel.'

'That's fine with me.'

'I'll book you into the Wailing Willows Hotel and we can meet in the Bull and Bullocks pub at 8pm.'

After packing a few clothes and photographs, Anushka took the mid-morning train to Witherington, sitting with her back to the engine so she could see the city fade into the distance. For the next hour and a half she thought about Boris and the terror she felt and all the reasons she should flee from him.

With a jolt the train stopped at Witherington station which seemed to be in the middle of a field of cows and deserted apart from two railway staff. She took the only taxi to the Wailing Willows Hotel. The hotel looked luxurious, like a stately home she'd seen on a postcard at a London station. It might have been a castle at one time, she thought. The grounds were like a park with many trees she'd never seen before. She paid the taxi driver and walked her case towards the reception where James Willows greeted her.

'Good morning, Miss Petrova, I had a call from Mr Serge Gallo. He told me you need somewhere to stay for a few days.'

'Yes, I need a job as well.'

'What a coincidence, I need a housekeeper if you're interested.'

'Thank you, I will think about it.'

James said, 'I pay good money.'

Anushka's eyes lit up. 'OK, I will take it.'

'I'll give you room 14. It's a small suite with bedroom, kitchen and bathroom. It's for employees and close to my quarters. Let me know if you need anything.'

'I need bread and milk and something for lunch.'

James wasn't used to employees making requests. 'I'll get you something from the pantry.' It was easier than explaining how to get to Witherington without transport.

The interior of her small suite was not a patch on the elegant flat Anushka had left this morning. She lay on the bed studying the pink roses and green intertwined stalks on the faded wallpaper, thinking it wasn't unlike accommodation she'd seen in Moscow. A little later, James knocked on the door and handed her a small package. She thanked him and took it without inviting him in. Inside the bag was enough food to make a sandwich and milk for a cup of instant coffee.

When Serge arrived at the Bull and Bullocks at 8pm, Anushka was waiting. Her eyes were puffy and her face red. She refused to tell him what was wrong. They skipped the pub and she got into his car. He wanted to get away from the town in case someone wondered why he was with a distressed woman. In the car she said, 'Serghei, I think I will die in Witherington.'

'But you haven't been here a day yet. And stop calling me Serghei. I'm not a bloody foreigner!'

'The only job for me here is cleaning cesspits for James.'

'Let's go and look for a stable where I can cheer you up. I can't wait to play out the grisly piece from William Morris's epic poem *Haystack in the Floods*.'

Serge parked in the lane near the farm and led her through a hole in the fence. The farm was in darkness except for a night light coming from the stables. She stumbled twice as her heels caught against dry mud. In the distance he could see what looked like a haystack but which turned out to be a heap of manure. He swore and made for the stables, pulled her inside and threw her onto a pile of straw.

Anushka looked around nervously. 'There is no haystack in here.'

'Just pretend there is one. It's the Hundred Years War between England and France. After the battle of Poitiers, I,

Godmar the nasty knight, meets Robert the good knight and I'm about to slice off Robert's head with my sword.'

Serge put his mouth close to Anushka's ear and whispered:

Godmar turned grinning to his men,
Who ran some five or six and beat,
His head to pieces at their feet.

Anushka shuddered. 'I don't like Godmar. I prefer you to be Robert, the knight I love.'

'Yeah but I don't want to have my head cut off and the shit kicked out of it at Godmar's feet.'

Anushka shivered. 'I'm a fair maid and I'd prefer to be in love with Robert.'

Serge swore under his breath. She always had to be in love.

'Do you prefer to give up your virginity to Godmar in his castle or do you want to be sitting in a chair waiting to be drowned in the Seine as a witch?' Serge said, gruffly, reciting in a suitably macabre tone in her ear.

Do you know Jehane, they cry for you,
Jehane the brown! Jehane the brown!
Give us Jehane to burn or drown!

Put poetically, Anushka decided to forget about love and get ravished by Godmar. Serge stiffened as the questions started. It was pedantic time again and he hadn't even got her blouse off yet.

'Godmar is wearing jeans?'

'For God's sake, Anushka, Godmar is wearing a suit of armour.'

'Then how do you screw Jehane with metal armour on crotch?'

'Just pretend we're in my castle and I've taken it all off.'

'How can Godmar climb stairs when heavy with metal?'

At that moment Godmar wanted to put his hands around Jehane's neck and throttle her.

The trip

White tureens had become Stanley's phobia. He dreaded opening the lid to find something he'd eaten three times in the same week. Santeros set two of them before him and opened the first lid to reveal several flat round lumps resembling anaemic beef-burgers. Santeros said, 'It's a chicken-burger.'

'What no beef?' Stanley lifted the lid on the second tureen. 'Fried potato skins? Where are the potatoes?'

'They're going into the pot for tomorrow's chicken soup.'

Stanley sighed. 'Perhaps speak to Mr Kim about some new recipes seeing as he's writing a cookery book.'

Santeros's purple-tinged lips tightened. 'In Cuba we eat whatever is put in front of us and I believe the same in your country. You also say a prayer – For what we are about to receive may the Lord make us eternally grateful.'

'Truly grateful,' corrected Stanley, rolling his eyes, sure the Lord hadn't meant him to eat chicken every day. 'Just try and beef up the chicken-burgers a bit.' He let it rest there and changed the subject, not wanting to sink into the quicksand of cultural sensitivities.

'Any new news worth listening to?' Stanley asked.

'Yes. There's a new woman in Witherington and she's a communist.'

'Where did you hear it?'

'In the pub. She's been sacked from her job at the Russian Embassy for wasting party funds. Her name is Anushka Petrova.'

'Good. You know what to do. I want to know about her

communist connections in Witherington and Russia and why she's here. Get the cocktail ready.'

'Which drugs?'

'You choose.'

In the basement, Santeros removed his white caftan and donned a long black robe ready to slip out into the night. Before such outings he usually killed a chicken and talked to his dead relatives for luck. Tonight he skipped tradition and called up the farmhouse's long-time-dead lodger. After three knocks on the wall, the axe-man stood before him, bitterly complaining about having to hang around on the gallows all day waiting for someone to spook.

Santeros said, 'Tonight a woman will arrive and you will stay away.'

The man brandished his axe and started to bluster his indignation until Santeros threatened to have him exorcised if he as much touched a hair on Anushka's head. Bowing to authority, the axe-man slid through the wall to the other side, leaving a whiff of putrefaction.

Anushka sat propped up against the bedhead reading a book on the history of the Wailing Willows Hotel which James had loaned her. A knock on the door disturbed her at an interesting piece about the Willows' family and a possible resident ghost. She took off the safety chain and opened it. She was expecting James, not a man in black with a balaclava. He rushed at her and pushed her backwards onto the bed, his hand over her mouth before she could scream. Her KGB training kicked in. She didn't hold eye contact. It could be dangerous. Never look your captor in the eye, she had been told. Her heart was thumping but she would not provoke. Neither would she react until an opportune moment. She was tightly pinned down as he was lying on top of her. She saw a flash of white and a damp chemical rag was pressed over her nose and mouth.

Anushka awoke in a whitewashed room with a neon light and no window, strapped to a shiny metal table. The room smelt of marijuana. Two men in white overalls stood over her. She screamed as one of them advanced on her with a syringe, which pricked her arm. Bright patterns moved around her head as she danced inside a giant kaleidoscope. In a myriad of lights she floated upwards towards a tree where a white chicken said, 'Anushka, you must leave here before it's too late.' But she didn't want to leave such a beautiful, colourful, peaceful place. She wanted to cry with happiness but the white chicken said she shouldn't or she'd cry all year long. A voice called softly to her through Caribbean music and she felt herself swaying rhythmically to the beat of her heart. The peaceful feeling passed and she felt afraid when a dark cloud moved around the ceiling. Perhaps it was night. A ghostly evil man in a yellow-and-black checked shirt had glowing red embers in his hair. She desperately wanted the colourful place back and the music. The myriad of lights surfaced, dispelling the black cloud. She was inside the kaleidoscope, which spun around her. A soft hypnotic English voice asked, 'How old are you, Anushka?'

'Twenty-three.'

She heard the soft voice whisper, 'Write everything down,' and a foreign accent say, 'OK, boss.'

The man asked her about her family in Russia and if they had ever been involved in espionage. Anushka felt the words tumble from her lips as if she'd no control over them.

'There was a family tragedy. It was the occupation of Stalingrad. My mother's brother, my uncle, was accused of being a spy for the Red Army. He was hung from a tree in front of the whole village. My mother saw it. She was eighteen.'

'Tell me about Boris,' said the man.

'I dreamed of going to university but my father was worried because I wanted to help the peasants in the countryside. He said I would clash with the State because of my progressive ideas. He asked Boris to get me a job at the embassy in London. Boris took me to London. His wife was very kind to me.'

'Did you sleep with Boris?'

'He sometimes visited me during the night.'

'Did you like it?'

'No. He was very rough. He was a beast.'

'Did he ask you to indulge in subversion?'

'Only to sleep with British diplomats and tell him news.'

There were more questions about communist friends in London and political contacts. She told the man she didn't have any other contacts and she couldn't give a damn about being a communist as all she wanted was a husband and a home.

'Who is Smirnov?'

'I met him once or twice.'

'What did he say to you?'

'I reminded him of his niece.'

'Did he ask you to become a spy?'

'No.'

'Is there anything you wish for the future? Perhaps you would like to work for the good of communism?'

'I would like to have a white wedding in a church in Rome near the place where the martyr of the war, the unknown soldier, is buried. I would like to have the photos taken inside the Trevi Fountain with wet wedding dress.'

She heard whispering. Then the foreign voice said he would touch her forehead with a chicken bone, after which she would fall into a deep sleep and remember nothing upon awakening.

In a distant recess of her mind, Anushka dreamed of being carried into a building and down a corridor. She knew it was a corridor as the person who was carrying her kept bumping her feet against a wall. The man was heavy-footed and smelt of roast chicken and incense. She was drowsy and couldn't see his face. A door clicked open and she was laid gently on a bed. She knew it was her bedroom as it smelt of her perfume.

Anushka woke up late the next morning to a knock on the door, wondering why she was still in her daytime clothes.

James shouted, 'Is anything wrong? You didn't make my breakfast this morning.'

She shouted through the door, 'I feel sick, as if I have a fever.'

James said, 'Take the day off, my dear, we don't want you passing your germs around.'

From horn to horn, and 'twixt the top and base,
Lights were in motion, brightly scintillating
As they together met and passed each other.

Dante Alighieri
The Divine Comedy: Paradise. Canto XIV

MAY 1986

Sex and the church

It was only 10am and Roland was dead on his feet, having spent most of the night thinking about Anushka and wondering if he'd ever get any sex before he died.

Serge greeted him with, 'Have a bad night, Roland? You look like shit.'

'Thanks, Serge,' Roland growled and sat at his desk.

Scarlett whizzed between desk and photocopying machine, while complimenting Roland on his parental rights and male bonding contribution.

Serge said, 'It was all one sided. It was all about women and domestic stuff. There was no question about a man's rights. And fancy getting stuck in the women's toilets.'

Scarlett replied, 'It was Roland's first mission, Serge. There were bound to be a few small glitches. He's still learning.'

Serge scowled and went back to finishing his article *Will female vets with menstruation survive the working week?*

Scarlett added, 'We've been inundated with letters from parents complimenting us on male bonding and the Women's Institute is calling for Veronica to be given a peace prize.'

Roland beamed and said, 'Artsy-fartsy Weirdo wants a planet renamed in my honour. He said Venus should be changed to planet Veronica.'

Scarlett smiled and Serge groaned.

Seeing as the atmosphere in the office seemed right,

Roland thought it would be a good moment to speak to Scarlett about having time off to help James with the siren for her aunt's project.

'Scarlett?'

'Yes?'

'Would you mind very much if I took half a day off on Friday?'

Her smile disappeared. Roland felt the atmosphere become heavy, with high depression on the lowlands or the other way round. A storm was brewing.

'Yes, I damn well would. I have an office to run and we're behind. Think about what you're going to write next.'

It was a slap in the face. He couldn't understand why she'd complimented him on one side and slapped him down on the other. He saw Serge smirk. He felt betrayed. After she'd defended him in front of the police over the siege in the ladies' toilets, he imagined she'd done it because she liked him. At the time, her musky perfume attracted him. Last night he'd made love to her in his dreams. At first he thought he liked her, but now he didn't. It was amazing how love could change in the span of a day.

She threw a letter across at him. The handwriting looked as if an insect had run across the page.

Dear Veronica,

I'm sick and tired of coitus interruptus. I'm just getting to my climax when he withdraws. It's not fair the man has all the pleasure while we women are worrying our minds in case we get pregnant. I think the church should get with it. Coitus interruptus should be banned in favour of pleasure.

Frustrated Fanny.

Roland was not in the right mood to deal with sexual problems. He said stiffly, 'I don't know a thing about coitus. I've never done it.'

Scarlett said, 'Neither have I, just use some imagination. Imagine you're making love with a woman and you don't want to get her pregnant. You are going in, out, in, out, and suddenly you're about to shoot the load. At that point you have to control yourself and pull it out.'

He started to say something but she interrupted with, 'If you don't you'll get her pregnant.'

Roland said, 'What about the pill and condoms?'

'The church is against them.'

'Can't you give the letter to Serge to reply to?'

'No. He knows even less than you.'

Serge raised his head. 'That's not true.'

Scarlett told Roland to get down to the library to do some research, following which he should interview the Bishop of Rottingham. He mentally noted there had been no 'please' or 'thank you' in their conversation.

The first thing Roland did after he'd calmed down, was to consult the library about the medical explanation for coitus interruptus. What he learned shocked him – over 30 million people worldwide were not getting satisfactory sex or orgasms. Before going to see the bishop, he wrote a few questions on his pad under the heading '*Sex and the Church*'. He pondered on his religious beliefs and doubts and didn't know if he believed in God or not. Neither God nor Jesus had been on his side on his eighth Christmas when he'd received a bike instead of a puppy after spending two months praying for it. Furthermore, his parents had ignored his questions about what happened to the puppy. A kind of communications shutdown had then drawn a dark cloak over their house when he'd complained that the notes sent up the chimney to Father Christmas did not mirror his requests. Frustration, tears and a feeling of loss and betrayal did nothing to soften their attitude. The fact that Father Christmas had drunk half a bottle of whisky left on the fireplace to help himself, only added to the list of questions he tried to ask his parents.

Talking to his mother had been confusing. 'Does Jesus live in the clouds?' She'd told him Heaven, being celestial, was a haven for those who didn't go to Hell. Roland wanted to know about the size of Heaven and how many people lived there and where they went to the toilet. To his question of, 'Where does God live?' she'd answered, 'In the heart and mind of each one of us.' Roland didn't really understand this and became disturbed thinking of someone wandering around his innards. When he'd asked for clarification, 'Which bit of us is he living in?' His mother had lost patience and said, 'Ask your father.'

When he'd got no answers he realised not everyone was blessed with communication abilities. Question – 'Dad, why didn't you buy me a puppy for Christmas?' Answer – 'Don't be so damn ungrateful, Roland, we bought you a bike didn't we?'

In his teens there were other questions left unanswered, mainly about his sexuality. He didn't bother asking his father about his wet dreams or he would have probably said, 'Ask your mother she's the one who washes the sheets.'

In any case, he resolved his sexuality problems by hand, the pleasure of which far outweighed the worry of going blind, according to an old wives' tale. When his era of loud music, long hair and dirge-type poetry began, he spent more and more time in his room with a '*Do not disturb*' notice on the door and mixed less and less with his peers. The boys didn't invite him to get drunk on a Saturday night and none of the girls wanted to kiss a hairy face. He did, however, find one who was happy to kiss the rest of him, down there, for a small amount of money. After the hell of adolescence, there was the awful fight with his parents about dropping out of college. The crunch came when he'd had to find a job and stop asking so many questions. Later on, the church was a place to hide when it was his turn to wash the dishes. It was also a place to think about the confusion in his mind about what was or wasn't sin. Being a half non-believer and leftist, he wondered if he really had the right to be in church.

The bishop's office was more sumptuous than Roland had expected. The dark wood desk commanded attention beneath red velvet window drapes in a celestial universe and the bishop turned out to be less intimidating than his elegant office. His plump soft face belied a man who seemed truly happy with his lot in life; a man who had never had existential problems or parents who'd obstructed his career or never listened to his needs.

Roland introduced himself by putting the bishop at ease with a human story. He told him the story of the puppy and how disillusioned he'd felt about praying so hard for it and finding out God had cloth ears.

The bishop replied, 'You have to pray harder, my son. You can't expect miracles.'

'I prayed hard my parents would drop dead but they didn't.'

The bishop smiled.

'I prayed girls would fall in love with me.'

The bishop nodded. 'You can't expect miracles, my son, try cutting your hair.'

It wasn't the reply he expected. He placed Frustrated Fanny's letter in front of the bishop and pointed to the word coitus.

'Your Eminence, I would just like to know what the

church thinks about women having more sexual satisfaction. Are they allowed orgasms? And don't you think coitus is a bit old fashioned now the pill has been invented?'

The bishop's tiny ears turned pink. He read the letter and handed it back.

'I suggest you talk to the archbishop. I'm not in a position to answer this question and if I were you, I'd leave sex alone.'

Roland left the bishop's domain feeling cheated. Life was running on two ambiguous parallel rails. Humanity was doomed to intellectual darkness. He rode his bike back to the office and, after much swearing, typed up his notes. He handed the draft to Scarlett to read. She liked it but Serge always had to be the party pooper. 'You can't use words like orgasm, it's taboo.'

'People want answers these days. I doubt the women of the world are happy with the in, out, shake it all about, thank you for my lost moment, Serge.'

Scarlett snorted impatiently and interrupted. 'Can we get some work done? It might be a good idea, Roland, if you interview the Reverend Pottering as well.'

'I'd rather walk over hot coals.'

An hour later he handed her his reply to Frustrated Fanny's letter.

Dear Frustrated Fanny, Re: coitus interruptus.

When God made the world, he made it so we could procreate. Nothing was mentioned about pleasure. Regarding coitus: there are over 30 million people worldwide who aren't getting satisfactory sex or orgasms but they aren't getting pregnant either (but the library can't confirm this). I agree the church should get with it but there's no reference to sex in the Bible (except for the stoning of harlots). There was one miraculous conception and some historians say Jesus got married but there's no mention of his mother-in-law.

The church encourages coitus interruptus so you never know what pleasure is really like.

Regards,

Veronica

Various revolutions

Yesterday Tallulah had chosen a few more recipes from her cookery book for the second lesson with Mr Kim. Such a nice man. Good manners. Quaint ideas. Well dressed. This morning he was wearing a casual brown corduroy jacket, white T-shirt and black trousers.

'You look very British today,' she said brightly, hoping he'd take it as a compliment and noticing he'd abandoned his black suit and tie. He said, 'Thank you Mrs Tallulah,' and followed her into the kitchen where she indicated a pile of recipes on the table. She wondered if he was trying to please her when he showed an interest in roast beef, Yorkshire pudding and peas. She put the kettle on.

'Roast beef is a very good choice. However, you must take good care not to put on the gas or electricity too high, for example over two hundred degrees. Everything has to be cooked slowly so as not to ruin the flavour or dry it out.'

'Thank you for your advice, Mrs Tallulah.' His manners were impeccable, she thought.

Mr Kim studied the recipe while she busied about taking cups, saucers, milk jug and sugar bowl from a cabinet.

'Will you be requiring a demonstration of my cooking or do you just need these recipes to make notes from?'

'For today, I will only make notes, thank you.'

She poured the tea and he asked her a question.

'Mrs Tallulah, Mr Stanley told me you are interested in cryonics and being put on ice and in a metal tube filled with chemicals while you are still alive. I find this very strange. Is it a British or American plot to get rid of old people?'

Tallulah laughed. 'Is that what your communist leaders tell you?'

'Well is it a plot or not?' Mr Kim insisted.

'The British and Americans do not suppress their old people, they usually send them to old people's homes.'

'Is it like a hard labour camp?'

'Definitely not. An old people's home is where they play cards and bowls before going for a long holiday in the sky.'

'It sounds truly horrible.'

' May I ask you a question?' Tallulah asked.

'Of course.'

'In your country, do you put your old people into hard labour camps?'

Mr Kim showed no sign of emotion. He said her question was impertinent and had she been in his country asking this question she would herself end up in such a camp. She decided not to prod him further when he mentioned, perhaps slightly maliciously, that she wouldn't be needing her cryonics canister, as the West was doomed to go up in a mushroom cloud before long, and was therefore a waste of money.

With the situation deteriorating on the cultural front, Tallulah decided to stick to inoffensive questions. She asked him how he was getting on with his revolutionary writing and cultural research.

'Thank you for your interest, dear old lady. I am very impressed as everything is big. Your women are also much bigger than ours and your babies much fatter. I am promoting British food so Korean ladies can have bigger breasts for giving milk to babies. It will be another revolution. We will call it "the big breast" revolution.'

'Won't you get into trouble for promoting our way of life?

I mean your country is not exactly open to foreign influence or criticism.'

'I am studying revolutions. My book will be acclaimed and will help understand revolutions in your country so we can take steps to avoid copying your disastrous politics and policies. Do you find it strange?'

'I certainly do. We've never had a revolution in the British Isles.'

'What about the Industrial Revolution?'

'Well, now you mention it—'

To avoid being caught up in a political quagmire, she said, 'Let's forget our cultural differences and have a nice cup of tea.'

Mr Kim told her he'd like some whisky to be added.

'I'll put the kettle on and maybe have a drop too.'

'Thank you, Mrs Tallulah, dear old lady, for your hospitality.'

'I'm not *that* old, I'm only sixty-eight,' she said laughing.

'In my country old people have a special place. The older you are the more respect you command.'

'I wish it were like that in my country,' she said remembering the times she'd been cast off and ready for society's scrap heap as soon as she'd turned sixty.

'I know, I do not understand why the capitalist countries do not respect their elderly,' he said.

'I don't understand either, but we have to put up with it.'

The cookery lesson was put aside as camaraderie began to develop. Tallulah realised their differences weren't all *that* different. Conversation turned to the various wars where, even though they'd been fighting for different reasons and on opposite sides, the outcome was the same – warriors died and their loved ones were left to pick up the pieces and carry on to rebuild over the destruction. It had always been so – build, destroy, build, destroy in a never-ending circle of bloody wars, with peace in between to give the population time to build and recover before another war destroyed everything again.

'I suppose war is necessary for the capitalist economy,' said Mr Kim, quoting building and supply contracts and mentioning the money made on the black market as well as rake-offs from illegal whisky and spirits.

Tallulah found herself relaxing in his company and let fly with a few political criticisms of her own about the population being sent to the front line to end up dead, maimed or psychologically crushed while the top brass were busy smoking big cigars and boozing at the old boys' club. Just like Stanley had done. She told him things she shouldn't have, but got it all off her chest.

Mr Kim commiserated and told her it sounded familiar, but was not allowed to say so openly as it could put his life in danger. He led the conversation away from dangerous politics, telling her how beautiful Pyongyang was in the spring and summer with flowering fruit-bearing trees. And the spotlessly clean streets without one piece of stray paper or garbage because the women were constantly sweeping them. He spoke about the Three Revolutions Museum and the Martyrs Cemetery and the Juche Tower.

He said, 'The Juche Tower symbolises the revolutionary philosophy of self-reliance which means that man is at the centre of his own destiny. We support the superiority of the collective over the individual which means the ability to act independently without regard to outside interference. National unity is indoctrinated into the children through our songs of wars and revolutions and tales of heroic soldiers. If you ever come to Pyongyang you will see the majority of people dressed in the uniform of the People's Army. We take our children to school and encourage them to be talented from a very early age.'

'It all sounds very regimented,' Tallulah said.

He laughed. 'Not always. Sometimes we have fun. We have a very good sense of humour you know. We are allowed to laugh and have fun as long as we are not poking fun at the government.'

She poured him another cup of tea and added some more whisky to keep up the interesting conversation. He started to sing 'Chollima on the Wing'. His voice was strong and sweet.

'Tell me what Chollima means,' she said after he'd finished singing.

'Chollima is a mythical winged horse. He is too fast to be mounted by a mortal. Horses have exceptional endurance and strength and Chollima can run a thousand miles in one day. He's the symbol of heroism and the way forward.'

'One day you will have to tell me some of your history and folklore,' she said.

'I will tell you about the three revolutions and the martyrs,' he said, taking his leave.

After Mr Kim had gone, slightly staggering, Tallulah immediately called Stanley. She told him about Mr Kim's amazing knowledge of world affairs and mythology and his wonderful singing voice.

'He doesn't need any re-education, as his knowledge of culture far outshines yours,' she said.

Stanley replied, 'Has Mr Kim been brainwashing you?'

Her voce raised an octave. 'I'm older than you and expect some respect.'

Then she slammed down the phone.

The whirling course

Fred was delighted when Ernest told him he was sending him on a two-day training course *How to materialise in front of the living*. 'Cecilia will take you to the whirling room where you can learn to be a good spirit,' Ernest said.

Fred could barely contain his excitement. He sought out Bertha Goodbody to ask her if she could stand in for him for two days while he was at the course.

He said, 'There's not much to do, except snoop around and poke your nose into everyone's business as you usually do. You can write up your notes and give them to Ernest.'

Bertha swore and screamed. 'My nose doesn't go around poking itself into every nook and cranny.' Fred told her to calm down and said he'd give her some free anger management classes when he got back. In reply, she swirled upwards as high as the church spire leaving a mist of bad breath behind her, shouting, 'I don't need any anger management and I hate writing reports. And tell dumb cluck Ernest I'm retired and have no intention of working with a chicken-brained cockerel.'

Fred felt offended, but happy she'd finally recognised he was a cockerel. She might have her faults, but at least she'd shown him some respect.

Cecilia was collecting wild flowers for her pot when Fred found her near the church.

'Ernest said I should see you about the training course. I

want to learn to materialise so I can make him proud of me,' said Fred.

Cecilia smiled and patted his crest. 'Well, you've come to the right person. Let's go to the whirling room right now. It's in the crypt.' She grabbed him by the neck and yanked him off before he could squawk his objection about dark spooky places.

Fred squinted in the darkness of the gothic crypt. His nose twitched at the smell of mould. The dank grey walls were claustrophobic. Dust covered the floor except for a circle in the middle. In the far corner were a few sarcophagi.

Cecilia gave a warning. 'The ceiling's a bit low so take care not to whirl too high, otherwise you'll bang your head. Stand back from the wall, the trainers are coming.'

Two men slid through the wall and stood in front of them dressed identically in a wide white skirt and short jacket. A high camel-hair hat, the shape of an overturned plant pot, completed their outfit. One of them held a set of bagpipes. Cecilia introduced them as Rory and Alastair Macleod.

'Rory and Alastair are Whirling Dervishes. Scottish but trained in Turkey where they adapted the music to the bagpipes. They even won the talent contest at Butlin's before they died.'

Rory and Alastair beamed and said they were at everyone's disposal. Alastair blew into the bagpipes while Rory took a few steps into the middle of the circle and began to turn clockwise with his arms outstretched. The sweet shrill music of the bagpipes began slowly then speeded up. Dust started to swirl. Fred's head followed the man around at an alarming speed, so fast he felt dizzy. Rory stopped and invited Fred to dance. Fred stepped into the centre of the circle and began to twirl, slowly at first until the bagpipes picked up speed. At forty-five revs per minute he lost his balance and fell against the wall ending up in a heap on the floor.

'Stay in the middle,' shouted Cecilia, but Fred was unable to stand up without falling over. He said he wanted to whirl in the opposite direction to get his balance back. Ignoring his plight, she said, 'Watch me and learn.' Unable to dance on her stump, she began to pirouette on her left foot, spinning until her white ballet dress clung to her and the dust on the floor moved outside the vortex of the whirlwind she created. She slowed down to the music of the bagpipes. 'Now you try it, Fred.'

Fred said he felt dizzy and sick and wanted to go home.

'We can try later if you like,' Cecilia said kindly.

Fred said he'd rather die. Later, Fred told Ernest about his experience.

'Well, did you pass the test?' Fred was forced to tell Ernest it was the most terrible experience he'd ever had and wild horses couldn't drag him back. Furious, Ernest grabbed him by the neck until Fred reminded him about freedom of speech.

An hour later, Ernest cooled down. It had been a trying day, he told Fred. He said he felt stressed and needed to connect with the universe and desperately missed his mother.

Fred said, 'If you want, I can sing to you like I used to sing to Ethel when she had a headache. What kind of a song would you like?'

'Something to help me relax.'

'How about "I'm on Cloud Nine", or "Staircase to Heaven"?'

'No, I'm not going to Heaven until I've wrapped up this case.'

'I've never sung to a dead man before. Give me a clue, I'm running out of ideas.' Fred developed a blank mind under pressure.

'Forget it, Fred, I'll sing to myself.'

Ernest slunk off back to his tomb thinking he'd never felt so alone. His job had been less complicated when he was alive because he didn't have to talk to dead people or dumb cockerels.

Dummy run

In her dream, Tallulah talked to the butcher about James's severed head which was sitting in a paper bag on the shop counter. She peeped inside to see his hair matted with blood. She said, 'This paper bag is dripping blood, can you please put it in a plastic one?'

The grocer smiled and helped her put James's head inside. Tallulah awoke with a start. The dream worried her. Was it an omen? Had James died during the night? She hoped not. At least not until he'd finished her cryonics project.

Scarlett dropped in for breakfast and found Tallulah without make-up and with bags under her eyes.

'Is there anything wrong? You look a bit pale this morning.'

'No, I just need to go and see how James is getting on with my project.'

'Did you give him any money?'

'Just a small advance. He said he's progressing.'

'I hope he hasn't run off with your finances.'

'No, but he's dragging his feet.'

'Sounds like Serge,' said Scarlett.

How's the office going?'

'Fine, *Sex and the Church* is in the pipeline for the June issue. Anyway, I have to go now. I'm going out tonight.'

'Enjoy yourself, dear. Are you meeting a nice young man?'

Scarlett smiled and threw her a glance which said, *Chance would be a fine thing.*

Later in the morning Tallulah rang James to make sure he was still alive.

'How's it going with my cryonics project, James?'

'Not so bad.'

'Good, because tonight we're going to do a dummy run. I'm going to fake a bad turn and you have to pick me up in the van and get me on ice and take me to Brighton to the cryonics facility before my brain dies. How's it going with the siren?'

'It hasn't been connected yet.'

'Then I'll call you by phone.'

At 11pm Tallulah called James to say, 'My breathing's failing. You've got four minutes to get here and put me on ice before I die. You don't have time to change out of your pyjamas. I hope you've got enough petrol to get to Brighton.'

James's brain went into a panic. He couldn't remember if she'd said they had to get to Brighton within four minutes or whether he had to change into his pyjamas first. In actual fact he already *was* in his pyjamas.

He jumped out of bed and ran to the garage only stopping to put on his slippers and dressing gown. His blood pressure started to rise. Yesterday, in preparation for *the call*, he'd removed a bath from room thirty-nine and bolted it to the floor of the van. Ice was needed but there weren't enough ice cubes in the freezer to cover the bottom of the bath, never mind a body.

James revved into gear and hit the accelerator. He reached Bluebell Vicarage within minutes, inserted the key Tallulah had given him into the lock and sprinted up the stairs. Tallulah was lying on the bed in a long white nightgown, her eyes closed. He lifted her up and carried her downstairs to the van. Placing her gently on the grass he fiddled with the keys to get the back doors open.

One eye opened and she said, 'The next time, James, open the back doors of the van first. My nightgown's getting wet and the grass is freezing.'

He lifted her into the bath.

She said, 'There's no ice in here.'

'Of course there isn't. Do you want your nightgown to get wet? You don't want to freeze to death before your time, do you?'

In theory they were on their way to a cryonics facility in Brighton. In reality they were just about to hit a roadblock at the Witherington roundabout.

A policeman waved them down. James stopped and opened his window. He gave the officer a smile.

'Good evening, officer, is something wrong? I have to get to Brighton. I have a half-dead woman in the back of the van.'

The officer asked James to get out and open the back doors. He looked at James's slippers and pyjamas and took out a notebook. There was a woman lying on her back in a bath bolted to the floor and she seemed to be dead. The police officer called Rottingham Police Station for reinforcements citing a dead woman in the back of a van.

James said, 'This is ridiculous.'

Tallulah sat up and said to the police officer, 'I'm still alive, you idiot, but I won't be for much longer.'

An embarrassing half hour passed before reinforcements arrived, by which time, theoretically, Tallulah would be brain dead. The reinforcements were treated to five minutes of her fury. At Rottingham Police Station, James was reprimanded for driving while not wearing appropriate apparel and Tallulah given a police issue blanket to cover her damp nightdress.

When Scarlett arrived at midnight to collect them, having cut short her evening, she found Tallulah hunched over a cup of lemon tea in Chief Inspector Dent's office.

He said, 'I gave her a blanket so she doesn't get hypothermia or a sore throat. The poor old lady reminds me of my mum. They're always a bit fragile at this age you know.'

Scarlett thanked him, thinking he knew nothing about old ladies. The Chief Inspector took her into another room and said in a quiet voice, 'We don't want to press charges given Mrs Millstone's age and the absence of a criminal record. Just keep her under control and get her to see a doctor, if you know what I mean.' He tapped his temple twice with his index finger. 'And by the way, please ask her to bring the police blanket back tomorrow.'

Scarlett drove home in silence with the two of them shivering on the back seat.

'We didn't make it to Brighton did we?' Tallulah announced.

Scarlett was too furious to reply and James said nothing, being intimidated by Scarlett's silence.

God bless America

The next morning Scarlett popped in to see how Tallulah was faring, worried she may have caught cold last night and to tell her to return the blanket to the police.

Tallulah said, 'There's no point in insisting, Scarlett, I've no intention of taking it back and that's final.'

'It's government property. It's stealing.'

'No it's not.'

'What on earth do you want to keep it for?'

'I'm not keeping it. The police blanket's going in the bin.'

'It belongs to the police.'

'Well it's mine now. I'm not going to be humiliated by taking it back.'

'Stealing is a sin,' said Scarlett.

'I'm just temporarily borrowing it.'

Later in the morning, Tallulah rode her bike to the Church of Local Martyrs and followed worshippers inside. The church hadn't lost its new smell and she noticed the sun was shining through the stained glass windows. She hoped Reverend Pontius Pottering would be able to enlighten her about the difference between borrowing and stealing a blanket and what parameters the church used. And it might be a good moment to ask him about the church's stance on cryonics. Tallulah liked him – the Reverend had always given her his time when she'd turned up unexpectedly, even though he'd talked very little about what was up in Heaven or down in

Hell as he said he personally had never been to either place. It was all in the scriptures, he said, and she should read her Bible more often. It was his way of side-stepping questions. He was fond of saying, 'Lucifer is right here in Witherington, enticing the congregation to the lair of sin where drunkards abide.' He meant the Bull and Bullocks pub.

The church service ran a bit late. Reverend Pottering's nose started to twitch impatiently, waiting for the crowd to settle. Tallulah noticed his usual habit of scanning his eyes over the congregation, counting heads, to see how much money he could expect in the offerings box. She walked down the aisle looking for a pew near the front in case she wanted to leave before the service finished. In the end she was forced to sit next to forty-year-old Florence of the Mothers' Union who always hogged the aisle seat to be near the exit and toilet. Florence was not someone who could blend into a crowd. Blowsy and noisy, she commanded attention wherever she went. Today she wore a psychedelic dress with splashes of turquoise and orange on a black background. Tallulah gave her a tight smile, stepped over her feet and sat down. The Reverend Pottering brought the congregation to heel by tapping a baton on the pulpit. His voice had a calming effect. It reflected his inner self which seduced and hypnotised the congregation for an hour. Many people said he was a bit too young at forty-five but he had a nice plain wife which made up for it, especially as her home-made scones were delicious. He started by asking who wanted to repent, waiting for someone to put up their hand. In the back row four youths in leather jackets whispered among themselves. Tallulah rallied her courage, stood up and addressed him. 'Well actually, I don't want to repent I just want to talk about—'

One of the youths shouted, 'Chickens?'

There followed some giggling from the congregation. Reverend Pottering said, 'Go ahead, Mrs Millstone, what's the trouble?'

'I'm so glad most of you have read the article in the paper about me and my cryonics project. I must confess I was interested in the Christian afterlife until I had a nightmare about being in Heaven with most of the people of Witherington.'

The congregation buzzed and the same youth from the back row shouted, 'Sit down, you old hag.'

Tallulah ignored the interruption and continued. 'Reverend Pottering, I turned to cryonics to have my body preserved until science can find a way of bringing me back to life. I have a few questions. If my body is suspended in liquid nitrogen for the next ninety years, can I continue being a Christian? Will my spirit still go to Heaven if I accidentally unfreeze? And what if only my head is floating in a canister – is it a problem if I'm without a heart? What's the position of the church and do I risk being excommunicated?'

She saw a blank look on Reverend Pottering's face. His eyes darted from side to side before he said, 'Thank you, Mrs Millstone, but questions and answers are on Tuesday at 7pm in the church hall. Anyone else?'

A short silence prevailed before Tallulah said, 'I haven't finished yet. I chose cryonics because I don't trust the religious burial procedure. Just suppose that, in my old age, I suffer from narcolepsy. I've heard of people being declared dead and waking up on a slab in the morgue. I wouldn't like to wake up six foot under and have a panic attack. So, another question is – after succumbing to a violent death in a coffin, would I move to the afterlife with a face looking like the back end of a bus and my nails worn away with scratching at the lid?'

A hush fell upon the congregation. An elderly woman in a drab green coat screamed, 'I don't want to be buried alive!' and ran out, arms flailing, followed by a man shouting, 'Bloody hell, I hadn't thought of that!'

Above the noise of collective chatter, Reverend Pottering shouted, 'Please turn to Psalm 23:4.' He began reading in a loud voice, 'And though I walk through the valley of the shadow of death, I will fear no evil, for you are with me—'

Tallulah waited until he'd finished and put up her hand. She saw Reverend Pottering nod resignedly, acknowledging her wish to speak again. She said, 'I want to know the difference between borrowing and stealing a blanket. What parameters does the church have?'

Reverend Pottering's nose twitched and he said he'd be glad to receive her after the service. Florence stood up, stepped into the aisle and spoke with a fog-horn voice, 'Tallulah Millstone should repent. She experiments on chickens and her niece writes filth.' She held up a copy of *Agriculture and Business Monthly* which had an illustration of a young couple in a passionate embrace on the front cover and a heading 'Where's the Church on Sex?'.

There followed a rustle of fabrics and shuffling of feet as the congregation turned to look at Tallulah. Led by Florence they began to chant, 'Repent, repent, repent.' The second inquisition had started. Tallulah waited until Reverend Pottering lifted his hand to silence them all before she stepped into the aisle and threw a punch. Florence clutched her nose, tottered and reached for the side of the pew. The congregation drew in breath and someone clapped. Tallulah's heels clacked as she trotted down the aisle towards the door. The stained glass windows no longer shone. It was obvious God had forsaken the church for today.

Storming towards home, Tallulah felt a tap on the shoulder and turned around to see Santeros. A shudder ran down her spine.

'Mrs Tallulah, you ran away from me when I was trying to teach you how to slit a chicken throat and make chicken soup.'

'No need, Mr Santeros, I'm quite an expert on slitting throats myself but with a difference – I don't use terror tactics to scare people.'

He said he didn't understand what she was talking about. 'Perhaps I can teach you how to cook *moros y cristianos*?'

'Christianos? Are you a cannibal?'

He laughed, exposing his straight white teeth. 'It is a Cuban dish – rice with black beans.'

'Well, thank heavens for small mercies. The British don't eat human meat. At least Stanley never did when we were married.'

'I like your sense of humour, Mrs Tallulah. Perhaps we can smoke special *Maria Warner* cigarettes and dance into stupor at sacrifices? I'm sure you can make good clean cut on necks.'

She said she'd never heard of *Maria Warner* cigarettes but suspected he meant marijuana.

'They are very special and make woman and man relaxed.'

He looked into her eyes and she saw the buildings behind him begin to fade, while the pupils of his eyes grew bigger. He seemed to tower over her like a huge black and white bird.

'You're not trying to hypnotise me are you?'

'I am looking for a good woman for making—'

'Well I'm not looking for a man,' she said in a tone which left nothing to the imagination except a curt 'no' to sex.

He leaned over her and held out his arms like two huge, all-enveloping wings which started to close around her. He replied in a sinister tone, 'The vulture is a patient bird.' She reckoned he must have been reading James Hadley Chase.

Tallulah returned home confused, disillusioned and still not knowing if she was committing a sin by not taking the police blanket back. By evening she decided to forget it all and get on with her project. Looking into an alternative to the facility in Brighton and to compare costs she decided to call a cryonics facility in Miami for advice. It would be about noon there. She called directory enquiries then dialled the number.

A man with an American accent answered her call. 'Kryonix. Good morning, this is the manager speaking. Welcome to the world of cryogenic flash freezing.'

Tallulah greeted him with, 'Good morning, America, I'm calling from Great Britain.'

A sleepy American dead-pan drawl said, 'Do you wish to place an order or are you requesting information about freezing?'

'I would like some information. Sir, I believe you freeze the un-dead in liquid nitrogen to preserve them for posterity?'

There was a momentary silence. 'Lady, this is Kryonix Catering and we only flash-freeze raspberries.'

Tallulah laughed. 'You Yankees will have your little joke won't you?'

'It's no joke freezing thousands a day.'

'Well it sounds as if you're good at your job. I want to ask you how much it would cost to preserve not one, but two bodies in the same tub for ninety years? Alternatively I'm interested in knowing the discount rate for freezing two or more heads instead of one. Hopefully by the time medical science has improved, we will be called back to life. The thing is I don't want my head to be in a tub with forty-five others. What can you suggest?'

What the catering manager suggested next offended Tallulah's ears. If he hadn't been on the other side of the Atlantic she'd have reported him to the police for vulgar language and sex and age discrimination.

Later she called Stanley and told him to keep Santeros away from her or she'd report him to the police.

Stanley said, 'I'm not his keeper.'

'He practically propositioned me.'

'Think yourself lucky at your age.'

MI5 MI6 or CIA?

An envelope without a stamp was sitting on the mat when Tallulah came down for breakfast. The message, in newspaper cuttings, read, *Sender: Anonymouse. Meet me gravy Sun: 1830 W7.* She decoded it. *Meet me at the graveyard on Sunday at 6.30pm at grave number W7.* Was it a hoax? She didn't know anyone with code name Anonymouse. Was the message from one of the secret services? Her suspicions stretched to Stanley, former MI6 and the Cuban Santeros – wasn't he from a little island with no religion and fifty missiles pointed at the White House? But was he capable of writing a coded message? Whoever it was must have news about the Cold War.

Grey clouds of dusk stole across the graveyard as Fred, Cecilia and Ernest watched Tallulah step between rows of tombstones wearing a thick green wool coat and matching short-brimmed hat against the cold. She moved towards Cecilia's tomb, looking behind her nervously as if expecting someone.

From behind Cecilia's headstone, a man in a long black coat, balaclava and Mickey Mouse mask appeared. Fred, Cecilia and Ernest saw Tallulah stumble backwards, obviously startled. They heard her say nervously, 'I suppose you're Anonymouse. If you're not from Disneyland you must be from the CIA. I've been watching the news lately. Ronald Reagan has signed legislation to outlaw the Russians. I suppose you already know the Soviet Far East Army is on alert and about to drop a nuclear bomb? Maybe we can avoid it if we send the Iron Lady or the United States President to talk to Gorby?' They heard the man grunt. She continued, 'I suppose it means I have to organise the Civil Defence in my area? Start battening down the hatches? If I may make a suggestion – get yourself some aspirin for radiation burns, no more than six a day, according to our government, as you won't make it back to the States in time.'

The man threw back his head and laughed in a sinister way. He said in a croaky voice, 'Cryonics,' and opened his black coat. All he was wearing underneath were grey socks and a pair of black fake-snakeskin shoes. By the light from the church, it was obvious his body was pink and quite young. The man in black wiggled his loins and penis as best he could and showed Tallulah his buttocks, which were quite hairy around his lower back. Cecilia covered Fred's eyes with her hands as the man's lower parts expanded. Ernest began to make notes. He heard Tallulah say boldly, 'You could have called me first instead of making a big thing about it. I'm interviewing prospective cryonics partners next Tuesday. You don't have to show me your body right now, just come along. I could marry you if you promise to improve your communication skills and shave off all that unsightly hair from your body. I could also introduce you to Florence of the Mothers' Union – she's the one hunting perverts in the park.'

The man shrieked and ran off.

The trio looked at each other wide-eyed.

Ernest said, 'I know who it is.'

'Who is it then? Don't keep us in suspense,' Cecilia said.

'Do you know old Mr Drury from the old people's home?'

'It can't possibly be him, he's too old to have an erection,' she said.

'Of course it's not. It's his nephew. I've seen them in church together and I recognise his shoes.'

'Is he the one who helps the plumber and grave-digger?' Fred asked. Ernest nodded.

Cecilia grinned. 'That means he wants Tallulah's body.'

Rottingham Police Station

Mid-afternoon Tallulah rang the Rottingham Police Station. She heard a young male voice reply, 'Rottingham Police Station. Good afternoon. How can I help you?'

He sounded like a young whippersnapper. There was no way she was going to tell him her business. 'I want to speak to Chief Inspector Dent. The one who gave me some lemon tea in the police station when I was in my nightdress. This is Tallulah Millstone, MBE, CBE, in that order. I was due for the Military Cross, but as a woman I was ineligible. Don't you think it's shocking after jumping out of a plane with a wireless set weighing a ton?'

'It certainly is, madam.'

She could tell he didn't really understand what she was talking about but at least he was polite.

She explained. 'The French gave me the Legion of Honour for killing a traitor.'

'Really?' The line clicked and there followed a two minute silence before he returned.

'Sorry, Mrs Millstone, but the chief's out on a case. He said I should ask you to tell me what it's all about.'

'If he's out on a case, how come he answered the phone?'

'He was just leaving but before he left he mentioned something about a blanket.'

Tallulah said, 'Can I speak to Constable Ernest Barnstable?'

'Sorry, madam, but sadly he's no longer here, he's passed to the police station in the sky.'

Later in the day, Scarlett called Tallulah to ask her if she'd called the Rottingham Police Station about the blanket.

'The Chief Inspector was out.'

'Call them again,' said Scarlett.

Tallulah couldn't believe her luck when Chief Inspector Dent picked up the phone. She expected him to greet her warmly. After all, they'd supped tea together in his office. Instead, his voice sounded officious. 'How can I help you, Mrs Millstone? I presume you're calling about the police blanket?'

'Actually I'm calling about something else but I'll bring the blanket back the next time I come. I can't bring it soon, as I've injured my back. I tripped in the graveyard when a pervert showed me his little willy.'

She heard an embarrassed cough. 'Sorry to hear it, madam. You should see a doctor.'

He sounded genuinely concerned. 'Please hold on, Mrs Millstone, I'll pass you to someone who can take down your statement.'

Tallulah didn't have time to say she didn't want to speak to the young whippersnapper when the phone clicked and the young man spoke. 'Mrs Millstone, Chief Inspector Dent has asked me to take down the details.'

Tallulah described briefly her meeting in the graveyard with a pervert sporting a Mickey Mouse mask who passed himself off as a spy and exposed himself. She mentioned the hairs on his lower back and his lack of communication skills and his disgustingly awful little willy. She threw in confidential information about a foreigner wanting to eat dogs and someone she couldn't name who had left toenail clippings in the bidet of a foreign hotel at the end of the war.

The young policeman listened patiently. 'We don't have much to go on.'

'I haven't finished yet. A man who's brainwashing communists threatened me about a lover I killed in the war. And a young leftist threw up into my sink.'

'Why did he do it?'

'Probably because I killed Fred.'

There was a momentary silence while the young policeman wondered how to handle his first murder case by a serial killer who had already killed two people.

He cleared his throat. 'Mrs Millstone, I have to read you your rights before sending someone to arrest you for murder.'

She snapped, 'Fred was a cockerel, you dumb cluck,' and hung up.

Another lousy fantasy

Boris Ustinov's hairy hand picked up the phone at the Russian Embassy in London and dialled a number in Rome. It rang eight times before a sweet young voice said, 'Good morning, this is UFO – the United Fruit Organisation. How can I help you?'

'Put me through to Smirnov.'

'Just a moment, sir.'

Smirnov answered with a hurried, 'Hello, Boris, to what do I owe this pleasure? It's great to hear from you but I'm just about to leave for a meeting. We've got a conference coming up soon. I'm hosting *Raspberry growing in developing countries*.'

Boris said, 'Then I'll be brief. I need your help getting someone a job.'

'No problem.'

'Remember Anushka Petrova? She was at your birthday party at the Russian Embassy in London. She was the woman in red with the black fishnet stockings?'

'The one who reminded me of my niece?'

'Yes, that one.'

'I remember her well.'

'She left London and she's now living in Witherington. Can you give her a job? Anushka doesn't know much about raspberry growing but she'd be a good person to have in your office for public relations.'

Boris refrained from telling Smirnov she was on the run and he wanted her back and in his bed. Or in a foreign bed.

Preferably with a wrought iron bedstead and a couple of restraining neckties.

Smirnov said, 'Boris, there's nothing I'd like more but my secretary might not like it. Irina's a bit jealous of her position. We have a special relationship, if you know what I mean,' Smirnov chuckled.

'I don't mean a job as a secretary. Anushka has experience of hand to hand combat and she's also good at removing people.'

'OK, I read you, Boris. I might be able to use her for a high-level job.'

'Can you get me a job there as well?'

'I'll have to look into it. We don't have many jobs going here.'

Anushka knew Boris would eventually track her down so it didn't come as a great surprise when she picked up the phone in her room at the Wailing Willows Hotel and Boris spoke. He told her he'd organised an interview in Rome for her.

'I don't know anything about raspberries,' she said, her voice trembling and hands shaking, remembering the fearful spanking session with his belt.

'You'll soon learn. I've asked Smirnov to give me a job too so we can work together again.'

Late evening, Anushka called Serge, repeating several times about her life being in danger and needing either to get married or have a steady job perhaps with *Agriculture and Business Monthly*.

Serge said, 'We don't need another journalist and you have no experience.'

'You promised to find me a job the last time we met.'

'I haven't had time. We've had lots of deadlines lately. You know what it's like working for a magazine.'

'No, I don't, I've never worked for one before.'

'Which is one good reason why I can't get you a job there.'

'Please, please, come to my suite and we can talk about it.'

'It's a bit late.'

'I can give you a fantasy. I'll let you in through the tradesmen's entrance so you don't have to meet James.'

'I can come for half an hour.'

Serge was punctual. Following Anushka into the living room he accepted a glass of vodka and orange, gulped it down and asked for another when she started talking about babies.

'Look, Anushka, I know you'd like to be married, but I won't make a good husband.'

She decided to change her tactics and make marriage sound appealing.

'Let's forget about living happily ever after and tell me what fantasy you want,' she said.

'Can we do Alfred, Lord Tennyson's *The Vision of Sin?* You can be a sexy barmaid pulling pints and I will be under the counter taking off your mesh stockings and suspender belt.'

'If you recite it to me, I will act it out.' Anushka unbuttoned her blouse then removed his belt and unzipped his trousers. During the kiss, they undressed hurriedly and got into bed with no preliminaries. Anushka fell silent, nestling her head in the crick of his arm. 'I am ready for the poem,' she said.

'I'm a bit tired so I'll start from the middle bit.'

Bitter barmaid, waning fast!
See that sheets are on my bed;
What! The flower of life is past:
It is long before you wed.

Anushka sat up tossing her short blonde hair. 'I am not a barmaid who cannot get married!'

'I haven't finished yet. It gets better as it goes along.'

Anushka lay back down and waited for the best bits to come.

Let me screw thee up a peg:
Let me loose thy tongue with wine:
Callest that thing a leg?
Which is thinnest? Thine or mine?

Anushka jumped out of bed and made for the kitchen. Serge heard her rummage around in the cupboards. She returned holding something behind her back.

She said in a husky voice, 'I want you to turn over and let me show you what a sexy barmaid can do.' Serge turned and lay on his stomach. She sat on the side of the bed and whispered in his ear, 'I am a sexy barmaid and I am in love with you. Then we get married and have many children.'

'What a lousy fantasy,' he replied, wanting to get up and get dressed. It was too late. He felt a sharp slap on his arse followed by burning pain. She clamped her hand over his mouth to stifle his scream and told him to shut up or James would hear them. She whispered in his ear, 'I am holding a little frying pan and enjoying my own fantasy of seeing you with pans in the kitchen.' She brought down the frying pan a second time when he said he didn't want to marry her and look after the children while she worked.

But Anushka was adamant. 'I will be a liberated woman and I will go to work while my husband stays at home and looks after the children. And if you don't get me a job with *Agriculture and Business Monthly* I will tell the world you are working with communists and Russian spies.'

Manipulator

Roland saw Anushka step outside her room as he was leaving for the office. Striding down the corridor quietly, he crept up on her to surprise her and smell her perfume. He wanted to be reminded of their afternoon of mad passionate love and his manly prowess on her bed.

When he tapped her on the shoulder she turned. 'Oh, it's you.' He thought she sounded relieved. Her eyes darted down the corridor.

'Sorry, Anushka, I didn't mean to startle you.'

'That's alright,' she said drily.

'What are you doing here? I never expected to see you again.' He wanted to take her in his arms and kiss her and smooth away her fears.

'I came here for a job interview at your office.'

'Why didn't you come to see me first? I'm just down the corridor. We can go to my room if you want. I can show you my rainforest.'

'I have a headache.'

'I can go to the chemist and get you some aspirin?'

'I am busy. I cannot have sex with you because I am going with Serge.'

Her words fell on him like a cold shower.

Scarlett shuffled papers on the meeting table while Anushka settled in the chair next to Serge. Roland arrived, his shoulders hunched, looking as if the office was the last place he wanted to be. All eyes were on Anushka who was wearing a bright red coat with black patent belt and matching boots. Her short blonde hair, combed into a bob, shone. As for her make-up, she'd been a bit heavy-handed with the black eyeshadow and red lipstick but all in all, her appearance was one of a young modern professional woman.

Scarlett introduced Anushka to Roland and Serge, gave them a copy of her curriculum vitae and asked Roland to take notes. She began by explaining the aims of the magazine before moving on to the job functions.

'We're looking for the right person to undertake some bookkeeping, help with the photocopying and dissemination of publicity. I see from your curriculum vitae you speak quite a few languages and have worked in the diplomatic service.'

'Yes, I speak Russian, Bulgarian, English and Italian. I kept accounts for diplomats. I gave job satisfaction.'

'Anushka, please tell us your good points.'

'I am a creative thinker. I can manipulate to get good results.' She stood up and removed her coat saying she was hot. Eyes were now on her breasts which threatened to pop out of her low cut black dress. Scarlett glowered at Serge and Roland who both sat mesmerised like snakes watching a snake charmer.

Scarlett said, 'Anushka. Would you like to tell us why you want this job?'

'I would like this job because I would like to help dysfunctional men and women with sex problems. And I like Veronica. However, she does not talk much about liberation. Actually I want to learn how to liberate myself from men who want only sex without getting married. I found no answers in your magazine. I want this job so Veronica can teach me how to get liberated.'

Scarlett glanced at Roland who was nodding his head

furiously. The last thing she wanted was Roland liberating Anushka.

'I don't think Veronica would have time as she's too busy with deadlines.'

'I can meet her after work then?' Anushka said.

Roland nodded again.

'I don't think so. After a hard day's work Veronica will be exhausted,' Scarlett insisted.

'Perhaps Serge can teach me?'

Serge said he would. The pan-spanking had been painful at the time, but now he longed for another session. Perhaps tied to the bed.

Scarlett kicked Serge under the table. 'Thank you, Anushka, but Serge will also be busy with deadlines.'

Anushka's voice raised a tone. 'Then what's the point of *Agriculture and Business Monthly* if you cannot teach me to be liberated?'

Scarlett said she'd let her know the outcome of the interview and showed her out. For less than an hour, the atmosphere had been what Roland considered '*harmonious*', Serge '*exhilarating*' and Scarlett '*disgustingly sexist*'. She tore up Anushka's CV and threw it in the bin. Roland and Serge understood Anushka would not be getting the job when Scarlett hissed, 'I don't want to have to knock on the door every time I walk into the store room.'

Roland beat a hasty retreat. Serge loosened his tie. 'Sorry, Scarlett, but she threatened me. She said I had to marry her or get her a job or she'd tell the whole world I work with communists and could end up dead.'

'She sounds like a troublemaker. Get rid of her. The next time you go to London take her and leave her there.'

Constable Barnstable's first sin

A hiccup and a sob came from the tree above Ernest's grave. Bertha's bare legs dangled over a branch. Her face was mottled red and eyes puffy from crying. Her hair seemed not combed for days. The Tartan dressing gown and matching slippers were rather grubby. Make-up was smudged around her face. She swayed back and forth, sobbing into a soggy handkerchief. Between hiccups, she was coaxed down from the branch. Once on the ground she threw her arms round Ernest's neck, burying her head in the shoulder of his police uniform. Rather incensed at her lack of propriety – he'd never have cried on her dress – he attempted to prise himself from her embrace. In the struggle, his helmet fell off onto the grass with a muffled thud. Releasing her arms from around his neck, she blurted out, 'I can't take the Pearly Gates Express dressed like this in front of everyone. I'll feel humiliated.'

Ernest agreed her dressing gown and slippers were inappropriate attire. 'It would be like the Queen of England meeting the Pope in her nightdress and curlers before she'd taken a bath,' he sympathised.

She sniffed into her hanky and blew her nose with a honking sound. 'I died in my best emerald green dress but Norman laid me out for viewing in my dressing gown. I think he did it out of spite.'

'I'll try and get your dress back from the funeral home, but I can't promise anything.'

'And don't forget my shoes, although I don't know how I'll get my feet into them after being in these slippers for so long.' She took off a tartan slipper to show him a red inflamed bunion, which, she said, became redder every time she got angry – which had been for most of her married life. She then went on about a whole list of Norman's defects and violent intentions, including standing on her bunions.

'I want him sent to the Stream of Snapping Turtles!' she screamed, her voice reverberating around Ernest's head.

'I'll retrieve your dress but I can't say which Terrace of Purgatory Norman is eligible for,' Ernest replied, heading for his tomb.

There was a full moon when Ernest glided towards the Goodbody Funeral Home. He wished he had his truncheon but on the other hand Norman wouldn't be a threat. Filled with trepidation and the feeling he was invading privacy, he slid through the front door, skirted the living room and drifted up the stairs.

Norman sat in a heavy dark-wood four-poster bed reading documents. Ernest's eyes fell on an insurance policy on Bertha's life with Norman as beneficiary. Opposite the foot of the bed was a built-in wardrobe. One by one, Ernest opened the doors until he found Bertha's clothes.

Norman saw the wardrobe doors open and Bertha's emerald green dress and red shoes float out in mid-air. Spooked, he jumped out of bed, knocking a shin on one of the bedposts and fled down the stairs. Bertha's dress followed him and the heels of her shoes hammered his head. Feeling total panic, he darted into the viewing room and quickly locked it. There was a bad smell from a dead woman in a coffin – Mrs J.C. Sarehole-Reape. He was scared. In her lifetime she had possessed a viperous tongue and unrelenting temper. She was the only woman in Witherington surpassing Bertha for sheer brutal cruelty to her husband.

Finding his voice, Norman shouted for help. He felt weak. His scalp tightened. The corpse leered. Her eyes moved from side to side and her lips twisted into a bitter smile. He stumbled back against a chair then tripped over a corner of the rug. Unable to steady himself, Norman precipitated forward towards Mrs Sarehole-Reape's coffin where his head smashed against the elegant polished wood and marked it with his blood.

Back at the graveyard, Ernest waited for Bertha to thank him for retrieving her dress and shoes but without a word she grabbed them from him and left for the family tomb to try them on. Cecilia and Fred exchanged glances, shocked at her bad manners. She reappeared shortly afterwards, smiling and completely transformed in her green dress, red shoes and matching make-up. They noticed a whiff of harem-type perfume. Quite unexpectedly she rushed at Ernest, her arms outstretched, the sheer force of her belly knocking him off his feet. He fell back narrowly missing a tombstone. Then she was on top of him. Cecilia and Fred stifled a giggle. Ernest had red lipstick from below his nose down to his chin. He pushed her off and stood up and announced breathlessly, 'I hereby inform you, Mrs Bertha Goodbody, that you are eligible for the Terrace of Lust, and, by the way, your husband is as dead as a Dodo.'

Bertha screamed and waved her arms and swirled until she was gone.

Ernest said, 'I'm perplexed. On more than one occasion she wished her husband dead.'

'Did you frighten Bertha's husband to death?' Cecilia asked.

Ernest blushed. 'No I did not.'

'You'll never go to Heaven if you tell a lie,' she said as if reciting a nursery rhyme.

'No you never will,' echoed Fred. 'And you can forget being gatekeeper.'

'Has the inquisition started again?' Ernest protested, not sure how to handle Cecilia's insistence on something which didn't concern her.

'Only if you've told a lie.' He realised Cecilia was going to continue probing unless he gave her a satisfactory answer.

'Oh, alright then, I admit I got some satisfaction from seeing a criminal get his due reward. I was annoyed because he was gloating over Bertha's insurance policy. But his death was an accident. He fell of his own accord against a coffin in the viewing room.'

'In other words you scared him to death – a sadistic policeman who couldn't control his anger,' Cecilia said.

'Hey, wait a minute, I didn't kill him on purpose—'

'I would say Ernest is innocent. He was just playing a funny game that ended in tragedy,' interrupted Fred.

'Shut up, Fred,' said Cecilia, directing her gaze at Ernest. 'It's time you went to the Church of Local Martyrs to confess your sins, otherwise I might be tempted to write to Saint Peter.'

Ernest paled. It seemed the tables had turned and now he was the one being interrogated. 'I don't want to confess inside the church in case I bump into Roland again.'

Cecilia won in the end. After having confessed his sins to an empty church, Ernest asked for forgiveness to the Creator. An immediate reply came through. He heard a voice say, *You have to save Bertha.*

'Did you hear that?' he asked Cecilia.

'Hear what?'

'The voice.'

'I didn't hear a thing,' said Cecilia.

'Neither did I, you must have been imagining it,' said Fred.

'Maybe it was his conscience talking,' replied Cecilia.

But Ernest was convinced the voice was telling him to save Bertha from her dead husband, who was likely to arrive soon. Cecilia said she'd better things to do than help save a mad woman. Fred, shocked at her language, called her selfish and said, 'You're in the house of God. Where's your sense of Christianity and all you've been taught about forgiveness?'

Cecilia said they'd be better off saving Norman from Bertha as she was rude, ignorant, controlling and not worth saving.

Unexpected developments

Anushka was surprised to receive a telephone call from Rome from a man with a Balkans accent who said his name was Anton. He told her she'd been referred to him by someone at the Russian Embassy in London, who she assumed was Boris. Anton explained that Mr Smirnov of the United Fruit Organisation in Rome wanted to interview her in connection with a remunerative job. She remembered Boris's middle-aged friend who she'd met at a party at the Russian Embassy. Not really attractive but well-dressed, with silver hair and rimless glasses. If it meant working with him she didn't mind. He had been nice to her.

Anton said, 'We're looking forward to interviewing you and you'll find a ticket at London airport's Alitalia desk for the flight to Rome. About your passport, the Russian Embassy in London has issued you with an Italian one in the name of Anna Petrone as it will save unnecessary British bureaucracy, if you know what I mean.'

She said 'yes', supposing that Boris had had a hand in it.

James lay in his bed thinking how fortunate he was to have Anushka working for him. He remembered the first time he'd seen her, looking like a lost child, pulling a medium-sized black case behind her into the reception area. She'd been wearing a short black dress with high boots and had a red coat bunched up over her arm. Clara had just given in her notice and he'd been looking for someone else to do the cleaning. Anushka had jumped at the chance. She had been with him from the end of April and all of May but it seemed much longer. Perhaps it was because he saw her on a daily basis and many times during the course of the day. He saw her more often than he used to see Cecilia or Clara. He liked her. Anushka made a good breakfast every morning and pummelled his pillows to make them softer and more comfortable and stripped off the sheets with the determination of a trooper. And she didn't pretend to be working when she wasn't, or leave fluff under the bed or in the corners of the room, like Clara used to do. At first he'd watched her to see if she was giving off any sexual messages but he knew Serge Gallo visited her on occasions and he considered her off-limits. He'd never stolen another man's woman. In any case she was young enough to be his granddaughter. On occasions she'd made him feel twenty years old. He was a young man inside an old man's body. Sometimes Anushka was a woman and other times she was a child. Her moods fluctuated. Her silences intrigued him and her laughter beguiled his foolish heart. He was happy with their strange platonic relationship which caused him no aggravation but lifted his spirits because it was pure, flawless and heavenly. He thought things might have been different had he been forty years younger, but now all he wanted was peace and quiet. Although he frequently thought about sex, he resisted the urge to think of her in a sexual way. He preferred to keep her at a safe distance so no animosity could come between them and ruin their perfect relationship. He wanted her to stay with him forever.

Anushka spent the night wondering what Boris had in store for her and why he would want her to go to Rome when he'd insisted he wanted her back at the embassy in London. It made no sense unless he was planning a transfer to Rome.

She realised she'd have to tell James she was going for an interview seeing as he'd have to get his own breakfast for a couple of days. She rather dreaded telling him as he had been nice to her in a fatherly way.

Anushka waited until James had finished his breakfast before unloading her news. She thought he would be very angry. But she could see he was controlling himself in the way the British do when faced with unfathomable odds.

James said, 'Go for the interview and let's see how things work out.'

'What if I get the job?'

'We'll cross that bridge when we come to it.'

Anushka thanked him for his understanding, wanting very much to embrace him. He reminded her of her father who had had the same sad expression when she left Russia – not knowing if he would ever see her again.

Upon the stern stood the Celestial Pilot;
Beatitude seemed written in his face,
And more than a hundred spirits sat within.

Dante Alighieri
The Divine Comedy: Purgatory. Canto II

JUNE 1986

Henhouse blues

Seeing as the day promised sunshine, Fred decided to visit Bluebell Vicarage and see how the hens and Gottfried were getting on. He left the early-morning hushed silence of the graveyard.

Ethel was crying in the henhouse.

'I miss Fred,' she sobbed.

Virgin, a small delicate Rhode Island Red, attempted to comfort her. 'Ethel, I'm sure he'll come back. He probably wandered off and got lost.'

Ms Prim, a haughty Silky, who prided herself on educating the hens said, 'One should say "he *became* lost" and not "he *got* lost".'

Ethel sobbed. 'He loved me the most.'

Virgin retorted, 'He loved us all. We were all his concubines you know.'

Ms Prim said slowly, 'If you are a concubine it means you are not a virgin.'

Virgin stuck her head forward. 'Yes I am. I don't need to be fertilised to lay eggs.'

Ms Prim came straight to the point. 'Are you sterile?' A dreadful silence ensued as they visualised Tallulah's soup pan.

Virgin began to shake. 'I'm not sterile,' she insisted.

Gottfried the bantam, overseer of discipline, intervened. 'In all my time living in a henhouse in the Black Forest, I've never seen such a lazy bunch of hens. Someone's not laying.'

Ethel said, 'As usual you've misread the message. It's got nothing to do with laziness. Someone's ovaries have packed up.'

'Well they're not mine,' said Virgin strutting to her perch.

Gottfried pulled himself up to his full height and puffed out his chest. I'm going to watch and see who's laying and who's not.'

Virgin looked down from her perch. 'You always were a little Hitler,' she said viciously.

Gottfried retorted, 'Please remember who's in charge. To sum up, we have here two sets of functioning ovaries and one sterile death sentence.' He strutted back and forth in a goose step mumbling, 'Someone's got dead ovaries.'

The hens shuddered. Virgin said, 'I would say Ms Prim is making a song and dance out of the situation because she's covering up for her own infertility.'

Ms Prim took a peck at Virgin, pulling out one of her tail feathers. Virgin screamed and clawed at her. Fred saw Gottfried step forward. Notwithstanding his size, the only thing he was good at was stopping riots. He scribbled in the dust *hens don't lay eggs every day of the week. They have one day off, not necessarily on the same day.*

'If one of you lays two in one day, the old lady will never know someone is sterile,' he said.

Ethel stopped crying. 'You must be joking, Gottfried, we can't work overtime. It's slave labour.'

Gottfried's back became a ramrod. He goose-stepped around Ethel. In a quiet threatening voice he said, 'I suggest you keep quiet and toe the line.'

Ethel, furious at the attack on her rights said, 'I don't agree with you, Gottfried. You can't gag us. I'm going to report you to the Cluckers' Union.'

Fred flew back to the graveyard and sat in the tree with his head under his wing. Who wasn't laying and who would be Tallulah's next victim?

'Problems afoot, Fred?' The question came from Bertha who materialised beside him. 'You can cry on my shoulder if you want.'

'I don't feel like talking. Please go away.'

'Sometimes it helps to talk and get it off your chest. It's not good to keep it bottled up and would you mind coming out from under your wing.'

Fred poked his head up and said he felt confused. First Ernest had tried to gag him and more or less said he couldn't have a mind of his own and now Ethel was in danger of being gagged and there was no free speech in the henhouse. He mentioned Virgin and Ms Prim who had the axe of Damocles over their heads.

'What a terrible situation,' Bertha sympathised. 'First the old lady chops off your head and now she wants to kill your chickens. I think she deserves to die. You could try haunting her and giving her a heart attack.'

'Ernest would send me to Hell.'

'Don't worry, Fred, I'll help you. Just leave it to me.' She was gone before Fred had time to stop her.

He asked himself if he really wanted Tallulah dead – wasn't it a sin? Was she worth roasting in Hell for? And what would Ernest say and do to him? The thought was definitely scary.

In the middle of the night Bertha whirled to Bluebell Vicarage and found the hens and Gottfried sleeping soundly. She slid into the henhouse and quietly took Gottfried from his perch. Carrying him into Tallulah's shed, she laid him gently on the table.

Gottfried's eyes half opened drowsily. He didn't know

where he was. Through the haze he saw a very large ghostly lady with a green satin dress and snakes in her hair. He tried to squawk but was paralysed. The ghostly lady stroked his crest and looked into his eyes, speaking with a mesmerising hypnotic voice. She told him to listen to her. In a whisper she said, 'At the next opportunity, when the old lady arrives to collect the eggs, you will attack her before she carries off Virgin. You can claw and peck her eyes out and leave her for dead. If you don't you'll end up in the soup pan with your hens. Nod your head if you agree.' He nodded twice and felt himself drifting away somewhere. The next morning he remembered nothing except falling asleep and dreaming he was in hot water up to his neck.

Women rule OK

Mr Kim arrived at the Vicarage to tell Tallulah he'd collected quite a few English recipes which were, to his taste, rather bland. He quoted rice pudding and semolina. He said he needed something a little more tasty. She asked him what he was used to eating in North Korea. He mentioned many dishes she'd never heard of.

'What fruit and vegetables do you eat?'

'Mushrooms, apples, pears and other things,' he replied.

'What about potatoes?'

'I find them bland. However, I will start a potato revolution if you can find me good recipes for them.'

Tallulah leafed through her cookery book, telling him his people would need to diversify and plant on rotation to avoid another Irish potato famine. To her surprise, he replied politely he was well aware of the consequences, having studied British history and the many dynasties and great British leaders of the past and also music. He gave her a rendering of 'O Danny Boy', in the Korean language and she joined in, singing it in English. It was a good start to the day.

Tallulah pointed to one of the recipes. 'As you can see, you can put a few sprigs of mint in the boiling water to give the potatoes flavour,' she said.

'I have never tasted mint.'

'What about baked potatoes with baked beans.'

'We do not have baked beans in tins but I could fill the baked potato with kimchi.' A fourth footnote was added as Tallulah said she liked kimchi and it was a good idea.

Mr Kim beamed and told her she was a true daughter of the revolution. He asked her about a mushroom recipe.

'I have just the recipe for you – a mushroom omelette.'

Mr Kim's face lit up. 'I think it's a perfect idea. Our mushrooms are the best in the world and the happy chickens will do their patriotic duty for the Fatherland by producing twice as many eggs than any capitalist state.'

Mr Kim showed his appreciation by asking for a cup of delicious Earl Grey tea, the likes of which he'd never tasted in all his time marching in the snow-covered mountains and digging ditches for the communist cause, he said.

Tallulah made him tea and began to warm towards him. He was a perfect gentleman and appreciated good British food. In the relaxed atmosphere they felt at ease with each other enough to venture on to the minefield of politics.

Mr Kim wanted to know why the British Isles were ruled by two women – the Queen and Mrs Thatcher.

'I find it quite strange,' he said in his perfectly gentlemanly stilted English, 'that women rule your island, unless they came to power through proletariat uprisings or secret revolutionary strategies.' Tallulah smiled at his charming, almost boyish, analysis of the British political scene.

She said, 'The Queen took office after her father died and Mrs Thatcher was voted in by the majority of the population.'

'So why does the population prefer a woman? Is it because your men are too weak?'

Tallulah stifled a laugh and explained about the voting system and democracy, which, Mr Kim again politely pointed out, wouldn't work in his country as the present Stalinist nepotistic dynasty couldn't be faulted.

He said, 'I think your country does not work well, as you have very big revolutionary subterfuges going on.' As an example he quoted the coal miners' strikes.

'In my country the coal miners are too patriotic to strike. We have the perfect system. It is the glorious Party which dictates democracy and everyone is happy. We believe in putting the State before everything else as we are working to make our grand country greater.' He went on to tell her about free education and many commodities provided by the State. He sang her a song, 'We shall go on the correct road to revolution'. And she replied she was impressed and had no idea communism made sense.

Following an explanation by Mr Kim about the advantages of Marxism, Tallulah made him another cup of tea and thanked him for the lesson, saying it had been a true eye-opener. She said he deserved an immediate lesson on how to cook a proper mushroom omelette.

'Just wait here while I collect some eggs,' she said beaming.

Tallulah entered the chicken-run to find Ethel, Ms Prim and Virgin huddled in their nesting boxes. Surprisingly there were only two eggs instead of three. One of them had not laid even one egg for more than a week. It meant one thing – it was time for the pot and some nice chicken soup.

When Tallulah yanked Virgin out of her box by her neck, the hen squawked and struggled, flapping and clawing at Tallulah's arms. Gottfried, alerted by Virgin and Tallulah's screams, came to the rescue. Diving from his perch, he flew onto Tallulah's head and plucked strands of hair from her head, pecking at her scalp at the same time. She screamed even louder and let go of Virgin who rushed back to her nesting box. Stumbling over a large stone, Tallulah fell on her front, squashing the two eggs in her apron pocket. Gottfried was clawing Tallulah's legs when Mr Kim, alerted by the chicken-run war, ran from the kitchen to help Tallulah. He wasn't quick enough to grab Gottfried who, seeing Mr Kim rushing towards him, flew over his head and through the open gate to freedom.

After witnessing the gravity of the claw marks on Tallulah's arms and legs and her pecked scalp, Mr Kim called Tallulah's doctor who came with his nurse to medicate her. When the nurse had finished bandaging her arms and legs, Tallulah asked if she could come to the house to medicate her on a daily basis. Although the doctor was sympathetic, he said he couldn't justify home help. Having been a doctor in the army, he suggested she carry on like a good trooper, get a friend to medicate her and keep out of the chicken-run as she risked infection. Mr Kim fussed over her and made her a cup of tea, saying how sorry he was to see her injured. It set him off on a train of thoughts about his army training. 'And now I will sing to you, Mrs Tallulah,' he said giving a zealous rendering of 'I will devote my whole life to being a soldier'. He said he dedicated the song to her as she had just survived a battle.

Scarlett arrived later with fish and chips wrapped in newspaper. Tallulah could barely hide her delight. 'It reminds me of when a friend and myself went on holiday to Southend-on-Sea in the fifties. We walked along the cockle sheds and ate cockles and mussels, taking them out of their shells with a pin.'

'I'm not sure I'd like them. They're a bit like snails aren't they?'

'Not exactly. And in any case you have to be by the sea to appreciate them.'

Scarlett opened the bottle of wine she'd brought with her. 'Roland gave me the wine to give to you when he heard you'd been injured.'

'How very sweet of him. How's he getting on?'

'He's doing OK. We have a good readership now. He rarely goes to Hyde Park. Too much work to do, what with all the deadlines.'

'Perhaps it's just as well. There's nothing but trouble going on in London. I see he's carrying his leftist ideas into his articles. I do read your magazine even if I don't agree with everything but I suppose you know what you're doing. It's a bit controversial though.'

'Women's rights are always controversial but I don't want to gag Roland.' Scarlett looked at her watch. 'I have to go now. We have a busy day tomorrow.'

Tallulah thanked her for the unexpected dinner and asked a favour. 'The doctor said I can't feed the chickens or I might pick up some nasty germs, so I was wondering if you could pop in once a day to feed them.'

Scarlett groaned inwardly. 'We're snowed under at work but perhaps I could organise it. I could ask one of the local cleaners or boy scouts, they're always looking to make some money and it's good for the local economy.'

Tallulah wrinkled her nose. 'Perhaps you could ask the paperboy. He always brings my newspaper before breakfast.'

'Done,' said Scarlett, making a mental note to tell the paperboy where to find the chicken-feed.

'Thank you dear, I don't know what I'd do without you to help me with the chickens.'

'Probably chop their little heads off?' said Scarlett with a hint of sarcasm.

Much later, Tallulah called Stanley at the farmhouse and lauded Mr Kim for heroically saving her from sure death.

'I could have had my eyes pecked out by Gottfried if dear Mr Kim hadn't saved me in time. I think you can cross him off your list as a dangerous communist. In fact, I'm beginning to think communists aren't so dangerous and are really quite harmless and nice. He deserves a medal.'

Stanley said, 'I see he's succeeded in brainwashing you.'

In cold blood

The alarm clock rang, quietly at first, before rising to a shrill crescendo. Roland's hand reached out for the table light before stabbing his palm over the clock to silence it. The only compensation for having to get out of bed was seeing the sun shining when drawing back the curtains.

Sleep had not fully left him when he entered the office to be confronted by a hyperactive Scarlett asking him if he could interview her aunt seeing as he might need some inspiration to write a letter for his column. He grunted and said it wouldn't be a problem.

Scarlett said, 'I know it sounds a bit like nepotism but she's had a hard time lately. She's been harassed in church and attacked by her hens and insulted and has received crank letters. Someone even exposed himself. She's almost afraid of leaving the house. I think it would be good for her self-esteem if you talked to her about her cryonics project.'

Roland squinted through the haze in his head and thought he'd have preferred writing about the devastated rainforests of the world rather than half-dead bodies floating around in canisters.

Scarlett said, 'My aunt was on the front line during the war and was dropped by parachute into France to set up contact with the French Resistance. She led attacks on the enemy and saved a lot of lives and got medals for it. She's a sure hit with a pistol and rifle.'

He nodded, not daring to say he'd never understood why people should get medals for killing their fellow men.

Scarlett picked up the phone and called Tallulah. 'Do you remember Roland? The one with the long hair and yellow fluorescent socks? Well he wants to interview you about your medals.'

He heard Scarlett say, 'I think 2pm will be fine.' Then a pause. 'What! He never told me that.'

Scarlett put down the phone after saying goodbye and turned to Roland. 'Lunch at 2pm. What's this about you vomiting into Aunt Tallulah's sink?'

'No idea,' he lied, 'she must have dreamt it. Old people tend to invent things.'

Having a room at the Wailing Willows Hotel, two floors below the office, had turned out to be a blessing for Roland when he had to change his clothes to go out. He didn't need to ride his bike across town. Pulling a smart white shirt from the wardrobe along with a blue cashmere jumper his mother had given him for Christmas a few years ago, he proceeded to make himself look decent, at least for an old woman.

It was a toss-up whether to buy Tallulah chocolates or flowers. Not knowing her preference for light or dark chocolate he decided to play safe with a bunch of yellow roses. In the end it was Marigold the florist who was key to what Tallulah would receive. She said there were only red ones left but she could let him have them for ten per cent discount. He took them. Then a logistical challenge presented itself – how to carry the roses seeing as he'd no basket on his bike. The problem was resolved by tucking them inside the front of his long black coat and keeping his fingers crossed their thorns wouldn't draw blood from his chest.

Pedalling furiously, it took Roland about fifteen minutes to reach Bluebell Vicarage. His hair, carefully combed before leaving home, flew wildly in the slipstream. The roses had a few petals missing by the time he rode through the gate but not so much as the old woman would notice. He wondered if she was watching him from behind the lace curtains. Seeing no sign of her, he took his comb out of his inside pocket and drew it through his hair. This time he rang the doorbell only once.

Tallulah opened the door sporting bandages around her arms and legs. Her eyes lit up when she saw the red roses. 'Come in, Roland dear, lunch is almost ready.' She placed the roses on the hall table and led him down the hall into the living room where a table had been set for lunch. Two glasses, a bottle of gin and two bottles of tonic sat on the antique sideboard.

'It took me quite some time to make the fire and set the table. Would you like an aperitif?'

Roland sympathised about her injuries and added, 'Thank you, Mrs Millstone, I don't usually drink heavy stuff at lunch-time, but I could make an exception as long as it's not vodka.'

'Please call me Tallulah. Would a gin and tonic be alright?'

'Thank you. More tonic than gin please.'

Tallulah poured them both a drink while keeping the conversation going. Her eyes twinkled.

'It's wonderful to be interviewed and have some positive publicity for my cryonics project. Perhaps you can find me a canister partner to share costs with. I don't mind male or female. It would have to be someone who James can put on ice within a short time. Preferably someone with interesting conversation to offer. I wouldn't want to be stuck with a bore for ninety years.'

Lunch followed – chicken with roast potatoes and peas. Roland hoped he wasn't eating Fred or Ethel. He led the conversation onto tested ground – her garden and love of flowers. Talk about the garden led her to conversation about the pig and cattle farm next door and the terrible smells coming from it.

After the sweet – chocolate pudding with custard, Tallulah invited him to sit by the fireplace in one of the armchairs.

She offered him a glass of port, which he accepted as he was anxious to ingratiate himself with her. He began the interview.

'I'd like you to talk about the glorious past and your medals.'

'Of course. I'm taking my medals with me when I go, although I don't know where I'll pin them seeing as I'll be in the nude.' She laughed and blushed at the same time.

He waited for her to continue about her wartime experiences but she seemed bent on diverting the conversation to her ongoing cryonics project and her vicious hens. She pulled back one of her bandages to show him her injuries and talked about Mr Kim saving her life.

'He deserves a medal. How strange, I'd never before thought of North Koreans or communists as being human. They'd always struck me as being terrorists.'

Roland hid a smile and said, 'Can you tell me how you earned your wartime medals?'

'What I'm going to tell you is very confidential of course.'

He nodded but didn't like to tell her that in the world of journalism nothing is confidential. Anything told in confidence was a scoop.

'Well, I had two affairs in France – one with a traitor and another with James Willows in a hotel in Paris – would you believe he used to leave his toenail cuttings in the bidet?'

Roland said he wasn't surprised. 'Tell me how you earned your medals. I'm sure you didn't get them for counting toenail clippings.' It was an attempt at humour which fell flat.

'No, I led attacks against the Germans and killed a man in cold blood.'

'Who?'

'My lover.'

A shiver ran through Roland. The hairs on the back of his neck stood on end. He made an excuse to leave to get back to the office because of a deadline. It was time to beat a hasty retreat.

At the front door Tallulah put her hand on his arm and said, 'You're welcome to share my cryonics canister, should you be at death's door in the near future. I can have you put on ice if you have an almost fatal fall down the stairs but not for mushroom poisoning. I don't want any poison in my canister. Of course you would have to cut off your long hair and leave your awful gothic clothes at home. Your legs are a bit long for the canister and might have to be sawn off. I like you because the red roses show you have a romantic streak and you're good at conversation, which is important as we will be living together for ninety years. By the way, we have to get married first, as I'll be in the nude,' and here she blushed, 'and I don't approve of sex before marriage. I'm offering twenty thousand pounds in advance to the lucky person, so think about it.'

Roland escaped into the garden and mounted his bike, pedalling at top speed down the lane, not stopping until he reached the hotel. As soon as he was back in his room he called Scarlett at the office to tell her he had a terrible headache and possibly a high temperature and wouldn't be in until tomorrow morning. It was an excuse of course. After all the stress, he needed to chill out.

She sympathised and asked him how the interview went.

'I hope you won't be offended, but your aunt is completely nuts.'

'I did warn you.'

'I can't write something based on her love life, toenail cuttings or her murderous tendencies. I need a bit more to go on.'

'I apologise, Roland, I should have known better. Take some aspirin for your fever and get a good night's sleep. See you tomorrow.'

She'd brushed him off just like that. Two hours later he called her again and asked if they could spend the evening together.

'I'd love to Roland but you have a temperature and I don't want to risk catching something.'

His lie had backfired.

She said, 'By the way, I want you to get another of your letters into the pipeline for the July issue. Perhaps you could do one on heroism, given all my aunt's been through.

Love thy neighbour regardless

Before leaving for the office, and inspired by a dream during the night, in which he made his peace with Tallulah, Roland picked up his pen and started writing a letter from himself to Veronica.

From an admirer:

Dear Veronica,

I am requesting your opinion on love and heroism. There's an elderly lady in Witherington who won medals for bravery during the Second World War. She also shot a man, which she said was in self-defence and was her duty as a Christian to do so. I am therefore confused about the church's teachings on their "Love thy neighbour" policy. About heroism – this woman was recently attacked by her vicious hens and saved by a foreign communist who, had they been in the trenches during the war, would have been shooting at each other. He bravely dragged the old lady out without thought for his own safety.

Which of the two do you think would make the best neighbour or the worst enemy?

Thank you.

A bit confused.

Roland proceeded to reply to himself.

Dear Confused,

Our magazine promotes peace and harmony. Being a pacifist, I don't subscribe to people getting medals for belligerent acts of war.

I realise mine is a controversial statement which could stir up a war of words from those who did their patriotic duty for King and country (hence the disclaimer below to avoid legal action from millions of people). The foreign communist is indeed a hero. During the First World War, British and German soldiers left the trenches on Christmas Day after a cease fire, and drank together and wished each other a merry Christmas. Then on Boxing Day, they went back to killing each other. This shows the mad side of the human race. With reference to the communist who saved the elderly lady in the henhouse, I would say he definitely deserves a medal and would make a good neighbour (if you happen to have vicious hens). I quote from the scriptures – 'There is no greater love than for a man to lay down his life for his friend' (I assume this also refers to women but at the time the scriptures were written it was a man's world with no space for women's liberation – which took almost two thousand years to get off the ground).*

Regards,
Veronica

**Disclaimer: This is the author's personal opinion and in no way reflects the opinion of the magazine. A note to my readers: any insulting letters will go straight into the bin.*

Roland hoped it made sense and that he hadn't mixed up too many issues. But he enjoyed stirring up discussions and annoying people from time to time. It boosted his self-esteem. In any case, Scarlett liked the letter and told him to rush it to the printers for the July issue.

Dead cold hands

Florist Marigold Birch closed the annex door of the Goodbody Funeral Home after the last of the mourners had left, anxious to get out and go home. The last thing she wanted was to be stuck in the viewing room with Norman Goodbody dead in a coffin. It had been a mistake to agree to receive grieving relatives to view Norman. She'd accepted only because there was no one else who wanted to do it and she never liked to say no and upset people. It seemed to be too much of a coincidence about Norman and his wife Bertha both meeting their deaths tripping against a coffin. There were evil spirits around, she was sure. Closing the door on Norman lying waxen on padded white satin, she hurriedly left.

Constable Barnstable watched Marigold leave. He slid into the viewing room, curious to see what kind of a job the undertakers had done on Norman. As he bent over the coffin a voice from behind him said, 'Come to visit me have you, Ernest?' He turned and saw Norman sitting in a dark wood, red brocade upholstered chair.

Ernest said, 'I've come to pay my respects and apologise for causing your death. It's part of my penitence.'

Norman gave a hollow laugh. 'Well, well, well. What a turn up for the books. A copper who killed a man after breaking and entering and taking women's clothes. I wonder how many years you'd have served if you'd been alive.'

'Look, Norman, I didn't mean it to happen, but you did trip of your own accord.'

'Yeah, after you scared me.'

'I thoroughly apologise. I went to church to confess.'

'Never mind, you did me a favour. Now I'm dead, I can see Bertha again. I do miss her you know. She was a good wife and ran the funeral parlour perfectly.'

'She said you beat her and put her down and dressed her in her tartan dressing gown for her funeral and stamped on her bunions.'

'Only sometimes. She kept calling me an idiot. I do have my pride you know. I dressed her in tartan because she said her dressing gown reminded her of our lovely holiday in Ireland. She said she loved it.'

'Well, she may have wished to be buried in something a little more apt.'

'You mean, in her emerald green working dress? Everyone in town had seen it at every funeral over the past year. You know what women are like. They don't want to be seen in the same dress twice.'

Ernest came straight to the point. 'Bertha doesn't want you in the family tomb.'

'What? You have to be joking. I've nowhere else to go.'

'You could go to Purgatory for posing as headless-Hannah's husband at the seance.'

'It wasn't me.'

'I saw you with Bertha's life insurance policy.'

'Well what did you expect me to do with it – burn it?'

'People might think you killed Bertha for the insurance money.'

'People have nothing better to do than poke their noses into things which don't concern them. They deserve to have their mouths washed out with battery acid.'

Ernest reined him in by telling him to focus on the present and what he was saying would be taken down and used in evidence against him. 'If you don't make it up with Bertha you'll never see her again as she doesn't want to see you.'

'Please don't separate us,' Norman pleaded.

'I thought you hated each other?'

'She was different when she was young. We were like two lovebirds.'

'Then what happened?'

'We got married. She was sweet and nice at the beginning but then with age she turned into her mother.'

'What was her mother like?'

'Interfering, mean, bad-tempered.' Norman chanted a list of his mother-in-law's bad points, which he seemed to have learnt by heart.

'Is it possible you were looking for excuses for your own bad behaviour and blamed your mother-in-law?' Ernest wanted to know.

'She deserved it. The old hag didn't want us to marry in the first place. She didn't want her daughter living with corpses in the house.'

'I think it's a fair comment from a mother who cares about her daughter.'

'She didn't want me touching her daughter with hands that were touching corpses from morning till night.'

'I see. Did you ever strike Bertha?'

'I'd just started the funeral business. I was going through a bad period financially—'

'Violence is never justified.'

'Bertha said her mother had been right about me all along. She said she'd had enough and stopped letting me touch her.'

Norman's voice broke off. 'I'll make it up to her I promise. I'll never hit her again. Just don't take her away from me. I missed her after she went. I missed her cooking and the clean ironed sheets. I missed her not being in my bed.'

'It sounds as if you were downright lazy and egocentric and never helped her with the housework. I may put you down for the Terrace of Sloth – treadmills over snapping turtles – but I'll see what I can do,' Ernest said, squeezing Norman's shoulder.

'Tell her I'm sorry and want to make it up to her,' replied Norman, rising from the chair and trundling back to his coffin.

Abandoned

It was the third time in three days Ernest had been harassed by Cecilia about her missing foot.

She said stonily, 'If I were a police officer I'd be asking specific questions.'

'I like to build up confidence first,' he replied.

'In my book it's called procrastination.'

He suppressed the urge to grab her by the throat. 'I would really appreciate it if you would leave the detective work to me. I have my methods.' She was pushing him over the top. In all his years in Witherington no one had ever called him a procrastinator and he was not used to bad manners. 'I object to your insinuations. If you continue, I'll have to arrest you for defamation.'

Fred intervened and told Ernest he was being unreasonable, while Cecilia scuttled off, saying she was going to take a holiday. There was mutiny in the air. Ernest longed to be in his warm bed at home, where he could pull the covers over his head to escape from the world. In the end he decided to pay his mother a visit.

He found her sitting on the settee watching television with Lovey on her shoulder. She smiled momentarily at something someone was saying on the television. He was sorry there were so many things he'd left unsaid when he was still alive. Things he'd put off because he felt there was plenty of time left. But there hadn't been. He'd regretted not having asked her more about his dad. At the time, life seemed eternal and there was always the next day. But they never seemed to get around to it. He had a vague recollection of what had happened. They'd been on holiday. His dad had been sucked down into quicksands on the beach. His mother had been helpless to save him. She told him later he'd inherited his dad's good looks and strength. She'd given him a faded photograph which seemed to confirm all of this. He wanted to know more but it was too late and he couldn't return to the past. And now, he wondered if he'd eventually meet his dad in Heaven and if he was still a young man of twenty-four. A burning question was – how would his dad feel about meeting his son, a middle-aged man? No doubt, if they ever met, they would find many things in common and it wouldn't bother him at all talking to a young man who had once been his father.

Upon returning to the graveyard Ernest looked for Fred, Cecilia and Bertha. But all he found was a letter on his tomb from Cecilia which read, '*You're making our lives a misery. We've had enough and have gone to the Eternal City (but not the one in the sky) to find out if I can take my washing machine to Heaven*'.

Ernest put his head in his hands. It wasn't just the fact that they'd left him in the lurch that bothered him. He was worried what the Holy Father in Rome would say about a foot-less ballerina visiting his bedroom in her ballet dress and, contravening Vatican dress code, would have no cardigan around her shoulders.

Raspberries with waffles

As Anton had promised, Anushka found a ticket for Rome waiting for her at London airport on the seventh of June. Serge had to buy his own.

After the hassle of check-in, security checks, passport control and an exhausting wait for embarkation, Anushka and Serge sat back to enjoy the two and a half hour flight.

At Rome airport, they sailed through customs and followed the instructions Anton had left in the envelope with her passport. At the exit to the terminal Anushka held a copy of *The Guardian* in front of her and looked around for a man carrying a copy of the *Bright Red Star*. In less than five minutes, a tall, dark, handsome man about thirty-three years old, approached and took their hand luggage. 'Please follow me. My name is Anton,' he announced with a trace of a Balkans accent, which Anushka recognised from the phone call.

From Fiumicino airport the autostrada whizzed by as the black BMW glided quietly towards the city. Upon reaching the outskirts and the wide lanes of the Cristoforo Colombo, the car sped past Mussolini-era buildings and old apartment blocks with balconies of flowering geraniums. June was a perfect month to go to the beach, perhaps to Ostia or Fregene, but there was no time.

Anushka said, 'In Russia all is grey,' adding that the next time she would like to go to the beach or perhaps to Lake Gandolfo in the Castelli hills to see the Pope's summer residence.

Anton turned into Via Grotta Perfetta and continued left at the traffic lights. After five minutes' drive, dodging traffic, he pulled up outside an elegant Roman building. 'Welcome to the United Fruit Organisation,' he said getting out of the car and opening the door on Anushka's side. 'The Raspberry Conference is in the conference hall. You can collect your security passes from the reception. Mr Smirnov's office is on the seventh floor overlooking the park.'

At the entrance to the conference room, a brass stand announced UFO Conference on Raspberries for Development – fluctuating temperatures in raspberry growing countries.

Young ladies in uniform handed out member-state flags. Microphones were tapped, switched on and blown into. The audience buzzed in anticipation. They found two seats near the back next to the aisle. Anushka commented on the colourful flags of member states flanking a raised dais on the stage. 'I would like to take a raspberry revolution to Russia. My mother has never eaten a raspberry. But have you noticed, there are no raspberries in flower?'

Serge nodded. He noticed there were raspberry plants everywhere but no raspberries. On the other hand there were television cameras from the BBC, CNN and some European networks.

Shortly afterwards a tall well-built man, around fifty-five years old with a white hair and wearing rimless glasses, walked onto the dais to thunderous clapping.

Anushka nudged Serge. 'He is Smirnov. I recognise him from the Russian Embassy party.'

The ovation died down. Smirnov launched into a diplomatic preamble of thanking delegates for their support in helping him steer a convoy of salvation through the waterless deserts of deprivation, hunger, poverty and under-development, without mentioning that many years down the line they were still no further forward in combating a multitude of disasters which could not be blamed on God. 'Today is International Raspberry Day,' he said to cheering staff, visitors and diplomats. Smirnov waffled on about the great challenges the organisation had faced and the years of sacrifice and dedication of staff who had given their all to develop under-developed countries, which, without his outstanding leadership would be still in darkness.

Serge whispered, 'They're spending a fortune and everyone knows raspberries will never grow in hot climates. Did you know our taxes pay for their bloody first-class travel? No one's interested in the moral bits. They're just interested in the money. It's shocking.'

Anushka whispered back, 'Since when did you care about the moral bits?'

Smirnov continued. 'I'm here today to tell you how I'm going to save the world from disaster. After ten years of research and pilot projects to test the usefulness, I have the answer here in this very box.' He pointed to a large metal chest sitting on the floor by his side. The air was electric. A man stepped in front of the audience with a board which read, 'Everybody clap'.

Serge got up from his seat. 'I know what's in there. Let's get out of here I've heard enough.'

'Can't we just wait until he opens the coffin?'

'That's no coffin. It's a load of fermented cow and chicken shit. I did an article on biogas last year. When he opens it there'll be a stampede to get out.'

Anushka decided not to argue and followed Serge. Making for the cafeteria, they heard a collective gasp and groan, followed by the sound of a herd of buffaloes making for the exit.

Bay of pigs

After having had a cappuccino and brioche in the lounge, Anushka and Serge took the lift to the seventh floor and searched the corridors until they came to a sign on a door *M. Smirnov, Raspberry expert and agro-meteorologist.*

At Anushka's knock, a voice shouted, 'Come in.'

A sumptuous pale green wall to wall carpet gave the office an air of tranquility. It was a colour Anushka associated with lunatic asylums to keep patients calm. The polished cherry-wood desk was bereft of clutter and there was nothing in his 'In' box.

Smirnov stood up as they entered, recognising Anushka. He looked pleased to see her. Anushka introduced Serge as a biogas expert who'd come to listen to the conference and the new approach to saving the planet. Smirnov reached over and pressed the telephone buzzer.

'Irina, could you please come in and escort Mr Gallo to the coffee bar as I need to talk to Ms Petrova about a confidential matter.'

Serge was about to say he was used to confidential matters and that he'd once, some time ago, signed the Official Secrets Act, until he saw Irina's black and white dress, high heels, bare arms and cleavage. She approached Serge, held out her hand and said simply, 'Irina.' He could see she was summing him up the way her eyes flitted from his eyes down to his crotch. At that moment he knew they'd give the coffee bar a miss and head for the park to have a tête-à-tête about succulent raspberries.

After explaining the workings of the organisation, Smirnov told Anushka there was a position in Human Resources as a clerk. The chosen candidate would handle international travel to raspberry projects.

'I have never before eaten raspberries.'

'In my office it's not important you are not a raspberry expert. You learn as you go along. Most of my experts have never eaten a raspberry either.'

'So what use is studying many years in specialisation?'

'None whatsoever.'

Anushka thought it a strange way to run an organisation but maybe it was the capitalist way.

'What is your experience?'

'I have been trained in hand-to-hand combat and surveillance.'

'Then I'm sure we can find a suitable job. Boris said I should take good care of you.'

Anushka shuddered. 'I could go abroad.'

She asked him if there was a job available in a warm country somewhere in Latin America.

'There's one in Cuba. We've set up a Raspberry Project near the Bay of Pigs, Bahia de Cochinos, on the Zapata Peninsula and are expanding it. The area is of interest to tourists, as in 1961 there was a failed military invasion sponsored by the CIA, during which armed Cuban exiles who wanted to overthrow the Fidel Castro regime, were abandoned at the last minute because of international pressure. Airborne support was pulled out and the Cuban exiles were sacrificed – either eaten by alligators in the swamp, shot by the local revolutionary militia or thrown into prison. The tourists like a bit of gore and we tolerate them because they buy raspberries. Getting back to our project – the swamp water is in abundance for irrigation. There are still a few alligators but every job has its risks and that's what they get paid for. Now and then an accident is reported. Only last week one of our consultants fell into the swamp. Such a pity. He was just about to spill the beans on one of our contractors.'

Anushka's hand flew to her cheek and she said, 'That's terrible.'

'We had to pay a lot of compensation to his widow.'

A few details of her job were discussed. Smirnov said she would be based in Havana and travel weekly to the project to look after staff and raspberry plants. She would also be responsible for repatriating bodies in the unlikely event of another accident.

She said, 'What about manure for the project? Perhaps Serge could set up a biogas plant in Witherington and export it to Cuba?'

Smirnov said drily, 'We have very high-level connections in Sicily for that.' She supposed he meant the mafia.

Anushka asked him when she should start her new job.

He replied, 'It's now June. I will let you know by the end of July if you have got the job. You must be patient, it takes a while to get the staff moving,' he said with a smile.

Anushka left Smirnov's office thinking she'd just landed the job of her dreams, apart from the alligators. But had she? Smirnov hadn't mentioned contract details.

After Anushka had gone, Smirnov summoned Anton to his office to tell him to prepare what they had discussed, in great secrecy, with their contact Archbishop Marius Conak in the Vatican City.

'She'll need a one-way ticket London/Rome/Madrid/Havana,' he said, asking Anton to sort out the administrative and logistical details of a political assassination.

Prisoner of the Vatican City

Pope Joseph's legs felt heavy and his ankle bones had disappeared into the swollen flesh. Just a little fluid retention, he thought, thanking the Lord he was reasonably healthy for his seventy-seven years, if he didn't count stomach pains from time to time.

He waited until evening before asking to be escorted to the Vatican gardens. Two Swiss Guards walked behind him at a respectable distance between bushes and flower beds, just in case he should fall or need to go back to the papal apartment in a hurry. He liked them being near him as he knew their dedication and loyalty would keep him safe.

It had been a trying couple of months. A short time ago his predecessor had died unexpectedly at the conclave. Following the duration of time for the funeral rites and lying in state, a second conclave had been held in the Sistine Chapel to elect a new pope. After many hours, when the votes had been counted, Cardinal Nkosi, an African, was elected. It should have been a joyous day, but Cardinal Nkosi who would have been the first black pope in recent history, dropped dead unexpectedly before the official proclamation. In a flurry of activity, the Vatican undertakers had been called and everyone sworn to secrecy. Subsequently, the body of Nkosi was spirited away to the necropolis and the cardinals had held another conclave. They were locked inside the Sistine Chapel for thirteen hours with very little food, to encourage them to get a move on. Some were as surprised as he was when he was proclaimed pope, given his humble background. Then their votes had been fed into the stove until white smoke rose from the chimney in Saint Peter's Square to cheering and much later, the announcement they had been waiting for – *Habemus Papam* – We have a Pope. The name he'd chosen for himself was Pope Joseph I. It was a name close to his heart – the Lord's father had been called Joseph, as had his own.

When the pomp and ceremony had died down, a serious problem raised its ugly head. A tragic situation had arisen whereby Cardinal Nkosi was not eligible to be buried in the Vatican Grottoes, having died before officially being proclaimed pope. Since being elected, Joseph had been trying to sort out Cardinal Nkosi's resting place but his progressive ideas hadn't gone down well with the Vatican hierarchy who made sure they dragged their feet. But he was determined to continue to fight for the right of a genuinely elected pope to be laid in a fitting place.

Perhaps a walk around the Vatican gardens might clear his mind of things not directly his calling – rules, regulations, administration, protocol, finance and other distractions his attention was drawn to. He pondered upon the long working week and religious tours which might eventually take their toll on his health. A slight surge of shame washed over him for being ego-centric when millions in the world were suffering or starving. And what were his problems in comparison to what Christ had suffered?

Nonetheless, he allowed himself a few inner thoughts which he would share with his confessor, a life-long friend – a holy man in a holy city. And the shame he would feel would be his punishment. There were many things he wanted to confess – his anger towards the constraints on his movements and not being able to walk freely among his flock; frustration at being confined to the Vatican City until security permission was given; a longing to walk alone in Saint Peter's Square as he'd done in Saint Mark's in Venice; wanting to throw off the shackles of a prisoner in the very place which was supposed to be a haven and heaven on earth but which hid political treachery. Only recently he'd asked his trusty driver to sneak him out of the Vatican City at night to take a drive to the park of Villa Borghese to look towards Heaven and talk to God and feel the holy presence around him. They'd both laughed like young boys playing truant. It was done in secrecy – an hour of peace, away from his suffocating prison to reflect on the needs of the poor, the sick and all of God's children. He wondered if it could be considered a sin.

His memory went back to the time he was innocent and pure of heart. Marco, the tenth child of a farming family in the north of Italy where his childhood had passed too quickly. His mother was glad when he'd entered the priesthood, although she'd had reservations of how long it would last, given his streak of rebellion and the inability to mind his own business. Not being able to keep his mouth shut when seeing injustice being dished out, he'd confronted bullies and defended the oppressed. The many times he'd gone home bruised, she'd marched him to church to confess his sins. It had turned out to be a blessing. The more he went into the church the more he liked it as each time he looked at the statue of Christ on the cross or the Virgin Mary, joy and elation had filled his body in a mysterious way and led him towards the Holy Spirit.

After he'd been ordained and as the years went by, he'd followed politics as an interested bystander and intervened when the struggles of his flock were a noble cause. His streak of rebellion came to the forefront when he'd upset the bishop by questioning the scriptures and the role of Pontius Pilate in Christ's death, by asking if Pilate had really washed his hands of Jesus or if he'd been instrumental in manipulating Christ's enemies, seeing as Philo the Greek in the first century had defined Pilate as being 'vindictive with a furious temper, corrupt and insolent' who had had his soldiers randomly attack, beat and kill Jews in an attempt to silence them. Another question was – could the whole of the Jewish race be blamed for the death of Christ, given the terrible evil the Roman Empire had unleashed upon them?

The bishop had looked at him stonily and had told him the scriptures shouldn't be questioned. The conversation ended with an admonition to read them more carefully. But in the years that followed, he couldn't be gagged. He publicly denounced the seven deadly sins; exploitation of the workers; corruption; the mafia; human trafficking; and human rights abuses. For his pains he'd been scorned, maligned and threatened by evil forces. The devil had captured the hearts and minds of the weak, weary, the undeserving privileged and had led the wayward down the dark path. His forward-thinking views inside the Vatican City had been trampled underfoot by the devil's disciples.

The walk around the Vatican gardens did little to clear Pope Joseph's mind of the many tasks ahead. But it was his destiny. It was God's wish he be the chosen one. Would God consider him weak if he added a little prayer asking for strength and patience to tackle his new job? And to reflect on why the Vatican and Holy See hadn't been quick enough to intervene on thorny matters and often turned a blind eye to racism and abuse. He remembered the Holocaust, Apartheid, and the many reports of genocide from around the world. All these things he wanted to address at the cost of treading on a few toes.

Returning to the papal apartment, he called for his confessor. It was not an easy meeting. He felt ashamed. He needed to confess his sins like every other mortal. He told him his earlier thoughts. He confessed to his yearning for freedom so he could meet his flock without constraints. His confessor replied that as long as he concentrated on the job and got results, he could be allowed a few small personal satisfactions to cope with stress, just as long as he prayed a bit more and asked God's forgiveness.

Pope Joseph slept well, having confessed his sins. It seemed unlikely he would be able to take an August Holiday this year at the papal residence in Castel Gandolfo with all that was going on. It was one place he could clear his mind of unimportant matters and focus on his flock or dodge security to sneak out some nights with his trusty driver to the hills of Castelli Romani or to paddle his swollen feet in the lake.

Hotel Hallelujah

In a modest hotel, not far from Porta Portese flea market in Rome, Fred, Cecilia and Bertha sat on a double bed listening to the splashing coming from the bathroom. Folding her arms over her bosom, Bertha said, 'What an untidy bedroom.' The splashing ceased and the silence was broken by Anushka moaning.

Fred said, 'She sounds like she's being murdered. Maybe we should go and investigate.'

Bertha put her hands over Fred's ears. 'You're too young to listen,' she replied, making a disparaging comment about what the world was coming to.

They watched Anushka, naked and dripping wet, enter the bedroom and throw herself on the bed. Serge followed, jumping on top of her, excited by her wet body and quoting the wettest, most horrible bits of Samuel Taylor Coleridge's long epic poem of the Ancient Mariner.

Water, water everywhere,
And all the boards did shrink,
Water, water everywhere,
Nor any drop to drink.
And every tongue, through utter drought,
Was withered at the root:
We could not speak, no more than if
We had been choked with soot.

Anushka complained she was going off it as it was bringing out his sadistic side.

'I don't like so much water or the withered tongue,' she said snappishly.

'I thought you might like a little rough tongue tickling,' he replied, telling her she was never satisfied. He jumped off the bed and made for the bathroom, bringing back a glass of water and pouring it over her face.

I looked upon the rotting sea,
And drew my eyes away:
I looked upon the rotting deck,
And there the dead men lay.

Anushka screamed as Serge rocked her from side to side in an imaginary flooded boat in a stormy sea. Bertha grabbed Fred by the neck and yanked him out of the room saying he was too young to be witness to such psychopathic behaviour. She took him into the corridor while Cecilia followed, screaming, 'I don't have time for all this, I have to talk to the Pope about my washing machine.'

Bertha told her to shut up. 'You won't have time and in any case we're leaving in the morning.' She left Cecilia sulking in the corridor and returned to the bedroom to find Anushka tied to the bedhead with Serge's socks and a terrified look on her face.

Anushka watched the hostess in her neat dark blue uniform walk up and down the aisle of the Alitalia flight from Rome to London, thinking of the day she'd be walking down a church aisle with a handsome husband. After yesterday's sadistic psychological torture, she wasn't sure she wanted to marry Serge. On the other hand, it would be difficult to find a man to marry in such a short time. She needed a stiff drink.

Turning to Serge she said, 'Shall we order vodka? I always have vodka when I am on a plane.'

'Always? You've only been on a plane a couple of times in your whole life.'

After a few drinks, Anushka forgot yesterday's fright and pain. She became maudlin and started talking about weddings and babies. Serge decided to humour her to avoid attracting attention if she became belligerent. He agreed to marry her.

'I want a big white wedding in Rome,' she slurred, 'and I want to be a virgin on wedding night.'

'You haven't been a virgin for years but I promise you a virgin fantasy if you keep it a secret until your birthday in August when we can announce it with a party.'

'I like secrets and party,' she said, kissing him.

Serge had two months to get out of a wedding.

Destined for Purgatory

Upon the investigation team's return from Rome and following a few days of silence, Ernest apologised to Cecilia and Fred for making their lives a misery but chastised them for leaving him without a proper explanation. He mentioned a challenge he needed help with – how to reunite the bickering couple Bertha and Norman, as his police training hadn't prepared him for peace-making.

It was with trepidation Ernest knocked on Bertha's family tomb later in the day. She materialised wearing her new outfit and thanked him again for retrieving it. He was happy to note she was in a good mood as she led him inside.

'Nice place,' he said looking at four coffins side by side.

'One is mine, two belong to my parents who've already moved on and the last one is for Norman, although I don't want him here,' said Bertha.

'Talking about Norman. He's hanging around looking for somewhere to sleep. He's sorry and wants to make amends.'

Bertha swirled around Ernest. Dragged him into an emerald green whirlwind. Spun his helmet upwards into the vortex. Whirled him to the outside and dropped him on the grass. For a few minutes he lay on his back struggling to get up. Where was his helmet? Staggering back to his tomb he sat down and fished in his inside pocket for his notepad. He prised open a page and added an annotation in the margin about Bertha and the Terrace of Wrath.

Then he heard the voice he'd heard in the church, whispering in his ear, *You have committed the sin of revenge. You'd better put it right.*

Ernest sighed and reluctantly crossed out the Bertha's name. He then wrote another note to himself – *Visit Bertha again.*

Bertha picked up Ernest's helmet from the grass, turning it around in her hands. Should she keep it or give it back? What would happen if he arrived at the Pearly Gates without it? Would he be in trouble? She decided it would be wrong to keep it.

The next morning she found Ernest wiling away time picking daisies for Cecilia. 'I've brought your helmet back,' she said handing it to him.

'Thank you, Bertha.' He took it from her trembling hands, wondering if she was symbolically handing him an olive branch.

She said, laughing as if in jest, 'It's a good thing we're dead and don't have to keep changing our clothes, otherwise I'd have to ask you to fetch the rest of my wardrobe.'

He took it as her way of thanking him. 'Yes, it's a blessing, but just in the line of duty,' he replied.

She asked him, 'Was it in the line of duty to talk to Norman?'

'I was trying to help you both.'

'Well, supposing people don't want to be helped. Shouldn't the request for help come from the other person?'

'Sometimes people are too proud to ask,' said Ernest.

'Then you should leave well alone unless it's a matter of life or death. I see no point in you playing the Good Samaritan.'

'I didn't expect to find Norman so upset about your death,' Ernest said.

'Norman? Upset?' she looked genuinely surprised.

'He said he's truly sorry about the way he treated you at the end. He said you were happy at the beginning and you loved the tartan dressing gown he bought for you in Ireland.'

'Well maybe I did. But maybe I didn't want to be laid out for viewing in it so the whole of Witherington could come and gloat.'

'Does it really matter what people think? You're dead. People have a knack of quickly moving on to more interesting gossip,' Ernest said.

'Mrs Sarehole-Reape had a good memory. She never stopped talking about me.'

'She's dead now.'

'I'll probably find her behind me at the Pearly Gates.'

'She has to pass through all the terraces several times,' replied Ernest, quick to pacify Bertha.

'How did it happen? With Norman I mean?'

'He tripped on the edge of the rug. Let bygones be bygones and forgive him for the past.'

'I don't know—'

'Look, Bertha, you can't hold a grudge forever. The hate will eat you up inside. You'll get worry lines, bags under your eyes and a tight ugly mouth.'

'Will I lose weight?'

'Probably, but you might look like an old hag or dried prune in the process.'

She said she didn't have much option than to meet with Norman. 'I'll listen to what he has to say but I won't promise I'll let him into my tomb.'

'I suggest you forget your grievances and be friends, unless you want to end up like Janice Sarehole-Reape – bitter, twisted, sour and lonely.'

After Bertha had left, Ernest retreated into his tomb and fell into an exhausted sleep.

Not having had seen Ernest for some time, Fred and Cecilia began to worry. 'Something must have happened to him,' she said gravely.

He's either dead or he's been kidnapped,' Fred replied.

'He's already dead and can't die twice, you dumb cluck. Sorry, Fred, I didn't mean to be offensive, I meant "you silly bird".'

'I'm not a bird, I'm fowl.' He paced up and down muttering to himself.

Cecilia told him to shut up. 'For heaven's sake, you silly bird, you're making me nervous.'

Fred glared at her. She'd called him a bird for the second time. The blood from his lower parts rose to his neck. Raising his crest, he squawked a shrill battle cry and flew at her. She lost her balance, wheeled over onto her stump and toppled onto the grass. Afraid she'd hit him, Fred retreated to the overhanging branch screeching for reinforcements while Cecilia screamed insults.

A further battle was derailed when Ernest materialised from his tomb rubbing the sleep from his eyes. 'What's all the noise about? I'm trying to sleep!'

Fred flew down from the tree. 'We thought you'd been kidnapped.'

'No we didn't,' interrupted Cecilia. 'I knew all along you were sleeping.'

Fred was raised on his claws and about to fly at Cecilia when Ernest stepped in. 'Stop bickering. I have enough on my plate with Bertha and Norman without having another war on my hands.'

'We didn't expect you to sleep for so long,' Cecilia complained.

In no mood to listen to recriminations about his behaviour, Ernest replied, 'Either you both kiss and make up or you'll be in for more punishment.' The tone of his voice left no doubt he was in charge.

Cecilia said she'd rather kiss a sheep's backside than kiss Fred, while Fred said he'd rather kiss a worm.

'Then shake hands,' said Ernest, starting to lose his patience.

Cecilia reluctantly held out her hand while Fred lifted his leg and offered her his right foot.

Cecilia screamed, 'Your wing, you filthy bird, your wing.' Fred relinquished all thoughts of being defiant when Ernest grabbed him by the neck and dumped him angrily in front of Cecilia.

'Fred, shake the lady's hand or I'll cuff your ear. And if I hear one more squawk from either of you, there'll be hell to pay.'

There was a moment of shocked silence before Cecilia said, 'Ernest, this is the second time you've lost your cool. You need to learn to control your anger. I suggest you go to church and confess your sins.' Cecilia added that if he didn't, he'd likely lose his job as forthcoming Gatekeeper of Purgatory. And the way she said it sounded like a threat.

Poison pen

Ernest tried to sleep on, but it was not to be. Cecilia arrived and accused him of being too taken up with Bertha and Norman to give attention to her missing foot. To keep her quiet he asked her if she was the one who sent poison pen letters to three local tradesmen which read, 'Keep that dirty bitch of a wife of yours away from the dances. She's going with the men'. But all she said was, 'Focus on who wanted me dead. It's hardly likely someone committed murder just because of a nasty letter.' In other words, she didn't want to answer.

'So, there were many who wanted you dead?' Ernest asked.

'Tallulah Millstone. She wanted me out of the way so she could marry James. Or perhaps Clara the cleaner who might also have wanted to marry James.'

'Was he having an affair with the cleaner?'

'Probably,' Cecilia replied, smoothing the front of her ballet dress.

'Can you be a bit more specific?'

'He was always hovering around the bedroom when Clara was making the bed. I used to walk past the bedroom door now and then just to check. I saw them many times.'

'How many times?'

'Twice.'

'So you walked past the door and saw them in the same room together. But did you see them making love on the bed?'

'She was fluffing up the pillows and he was standing behind looking at her legs.'

'It doesn't mean they were having an affair.'

'My guess is they wanted to kill me because they were having an affair.'

Ernest now had two scenarios: James and Clara had pushed Cecilia from the window because she'd accused them of having an affair or James and Clara were having an affair and Cecilia committed suicide out of jealousy.

'Is there anyone else who might have been in love with James?'

'I'll have to think about it.'

He asked Cecilia one more question. 'Is it possible you committed suicide because you believed James was having an affair with Clara?'

Cecilia swirled and screeched, refusing to answer further questions. Ernest was tempted to grab her by the throat but restrained himself. There had been many times during his lifetime when he'd been tempted to bash, pulverise and lynch, but he'd always exercised self-control becoming of a police officer and had never laid a finger on a woman. It was time to interrogate James.

Ernest sat on James's bed until he'd fallen into the dark pit of nightmares. Speaking to James through his sleep paralysis, he prompted his memory, 'Tell me about Clara, the cleaning woman. What was she like?'

James, breathing shallowly, said, 'She was beautiful… a great pair of knockers… and shapely calves that disappeared up into her skirt, a dark secret place where—'

Ernest interrupted. 'Can you please be brief, we don't have all night.'

'These things can't be rushed.'

'Cecilia seems to think you were having an affair with Clara.'

'Chance would be a fine thing.'

'So you fancied her?'

He nodded. 'But I never touched her. I came very close to it the day she was bending over the bed to change the pillowcases when her billowing skirt raised a few inches to show—'

'That's enough thank you.' Ernest cut him short as he'd no way of verifying James's story. He was tired. He missed working at the police station. At least he got paid for it and all his suspects were alive. He decided to press on.

'Cecilia, your wife, said you had an affair with Tallulah during the war just before you and she were due to marry.'

'So what?'

'Do you think Tallulah had a reason to push your wife from the window?'

'No.'

'Could Tallulah have murdered Cecilia because she received a poison pen letter?'

'What poison pen letter? I know nothing about it.'

'I would have thought, being married to her—'

'Cecilia had many secrets and she kept them from me.'

'I see.'

In fact, Ernest didn't see at all. The investigation had too many twists and turns and the plot was becoming contorted. He closed the door on James's fantasies. Piled on top of the confusion was the exasperation he felt at having to receive Bertha who had information about the dark side of James's character.

Bertha told Ernest that she and James had had a short love affair in their teens. She'd been a virgin at the time. On more than one occasion he'd put his hands around her throat.

'So James was a violent person?'

'Yes, he tried to strangle me.'

'Did he have good reason?'

'Absolutely not. I was a sweet girl.'

Ernest rolled his eyes, secretly doubting James could put his hands all the way round Bertha's neck given the circumference of it. He asked her if she knew any other reason for which James might be violent towards Cecilia.

'She was having an affair with the night watchman.'

'Did anyone else know?'

'Yes, the whole of Witherington.'

'I never heard a word. Did James know?'

'Probably.'

'I don't remember hearing any gossip when I was working in the police station.'

Bertha told him a further succulent piece of gossip – the plumber's assistant had walked into room sixty-nine to find Cecilia and the night watchman in a sixty-nine position, following which, her lover had grabbed a piece of drainpipe from the man and threatened him with it.

Ernest asked, 'What was the plumber's assistant doing with a piece of drainpipe in a hotel room?'

'He was going to fix a drain.'

'But aren't drainpipe's fixed outside?'

'The man told me he was violently assaulted with a drainpipe.'

'How come it wasn't reported?'

'The usual reason – no one wanted a scandal. All I know is what he told me, plus that the two of them then rolled around the garden in the mud completely naked.'

Ernest asked her why they would do such a thing in the middle of winter when the temperature was at freezing point. Bertha then changed her tune and said the plumber's assistant had probably invented it. She said he liked to talk dirty and was a shit stirrer and had probably been watching them through the window.

Ernest changed the subject, taking account of her reputation for embellishing half-truths. 'Tell me more about James.'

'He wanted to kill Cecilia.'

'Did this come from your mouth or Cecilia's?'

'Hers of course, she's my friend.'

'Did she put you up to it? Or have you invented it because you hated James?'

Bertha breathed her foul, drain-smelling breath on him and left, shouting he'd been happy enough when she'd been useful to him collecting information.

Moral blackmail

Stanley called Tallulah and asked her sarcastically if she wanted to come over for some re-education, seeing as Mr Kim had contaminated her with the Stockholm Syndrome. In his opinion, Mr Kim had brainwashed her into feeling sympathy for him in order to lure her towards his communist beliefs.

She replied sarcastically, 'You're losing it, Stanley. Check your dictionary. The Stockholm Syndrome is all about survival in a hostile environment. It applies to desperate captives who fraternise with their violent captors. I was not captured by Mr Kim and held in isolation. We were in my kitchen looking at recipes.' She called Stanley a beast for not enquiring about her terrible incapacitating wounds and told him to get himself a life.

'You never did have a sense of humour, Tally.'

'What do you want?'

'Anushka Petrova has been for a job interview with a Russian spy at the United Fruit Organisation in Rome and I suspect she'll make an attempt on the life of the Pope because he's interfering in international affairs.'

'You mean because he won't let the Vatican bank launder any more dirty money?'

'Precisely. You have to get rid of her. Get your gun out of wraps.'

'Can we talk about this some other time? It seems a bit pie in the sky. And in any case, I'm more interested in defending children from perverts. I've a meeting with the Mothers'

Union. A man exposed himself to me in the graveyard.'

'The organisation is a front for political assassinations.'

'You couldn't give a damn about me could you?'

'I'm tired out.'

'Then I suggest you take a holiday in Rome. The Italian economy is dreadful and your pound will go further.'

'Are you kidding? They have workers' strikes every five minutes and I don't want to get caught up with the red banner waving. I'll be surrounded by communists. If they find out I used to work for Her Majesty's secret service they might bump me off.'

'Stop being pompous, Stanley. You couldn't possibly be a danger to their cause. Why don't you call the security office at the Vatican City and tell them an unemployed spy from Witherington wants to kill the Pope, but get your facts right first, because if you don't you could be arrested for disseminating false information.'

Tallulah could just imagine him calling the Vatican.

'Good morning. My name is Stanley. I can't tell you my real name as I'm bound by the Official Secrets Act and by the way someone's going to bump off His Holiness.'

The person on the other end of the phone would reply:

'Please hold on while I transfer you to the Military Police, the Carabinieri.'

The Carabinieri would likely inform Interpol and Stanley's former superiors, who would have him committed to a lunatic asylum.

Stanley said, 'I want you to shoot Anushka and bury her somewhere – Bluebell Wood perhaps?'

'I don't have time, I'm busy with my cryonics project. Why don't you bury her at your place?'

Stanley's voice turned stony.

'Perhaps the people of Witherington might be interested

in your little secret? Should I mention Thierry of the French Resistance?'

The most despicable part of Stanley was his capacity to dredge up secrets from her past. She felt her hackles rise. She knew what he was referring to. It was tit-for-tat.

'There was a war on, Stanley. He was messing with my radio set and I shot him in self-defence.'

'You shot him in the back, Tally.'

'I didn't shoot him in the back.'

'I know you did.'

'He was a traitor.'

'Was he? My records show he was on our side.'

'You're lying as usual.'

'Am I?'

'You're wrong. I didn't shoot him in the back. I looked him straight in the eye before pulling the trigger.'

Painful memories flooded her mind. She recalled France 1944 – the steaming tin bath shared with Thierry of the French Resistance in the barn; the smell of sweat on their clothes, the grey tide-mark and the romp in the hay afterwards. Then a terrible sense of betrayal when she'd caught him fiddling with her radio set. She'd waited until they had finished eating the farmer's cat before shooting him. At least he'd died on a full stomach. These were things she'd never tell her mother – eating a cat or, even worse, losing her virginity to a foreigner.

Tallulah wanted to grab Stanley by the neck and sink him in cement.

Sex and blasphemy

According to the news last night, the British Isles could expect a storm today. Roland interpreted it as divine intervention for his article on *Sex and the Church*. His prophesy turned out to be right when ten members of the Mothers' Union marched into the office before high noon, without knocking.

He slid into the store room and left the door slightly ajar. He watched as Florence thrust a copy of *Agriculture and Business Monthly* in front of Scarlett, her chubby forefinger jabbing at Veronica's name. After giving Scarlett enough time to see the title *Sex and the Church*, Florence grabbed it back and began to read aloud Veronica's reply to *Frustrated Fanny*, pointing to line four: *there are over 30 million people worldwide who aren't getting satisfactory sex or orgasms.*

Florence finished reading and threw the magazine on Scarlett's desk. 'We want to speak to Veronica about this piece of filth.'

'You can talk to me. I'm responsible,' she replied stonily.

Florence's lips tightened. 'We want to speak to the woman who wrote it.'

'She's on holiday.'

There was a collective murmur.

Florence said, 'We object to having the word "orgasm" in our front rooms.' Scarlett reminded them *Agriculture and Business Monthly* was intended to be available to men and women alike, including teenagers. She requested it not be put in the downstairs toilet to be read as it was meant to open inquisitive minds, not bowels.

Florence said it sounded like a pile of shit.

Scarlett asked why it had taken so long for them to complain.

'We had to take a vote on it.'

Scarlett said, 'The next time you want to descend on my office, I'd be grateful if you could call me first.'

There were murmurs of dissent. Florence looked as if she was having a hot flush. She shouted loudly about blasphemy and Jesus's mother-in-law.

Realising conflict resolution was needed, Roland forced himself out of the store room. Coughing loudly, he drew himself up to his full height and faced them. 'Ladies, the purpose of the magazine is to promote freedom of speech and equality of the sexes.'

Florence looked at Roland and spat out, 'Look who's talking – the great liar himself.'

Roland, used to hecklers at Speakers' Corner, said, 'Let she who is without sin throw the first brick.'

Florence thrust out her bosom. 'I don't remember reading about bricks in the Bible.'

Roland said, 'We're not here to pander to individual needs. Our objective is to show both sides of a coin. We cannot show the head without the tail. Sex and the Church was written with this in mind because many people were asking if Jesus had a mother-in-law. Is it blasphemy?' He pointed to one of them and asked, 'Do you think Jesus had a mother-in-law?'

The woman said, 'I think it's quite possible.'

Florence glared at her. 'Don't be ridiculous, Mary, Jesus wouldn't have had a mother-in-law.'

Mary said, 'Why not? We've all had one.'

They all spoke at once and some were arguing.

Roland raised his hands to silence them. 'This is a very important matter and I see there are two different camps here. If you have any doubts I suggest you go and discuss them with Reverend Pottering as he's well versed with the scriptures.'

They all nodded except Florence who shouted, 'The Vicar doesn't even know what time of day it is.'

The delegation ran out of questions and trickled out into the corridor. Florence called them to heel but mutiny was in the air. She grabbed Mary's arm and tried to drag her back inside. 'I haven't finished yet, Mary, I want to ask about coitus interruptus.'

Scarlett heard Mary reply, 'You can ask the Reverend Pottering about that.'

After they'd gone Scarlett said to Roland, 'I didn't know you were good at crowd control.'

'You haven't seen me at Speakers' Corner.'

'No I haven't, but I'd like to. I wish I had your guts.' Scarlett thanked him for defending her and keeping the hissing vipers at bay. She left her desk and hugged him, thinking he deserved it, realising he was no longer the confused boy she thought he was. Roland was every inch a man.

Reading the admiration in Scarlett's eyes, Roland pulled up her chin and kissed her on the lips.

After the kiss, Roland thought maybe he was in love with Scarlett after all. This morning, after spending the night with her, he'd had to drag himself to the office. As he came through the door she said 'good morning' and never mentioned last night as she was busy reading something. He was a little hurt and wondered if she'd already forgotten. It was as if their mad passionate embraces had never existed. Another half hour went by and Serge arrived looking as if he hadn't slept all night. The first thing he did was to present his ticket stubs to be reimbursed for his trip to Rome with Anushka. Scarlett said she refused to foot the bill for his dirty weekends.

'She had an interview at the United Fruit Organisation and I interviewed the Director-General so it's work-related,' insisted Serge.

'About what?'

'About raspberry growing in developing countries. I thought it would make a good article and they're looking for new biogas possibilities in rural areas. It might be interesting for Witherington.'

'Sounds like a load of bullshit to me,' said Roland.

Scarlett threw him a warning look and said to Serge, 'Where's she now?'

Serge coughed nervously while he rummaged in his brain for a good excuse as to why he'd brought Anushka back to Witherington. 'She didn't get the job and I couldn't leave her penniless, homeless and probably pregnant on the streets of London.'

Scarlett raised her eyebrows. 'Pregnant?'

'Yes, she's in her room unwell.'

Roland felt the blood rush to his neck. He said he had to go and see the printer and left the office. The printer was the excuse he used when things started to get tough.

Five minutes later Roland was banging his fist on the door of room fourteen. Anushka's voice called, 'What is going on? Is there a fire?'

He heard the lock click as she opened the door. She stood barefoot in a short white silk under-slip with narrow shoulder straps. Roland looked at her belly for signs of pregnancy and walked into her room without being invited. 'You could have told me,' he said, remembering their passionate afternoon at her flat and amazed his sperm had hit home the first time around. 'When's the happy event due then?'

'Are you talking about marriage? Serge told me not to tell anyone until my birthday.'

'So you've been sleeping with Serge?'

'I will marry him. I am going to have big white wedding dress.'

Roland felt a surge of hatred mixed with envy overwhelm him. He felt dizzy.

'Is the baby mine?' he said, steadying himself.

'There is no baby.' She said it pan-faced, as if she was unaware of the pain he was going through. Then she asked him to leave.

Two hours later, after visiting the Bull and Bullocks pub, Roland returned to the office. Luckily Serge wasn't there otherwise he'd have pushed his head into the toilet bowl. Scarlett wanted to know what he'd brought back from the printers seeing as she couldn't remember anything being outstanding.

'When I got there he said he'd made a mistake.' He could tell Scarlett was starting to get annoyed when her voice raised a tone. 'You can't just walk out and stay out for two hours. We've got deadlines today.'

She'd already forgotten about the hours spent in bed. Roland cursed silently. Life seemed to be full of bloody deadlines and insensitive people with their own agendas. It had been a mistake to sleep with his boss and he couldn't even retreat into his tree because she'd destroyed it.

After sifting through a pile of fan mail from women and men who had written to Veronica, he picked out one from a man whose frame of mind matched his own. It would do for a future issue.

Dear Veronica,

I'm heartbroken. They say it's unmanly to cry but I cried all night when my girl went off with another man and got pregnant. Does it mean I'm unmanly because I cry? I want to end it all.

Regards,

Macho Man

The letter disturbed him. It seemed that the man was talking directly to him in all his deep despair. He penned a reply from the heart.

Dear Macho Man,

I understand your pain. If you are thinking of doing yourself in, you might want to reconsider, as most solutions are painful or wrought with challenges:

Hanging: If you don't tie the knot on the noose right (refer to some cowboy movies for the correct way) you could end up dangling for hours unable to scream.

Gassing in the car: The petrol might run out.

Drowning in the bath: Sliding under water is not a good option if the plug leaks (and getting water up your nose can cause instant death according to a book I read on murders in the bath).

Slitting wrists: I'm told, is only for women (but I shouldn't say this).

Driving off a cliff: Difficult if you only have a bike (and there are no cliffs in Witherington).

My advice to you is go to the pub (try the Bull and Bullocks) and cry into your beer. If you buy a round for everyone, no one will notice your red tearful eyes – they'll just think you're drunk. I suggest you get another woman or find yourself a sexy man.

Good luck.

Veronica.

Roland silently thanked Macho Man in advance for listening to his fears. He was about to throw it in the bin when Serge came past his desk and grabbed it. He read it aloud and said, 'What a load of tripe. There aren't any queer-boys in Witherington.'

Scarlett said, 'Stop being politically incorrect Serge, they're called homosexuals. Get out of your mind-set, we're here to address all kinds of needs.'

'The church won't like it,' he replied.

'We're not here to serve the church but to serve the people.'

Serge threw the letter on Scarlett's desk and walked out.

Scarlett's eyes ran over it. She turned to Roland and hesitated a moment.

'It's too strong. We don't want to encourage people to think about suicide options, even though you gave a good reply about the pub.'

'Can't I just cancel "*find yourself a sexy man*"?'

'No. To be blunt, the whole article is crap and you risk opening a can of worms. We'll have the Mothers' Union marching in here to ask what kind of example we're setting for children. I don't think I could face Florence again.'

Roland gritted his teeth and couldn't help a touch of sarcasm. 'If I remember rightly, I was the one to face Florence.'

'Scrap it!' said Scarlett.

So I gave way beneath that heavy burden,
Outpouring in a torrent tears and sighs,
And the voice flagged upon its passage forth.

Dante Alighieri
The Divine Comedy: Purgatory. Canto XXXI

JULY 1986

Political hot potato

A sense of calm reigned over the office. Roland was pleased to know his *Love thy neighbour regardless* letter had gone down well and was already in homes across Witherington.

Scarlett handed him a letter addressed to Veronica. 'I'm not sure about publishing it, seeing it's from a person who's signed it "anonymous". It's far too long and the language is weird.'

Roland took it from her and read it. 'It's long but interesting. The style shows a tidy mind.'

'It could be from a crank trying to stir up trouble. It's a political minefield. Wars are known to have been started for less.'

'Come on, Scarlett, remember about liberation and equality. Everything the man says is true. All we have to do is reply and print the usual disclaimer to avoid people descending on us.'

She finally relented but said she'd hold him responsible for any media disaster resulting from his reply to 'anonymous'.

From a Foreign gentleman.

Dear Veronica,

I am doing some research to compare our two countries. In my country we support the workers' struggle for the betterment of the Fatherland. Our young people are hard working. They work the paddy fields with dangerous mosquitoes during summer holidays and make roads and dig ditches for sanitary purposes and sing revolutionary songs and wave red flags while following the tractors. The girls dig trenches and carry heavy rocks to see who can carry the biggest load and because they win a prize. Old ladies are proud to carry heavy bags of commodities on their backs because they bravely fought in the Fatherland War against the evil imperialist aggressors.

In contrast, your country is divided (England, Scotland, Wales and Ireland). Your prisons are full of layabouts who would benefit from hard labour. Subversives at Hyde Park Corner denounce the government and are not arrested. Young people listen to pop music (which we do not officially approve of except in secret discotheques in the city).

It is rather strange that, notwithstanding the disaccord in your government, the interference from the church, and multiple protests over human rights, your glorious country has survived. It is amazing to see people smiling in the face of adversity when the Welfare State does not measure up to their expectations. Your country is held together by the Royal Family who strive to foster international relations, thereby distracting the populace from the aforementioned problems and subversive protesters (whom my country approves of – but only in other countries).

Signed: Anonymous foreigner

PS. I am looking for someone to edit and publish my cookery book (which will eventually be translated into my language). I hope you can help me.

Roland thought the letter was interesting and deserved a reply. After all, it wasn't every day they had a serious communist in their midst. Most of the ones in the West were too busy indulging in the fun game of rebellion. Roland quickly wrote a reply to get to press before the end of the month for the August issue.

Dear Anonymous foreign gentleman,

Our young people do not pull rice from paddy fields (because we have none). In the fifties and sixties, young people collected potatoes in the fields for ten shillings a day. Today it's considered child cruelty but after the war this contributed to the family economy and the kids enjoyed making a bit of pocket money. Yes, we have strikes, freedom of the press and protests marches. These may create tensions in political ranks, the police and the secret service, but we call it democracy. We go to war to defend our principles and we haven't been invaded by a foreign power except for the Roman Empire and the Vikings (but please check this information in Encyclopaedia Britannica).

Please send your book to me for editing.

Regards,

Veronica

**Disclaimer: This is the author's personal opinion and in no way reflects the opinion of the magazine.*

Scarlett read it and told him to get it ready for the August issue. 'You never mentioned the layabouts,' she said with a cheeky grin.

'I don't want to start a class war in the suburbs. They'll all be descending on us before we know it and Florence will be in here with the Mothers' Union as well.'

She put a hand on her hip and tilted her head. 'I thought you said you believed in free speech.'

'It depends,' he said, tempted to kiss her.

In the afternoon Scarlett handed Roland a package with a full manuscript inside. It was from a Mr Kim, who Roland assumed was the 'anonymous foreigner'. The title was most unusual but the text was written in almost perfect English, punctuated now and then with quaint words like 'revolutionary', 'imperialist aggressors' and 'Yankee underdogs'. The main thing was it made sense and he was not going to quibble about a few foreign expressions. He quickly worked through it and made notes in the margins about the strange photo of terrapins sitting in holes in a Yorkshire pudding. Roland phoned the author about a few queries. After three rings Mr Kim answered the phone. Upon being prompted to furnish some information about himself, he gave a short verbal biography and said he was from North Korea and presently on a cultural visit to study the British way of life. Roland complimented him on his book and, after an interchange of patronizingly polite small-talk, which only the British are capable of in their mission to show their human side to the foreigner, Roland put him at ease and asked him for his full name to put on the front cover.

'My name is Comrade Kim,' he said with hardly a trace of a foreign accent.

'Could we not just call you Mr Kim?'

'No, because nearly every man in my country has such a name.'

'How about just being called Kim.'

'No, because there are also many Miss and Mrs Kims.'

'So what name would you like to have on the book?'

'I would like Glorious Revolutionary Comrade Kim.'

'It's a bit long,' said Roland. 'So let's call you Comrade Kim. I'm a little curious about the terrapins.'

Mr Kim said, 'I took Mrs Tallulah's recipe of toad-in-the-hole and adapted it. If you look on the bottom of the page, I have added another footnote.'

Roland paused for a moment before saying, 'I see you're calling your book *Glorious Revolutionary Recipes from a Pissing Little Island in the North Sea.*'

'Correct.'

'Could you kindly tell me how you arrived at such a creative title?'

'Well you see, Mr Roland, I met a nice Italian gentleman in a pub in Rottingham who said he was born in Sicily where they eat very well. He asked me what brought me to this pissing little island. I told him about my cookery book and he was very interested. He helped me write the title.'

'Were you both pissed at the time?' Roland asked.

'We were merry. The wine and whisky were of excellent quality. However, if you do not like the title, we can replace "pissing little island" with "merry little island".'

Roland said, 'Can we just call it *Revolutionary Recipes*? There's not much space on the front page for a longer title considering the length of your name.'

The war and peace process

Reading notes he'd made over the past twenty-four hours, Constable Ernest Barnstable thought he was ready to tackle a thorny peace-keeping mission between Bertha and Norman. The strategy he'd chosen might or might not work. It consisted of convincing Bertha to be calm and collected, but he wasn't sure how to go about it without her going into one of her spins.

Seeing her shortly afterwards, he told her Norman would drop in soon. In her typically belligerent way she said, 'I may not agree with everything he says but I suppose we'd better go back to my place and wait for him.'

Norman was waiting at the family tomb and the talks began by Bertha insisting that Ernest take notes.

Norman set out his defence. 'I want to make amends and be together again as I've nowhere to sleep and I've a right to rest in the family tomb.'

Bertha's nostrils tightened and her voice rose a few octaves. 'I can't have you here. You never got on with my mother.'

Ernest reminded them of their wedding vows and the happy holidays together.

'We weren't always happy,' she said with a snort.

Norman began to turn the knife. 'That was because your mother was forever interfering.'

Ernest stepped in. He was aware of the dangers connected

to mothers and mothers-in-law. They regularly took the brunt of conjugal frustrations.

'Can you both forget the past and come to an agreement? Otherwise we'll be here all night.'

Ernest realised Bertha was procrastinating when she said, 'I think we should sleep on it and meet tomorrow. I don't like making rash decisions.' But Norman insisted they take an immediate decision as he didn't want to sleep on the damp grass tonight. During the following hours of extenuating discussions and arguments, Ernest attempted to extract an agreement from Bertha allowing Norman to spend the night in the family tomb.

'I'll agree if it's only for tonight. But I'm not sleeping with him.'

Norman desired more. 'I want a long-term agreement and without your parents visiting when they feel like it.'

'I can't stop them coming and they have a right to visit me when they feel like it,' said Bertha. The stumbling block was Norman's refusal to include Bertha's parents in their new life. One thing Ernest learned from the experience was that a peace agreement between two warring parties, if left unsigned, is tantamount to a declaration of war.

Norman refused to sign.

Following the inconclusive meeting, Ernest decided it was time to call Cecilia and Fred to flesh out a policy. He found them completely ignoring one another. Desperately needing to get the peace process off the ground, he begged them to collaborate and put forward a strategy. 'We have to decide roles. We need a negotiator, a mediator and a legal observer,' Ernest said.

Fred puffed out his chest and said he was the best one to lead the negotiations having spent so much time in the henhouse sorting out petty female problems. Cecilia gave a disparaging throaty laugh and reminded them about her missing foot and the precious time being wasted on a lost cause.

'There's no such thing as a lost cause,' rebutted Ernest.

'I fully agree,' chimed Fred.

Ernest told Cecilia she was quite welcome to leave if she wanted to. She glared at them both and said she'd stay as an observer to make sure things didn't get out of hand. Therefore Fred was given the job of negotiator while Ernest said he was quite happy to sit by and mediate when things got hot.

Norman and Bertha arrived shortly afterwards. Norman's face was a blustery red, his hair in disarray and his grey suit creased. His tie was missing. Bertha strutted towards them in her emerald green dress, staggering on her red high heeled shoes which threatened to sink into the turf at each step. She explained they'd done nothing but argue. She cursed and pulled off a shoe, removing earth from one of the heels. Ernest wanted to know what they'd been arguing about.

'Just this and that,' Bertha said, defiantly refusing to go into detail and saying it was none of anyone's business. Fred, the negotiator, pulled two chamomile daisies from the grass.

'Eat these and they'll calm you down,' he said grinning.

Bertha threw hers on the grass and stamped on it. 'I don't need calming down,' she shouted before going into one of her spins and tottering off in bare feet, baring her inflamed bunions. Norman sat on the grass eating his daisy, saying it wouldn't be good for his blood pressure if he had to spend any more time with his dead wife. The peace process had failed. Norman was now homeless and staring into space. Fred sat next to him and put a wing around his shoulder. 'It looks as if you'll be sleeping under the stars with me tonight.'

Norman and Fred spent the night huddled up to each

other on the grass under a tree, their bodies keeping each other warm during the dark windy night. At dawn the sun began to rise on a day without wind or rain. Norman stirred as a cock crowed.

'That sounds like Gottfried,' Fred announced.

'Who's Gottfried?' Norman enquired stretching his body.

'He's the one who's always arguing with the hens. They never agree.'

'Sounds familiar.'

'He hangs around Ethel.'

'Who's Ethel?'

'She's my dancing partner.'

'I've never danced,' said Norman with sadness in his voice.

'It's easy. You should try it.'

'I don't have a dancing partner.'

'I'll teach you.'

Fred stood up and stepped into a waltz counting one-two-three, one-two-three.

'Watch me and follow my steps and turn as you're doing them.'

Norman began uneasily to copy Fred's steps. He stumbled a few times before he got the hang of it.

'Now lift your right hand and pretend you're holding a woman's hand. Then put your other hand around her waist. And stop looking at the ground, you have to look into her eyes,' said Fred, humming a popular waltz.

Norman stepped and turned. 'I've never had so much fun in my life,' he chuckled. The waltz turned to a cha-cha-cha and before long they were both trotting around, humming and laughing uncontrollably. Their gaiety attracted the attention of Ernest who was rudely awakened from sleep and asked them what the hell they were playing at, given the unholy hour. Cecilia arrived as if on cue and said she'd been disturbed too. Norman laughed good-naturedly and asked her to dance.

'I can't dance until I've found my foot,' she said looking at her stump, 'but when I do I'll be happy to dance with you. I used to be a ballerina you know.'

Norman sympathised. 'Forget about your missing foot, I'll hold you up.'

He grabbed her and hoisted her off the ground and spun her into a waltz. She squealed in mock horror and said her white ballet dress wasn't exactly the right dress for a waltz but Norman said it was perfect and he'd be glad to dance with her at the community party in September.

Bertha arrived, also having been woken up by the noise. She watched Norman and Cecilia for a moment.

'You've never danced with me the way you're dancing with her,' she said peevishly. Norman put Cecilia down gently and approached Bertha. 'Then let's dance, there's always a first time.'

'I've never danced before.'

'It's easy, you just count one-two-three, one-two-three and turn. Put your right hand into mine and your left hand on my shoulder. Now look into my eyes.' He put his hand around her waist and started slowly to show her the steps.

Ernest whispered to Cecilia, 'I thought you said they were a lost cause.'

'It's thanks to Fred they're together. I have to admit he's a good negotiator.'

Ernest nodded and smiled.

When the dancing finished, Cecilia approached Fred. 'I'll try and find a new home for Norman,' she said, stroking his head.

Fred said, 'I don't think you need to. Just look at them.' Bertha's head was on Norman's shoulder and she was crying. Norman looked in seventh heaven.

'Quick, get them to sign this,' said Ernest pulling the peace agreement from his pocket. Fred snatched it and tore it to shreds.

'I don't think they need it now,' he said triumphantly.

Recycled presents

Questions about Cecilia kept popping into Ernest's head. Who in the community wanted her maimed? Why had her right foot and not her left been severed? Was it to do with her ballet dancing? Had a wild animal taken it? A pig from the farm? If the occupants of the graveyard were to be believed, Cecilia had many enemies. She was proud, mean, aggressive and vain. There was a list a mile long of people who had had it in for her. On the contrary, she considered herself the saintly hard-done wife of James who put everyone else before herself. She said she was a loving, giving person and the perfect friend.

On a darker note, Ernest knew Cecilia had recycled birthday and Christmas presents by selling them to charity shops to spend the money on herself. His mother had once given her and James a Christmas present – two antique brass candlesticks. Then he'd seen them, not six months later, at the church bazaar with a price tag of three pounds, far below their worth.

Later in the day he questioned her. 'Tell me about the candlesticks,' he said gruffly.

'They were scary and kept toppling off the mantelpiece. It was an omen of death.'

'What about the china tiger?'

'It was positively frightening.'

'I saw it at the church bazaar with a price tag of only two pounds. It probably cost someone a fortune.'

She bit her lip. 'I've been scared of tigers since I was a

child. They give me nightmares and I was worried I'd meet one sooner or later.'

He said, 'There aren't any tigers in this country.'

'One could escape from a circus or a zoo.'

'It's never happened.'

He didn't tell her he knew, from village gossip, she'd sold the china tiger out of jealousy, simply because James had received it from Tallulah Millstone. It was time to speak to James.

Ernest waited until 2am before entering James's bedroom. He sat on the bed and asked him a question.

'Why did Cecilia sell the china tiger Tallulah gave you?'

James stirred and mumbled. 'Because she was jealous. Tally and I had a fling. She said I was as strong as a tiger – it was a symbolic present. I hid it in the wardrobe but Cecilia found it.'

'What did you do when you knew Cecilia had given it to the church bazaar?'

'We had an argument.'

'Did you threaten to kill her?'

James screwed up his face. 'I could have killed her.'

'Did you?'

'No. Now leave me alone.'

Ernest left James's bedside, frustrated at the lack of collaboration.

Back at the graveyard, he asked Fred to sing to him. 'It's a bit late and I'm worn out after teaching Norman to dance,' Fred said, shaking his crest in a definite 'no'.

It seemed to Ernest he was always at the disposition of others but no one was at his. 'Forget it, Fred, I'll sing to myself,' he said, shuffling back to his tomb, feeling beaten at not having had the strength to deal with insubordination.

Blessing of the beasts

When Ernest informed Fred and Cecilia he would attend the Blessing of the Beasts church service, they said they would give it a miss. 'We don't want to be in a church with potentially stampeding animals,' Cecilia said, reminding him of her disabled foot. Then she hobbled away before Ernest could open his mouth to object. It seemed he was destined to go it alone.

At the entrance to the Church of Local Martyrs, Ernest saw his mother holding a cage with Lovey inside. He longed to put his arms around her and place his head on her shoulder. He touched her sleeve and whispered in her ear, 'I miss you, Mum,' but she gave no indication she'd heard him.

Scarlett and Tallulah waited outside the church for Roland to arrive. Serge had refused to come. Tallulah held a cage with a subdued Ethel inside. 'I gave her some Valium so she won't make a noise in church,' she said as Ethel keeled over and lay on the bottom of the cage.

'Just make sure she doesn't pop her clogs,' Scarlett said, 'or there'll be hell to pay.'

Roland turned up holding a small cage with a hamster inside. 'I borrowed it from the vet,' he said sheepishly, avoiding Tallulah's eyes as they walked towards the entrance.

Inside the church, all pews had been removed to the crypt. A police cordon with *Do not cross this line* provided a dividing line down the middle between the altar and the church door.

An attached notice warned that small animals were to stand to the right and large animals to the left to avoid crushing. Pinned inside the front door were a few rules:

All beasts attending must be accompanied.

Owners are encouraged to confess on behalf of their beast/beasts and are not allowed to bring more than two of the same species.

Owners are responsible for collecting droppings.

It had been reported in the local paper that Reverend Pontius Pottering had been hosting the Blessing of the Beasts service annually for the past five years. It had been an uphill climb to convince the hidebound that church organ music would be calming to their animals, help them produce more milk, tastier cheese, bigger eggs and incredibly tender meat. Of course there had been the odd vegetarian who objected to the tender meat and slaughter and refused to adhere to the initiative because of animal cruelty. Consequently he'd given a sermon about Muslim and Jewish ritual slaughter which was carried out in a manner not to cause undue suffering to the animal. It was predictable that the sermon couldn't please everyone and had risked starting a holy war.

Walking down the aisle towards the altar, Reverend Pottering found a dark-skinned man in a white caftan barring his way holding a chicken in a cage. Introducing himself as Santeros, the man said he was a Cuban exile wanting to introduce Santerian voodoo practices to Witherington. He said he'd heard the sermon about humane slaughter and wanted to introduce the Cuban way of culling chickens.

'I can give the congregation a demonstration at the altar of how to slit a chicken's throat humanely and drain its blood.

There will be no waste. Your wife can make the carcass into a broth and I will give her onions and carrots.'

He was halfway to offering a stock cube when Florence of the Mothers' Union bore down on him shouting, 'I'm going to report you to the RSPCA!'

Santeros towered over her and looked deeply into her eyes whereby Florence shrunk and shuffled away as if in a trance. The Reverend quickly intervened. 'I'll have no voodoo in this church,' he said, moving towards the altar where he asked the congregated to take their places. 'The blessing is about to begin.'

While waiting for parishioners and their animals to settle, Reverend Pottering looked around. Today there was a full house – cats, dogs, birds in cages, tortoises, hamsters, sheep, pigs, goats, horses, cows and thankfully no ostriches. He waited for silence and spoke from the pulpit.

'And the animals came in two by two, and yea the beasts of the field have looked up to thee, as a garden bed that thirsteth after rain. Let thou rule over the fish of the sea and the birds of the air, over the livestock, over all the earth, and over all the creatures that move along the ground.'

Some blank faces showed they were confused by the 'yea' and 'thirsteth'. He stopped reading further and led them into singing 'All Beasts Bright and Beautiful'.

The next piece from the scriptures was about loaves and fishes. After blessing a few goldfish in glass bowls, he led the congregation into prayer and asked parishioners to come forward two by two to confess their animals and have them blessed. Had the Reverend Pottering not skimped on his morning prayers, he might have received a warning from the Almighty that the blessing service was destined to be short.

A hand-held microphone was passed to Farmer Wormsley in the front row, who shuffled and cleared his throat nervously. 'I'm speaking on behalf of Porkchop my pig and my wife is speaking on behalf of Pancetta, Porkchop's wife. First I will confess on behalf of Porkchop.' He blew into the microphone and began his confession. 'My name is Porkchop and a little while ago a stranger wandered into my pen. I think I ate the bugger. Well actually I think he was female as I found a red toenail hanging by a hair from my rectum.'

Elsie put her mouth in front of the microphone and added, 'It's the first time it's happened so don't worry about our sausages. There's no human meat in there.'

There was a sudden hush as the information sunk in. A scream came from Florence of the Mothers' Union, 'I had sausages for breakfast.'

All heads turned in her direction like a flock of sheep. They watched as she rushed down the aisle to heave into the flower beds. The human stampede started when someone else shouted, 'I had some yesterday.' It seemed the whole of Witherington had eaten the Wormsley's sausages. Parishioners left in a panic, leading or carrying their animals. Elsie was ticking off her husband for starting it, while Porkchop wondered why everyone was running scared just because he was suspected of eating a bit of human flesh.

In the mayhem that followed, Roland wandered around looking for the vet's hamster which until a few minutes ago had been sitting in its cage between the pew and the prayer mat. When the Reverend pulled out the little beast from behind the altar, Roland wondered if divine intervention had brought them together so he could speak about outstanding questions on the church's teachings. The Reverend sat gloomily on the altar steps and agreed to listen to Roland, seeing as there was nothing else to do at that tragic moment.

Roland said, 'Reverend, could you kindly tell me about the Church's teachings regarding coitus, wet dreams and masturbation?'

The Vicar looked more in a trance than shocked. 'So sorry, Roland, but question time is on Tuesdays in the parish hall. You're welcome to come but I may not be here this Tuesday as I need a rest. I suggest you get in touch with the Bishop of Rottingham.'

It wasn't the answer Roland was looking for. He picked up the vet's hamster and walked out, no further forward in understanding the ways of the world and feeling frustratingly ignored. The clergy, his parents and the office, had let him down. The list was endless. It was impossible to get clear answers.

At home, Pontius Pottering complained to his wife about the abandoned droppings. There was no money in the offerings box to pay the cleaner.

The good woman said, 'Don't worry, dear, we can clear them up ourselves.'

He groaned at the 'we', reflecting that, in the scriptures, none of God's messengers had ever been asked to sweep up piles of dung.

Porkchop on death row

Elsie Wormsley had just finished washing the dishes in the sink under the kitchen window when she heard a car draw up outside. Pulling up the corner of a lace curtain to see who it was, she gave a short squeal.

'There's a police car by the back fence, Bert. They must have come for Porkchop.'

Bert jumped up from a kitchen chair almost knocking it over in his haste to peep through the curtains. 'I hope they're not here for my whisky.'

She screamed at him, 'Our pig is suspected of eating someone and all you can think of is booze?'

'I was just worried in case they might want to look in the barn.'

'You've not been making moonshine again have you, Bert?'

'Of course not, luv, but the equipment's still there.'

With a shaking hand, Elsie pulled the curtains back into place. 'They're coming up the path. There's two of them.'

Bert dashed to the front door as the bell rang. Coming face to face with two uniformed police officers, he said, 'We were just going out.'

'It won't take long, Mr Wormsley. We're just making routine enquiries. We've had some complaints about your sausages—'

'There's nothing wrong with my sausages, the whole town eats them and says how good they are.'

'We believe your pig ate an intruder and there's human meat in the food chain.'

'Our pig never ate anyone.'

'You and your wife said quite a bit in front of a lot of people, so unfortunately, sir, we're forced to investigate.'

Bert stood back. 'Then you'd better come in.'

The police officers followed Bert into the kitchen where Elsie was setting the table for four. She smiled and said, 'Would you like biscuits with your tea?'

'No thanks, just tea,' said the tall police officer taking a seat at the kitchen table.

'Mrs Wormsley, we've interviewed a few people who are ready to swear your pig ate a person.'

'They're all gossipmongers.'

Bert interrupted. 'Just because she found a toenail hanging from our pig's rectum doesn't mean he ate someone. He could have sat on a dead body. He spends most of his life sitting in different places.'

The short officer said, 'We're not investigating a murder as yet.'

Elsie poured the tea and listened while the officer told her they were looking into every possibility.

'Notwithstanding, we'll have to take the pig into custody and have him examined internally by the vet. If you still have the toenail please hand it over as we'll need it for the investigation.'

Elsie's hand began to shake and the teacup she was holding rattled. 'I threw it in the bin,' she stammered.

The two policemen raised their eyebrows and looked at each other. The short one took out a pad and pen from his pocket and wrote *Evidence destroyed.*

He said, 'Can we have a look at the pig?'

Bert replied, 'Sorry, officers, but he ran off yesterday.'

The policeman wrote, *Suspect missing – possibly on the run.*

Elsie took two paper bags from the fridge and placed

them on the table. 'There's a pound of sausages each. They'll go down nicely with eggs and bacon for breakfast. All our customers are very happy with them.'

'Thank you very much, Mrs Wormsley. These sausages will be analysed for human remains and used in evidence if any are found. You'll be hearing from us in due course.'

Elsie's face fell and she swore under her breath *ungrateful bastards*. Showing them out, she watched the police car disappear from sight, along with the sausages.

Bert put his hand on Elsie's shoulder. 'Another cup of tea would be nice, Elsie luv. By the way, where did you get them sausages?'

Elsie managed a smile for Bert. 'I bought them at the butchers yesterday. There's no human meat in those.'

Bert laughed. 'Do me a favour will you – go and let Porkchop out of the barn.'

Elsie was quite sure she'd heard the last from the ungrateful police officers until the phone rang the next morning.

'Mrs Wormsley, we met yesterday, remember?'

'Of course I remember. You took my sausages without saying thank you.'

'So sorry, it was very rude but we have a job to do. I was wondering if your pig has turned up?'

'Not yet.'

'Please let us know if he does. All police cars are presently on the alert and searching for him at a great deal of expense to the taxpayer.'

'Porkchop won't be caught easily. He runs very fast.'

'Perhaps, but our police cars are faster and he won't evade them for long.'

Elsie hardly dared ask the next question. 'What'll happen when he's caught?'

'It depends. He'll be taken to the vet and if he's free from human remains he'll be returned to you, otherwise he'll be suppressed and incinerated.' Elsie screamed and dropped the phone, her legs crumpling under her. Bert picked her up off the floor. 'Don't worry, luv, they'll never find Porkchop.'

She was crying. 'But we can't keep him locked up in the barn forever.'

'Oh, I forgot to tell you. I had a telephone call from a bloke called Stanley who wants to buy him.'

'What for?'

'Well he said he wants him for something to do with removals. He'll give us two grand for him.'

Elsie slumped down on a kitchen chair. 'That's a lot of money for a pig.'

'Our Porkchop's no ordinary pig. He's won a lot of prizes. He's worth more than gold.'

'I don't know, Bert. I'll miss him.'

'Stanley told me we'll be saving him from horrendous torture when the vet gets up his rectum – there's sure to be splintered bones inside him.'

Elsie visualised Porkchop with a rope tied around his neck being led into the vet's surgery struggling every inch of the way, and then the splinters of bone. She put her head in her hands and closed her eyes as tears welled up. 'I don't want to think about it or I'll be having nightmares all night.'

'Don't cry, love, think about poor Porkchop and let's do what's best for him. If he stays here he'll be caught sooner or later.'

'Alright,' Elsie sobbed, 'call Stanley and tell him he can have him.'

'Just promise me you won't breathe a word about where Porkchop's going or the money. And don't mention it in church.'

She thought for a minute. 'I promise not to breathe a word if you buy me a fur coat with the money. I'd love to have one. Florence has one.'

Bert was too busy thinking about Porkchop to be alarmed at the implication of her sporting a new fur coat in church which, under normal circumstances, they couldn't afford.

'I wonder who it was he ate. You don't suppose it was Cecilia Willows do you?'

On the roof of Bluebell Vicarage, Cecilia pushed her ballet dress down over her legs and waited for Ernest to speak.

He said, 'It's quite possible Porkchop chewed your foot off as a red toenail was found hanging from his rear end.'

A shocked silence ensued before a long scream reverberated through Ernest's head. Then Cecilia calmed down and said, 'But I never used red nail polish.'

The wedding dress

James finished his breakfast and watched Anushka clean egg from the stove. She took off her apron and hung it next to the tea towels, wrung out the dishcloth and tipped the soapy water down the sink.

'I will get married soon,' she told him. It was a shock. But the good sport he was, James said, 'That's wonderful news. Of course I'll miss you, Anushka.' In reality he was devastated.

She gave him a little-girl wide-eyed smile. 'Could you please give me an advance of three months' salary? I need it to buy a wedding dress in Rottingham.'

'Of course.' He gave her the money without asking when she would pay it back. She took it gently and put it in her pocket. 'James, can you walk me down the church aisle as I don't have a father?'

How could he not accept? At first a distant foreigner, he now saw her as a lonely girl who needed a father. He felt privileged, never having had children of his own.

'I would be honoured,' he said proudly.

She kissed him on the cheek. 'I would now like to go to Rottingham.'

James dropped Anushka at the bus stop in Witherington, wondering if he shouldn't have driven her to Rottingham considering she'd encumbered him with such a weighty responsibility. He wanted to hug her and tell her everything would work out fine but the bus arrived and she was gone.

Upon reaching Rottingham, Anushka hurried to the bridal shop, excited at the thought she would marry and not have to run and hide any longer. Once inside the shop she pointed to the wedding dress in the window and said she'd like to try one on in her size. In the changing room, in front of the mirror, she slid into the soft silk and organza dress embroidered with pearls. The assistant told her she looked like a princess and a graceful white swan all rolled into one. Her heart almost burst with joy at the thought of walking down the aisle into a new life.

Before leaving the shop, carrying the wedding dress and veil, she pulled out the money James had given her and handed it over.

Serge sat on his bed thinking of how he was going to save himself from a life of drudgery on the home front and in the office. Six months ago the call of the countryside had been irresistible. Tramping around the fields of Witherington had been exhilarating until he'd had to clean cow pats from his boots. At first the smell of newly spread silage filled his senses but over time it lost its romantic bucolic perfume and now just smelt like shit. The call of the wild had been replaced by noise, rules, regulations and parking tickets. Then there were the women – mostly married, who wanted some respite, in the form of extra-marital sex to brighten up their boring nuptials. Living in a small town, however, he couldn't allow himself any type of scandal. And so it was – his sexual frustrations drove him into Anushka's arms. He was now at a crossroads and had to make a decision – to get back to his roots or marry Anushka. Last night he'd had a nightmare. He was shut in a house with no doors or windows. A woman nagged him about his not spending enough time with her. She said he didn't love her any more because he'd forgotten her birthday.

Serge pulled out a pen and paper from the sitting room desk to try and work out what he didn't want from life. It wasn't long before he realised he needed to get back to his roots on the Isle of Wight and count seagulls for a while.

Abominable coward

James was watching the BBC news when he heard a blood-curdling scream coming from room fourteen. He rushed down the corridor and banged on Anushka's door shouting, 'Anushka, are you alright?'

She slid back the bolt and threw herself into his arms sobbing hysterically. In her left hand was what looked like a crumpled letter. He prised her arms from around his neck and took it from her and read it. It was from Serge.

Dear Anushka,

I'm sorry I can't attend our wedding as I have to leave Witherington forever on an important journalistic mission for the United Nations which will take me to the Himalayas and Mongolia in search of the Indomitable Abominable Snowman (Bigfoot). Should I not survive the below freezing temperatures, the crevices, the deadly caves, the prowling tigers and the short-sighted hunters, please remember I have always loved you.

Serge

Anushka said, 'I cannot now stay in UK and become a British citizen. Serge has gone to look for big feet in Mongolia.'

James stroked her hair. 'I think you may be mistaken, dear. Serge could never survive in Mongolia.'

'We were to get married.'

James gave her his handkerchief. She hurled herself on the bed and thumped it several times while he was at a loss as to what to say to a distressed woman.

'You'll soon find another man,' he said softly. It was the wrong thing to say. She tossed his handkerchief, now sopping wet, back at him and rushed to the dressing table to search for the handkerchief with the pale violets. She fished it out and blew her nose into it with a loud honking sound.

'I will be an old maid and never be able to make sex again.'

Her frankness embarrassed him. He searched his brain for a suitable solution.

'What about marrying Roland?'

He wished he'd kept his mouth shut when she started howling. 'I cannot marry a man who gets sick with vodka. If he does not drink a lot of vodka on the wedding day he will embarrass me. Roland will be like a eunuch and not accepted by my family.'

It was obviously a cultural thing that Roland would have to show he was a man by drinking gallons of vodka until he passed out. James gave up and left her grieving and shouting about what she'd do to Serge if she ever caught up with him.

During the night James pondered upon how he could help Anushka and himself, considering he'd just been deprived of his new role as her adopted father and would no longer be walking her down the aisle. For the first time, he couldn't wait to get into bed and drift down into the dark dungeon. Any nightmare was better than this. His spirits picked up when Ernest, or rather Constable Ernest Barnstable, deceased, arrived shortly afterwards and sat on his bed. James poured out his troubles and asked Ernest for some advice.

'You have to think how you can make the most of a bad situation,' Ernest suggested.

'Short of dragging Serge back from Mongolia, there's nothing I can do. In any case I'm not even sure he's gone to Mongolia.'

'You could try asking the travel agency in Rottingham, they would know. You have to follow up on every little clue,' said Ernest, happy to be imparting some detective information.

The next morning James ate a hurried breakfast and drove to Rottingham. Apart from himself and the travel clerk, the agency was empty. The clerk was making herself a cup of tea and asked him if he wanted one.

'No thanks, I've just had breakfast. Actually I've come to ask you if Serge Gallo has booked a ticket for Mongolia.'

'Never heard of him.'

'He left on an important journalistic mission to find Bigfoot.'

'There aren't any in Mongolia.'

'Then perhaps in the Himalayas?'

'Hardly likely.'

James gave her his card and asked her to call him if she had any news.

'Certainly. How's business going with you at the Wailing Willows?'

'Not so good. Most of the rooms are empty.'

The clerk said her business wasn't going too well either. 'We need to invent some interesting events and initiatives. Tell me more about Mr Gallo, he sounds interesting. Perhaps we can cash in on his courage to advertise your hotel rooms.'

James said it sounded like a good idea. When his business acumen kicked in, he imparted a juicy piece of information – Serge Gallo had Italian connections and it was rumoured his father, while still married to his mother, had seduced the daughter of a local mafia man of honour and had been fed to the pigs. James didn't know if it was true or not but it sounded an idea which would sell.

A few days later the travel clerk rang to book ten rooms. Serge's history had been useful in her publicity campaign to encourage the adventurous. She foresaw dozens of calls from people wanting to visit Serge Gallo's living quarters and office and a few women perhaps wanting to marry him. James contacted Serge's ex-landlady who said she'd be glad to charge a pound a head to let visitors see Serge's room. For an extra pound, tea and biscuits could be served in the garden or lounge if it rained. Taking advantage of Serge's imprint around Witherington, James called Scarlett in the office and asked her permission for a group of people to stand quietly under the window where Serge had worked. Her answer reflected her mood.

'What the fuck for?'

'Well where else can I take them?'

'Try the Bull and Bullocks.'

She added that if she ever got her hands on the lazy double-dealing bastard, he'd end up dead and buried under a pile of cow shit. 'Why should a lazy son of a bitch get such attention,' she ranted.

'It'll keep people's minds off poverty and the economy,' replied James citing the role of the Royal Family and film stars as a fairy-tale diversion for the realm's poorest dreamers.

'He's hardly bloody royalty,' Scarlett snapped.

The travel clerk rang James later to suggest having T-shirts and balloons with 'Serge Gallo worked for *Agriculture and Business Monthly*' printed on them and released from a hot air balloon. It would be at his own expense of course. James said no thanks. Apart from the expense, he was sure Scarlett would go bananas.

Stormy weather

The atmosphere in the office could be cut with a hatchet and it was only 9am. Roland retreated into his mind and pictured himself in the Amazon jungle. He noticed Scarlett's eyes were red as if she'd been crying all night. They were one man short, if Serge could be called a man. Heavy clouds hung over the Wailing Willows Hotel. Before going to work, he'd been tempted to knock on Anushka's door but didn't have the courage when he'd heard her sobbing. Two women sobbing for Serge for different reasons. And while he was glad Serge was out of the way, he was furious Anushka had been treated badly.

He returned to the real world when Scarlett broke the silence. 'Who's going to write Serge's articles now?' Roland read the underlying fury in her voice. He didn't blame her, Serge had done a bunk without giving six months' notice.

He replied, 'Let's start with getting an advert into the local paper for a temporary replacement seeing as we have so many bloody deadlines,' he said sarcastically.

When she handed him the details on a hand-written A4 sheet, he said, 'You'll have to offer a bit more money, it sounds like peanuts.' He thought he was taking the lead, seeing as she seemed a bit lost, but immediately regretted misreading her apparent vulnerability when she glared at him with the look of a bull bearing down on a lost traveller. 'We can't afford it. We'll just have to work a bit harder and come in at the weekends.'

She was riding roughshod over his rights. 'I have to go to Speakers' Corner on Sunday,' he said stiffly.

'You haven't been there for weeks!'

A short silence.

'By the way, I can't pay you overtime,' Scarlett continued.

'I'm not here just for the money,' he replied, storming out of the office.

Having spent the rest of the day shut in his room meditating on the meaning of work and the boss/employee relationship, he wondered if he wouldn't have been better off leaving for the Amazon on the next flight.

Late evening he rapped on Scarlett's door intending to clear the air. When she didn't answer he called out, 'I see you're in a bit of a state, we'll sort it out tomorrow,' and went back to his room knowing he wasn't going to get much sleep.

Scarlett didn't hear Roland's knock as she was in the bath studying the mildew on the ceiling and wondering if she wouldn't have been better off employing two women instead of two men. Serge had let her down and Roland was becoming rebellious. Or was he? Maybe he was just being himself. Perhaps she'd stifled his true identity and trampled on his feelings?

Half an hour later, when the heat had gone out of the bathwater, she dried herself and slipped into a white cotton dressing gown. Putting an ear to the connecting door, she listened for movement. The longing to see him and make amends was great and eventually she knocked on his door. Roland pulled it back with force. Slightly surprised, Scarlett found herself looking into dark eyes wide with anger. Roland was wearing a black bathrobe which matched his mood. His hair was wet around his shoulders.

'I'm sorry I was so rude, Roland,' she said, walking in as he stood aside to let her past.

'You can't take out your problems on me.' He closed the door behind her.

'What do you mean?'

'I mean it's not my fault you have multiple problems of your own making.'

'If you're talking about my aunt and Serge, I—'

She left the sentence hanging, feeling exhausted and not wanting to drag up emotions. She followed Roland into the bathroom where the smell of manly soap filled her nostrils.

'Roland, just for tonight, can we forget I'm the boss? I don't like having an atmosphere between us.'

Returning to the bedroom with Scarlett trotting behind, Roland picked up a hairdryer from the bed and plugged it into the nearest socket. She took it from his hands and began to dry the back of his hair. Her fingers touched his neck. He recoiled, not sure whether it was her cold hands or body contact which gave him an electrifying thrill in his lower parts. Standing in front of him, Scarlett took some strands and placed them behind his ears. What happened next was governed by his galloping hormones. Roland removed the dressing gown from her shoulders and watched her startled expression as it fell to the ground. Any animosity between them melted away when he opened his bathrobe and pulled her inside.

Dangerous agendas

When Tallulah called James to ask how her siren was proceeding, she was surprised and horrified to find he was dedicating himself to putting Witherington on the tourist trail. He justified it by mentioning Serge Gallo, the cream teas and an economic boom for Witherington.

Tallulah let an hour pass. She never acted upon anger. When she'd calmed down she grabbed the phone and called Scarlett at the office.

Roland answered. 'Sorry, Mrs Millstone, but Scarlett's unavailable right now.'

'Just tell her I'll end up in a coffin if James continues with his ridiculous new project about Serge Gallo. I want her to speak to him as I'm too angry to do it myself.'

'Scarlett doesn't see James every day, so I suggest you call him your good self. May I warn you not to talk to her about Serge as it's a sore point.'

'If you don't let me talk to my niece, I'll tell her you vomited into my sink the next time I see her.'

'Don't worry, I'll tell her myself.'

'Didn't you say you wanted to share my cryonics canister?'

'No I didn't. I'm in love with your niece. Thank you for not calling in the future.'

The phone went dead. Tallulah put down the phone, picked up an inexpensive vase from the sideboard and launched it against the fireplace.

The nightly search for solutions was helped by the odd glass of red wine. Tallulah fell asleep at dawn without dreaming and slept until about 10am before getting up and filing her sorrows in the recesses of her mind. Life had to go on. Sitting at her desk, she penned a second advert.

Cryonics Manager required to replace incompetent bastard. Then she tore it up and threw it into the waste bin. It wasn't good manners and protocol required she write something more polite.

It was much later in the day when Tallulah opened the door to a young woman in a tight-fitting red coat with black patent belt, showing a great deal of flesh between ankle and thigh. She introduced herself as Anushka Petrova.

Tallulah snapped, 'I already have a set of *Encyclopedia Britannica* and I don't want any religious nonsense.'

'I have nothing to sell and I am not religious. In my country we have no God. May I come in? I hear you are looking for a cryonics partner to share your canister.'

Tallulah nodded and led her to the living room where Anushka lowered herself into an armchair. 'Mrs Millstone, is it not? I believe you are offering much money for a cryonics partner and I'd like to offer my services.'

'Well, I'm not sure I want to share it with a foreign woman and in any case aren't you a bit young to be thinking of spending ninety years in a canister?'

Anushka said she wasn't. 'I'm willing to put my body into the hands of science to help future generations. I will soon die.' She drew her hand across her eyes in a dramatic sweep.

Tallulah said, 'Is it catching? I mean I don't want any germs in my canister.'

Anushka took out a hanky and dabbed at her eyes. 'No germs, I have a minor genetic illness. I need money for my mother who has also the same illness who is also dying.'

Tallulah wondered why her mother wasn't already dead seeing as the family had such a short life-span. Stanley had mentioned Anushka several times but had said nothing about her being ill. Why would he want her dead if she was going to die anyway?

'I think we should discuss this over lunch,' said Tallulah sweetly.

'Of course, I would be honoured.'

They talked for a while and had a cup of tea before Tallulah accompanied her to the door.

'It was a pleasure meeting you and I look forward to seeing you at lunch very soon. By the way, do you like roast chicken?'

'I love chicken. It is to die for.'

Tallulah was sure of one thing – Anushka was a liar, dangerous and after her money. It was just a matter of time before she'd invite her to her last lunch in Witherington.

Much later, she received a call from Stanley who told her he was making an emergency plan in the event of a communist invasion and the impact on the economy.

'We've got enough of them here already. I'm accountable for every subversive in the land and can't cope with any more.'

'Accountable to whom?'

'To Queen and country. The prime minister would go berserk if I let one of them bloody foreigners slip through our hands.'

'I'm sure they have more important things to think about than people who officially don't exist.'

'I called to tell you I've bought Porkchop for two grand. He's got a good appetite for human flesh.'

'It's a lot of money for a pig.'

'It's coming out of the Special Operations Fund. The one connected to removals, if you know what I mean.'

She knew what 'removals' was but she didn't know where

the money was coming from. He asked her if he could put Porkchop in her shed for a few days.

'Why?'

'Otherwise I have to build a pen in a field behind the farmhouse or Santeros will make bacon out of him.'

'So?'

'I need Porkchop for waste disposal, if you know what I mean.'

Tallulah was used to reading between Stanley's lines. In plain language, Porkchop would soon be feasting on communist flesh.

'Could you add Anushka to your list? She's trying to defraud me.'

Stanley said he was glad to hear she'd changed her tune. He said, 'No problem, seeing as she's sleeping with James Willows, who's probably passing on secrets to the Russians. We could also feed James to Porkchop.'

'Touch James and you're dead. He's my cryonics manager,' Tallulah said with a hiss in her voice.

'I'd be doing you a favour seeing as he's so incompetent.'

'Mention it again and I'll go public with your big secret. I'll be talking to a few journalists about *your* incompetence at not noticing your boss was passing secrets to the enemy during the war.'

There was a short silence which was broken by Stanley's bloody-minded cheek.

'Well, can you look after Porkchop for a few days or not?'

In late afternoon, Tallulah called James and said, 'I'd like to invite you and Anushka for a cooked lunch tomorrow.'

'That's fantastic. Can I bring a bottle?'

'No, just yourselves. I hope you like roast chicken,' she said, making a mental note to take frozen Fred from the freezer.

Murderous Operandi

Fred sat on top of the fridge watching Tallulah lift his bare defrosted body from the draining board.

'It's just a carcass,' said Cecilia dismissively. Fred howled. Ernest said, 'Why don't you go home, before she puts you in the oven.'

Fred said he felt faint. Cecilia put a protective arm around Fred and flew at Ernest shouting, 'Constable Ernest Barnstable, how could you be so insensitive?'

'I was just speaking my mind.'

They watched Tallulah heat the oven, smear fat on Fred's carcass and place him on a tray surrounded by par-boiled potatoes cut in half. The kitchen smelt good. They noticed one odd thing – although it was only July, the kitchen and living room were decorated as if it was Christmas.

Knowing James sometimes had lapses of memory, Tallulah picked up the phone and called him to make sure he hadn't forgotten about lunch.

'I've made a roast with a Christmas theme just in case I peg out and have to be put on ice before then,' she said, also asking if Anushka was coming.

'I hope so. She's in mourning at the moment.'

'Oh?'

'Her husband-to-be left her in the lurch. She said he's as good as dead.'

'I didn't know she was going to get married. She told me she was dying of an incurable illness.'

James sounded genuinely shocked. 'I had no idea—'

By midday the dining room table had been set and the fireplace decorated. James arrived and handed Tallulah a box of Black Magic. 'Anushka will be along when she's finished hacking at her wedding dress with the scissors,' he said, kissing Tallulah on the cheek.

'Dear, dear, what a waste, those things cost a fortune.'

Anushka arrived half an hour late but beautifully groomed, her short blonde hair contrasting with her V-neck black dress. She handed Tallulah a bunch of chrysanthemums and managed a smile. Tallulah thanked her, mentally noting they were graveyard flowers in some countries. She led Anushka to the lounge where there was a blazing fire in the grate even though it was July. 'Are you all right, dear, you look a bit pale?'

Anushka dabbed at her eyes with a linen handkerchief. 'I am dressed in black because the son-of-bitch is dead.'

'Oh dear, when and why?'

Anushka ignored her and went to study the decorations on the mantelpiece.

James nudged Tallulah and whispered, 'He's not dead – he left her.'

Tallulah enquired, 'So where is the son-of-bitch now?'

Anushka sniffed into her hanky. 'I hope floating in the river. I hope fish gnawing eyes and balls.'

Tallulah recoiled and shuddered. 'As we're about to eat, perhaps we could talk about something else?'

Anushka went into a full-blown howl. She only calmed down when James put his arm around her and said, 'There,

there, don't cry. I'm so sorry to hear you're terminally ill.' He said it as if he were talking to a daughter. Anushka didn't reply and he distracted her by taking her to see the nativity scene on the mantelpiece.

She said, 'Why is cow standing over baby in the cradle? Cow has bovine spongiform encephalopathy.'

James said, 'My goodness, what a mouthful!'

'In Russia, the government feeds cows to prisoners.' She then added more detail. Tallulah lost her appetite upon hearing Anushka describe the sick, staggering cows and retreated to the kitchen.

James's eyes lit up as Tallulah brought in the food. Roast Fred lay on a silver platter surrounded by Brussels sprouts and sage and onion stuffing. James ate his food with appetite while Anushka just picked at hers. Having been brought up on good table manners, Tallulah noticed James held his fork correctly, while Anushka grasped her knife in her fist like a dagger. She stabbed at the Brussels sprouts so it didn't come as surprise to Tallulah when she said, 'I am stabbing Serge's balls.'

Tallulah ate the potatoes and Brussels sprouts and avoided eating the roast, seeing as Fred had been sedated before she killed him. She kept the conversation away from Anushka's stomach-turning tales by recounting some of her own wartime experiences. She told them she ate the farmer's cat then murdered Thierry in cold blood in the barn in France. James looked appalled.

'When we were in Paris you never told me you killed a man in cold blood or ate a cat. I bet the War Office wasn't too happy.'

'It was a French cat,' she replied.

Delving into her past threw up ghosts. Tallulah knew she shouldn't have revisited it when Thierry's face flashed through her mind. Thierry, the cat, the bovine spongiform and Serge's balls had ruined her appetite. She excused herself to go to the bathroom. A previous arrangement with Stanley had been agreed upon after Tallulah told him about the attempted fraud. The modus operandi suggested by Stanley sounded fine. All she had to do was wait until midnight to put 'The Plan' into action. Stanley had always said, 'You can't bump-off someone without first making a plan.'

Tallulah waited in the bathroom for the sedative inside Fred to take effect and almost an hour later she returned to the dining room to find Anushka and James fast asleep on the settee. They were still sleeping when midnight came and there was no sign of Stanley. At 1am Tallulah rang him in vain and at 2am she drank a coffee to keep herself awake. An hour later, after covering James and Anushka with a blanket, she went to bed.

At 6am she called Stanley again and this time he picked up the phone.

'Stanley! I was awake all night.'

'Sorry, Tally, I had an urgent call out. I had to track down a leftist. It was urgent.'

She knew he was lying. Most likely stoned on *Maria Warner* cigarettes. 'I've got two people here. They're out for the count but they'll soon be awake. What on earth am I going to do with them?'

'Use the hammer. Knock them on the head.'

Stanley's modus operandi was always extreme. 'You've got to be joking. There'll be blood all over my settee. I cannot, repeat cannot, take out James. I need him for my cryonics project. He hasn't finished it yet.'

'I thought you said he was procrastinating and you wanted him dead?'

When her voice took on a quiet high pitched menacing squeak, he agreed to be at her house at 10am. 'Hurry up, as I have to run the vacuum cleaner around this morning and they're sprawled all over the place.'

'Tally, what happened to the young girl who was good at troubleshooting? Just lift up their damn legs and hoover underneath. Use a bit of initiative.'

Tallulah hated Stanley when he was being patronising.

Awakening from a sedated sleep on the settee, Anushka struggled to sit up and said, 'I feel as if I am run over with a double-decker bus.'

James said he had a steaming headache and had never felt like this since Cecilia's death. In a spin waiting for Stanley, Tallulah asked them if they would like some tea.

James said, 'I had a strange dream last night, Tally, I dreamt you tried to kill me.'

'How ridiculous,' she replied, 'why would I want to do that?'

'It was just a dream.'

Anushka had to put in her two-pennyworth by saying, 'Sometimes dreams are true.'

'Well do you two want a tea or not?' Without waiting for an answer Tallulah made for the kitchen to put on the kettle. She hurriedly prepared the teapot, cups, saucers, sugar and milk. When the tea was ready she called James to carry it to the living room table.

He staggered slightly. 'I hope I don't spill it all, I'm feeling a bit groggy.'

At a quarter past ten, Tallulah heard a van come through the double gates. She excused herself and told Anushka and James the insurance man had just arrived. James said he felt sick and wanted to go home. He asked Anushka if she'd like a lift but she seemed to be snoozing.

'Don't worry, James, I'll see she gets home,' said Tallulah.

Anushka opened her eyes. 'I will go home with James for fresh air.' She left with James, ignoring Tallulah's desperate insistence to stay.

Tallulah found Stanley sitting in his black removals van writing in a diary.

'Just making a note of how much petrol I used to get here. I have to account for every penny you know.' Tallulah sighed at his lack of urgency, but on the other hand he'd always been pedantic and a foot-dragger in the office. He finished writing and said lightly, 'By the way, I have Porkchop in the back of the van. Can I put him in the shed? He's starving and Anushka will make a nice lunch for him.'

Tallulah told him Porkchop wouldn't be eating anyone as Anushka had left to go home with James. 'The Plan' had gone awry. By the time Stanley had finished raining verbal abuse upon Tallulah about not restraining Anushka, Porkchop's breath had steamed up the back windows.

Stanley said, 'Have you any food to give him, he hasn't eaten since last night?' He got out of the van without waiting for a reply and opened the rear doors. The pig seemed lethargic. He let himself be led to the back garden and into the shed where he flopped down on the wooden floor. She told Stanley she didn't have any animal food except what was in the garden. 'I only have apples but you'll have to get them yourself from the tree.'

'You'll have to give me a ladder, Tally.'

'It's behind the shed.'

Stanley fetched the ladder and propped it against a branch.

'Don't worry, I'll hold it for you,' Tallulah said.

Stanley climbed up to the top rung of the ladder and reached for the biggest apples.

'Tally, you *are* holding the ladder aren't you? I just have to lean over a bit further—'

As he did so, she thought about how she'd be saving Her Majesty's Government from paying him a pension if he died. She'd no idea how many thousands of pounds but the mere thought of it was enough to succumb to temptation. Without a second thought for the consequences of not having a logical plan, she pulled the ladder away from under his feet. A strangled cry came from Stanley. He tottered and flailed his arms, trying to grab a branch. She threw the ladder on the ground. He managed to grab one branch but it bent under his weight and he came down with a thud. He was out cold. The hardest part was dragging him towards the shed by his legs. Tallulah was exhausted by the time she got Stanley to the door. How could she get the door open without Porkchop escaping? He was huge and might trample her on the way out. She peeped into the shed and saw him prostrate on the floor – most likely weak from the journey and lack of food. Dragging Stanley inside, she expected the pig to seize him and start chomping, but he seemed without appetite.

Tallulah barely slept. She spent the whole night imagining the crunching of bones between one horrible dream and another. The next morning, she made herself a cup of tea and wondered what she was going to do with Stanley's van and what was left of his body. She regretted not making a plan.

A tapping at the kitchen window startled her. She turned and saw a face squashed against the glass. She screamed and dropped her teacup which bounced on the floor and broke. The face at the window belonged to Stanley. He tapped again and shouted, 'Tally, for God's sake let me in.'

She shouted, 'If you're dead just glide through the window.'

He swore and said, 'I'm not bloody-well dead. Let me in.'

When she opened the door, Stanley looked thunderous. He stank and there was a hole where his trouser pocket should have been.

'Did you try to kill me, Tally?'

'Of course I didn't. You fell from the tree and I couldn't just leave you lying in the garden all night. I put you in the shed because you were too heavy to carry into the house. The pig was sleeping. I was afraid you'd freeze to death.'

He said, 'I froze to death anyway.'

After telling Tallulah what a terrible time he'd had with a hungry pig during the early hours, he informed her the pig was dead after eating a cyanide pill from his pocket.

'Luckily the remaining ones were in my other pocket.'

He started to shiver and Tallulah put the kettle on. He pulled out the remaining cyanide pills from his other pocket and gave them to her for safe-keeping. She was tempted to put one in his tea but then she'd have the problem of getting rid of the pig, the van and Stanley.

She said, 'You can't leave Porkchop here so I suggest you take him to your mother's place. You can bury him in her garden.' Stanley quashed the idea of letting his mother see a deceased pig as she was easily upset when it came to dead animals. Tallulah suggested they brain-storm, but his brain seemed slow. She guessed he was in shock. She had to keep repeating things before the penny dropped. 'Now remember, he's full of cyanide. You can't just dump him in the countryside otherwise wild animals will eat him and you can imagine the consequences. And I can't have him lying around in the shed. If the rats eat him and the cats eat the dead rats and the dogs eat the cats, there won't be one animal left in Witherington.'

'I could dump him in the reservoir?'

'Stanley!'

'Yes?'

'He's full of cyanide. The reservoir water goes into your tap.'

'Can't I leave him outside the Wormsleys' front door?'

'No.'

Tallulah said 'absolutely not' to his ridiculous initiative of burning down the shed and having the police around to eat roast pork sandwiches, although he laughed and said he was joking. Getting rid of a poisoned, potentially hazardous pig was going to be the biggest challenge they had faced since World War II. Tallulah suggested another possibility – to have him stuffed by a taxidermist. It seemed the most fitting end and all they had to do was find someone to give him to as a present.

Tallulah made Stanley some coffee, hoping he'd wake up a bit and after two cups he seemed to be coming to his senses. With difficulty, they dragged Porkchop to the van using ropes, then slid him onto an old door, using a pulley soldered to the roof of the van to winch him in. Stanley wiped the sweat from his brow. 'Can you give me the taxidermist's telephone number? I need to call him urgently before Porkchop starts to go off.'

Tallulah sighed impatiently. 'He won't go off if he's full of cyanide. I believe they use it in the stuffing process,' she said, although she wasn't altogether sure.

Stanley drove Porkchop to the taxidermist who called a day later to say he'd found suspected human bones in the pig's lower intestine.

'If you don't want it reported to the police, I could overlook it but it'll cost you extra.' Stanley told him to forget he'd ever found the bones and to go ahead.

'Of course. Who shall I send the bill to?'

'Call me and I'll pass by and pay cash,' Stanley replied,

not wanting any trace of payment. 'Just make sure he's crated. He's a present to friends. By the way, are you any good at stuffing humans?'

'Of course I am. I stuffed my wife when she popped her clogs.'

Holy wars

Anushka gave a start as knuckles rapped her door. A shiver ran through her, thinking it might be Boris. He knew she was staying at the Wailing Willows Hotel.

Her voice shaking, she called out, 'Who is it?'

A familiar voice replied, 'There's a letter for you.'

Opening the door to James, he handed her an airmail letter with a Rome franked stamp dated 20 July 1986. With a squeal of delight she tore it open and read it aloud. *The United Fruit Organisation has the pleasure of offering you a contract as Raspberry Expert in Cuba. The contract will start from your date of travel to Rome on 25 August 1986. An air ticket will be waiting for you at London airport for London/Rome/Madrid/Havana. The duration of the contract is for two years, renewable upon satisfactory performance. You will receive a daily subsistence allowance (DSA) for Rome and DSA for one month in Havana to cover hotel expenses while you find suitable accommodation.*

It was signed by Smirnov. Throwing her arms around James's neck, she kissed him on the cheek.

'I'm happy for you, my dear. I'll miss you of course,' he said like a good sport.

'Perhaps if I get married you can come and give me away like a father.'

'I'd be delighted but might find it difficult coming to Cuba on my British passport.'

'I'll find a nice diplomat in Havana to facilitate matters,' she replied with a grin.

James beamed. 'Would you like to go for dinner tonight to celebrate?'

'I would be so honoured and happy,' Anushka replied.

At 7pm, wearing a slinky electric blue dress, Anushka knocked on James's door. He was wearing a light grey suit with pink tie and looked years younger. He told her she looked stunning. 'It's a long time since I took a beautiful woman to dinner. This calls for a special occasion,' he said, leading her to the basement garage.

The car was covered with a tarpaulin which smelt of mildew. 'I haven't driven it for some time, since Cecilia died, but it still works.' He pulled away the cover to reveal a shiny vintage Bentley. Anushka's eyes widened and she ran her hand along the bodywork and said she'd never seen such a beautiful car.

'A beautiful car for a beautiful woman,' he replied, holding the passenger door open for her. It took a few clicks of the ignition to get it started and then they were out of the garage and heading for Rottingham to an Italian restaurant in the centre of town.

'They make a delicious octopus starter with chopped raw carrot and celery. We could then have baked calamari – that is, squid stuffed with breadcrumbs and parsley, washed down with a nice bottle of wine and some Prosecco to celebrate your new job.'

The restaurant interior reflected the colours of the Italian flag – green, white and red. Anushka looked in awe at the elegant table setting – black-handled cutlery on a pristine white tablecloth, crystal glasses and a centrepiece of red and white roses around a green candle. A young waiter with a charming Italian accent pulled out a chair for her and poured Prosecco into their glasses. On a nearby table a richly-dressed older woman chatted to a young fascinatingly handsome Latin man.

After the octopus and squid starter, the waiter suggested the fish dish of the day and side plates of fried zucchini and roasted aubergine. For the dessert, it seemed they both had the same taste when they chose the cheesecake, decorated with woodland berries.

At the end of the meal, James excused himself to go to the car. He came back carrying two packages. She opened the smallest first, to find a gold brooch – a bird of paradise with flowing tail. Tears filled her eyes. No one had ever given her such a lovely present.

'It's just a small present as a thank you for all you've done for me.'

She blinked back the tears and opened the second package. Inside was a small book bound in soft black leather. On the inside page was a dedication, *To Anushka who has brought joy into my life. With love, James.*

He said he'd been honoured when she'd asked him to be her father and walk her down the aisle. He placed his hand on hers and squeezed it in a fatherly way. 'It's the Holy Bible and I thought you might like to read it. It's good philosophy and the foundation stone of Christianity and Western culture.'

She thanked him and leaned across and kissed his cheek. 'In communist countries we are unbelievers. We are brought up to believe there is no one higher than our Leader. He's our only God and the only saints we have are the martyrs of the resistance.'

James said he understood why her godless country was going to the dogs, adding, 'This book will help you understand many things about love and forgiveness.' She answered that she might have a problem forgiving Serge and Boris but that if she studied the Holy Bible it might help her get a white wedding in the Holy City.

The drive back to the hotel passed in comfortable silence, punctuated now and then by thanks and comments about a wonderful evening. He told her he'd sleep well tonight and hoped he hadn't gone over the top with the wine because if they were stopped by the police he might be arrested for drunken driving. Anushka laughed and said it was hardly likely, as it was she who had drunk more than half a bottle of Prosecco and quite a bit of the wine.

He escorted her back to her room and kissed her lightly on the cheek saying he hadn't had so much fun in a long time and she said she hadn't either.

Before falling into an inebriated sleep, she plumped up her pillow, sank her head into it, closed her eyes and smiled. Life had never been so good.

The next morning she awoke late. James had said last night he would get his own breakfast so she propped two pillows against the bedhead, opened the Bible and flicked through it. In the Old Testament, she found the wars and pestilences disturbing, ditto for the locusts, rivers running with blood and the Lord God's terrible threats in Leviticus, Chapter 26 paragraphs 28 and 29: *Then I will walk contrary unto you also in fury; and I, even I, will chastise you seven times for your sins. And ye shall eat the flesh of your sons, and the flesh of your daughters shall ye eat.*

The mere thought made her shudder. Gulags and firing squads seemed more civilised. If the Bible was the foundation stone of Christianity, she was glad to have been brought up a heathen in a country free from devastatingly hungry flying insects, plagues and forced cannibalism. The only thing she could relate to were the blood-filled rivers of past wars. She skimmed over the casting down of their carcasses and the desolation.

The New Testament was slightly less violent as there didn't seem to be much going on except towards the end. But it was a good source of the history of forgiveness. The Bible had been outlawed by the censors in communist countries. Forgiveness had meant being sent to the gulag instead of facing execution. In these countries there could never be '*love thy neighbour as thyself*' as long as neighbours secretly reported on each other, fostered by state paranoia against subversives and foreign spies. She considered this the biggest sin – to be responsible for sending a neighbour to prison to inevitable torture. On the other hand, she reflected, the holy Catholic Church of Rome had had its hands stained with blood between inquisitions and papal wars. In Moscow, instead of warring Popes they'd been plagued by the KGB whose mission was to lock up the outspoken and keep the peasants down. More or less the same thing, she thought, remembering the fortress, the Castle of the Angel, where in the distant past, the Pope's enemies had been tortured. In Moscow they had such a prison. But now she had to focus on the positive parts. The new Pope was a good man.

Ah, souls deceived, and creatures impious,
Who from such good do turn away your hearts,
Directing vanity upon your foreheads!

Dante Alighieri
The Divine Comedy: Paradise. Canto IX

AUGUST 1986

Porkchop goes home

Porkchop hovered over the taxidermist's table, watching the man with rimless glasses put finishing touches to his carcass on the pedestal. It was the first time he'd seen himself from a distance rather than just a reflection in a puddle. He marvelled at his enormous pink belly, cute curly tail and upturned snout, which gave him a regal look.

Fred arrived saying he'd been dispatched by Ernest to find out what was going on and if the bones found in Porkchop's nether region belonged to Cecilia. Luckily, they didn't. In any case, Fred offered his condolences.

Instead of being upset, Porkchop said, 'I don't want any condolences. Just look at me. Don't you think I'm magnificent? I'm far more handsome dead than I was when I was alive. I look like a prince.'

Fred had to admit he was also a lot cleaner. 'It's better to be embalmed than hang from a butcher's hook,' he said.

Porkchop was beside himself with excitement at the thought of going back to his roots where the whole of Witherington could come and admire him. He took one last look at himself on the pedestal and said, 'Let's go home.'

Fred jumped on his back and goaded him gently with his spurs. Porkchop roared with laughter and chastised Fred good-humouredly for tickling him. No one saw the ghostly couple drift upwards and out through the roof.

Whooping with joy, they did a full roll, headed north over the motorway towards Bristol, by-passed it and continued flying north-east, leaving behind the Bristol Channel.

'Can you slow down a bit?' shouted Fred over the whooshing of the wind, which was often quite strong in those parts.

'I can't, the wind's pushing us. At this rate we'll be there in about half an hour. We might have a bit of a bumpy landing though.'

Fred's crest stood on end thinking the last thing he wanted was to end up in a filthy muddy field by a pigsty. 'Can you land in the graveyard near Ernest's tomb?'

'I'll try, but I can't guarantee we won't end up in a tree.'

'Give it a try,' replied Fred, preferring the tree to a field full of slops.

Elsie Wormsley awoke with a start. Bert was snoring. She shook him. He turned over, half-asleep.

'What's going on?'

'I heard a van.'

'What time is it?'

'It's time you were up for work,' she said, sitting up in bed in the dark.

Bert groaned and pulled the covers over his head while Elsie slid her legs over the side of the bed and felt around for her slippers. She knew where her dressing gown was hanging with her eyes shut.

'Get up, Bert. They could be running off with our cows.'

He wanted to get up. His cows were precious. But he seemed to be a ton weight on the bed.

Elsie said, 'I'm going to have a look.'

Bert tried to dissuade her telling her it was her imagination, but she told him it wasn't.

'Can't you hear them?'

'No.'

Bert was half deaf.

Taking a small torch from the bedside table, Elsie crept stealthily down the stairs, quietly slid back the bolts on the back door and looked outside. There was a chill in the air but no one in sight. She took Bert's shotgun from the laundry room and moved slowly on the path leading to the front of the house. By the light of the August moon she could see a black van with 'Removals' written on it. Four burly men had a crate on their shoulders, as if they were carrying a coffin. With a menacing voice and brandishing Bert's shotgun she said, 'Get your hands up, you bloody criminals.'

One of them said, 'We can't, we've got our hands full.'

She felt their pockets to make sure they weren't armed. The first man spoke. 'It's a gift from a well-wisher. There's a note attached.'

Elsie said, 'Wait here,' and retraced her steps. She opened the front door from the inside and told them to bring the crate inside.

'Where do you want it, missus?'

'Just put it in the living room.'

After the men had left, she tore open a note on the crate and read it.

Dear Mr and Mrs Wormsley,

I write to thank you for giving me Porkchop, who kept my mother company for some time. Porkchop was her pride and joy and they became very good friends. He was happy with all her attention. I don't think any pig could have wished for a better life. I'm sending him back so he can be in the place he loved the most. Enjoy his company.

Yours sincerely,

Stanley.

Elsie imagined Porkchop running around the field and

wallowing in the mud. She gave a cry of joy and started to remove the tape on the crate. She shouted up the stairs, 'Come quick, Bert, come and see who's home alive and well.'

She couldn't wait to kiss her darling Porkchop and give him his breakfast. She certainly didn't expect to see him dead, stuffed and mounted on a pedestal.

Her screams could be heard clear across Witherington and it was only 5am.

A looming divorce

Councillor Ignatius Wheeler came home to his wife, the second sobbing woman today. His assistant Mrs Horsefield had cried on and off all morning without knowing why. He'd heard her muttering about 'the bloody curse,' whatever *that* was.

He hung up his coat in the hall. 'How was your day?' he asked Gladys.

'So, so,' she replied. It was the usual question with the same answer but her expression was different.

'What's up, Gladys?'

'Oh nothing.'

Two little words which often led to a tempest blowing through their house.

'Out with it.'

'I feel lonely, Ignatius. You're out all day and Roland hasn't called me for a while.'

As soon as Roland's name was pronounced, he made for the stairs and locked himself in the bathroom.

She ran after him and thumped on the door screaming, 'I want a divorce.'

'Don't be ridiculous, Gladys, we're having a community event soon. You can wear your new dress.'

She stopped in her tracks. 'You didn't tell me you were organising a party.'

'I was going to tell you when I get back from the pub.'

'You're always in the pub these days.'

He told her he wouldn't go there if she wasn't always snivelling about Roland.

Gladys burst into tears. 'I never talk to a soul the whole week apart from next door's dog and the postman.'

'I'll buy you a dog of your own for Christmas if you stop being ridiculous,' he said, unlocking the bathroom door.

'Roland wanted a dog but you said they were running with fleas.'

He said, 'Mention his name one more time I'm going out.'

Gladys did mention Roland's name once more and Ignatius left for the pub slamming the door behind him. Refusing to be treated like a doormat, she decided she definitely wanted a divorce. Roland had a decent job and would help support her or maybe ask her to live with him. Sitting in front of the open grate, she wondered how she could wear her evening dress at the community event with Ignatius and be divorced at the same time. Shortly afterwards she put on her cardigan and headed for the Bull and Bullocks. She needed an excuse to get divorced and if he was always in the pub it meant just one thing – he had another woman.

Sneaking around the outside of the pub, she looked through a window and saw him sitting in an alcove with an empty beer glass. Pacing up and down for ten minutes she looked in again. He was still alone and sitting over another pint staring into froth, his face tight and drawn. He blew his nose into a handkerchief and put his head in his hands. She waited another fifteen minutes and knew there was no other woman. She actually felt sorry for him.

Walking inside, he didn't look up as she strode over to his table and sat opposite. She put her hand on his arm. 'Let's talk about the good times, Iggy.'

Looking surprised, he said, 'What will you have?'

'The usual gin and tonic.'

'Mother's ruin?' It was corny but they both laughed. He went to the bar and came back with two gin and tonics and some crisps. A comfortable silence ensued as they drank and picked at the crisps.

He said, 'Do you remember the day we went fishing and I fell into the river and got tadpoles in my boots? It was a lovely day. I remember the picnic and the cake you made with seven candles for Roland's birthday.'

'Yes, I do,' she said, pleased he'd mentioned Roland's name without heading for the toilet.

It was almost closing time when they left the pub. Outside, Ignatius put his arm around her shoulder. 'You were a good mother,' he said.

Gladys noticed he didn't mention whether or not she'd been a good wife and left it at that. No point in spoiling a beautiful evening.

Inside the house they hugged each other and Ignatius went up to use the bathroom first. Gladys quickly put *Agriculture and Business Monthly* on the breakfast table and left it open at Veronica's letter on coitus. They climbed into bed and slept closer together, both feeling the need for some human warmth. At some time during the night she felt her nightdress sliding down and Ignatius' warm naked body next to hers.

The next morning Gladys didn't get up to make his breakfast and he didn't wake her. Relaxed, she slept in until around 10am. When she went down for breakfast the magazine had gone. It was time to change her life and write a letter.

Dear Veronica,

Last night I became sexually liberated but now I want to be liberated from the kitchen sink and male mindsets. I am an avid reader of your magazine, but I fail to see anything of interest about women's liberation in your columns. This is deplorable for a magazine which supposedly addresses women's rights and equality. I would like to smoke a pipe but my husband doesn't allow me to do anything. By the way, my son and husband are still not speaking to each other.

Regards,

Quite dissatisfied.

Respect thy awful elders

Anushka's decision to leave had left James slightly depressed. On top of that, the travel agent continued to harass him for a decision over the Serge Gallo balloons and payment for flyers to advertise the rooms. There was too much going on and he felt giddy just thinking of Tallulah, the cryonics project and the four-minute warning siren.

Last night, after 10pm, an hour he considered beyond the rules of decency, Tallulah had shouted down the phone and asked when the siren was going operational. 'Soon,' he'd replied. The lie had been an immediate panacea but the night was long and he spent it thinking of excuses as to why he hadn't yet delivered.

Her call came the next morning. She skipped the niceties and said in her usual brusque manner, 'Are we going on another dummy run?'

Luckily, during the night, he'd rehearsed his reaction to any pressing questions.

'I'm afraid I'm ill. I have serious sciatica.' His theatrical voice faded feebly.

Tallulah said, 'Can you come and pick me up tomorrow?'

'My knee hurts and I can't press the accelerator.'

'Call me when you're better.' She rang off.

James wiped his brow and walked along the corridor practising a limp. As the morning progressed, it was to be expected that Roland would be in the shower when he needed him most.

'I'm dripping wet, James, can I call you back? It'll take me a while to dry my hair.'

'Cut it all off, it's far too long. It'll be past your shoulders soon. In my day—'

'Thank you, James, when I need your opinion, I'll ask for it.'

When Roland finally called back, James could tell by the tone of his voice that the day would deteriorate even further. He asked Roland when they could get the siren sorted as Tallulah was putting him under pressure.

Roland said, 'We've permission to build it but the police won't allow it. It'll make too much noise if it goes off in the middle of the night.'

James felt a panic attack blowing through him. 'I've got a commitment to fulfil and I couldn't give a damn about waking people up in the middle of the night. If your father signed it, then it's legal. No one's going to complain about a bit of noise.'

Roland replied stonily, 'Dad was under duress when he signed it.'

James certainly remembered. He'd been threatened by Councillor Wheeler for calling Roland a liar.

'I'm entitled to build a siren, no matter how noisy, on my property and why are you defending your father? I thought you hated him?'

Roland said, 'What would you do if he was your father? Wouldn't you defend your own flesh and blood?'

It seemed denial ran in the Wheeler family.

James said, 'My father was an upstanding member of the community and I never lied, so we never had this problem. It's probably because we were nobility; we were brought up on good honest morals and manners.'

'Get lost, James.'

'You should have more respect for your elders. If you're staying in my hotel it's thanks to me and my upstanding family you're here.'

'Get stuffed. I don't get the room for free. And if I don't tell you to fuck off it's because I'm a gentleman and respect old people.'

The line went dead and James's palpitations started.

Blatant fraud

Arriving at the town hall before opening hours, Mrs Horsefield collapsed into her chair. It was 8.30am and she was tired and irritable. The morning had started off badly when her fifteen-year-old son Webber had made a comment 'Britain would be better off with a communist government' and, losing her temper, had offered to buy him a ticket to visit Stalin's concentration camps. Expecting a further deterioration to her day, she was pleasantly surprised when Councillor Wheeler arrived whistling and smiling. He asked for his coffee and made a request.

'I'd be grateful if you could organise a community party and ask Veronica to be our guest speaker.' It was the first time she'd seen him looking happy since he'd kicked Roland out of the house.

'Who do you want to invite? We don't have enough funds for a lot of people.'

'Invite those who've made a contribution to Witherington or who've done something outstanding.'

'Does it mean I have to exclude the other councillors?' she said sarcastically.

He rolled his eyes and waved her out of the office.

For the second morning running, Mrs Horsefield awoke with doom's dark cloud hanging over her. She was barely through the town hall door when Councillor Wheeler asked her if she'd organised the community party.

'I can't perform miracles. We don't have a date yet,' she snapped.

'Never mind. I've been reading Veronica's articles and I'm impressed. She's got a good head on her shoulders. I want her to give a talk on *love and harmony in the family*. Write her a letter and get a venue.'

'It won't be easy. I have other work to do as well. There'll be crowds and queues in here any minute now.'

'Put everything else on hold and just do it.'

Quickly scribbling a notice which read, 'Town hall closed until further notice', she taped it to the outside door while braving the disgruntled hordes and running the gauntlet of abuse.

Thumping on her Olivetti, she drafted the letter and put it in front of him.

Dear Veronica,

Councillor Wheeler has the honour to invite you to speak at a cultural evening at ...... on .... 1986 to talk about.......

She left out the date and venue to fill in later, knowing it would change several times before he'd make a final decision.

Councillor Wheeler studied his pen. 'I was thinking of inviting the local Masonic lodge.'

Mrs Horsefield said she wasn't into lodges. 'I thought it was going to be a cultural evening for the whole community? We don't want the Masons here. They don't have any women in their ranks,' she objected, deciding to speak up for women's rights.

Councillor Wheeler stared at the ceiling and muttered, 'I don't want to invite all and sundry and every Tom, Dick and Harry, however, I have to think of my re-election.'

'We could have the party in the streets of Witherington, you know, like after the war,' she said.

'Absolutely not. Who's going to pay for all the rubbish left on the streets the next day?'

'We can get the girl guides and boy scouts out.'

'We'll be accused of child labour.'

'We could hold it in the school playing fields?'

'Just get on and organise it. We'll think of the logistics later. We can always do a raffle.'

Mrs Horsefield felt her face getting hot. 'I don't like loose ends. It's no use inviting Veronica until we get things sorted out, if we don't know where the venue's going to be,' she said, her vacillating hormones giving her courage to speak out.

'Just be vague. We want to book her in advance in case she's got a full diary.'

Mrs Horsefield called in to see Antonio who was stocking up his shop just in case Gladys Wheeler, the British Godfather's mad wife called about food for the nuclear shelter. He'd just got back from Sicily and beautiful weather. 'Very good food and wine,' he told her.

She outlined the plan in simple language. 'We are having a community party with sandwiches on plastic plates in the streets. I want to order food on behalf of Councillor Wheeler.'

Antonio's neck turned red. He grimaced and asked her how much food.

She said, 'No pasta. No buns. We need thin bread and margarine and tinned fish, big fat wurstels, small gherkins and chucky eggs.'

Antonio began to sweat. First the British Godfather's wife had ordered him around and now it was the Godfather's horsey assistant. He picked up the pen next to his order book and doodled an aeroplane in flight towards Sicily.

'For how many people?'

'About one thousand.'

Antonio drew an airline ticket on his pad. 'Who is going to pay?'

'To be truthful I don't know yet.'

Antonio felt the sweat recede and he relaxed. 'Then I cannot order food.'

She told him the money would come from the raffle.

'The order is too big for my van. You can ask a catering firm. In my country we do not stand around with little sandwiches on plastic plates. We sit down at community tables in countryside and have big whopping meal. We sit down and eat for four hours. We sing and dance and drink good wine then we make love. Our women know their place.'

'You are lucky to have such a faithful wife,' she replied.

She saw his right hand disappear below the counter and imagined he was grasping his balls superstitiously, in the true Italian fashion, to stave off the evil eye and, in this case, to keep his wife pure and himself from being added to the list of village cuckolds. She tried to pacify him by saying, 'Antonio, you are as handsome as Al Pacino,' but Antonio's lips tightened. He made it clear he was proud and didn't like to be compared to a short-arsed American actor fraudulently posing as a Sicilian. He was a man of honour.

The long and short of it was a major disaster looming as long as Antonio refused to supply the food.

Mrs Horsefield decided to call Councillor Bacon's wife, who she knew she could count on to do some catering, being a woman of good sense. After asking her if the Women's Institute could make some smoky bacon sandwiches for the buffet dance, the first thing Mrs Bacon said was, 'Who's footing the bill?'

'Probably the council.'

The woman asked indignantly why the money was coming out of council coffers and didn't see why the taxpayer had to foot the bill. Mrs Horsefield then corrected herself, apologised and said it was probably coming from a raffle.

'How many people are coming?'

'About one thousand, but they may not all come. In September a lot of people might be on holiday.'

Mrs Bacon drew in breath and breathed fire down the phone. Her breath could have cooked a ton of rashers. 'It sounds a ridiculous idea to me. Where did you say you were having it?'

'We haven't decided yet.'

Mrs Bacon's breath got hotter. 'Call me when you decide.'

It started to look as if the community spirit had gone elsewhere when the school gave a sharp 'No' to her request to hold the party in the playing fields, stating the mess afterwards. The only other possible venue was the grounds of the Church of Local Martyrs but she suspected Reverend Pontius Pottering was more interested in saving souls than having the community tramping across his pitch. In any case Councillor Wheeler was against it. 'Find another venue,' he said tersely.

'Can we decide on a date?'

'When we've found a venue.'

'I can't until we have a date.'

Suffering from nerves and exhaustion, Mrs Horsefield took the next two days off sick and only returned to inform her boss the community party would be held in the streets of Witherington whether he liked it or not. The first thing she decided to do was to hold out an olive branch to Antonio just in case she needed him in an emergency but Antonio didn't answer the phone and there was a notice on his shop door, 'Closed for holiday'.

In the absence of Antonio, offers flooded in to help with the catering. The Mothers' Union and Women's Institute agreed to provide sandwiches and sausages, while Reverend Pottering's wife said she could organise the baking of pasties, cakes, scones and some foreign food. Mrs Horsefield busied herself organising a local band which would charge two pounds each to cover costs and any monies left over to be donated to charity. The Lions Club of Rottingham agreed to support any community initiative and could supply tables and chairs at no cost, to be delivered and placed all the way down the High Street to the town hall. They generously offered to hang lights and flags and throw in gallons of wine, beer and soft drinks, their wives helping with the serving.

Councillor Wheeler wasn't so pleased. 'I hope they're not going to interfere with our politics,' he said grimly. At the end of her tether for the day, Mrs Horsefield snapped and told him to shut up. Councillor Wheeler opened his mouth to reply but kept quiet, fearing mutiny in the air and worried he'd be left organising everything himself. He said, 'Just get on with it and have some respect for authority. I don't like your tone.'

Mrs Horsefield downed tools and picked up her bag.

'I've had enough for today. And if you don't like it you can lump it.'

Councillor Wheeler, left with his mouth open at her subordination, said feebly, 'Make sure you're here early tomorrow. We have to send out the letter to Veronica now we have a venue.'

She said, 'I've already sent it.'

'But I haven't signed it yet.'

'I forged your signature.'

Backing Britain

Scarlett handed Roland two letters. One was from a dissatisfied woman who had just been sexually liberated and needed advice and the second was from Councillor Wheeler, inviting Veronica to give a speech at the community party on love and harmony in the family. Roland's lips tightened and he swore under his breath. 'I'm not dressing up as a bloody woman.'

'Remember we're here to also represent the people of diverse genders.'

'You never mentioned that when you gave me the job.'

'I didn't say it explicitly but I expected your brain to open a little and read between the lines of what equality means.'

'You never said I'd have to dress up as a woman and make a fool of myself.'

'No one'll know it's you and it'll be good publicity. Sales will rocket.'

'I'm not doing it. It was a mistake to write under a woman's name.'

'You didn't seem to mind when you desperately needed a job.'

Roland said, 'I need a holiday,' and stormed out.

Scarlett shouted after him, 'Get your life into perspective.'

At the Hammock Travel Agency in Rottingham a big poster in the window read *Back Britain and uphold the economy*. The travel clerk looked over the top of her glasses at a young man with long hair and a black coat who said his name was Roland.

'I want to get away from Witherington for a week or so,' he said.

'We have a cheap weekend in Blackpool.' She handed him a brochure. Roland shook his head. He said a place where the British mafia raked in the money was the last place he wanted to be. She told him he had got it wrong.

'I was thinking more of swaying palm trees. Something a bit more exotic?'

'How about Clacton?'

Roland said he'd never been there but that the name sounded unexciting and conjured up 1960s donkeys on the beach and cylinder-shaped rock with 'Clacton' running through it. This time she laughed and told him he didn't know what he was missing as it wasn't at all like that.

'What about the Amazon rainforest?' he asked hopefully.

'You'll love it if you don't mind giant spiders, snakes, leeches and piranhas which you can see at London Zoo. I have a B&B in London at a special price?'

'No thanks.'

She said, 'What about the Wailing Willows Hotel in Witherington? There's a special offer and the chance to have tea and scones for an extra pound at a house where Serge Gallo the intrepid explorer used to live.'

Roland stifled a few swear words, picked a brochure out of politeness and left. A delicious smell led him to a chippy. Where else in the world could he get real fish and chips? Definitely not in the Amazon. He sat on a bench in Rottingham park and ate his fish with gusto. The park bench turned out to be a lesson in living. Next to him a tramp was feeding pigeons with what was left of his sandwich.

'Would you like some chips?' Roland asked. The man looked at him with a smile.

'No thanks, my pigeons don't eat rubbish.'

Roland thought the man's philosophy sounded like good sense and he left him there, while pondering on the meaning of honest cleaning-living life. The bus ride back to Witherington cleared his mind and the first thing he did upon entering the office was apologise to Scarlett for walking out. When he said he would dress up as Veronica, she forgot her anger and said she was delighted. 'Veronica is important to the people of Witherington. You can make a difference. You can change mindsets. You're a celebrity now and it doesn't matter whether you're a man or woman.'

Tottering inferno

In preparation for his debut as *Veronica* at the community party, Roland was foolish enough to sleep all night with plastic rollers in his long hair. The next morning it took half an hour to untangle his locks. At the office by 9am, he told Scarlett it had been the worst night of his life and akin to sleeping on a hedgehog.

She wasn't sympathetic. 'Women throughout the British Isles and probably the rest of the world, sleep in them every night, so stop complaining.'

'I want a wig,' Roland insisted. Scarlett sighed and said she had an old blonde one and she'd call Tallulah to retrieve it. The next step, she said, was to get *Veronica* to practise being sexy or at the very least, fascinating. Delving into the filing cabinet she brought out the green velvet dress and purple feather boa Tallulah had provided and a pair of red shoes with five inch stiletto heels and pointed toes.

'Put these shoes on, I'm going to teach you how to walk like a woman,' she said, brushing off his groans and complaints as he took off his socks and forced his feet into them. He stood up and tottered and then sat down again.

'These winkle-pickers are killing me. They're like walking on stilts.'

'You'll get used to them. For heaven's sake, try and walk with grace. Ginger Rogers danced backwards on them, so stop whining.'

Roland stood up and took a few steps across the room towards the window, holding onto chairs, waxing poetry. '*She left the web, she left the gloom, she took three paces through the room—*'

'Stand up straight and roll your hips a bit more,' Scarlett said, as Roland swayed from side to side grumbling he'd have a dislocated pelvis before long.

Their appointment at the town hall was for 11am. After having had his face painted, he lurched across the office towards the bathroom. Looking at himself in the mirror, he certainly looked like a sexy young woman, except for the missing tits.

'Don't worry we can pass by the greengrocers on the way and pick up a couple of oranges,' Scarlett said.

'I'd prefer a couple of melons. Everyone'll be too busy looking at my tits to notice if I talk a load of rubbish.'

'You're not supposed to have a mindset about sexist attitudes. But if it means it makes you more confident, then I suppose we'd better go to the shop.'

In the end they chose two identical unripe cantaloupes. Driving down the High Street in Scarlett's car, they noticed a poster stuck to a wall announcing an event in Witherington being attended by Veronica. Sensing Roland's nervousness, Scarlett said, 'You'll be in the hall of fame before you know it.'

Roland said he wasn't keen on his true identity being completely obliterated.

After parking the car, Scarlett took Roland's elbow as he tottered towards the town hall saying his toes were on fire. 'Remember, walk with grace and stand up straight, you're hunched like an old woman. You're now Veronica. Forget Roland exists for the moment.'

'Can we spend the night together after this charade?' he asked.

'Concentrate on what you're doing.'

'Well can we?'

'Oh, all right.' She wished he'd think of something other than sex, although she did always wake up feeling good afterwards.

Roland decided then and there, he wanted to marry her.

Scarlett said, 'By the way, I forgot to tell you. On the day of the party if you want a pee, use the ladies toilet and keep out of the gents unless you want to start a stampede in your direction.'

Roland shuddered at the mere thought of the ladies toilets. It reminded him of the nasty incident swatting Goliath from under the toilet door with his notepad and being stuck there until the police rescued him.

Mrs Horsefield showed Scarlett and *Veronica* into Councillor Wheeler's office and sat down in his chair, inviting them to make themselves comfortable in the two chairs on the opposite side of the desk. Apologising for the councillor's absence, she went over what they could expect on the day of the party and added, 'It's to drum up the community spirit many people experienced when the war ended in 1945. However, I want to make it clear that it has nothing whatsoever to do with Councillor Wheeler's re-election campaign. The party will start in late afternoon and go on until midnight and people will pay two pounds each to cover the cost of the band.'

Mrs Horsefield addressed Roland. 'Now about your speech, Veronica, I was thinking of around 6pm. What do you think?'

Roland put on his best falsetto voice. 'Fine with me. As long as there's still food on the tables. I don't want to be talking to a ferocious crowd of starving farmers.'

Under the wig, his head started to itch. The itching spread to his neck and shoulders. He jumped up and tottered towards the door saying, 'Sorry, I need to spend a penny.'

Scratching his crotch, Roland rushed into the gents forgetting he was supposed to be a woman. He came face to face with his father, Councillor Wheeler, who was buttoning up his flies.

Waiting for *Veronica* to return, Scarlett made small talk about the local band and monies in excess. They agreed upon a donation to an animal shelter and the old people's home. In the middle of their discussion, the door opened and Councillor Wheeler walked in with *Veronica*. Mrs Horsefield noted he was smiling, even though she was sitting in his chair.

'Has the party started already?' he asked good-humouredly.

Mrs Horsefield offered him a cup of tea.

'Yes please and make one for Veronica too, I caught her in the men's toilets.' He gave Veronica a wink. *Veronica*'s face turned bright red and looked sweaty. Alarm bells rang for Scarlett. She'd forgotten to apply deodorant to *Veronica*'s hairy armpits. Luckily Tallulah's dress was permeated with Eden by Cacharel and she hoped it would cover perspiration odours.

The perfumed Garden of Eden now hung in the office and seemed to have a strange effect on Councillor Wheeler who moved closer to *Veronica* to get a better sniff.

The mad British

Mr Kim was not impressed. He was surprised at the slowness of the British postal service, considering everything else in the British capitalist Isles seemed to be working beyond his expectations. Was it possible someone in the house, Stanley or Santeros, had steamed his letter open, read it and forgotten to replace it for a few days? Inside the envelope was a short letter from Veronica saying his book was ready and available at her office.

After dressing carefully in his best black suit and tie, a short drive took him to the Wailing Willows Hotel where James Willows tore greenery from the ground in front of a rhododendron bush. Mr Kim was about to compliment James on collecting herbs and edible grasses for lunch when he realised he was pulling weeds. It was another mystery of the British Isles. In *his* glorious country the whole community scattered seeds, reaped and collected the food and edible grasses. Time was precious and divided between work and education sessions. There was no time to waste on futile independent activities. When there was weeding to be done, the peasants would move like a plague of locusts across the communal land singing 'Song of the Red Flag'. The onus was on collectivisation and community harmony. It was no place for dodgy free-thinkers. Upon his arrival in the United Kingdom, Mr Kim had expected to see only cows, green fields, cabbages and rain and so it was a nice surprise to find automation and efficiency in many parts. In the latest diplomatic dispatches to his father at the United Nations in New

York, he'd mentioned the amazing British economic *Great Leap Forward*, which he hoped would not end in disaster like the great leap backward of Mao Tse-tung.

Poking his head out of the car window, Mr Kim greeted James. 'Good day to you, old man. I wish to pay you my respects.'

'I'm not *that* old,' replied James, adding, 'If you're looking for the funeral home, it's not here.' Mr Kim smiled and regretted being dressed entirely in black. 'I wish to speak to Miss Scarlett.'

James stuttered, 'Good heavens, is Tallulah dead? She was supposed to call me first.'

Mr Kim couldn't understand why James then staggered and propped himself up with the rake.

'I wish to speak to Miss Scarlett,' he repeated.

'Of course, come in, come in. I'll take you to her. She should be informed.'

When the office door was flung open, Scarlett was talking to Roland, who was wearing Tallulah's dress – the one she'd worn in Paris and her high heeled shoes. James threw his arms in the air and shouted, 'She's not long gone and already you're dividing up her things.' He then fled, leaving Mr Kim perplexed and wondering if all British people were mad. The office fell silent. He supposed the one with the shoulder length red hair was Miss Scarlett.

He said in stilted English, 'Mrs Tallulah is not dead. At least she was not the last time I saw her.'

Scarlett said she felt faint and rushed for the phone. She called Tallulah's number. Someone answered and words were exchanged. Scarlett said she would pop by this evening. She replaced the phone and sank into her chair. 'She's still alive,' she announced.

Mr Kim said, 'Perhaps Mr James has mental illness of imaginings because he lives alone?'

Scarlett nodded.

'We do not have such problems in my country. Our old people are taken care of by the family and they do not live alone.'

Scarlett couldn't verify the facts and was too stressed to explain about independent choices.

Mr Kim said, 'I have come for my book and to meet Veronica.'

Scarlett pointed to Roland who tottered across the office in high heels and held out his hand.

'I'm Veronica,' said Roland, 'and proud and honoured to meet you.'

Mr Kim looked at Veronica's hand. It was very large and she had stubble on her face as if she was growing a beard. She had a deep voice and hairy legs and walked as if her legs were not well connected to her feet. In his country women were more feminine and demure. Perhaps she was a half man? In his country, men didn't dress like women and wear heavy make-up. Nor did they have breasts like melons.

Scarlett said, 'I suppose you've come for your book, Mr Kim?'

He bowed politely. 'Thank you.' He took it from her, turned on his heel and quickly left.

In the car on the way home, Mr Kim reflected on his encounter with the old man who should be in a lunatic asylum and the strange young man/woman who should be there also. On the other hand, he'd had first-hand experience of the diversity of aspects of the British culture. If he'd known then what he knew now, he'd have added it to his book – *The proud British race sometimes digresses from normal practices. Imperialistic democracy affects their brains.*

A new thought materialised in his mind. Perhaps this new experience and understanding of the capitalist world would qualify him for a job as a diplomat at the United Nations, seeing as some Member States hadn't yet worked out how to be diplomatic with North Korea.

After work, Scarlett called in to tell Tallulah about James's bizarre reaction to seeing Roland in her dress.

'James seems to be losing his marbles. Do you trust him?' Scarlett asked.

In reply Tallulah said, 'Let's open a bottle of red wine and forget about the rest of the world.'

'I didn't bring any red wine.'

'Then I'll bring out the gin and tonic.'

Tallulah disappeared into the sitting room and came back with two glasses and the two bottles. She poured them both a drink. 'Here's to us and sod the rest of them.'

'Yes, here's to us and let's forget the bloody idiots. By the way, can I spend the night here as I don't want to be breathalysed on my way home?'

'Your bed's already made up and you can move back in if you want.'

'I'm almost living with Roland,' she blurted out, not quite sure why.

She expected her aunt to make a disparaging comment but all she said was, 'Let's celebrate then. I always liked him. Are you getting married?'

'He hasn't asked me yet.'

Tallulah gazed into space. 'How nice. I remember when I first met Stanley, he was so handsome and romantic—'

'I thought you hated him?'

'That came later.'

They retired to the living room where Scarlett flopped

exhausted into an armchair and dozed off helped by the drone of Tallulah's voice as she recounted the most romantic moments of her life.

Wild expectations

James didn't expect the electrician to laugh so heartily when he asked the man if he could connect an electric cable between Tallulah's house and his by Friday.

'You must be joking, mate. You can't get anything done in a hurry around here. First you have to get permission to put a cable across someone's land and then you have to ask the electricity board to do it. Months or years could pass.'

'What about laying it under the ground?'

'It'll cost you a fortune.'

The first thing James did was to call the Wormsleys to ask permission to cross their land with the cable. 'I can offer you one thousand pounds as compensation.'

Bert thought for a moment. 'I'll have to ask Elsie.'

James heard Elsie mumbling in the background, 'Yes if you buy me a new settee.'

Bert came back with, 'That's fine with me. Just make sure you're not doing anything illegal because if you are, I'll deny I ever spoke to you.'

'I'm sure it's not illegal.' But James wasn't sure. And what if he electrocuted the cows?

Sitting on the settee in the living room, James took stock of his health. All seemed to be functioning properly except his brain. He could remember things in the distant past like Cecilia dancing *Swan Lake* and Tallulah crying in the lobby of the Paris hotel when he left her, and Vera Lynn crooning about meeting someone again somewhere. But he was unable to recall more recent events such as the lead-up to Cecilia's death. As for his new job as cryonics manager, he couldn't seem to reconcile the planning with the practical side. Spending nights in his cold lonely bed had only accentuated his desire to share it with someone. But it seemed he was destined to sleep alone.

Tallulah received a call at 9am as she was about to go into Witherington. In a rush she picked up the phone and shouted, 'For heaven's sake, Stanley, what do you want? I'm already late.'

She heard James's voice say, 'Who the hell is Stanley?'

'He's a friend of mine and it's none of your business. Did you finish the siren?'

James replied, 'Not yet.'

'I could be dead and buried by the time you get it finished.'

'Sorry, but it won't be long now. I'm waiting for some inspiration.'

'Get your act together or you'll be fired.' Her words shook him down to his slippers.

He was on a last-ditch stand. 'Tallulah, I apologise for jilting you. I want you to warm my back. I want to invite you to spend the night with me. I want to feel your body next to mine.'

Tallulah put on her icy voice before she put down the phone. 'Have you taken leave of your senses? You're not getting anywhere near my body.'

It was predictable Stanley would call.

He said, 'The end is nigh for democracy. We've been sold out. The communists are winning. We'll all be bones and dust before long. The world and Christianity is coming to an end.'

'What's going on?'

'According to the CIA, in the next few days, a probable nuclear attack will be on the agenda of the United Nations.'

Tallulah snorted, 'I've never heard such rubbish. The United Nations don't get their agendas together *that* quick.'

He replied, 'If we're all going to die in a fireball, we might as well enjoy ourselves. How about spending the night with me? Remember our wonderful romantic times together?' Stanley asked.

'You never were romantic and I've already accepted an offer from James,' she lied.

Hard dirty talk

Today, Ernest felt well disposed towards Cecilia. She'd helped him clean up his dusty police uniform and helmet by combing them with twigs. Her attention had then turned to Fred who was complaining about mites until she dragged him, clucking and protesting, into the nearest pond. She seemed to be in the mood of wanting to please. Ernest took advantage and visited her later holding his Serious Incident Report. 'Tell me about the night you died. Start from when you got up dead from the driveway,' Ernest prompted Cecilia.

'After I died, I wandered around the garden looking for the night watchman.'

'The one you were intimate with?'

Cecilia blushed. 'He wasn't there and I supposed he'd gone to the pub.'

'Wasn't he supposed to be guarding the hotel?'

'It was his night off.'

'About your missing foot. Is it possible he cut it off because he had a fetish about feet?'

'No. He said mine were beautiful.'

'When was the last time you saw him?'

'The night before my death.'

'Where?'

'In his room.'

'Tell me about the plumber's assistant.'

'He was a horrible young man who talked dirty double meanings. He kept looking at my legs.'

'Did he find you in room sixty-nine with the night watchman?'

'No.'

'Did you roll around in the mud naked in the middle of winter?'

'Don't be ridiculous, Ernest, it was bloody freezing.'

'He seems to have told the whole of Witherington you did.'

'He was shit stirring.'

'Could he have had a reason to sever your foot?'

'I can't think of one. But he did say once, I looked good enough to eat.'

The interrogation of Cecilia had turned out to be frustratingly inconclusive and Ernest decided to pay James a visit. He waited until he'd slipped into the dark dungeon of nightmares, before asking if they could go over what happened the day Cecilia died and if he'd anything to add. James mentioned a ghostly shadow on the wall as he chased Cecilia up the stairs.

'Did you mention it to the police?' Ernest asked.

'Certainly not. I could hardly tell them I see the dead.'

'Is there anything else you didn't tell them?'

'Yes, a knife was missing from the kitchen. It was antique and had the Wailing Willows crest on it. I didn't immediate notice it wasn't there.'

'Did you use the knife to cut off Cecilia's foot?'

James stiffened and his nostrils widened. His face flushed as blood rushed up his jugular. He was about to blow a fuse. Ernest was quick to take the emergency in hand. 'I'm not accusing you but I need to eliminate you from the investigation by asking certain questions.

'I had no reason to want her foot. I'm not into touching the dead. As a police officer you should be asking yourself who had a compelling reason to remove it. Perhaps someone who has a fetish for feet? Or someone who's used to managing knives like the butcher. Or someone not afraid of touching corpses – try the funeral home. Just for your information I hate the sight of blood and would have used poison instead if I'd really wanted to get rid of my wife.'

Ernest scribbled James's answers on his pad, adding, 'If you are found to be withholding any evidence, this interview may be used against you in a court of law.'

'Don't be bloody stupid, Ernest, you can't arrest me. You're no longer a police officer and in any case you're dead.'

Ernest slunk off to look for a comforting friend.

Back at the graveyard Ernest looked around for Fred but all he found was a tail feather sitting next to a letter – an apology for his absence. It explained in brief about Bertha's incursion into Witherington to listen to the latest gossip. The information she'd picked up was alarming. Anushka Petrova was about to depart for another trip to Rome to visit an organisation known for political assassinations. Consequently, Cecilia, Bertha and himself had decided to investigate. And, if they had time, they'd visit the Pope to ask if Cecilia could take her washing machine to Heaven. A postscript had been added – Cecilia couldn't take any more of his interrogations which she said were 'extenuatingly invasive and downright nosy.'

Ernest took to his bed.

Flight to danger

Today was 25 August, the first day of her contract. She was going to Rome on the first leg of her journey to Cuba. Leaving her room, Anushka saw Roland staring perplexedly at her suitcase in the corridor. She hadn't told him she was leaving. He gave her a cursory glance then turned his back on her and walked away.

'Roland!' she shouted running after him.

He turned sharply and raised his hands. 'Don't bother explaining or apologising. I'll get over it.' He stomped down the corridor and she let him go without a word.

James drove Anushka to London airport where they bid a sad farewell. He pressed an envelope into her hands. It contained two hundred pounds on top of an extra month's salary she wasn't really entitled to. He took her hands and kissed them.

'What about the money I owe you for my wedding dress and the rest?' she asked.

'You can give it to me the next time we meet.' She knew he was being kind as there was no guarantee of ever seeing each other again. She imagined he was watching her as she walked towards the terminal.

At the ticket desk, Anushka collected her tickets for Rome/Madrid/Havana. After checking in her baggage, she walked through the security check without incident and headed for passport control. No one noticed her false passport and she was free to take the flight to the Eternal City.

Two and a half hours later her flight landed in Rome at 5pm with three stowaways aboard – Fred, Cecilia and Bertha. Taking a taxi from the airport to the Castle Hotel in Piazza Cavour, Anushka had no idea she had three free-riders. The trio alighted at the hotel and flew towards the Vatican City, a few minutes away as the crow flies.

The hotel room was basic but comfortable. This one didn't have ugly wallpaper or mould in the bathroom. The walls were white, the furniture dark wood and the furnishings reflected good Italian taste. She was about to climb under the pristine white sheet when the phone rang.

'Good evening, Anushka, this is Smirnov. I hope you've settled in and have everything you need.' She told him she did and they made small talk for a few minutes until Smirnov said, 'Tomorrow Anton, my assistant, will pick you up at midday and take you for lunch and a tour, if that's convenient to you?'

'It's perfect. Thank you, Mr Smirnov, for being so kind.'

'Don't mention it, my dear, we like to keep our agents happy.'

Before turning out the light, she hung a 'Do not disturb' notice on the door as tomorrow morning she intended to sleep until 10am.

Anton arrived punctually at midday, smartly dressed in a black suit and burgundy tie. To be prudent, she sat in the back seat of the black BMW in case he should get the wrong idea about her friendly banter. As he drove along Lungotevere, the road next to the River Tiber, he told her they were going to a simple restaurant in an old part of the city where in ancient times boats came from Ostia Port bringing wares and food to the city. He said he was taking her to the area called Testaccio to eat a renowned typical Roman dish – *Coda alla Vaccinara*

– oxtail stew made with celery, carrots, aromatic herbs, tomatoes and red wine. A short walk from the parking space to the restaurant was a slalom on foot, weaving between cars half parked on the pavement. Now and then his arm went around her waist as he guided her to avoid holes in the road and cracks in the pavements. She didn't mind him touching her and took it as a gentlemanly gesture.

The restaurant was not quite what she expected. It was rather basic – far from the elegant restaurant James had taken her to. Anton translated some of the menu. He was helpful, polite, amusing and oozed charm. She felt comfortable with him.

'Don't take any notice of the paper tablecloth, this is a special place where they cook traditional ancient Roman recipes. Once, only poor people ate such food but now people come from far and wide to eat here. You can also eat tripe and entrails if you want.'

'I eat everything,' she said, remembering the time she never turned up her nose at food back home because there was nothing else to eat except what was on the table.

Before the main course, they chose two starters – *Fiori di Zucca* – zucchini flowers filled with mozzarella cheese and anchovies dipped in batter and fried; and *Baccala* – salted cod in batter, which they shared. The *Coda alla Vaccinara*, the oxtail stew, was soft and tender and falling off the bone. The whole meal so far, accompanied by red wine, was well worth the trip to Rome. The dessert – *Crostata di ricotta* – cheesecake made from unsalted sheep's cheese and Marsala, turned out to be the perfect finish to a simple Roman culinary experience.

Over coffee – black and strong, Anton said he would take her this evening to visit Castel Sant'Angelo. 'The name in English means "the Castle of the Holy Angel". It was originally a mausoleum for the Emperor Hadrian and his family until transformed into a fortress to protect the Holy City from its enemies. Many of them were tortured and died in the prison dungeons. On the top of the castle you will see the statue of Archangel Michael sheathing his sword after the end of the plague.'

Anushka listened enthralled. 'How exciting. I can't wait to visit.'

Anton paid the bill and escorted her back to the car. His hand lingered longer around her waist. 'I'll collect you from your hotel at 8pm. In the meantime you should enjoy a siesta like the Romans. I don't advise you to go out in the afternoon sun and in any case the shops will be closed until around 5pm.'

He took her back to her hotel and this time she sat in the front.

Bertha's bunions

At dusk, Fred, Bertha and Cecilia were sitting in Boudicea's chariot on top of the Victor Emmanuel Memorial in Piazza Venezia. Fred settled himself on top of one of the gigantic horses and said he'd never been on a horse before. The night was clammy, prompting Bertha to grouch about the level of humidity. 'I've never been so hot and sweaty in my whole life and my feet are killing me.'

'Take your shoes off, Bertha,' Cecilia barked, on a short-fuse and in a no-nonsense mood.

'I'll never get them on again.'

'Then stop complaining.' Cecilia made a grab at Bertha's feet, wrenched off her shoes and threw them over the side where they landed in Piazza Venezia then quickly flew up and sat next to Fred out of reach. Bertha screamed abuse and said she'd get her own back while Cecilia pointed out that neither she nor Fred wore shoes so why should she be so privileged.

It was mid-morning before they awoke to the sound of honking horns and a whistle-blowing policeman on a small raised platform in the middle of the square, doing his best to direct unruly motorists. Keen to get away from the noise and confusion Cecilia suggested they fly to the Vatican and sit on top of the Basilica.

She said, 'The only thing that worries me is that the Vatican dress code means I have to cover my bare arms and I don't have a cardigan.'

Bertha had the answer. She spun around Cecilia and yanked the top layer of tulle off her ballet skirt pulling it away from the seams around her waist.

'That'll teach you to throw my shoes away,' she said triumphantly throwing the tulle at Cecilia. She didn't expect Cecilia's reaction, which was to throw her arms around her and thank her for her new stole which meant she could go and see the Pope tonight.

Fred suggested they make for the Vatican gardens as he was hungry and wanted some worms.

Bertha bleated, 'That's all very well for you, Fred, but what are Cecilia and I going to eat?'

'Roses, which are good for the complexion,' he replied.

'Not a bad idea,' Cecilia acknowledged.

Bertha thought for a moment. 'Will I have time to make some rosewater for my lovely face?'

Cecilia said, 'Definitely not, we have to go and talk to the Pope about my washing machine.'

'He won't be able to see you. You're dead,' Bertha replied spitefully.

Before Cecilia could open her mouth to reply, Fred intervened, 'Cecilia's good at materialising. She's been on a training course. In any case, you'd be wasting your time making rosewater for your face. You're not exactly a spring chicken.'

Bertha's patience snapped at Fred's remarks. With a well-aimed kick, she propelled him into space where he slowly tumbled down in a heap next to the Vatican Post Office. Cecilia swore at Bertha for kicking Fred and cursed her evil temper. Bertha replied she'd never been so insulted in all her life as her self-esteem had been destroyed by their callous comments. She tore another layer of tulle from Cecilia's dress and threatened further action for her inflamed bunion after kicking Fred.

Bertha turned her back and flew up towards the statues of the twelve apostles to sit next to John the Baptist. Cecilia watched as a ghostly young woman approached Bertha. She was sensually dressed in seven veils and offered her an oval-shaped silver plate. A few seconds later, Cecilia found Bertha sitting next to her, shaking uncontrollably and babbling about Salome offering her the blood-spattered severed head of John the Baptist which was sitting on a silver platter ready to be put in the oven.

A scary encounter

In her hotel room, Anushka tried on several dresses before she chose a below-the-knee black skirt and a white blouse with long sleeves just in case Anton took her inside Saint Peter's Basilica which observed a strict dress code – no bare arms, midriffs or breasts. He had asked her not to wear make-up and she wondered if it was part of the dress code too. In the full-length mirror she turned this way and that and decided she looked suitably demure. The skirt and blouse was set off by a pair of black patent leather high-heel shoes and matching handbag and she was ready to go.

At 8pm, Anton was waiting outside in the car. He opened the rear door for her and handed her a pair of dowdy flat black shoes and told her to take off her high heels and put them on. 'When we get to our destination, leave your handbag in the car, you won't need it.' She wondered what the mystery was about but complied as the shoes were more comfortable than her own.

Anton parked the car on a street flanking a low wall at the side of Castel Sant'Angelo. Taking her hand he kissed it. 'You are beautiful even without make-up,' he said, not letting go of her hand. She felt a thrill. He led her down some steps but her heart was beating too quickly to register her surroundings. A side door was ajar and they slid inside. It was 8.30pm and the tourists had long gone. The stone walls towered above them.

They were alone in the semi-darkness in an inner courtyard. The narrow pathway was lit by one street lamp on the right-hand wall. Against the skyline she could see the statue of Archangel Michael sheathing his sword.

Anton said, 'The guide is waiting for you. Marius will tell you some history of the castle. And be careful of the steep steps, Smirnov wants to see you back in one piece.'

He led her into a well-lit but dusty room in an office with keys in a cabinet behind the desk. Anton introduced her to Marius and she mentally profiled him – six feet tall; close to age sixty; light brown thinning hair specked with grey; face as smooth as a priest's; heavy lidded eyes, icy blue, probing, glittering and calculating; lips disgustingly moist; ambiguous smile; sweaty rubbery handshake. On the whole, body language of lascivious malevolence.

Anton said, 'Marius will explain why you are here. Unfortunately I have to get back as Smirnov's waiting for me. I'll be waiting for you outside from 10pm onwards.'

She wanted to ask him why he was leaving her there with Marius if Smirnov wanted her back in one piece, but he'd gone before she could open her mouth.

Marius invited her to sit down and proceeded with a history lesson.

'Below this office are the dungeons – the prison where in past times the Pope's enemies were taken to be tortured to extract confessions. They were politicians, intellectuals, soldiers, spies and ordinary people accused of treason or lesser crimes. The cells were dark and damp. There was no toilet. Some cells were so small they couldn't stand up or lie down to sleep. Meals came once a day. As for the women, what they did to them was—' Marius laughed, leaving her feeling uneasy at the sexual inference from a man she hardly knew and the way his eyes flitted over her body.

He continued. 'There's a secret tunnel between Castel Sant'Angelo and the Vatican City. It's called the *Passetto di Borgo* – the little passage. In 1527, the Vatican City was invaded by enemy soldiers during the *Sack of Rome*. The Swiss Guards saved Pope Clement VII by taking him down this passage. More than one hundred and eighty of them were slaughtered defending the rear guard. There were only forty-two survivors. A real bloodbath. The *Passetto* was also used by the Borgia Pope's lovers.' He gave a hollow laugh and his eyes glittered. 'Secret sex, not bad eh?'

Anushka began to feel afraid. He opened his desk drawer and pulled out a plastic bag with something soft in it and took a set of keys from the cabinet above the desk.

'These are to unlock the seven gates along the *Passetto*. Now, please follow me.'

Anushka followed Marius through the courtyard, past a marble fountain and up a wide stone staircase under a domed roof, of the kind built for soldiers to march abreast or horses to gallop up. Two lights on the wall gave out a sad, faded yellow light and it took her a couple of minutes to adjust to the gloom. At the top of the stairs, a door led out onto the battlements, lit by the street lamps below and the moon above. In the distance Saint Peter's Basilica stood out against the cobalt-blue sky.

They left the battlements to descend a flight of stairs where a narrow corridor stretched for perhaps half a mile, blocked occasionally by iron gates.

He said, 'This is the *Passetto* and we are heading towards the Vatican. Welcome to the *Inferno*. He explained that *Inferno* meant Hell and was quoted in Dante Alighieri's *Divine Comedy* where sinners languished, were tortured and roasted in the devil's fire. She wondered why he was comparing the Vatican to Hell and thought perhaps he was an unbeliever. Or maybe he just enjoyed scaring her.

The temptation to run in the opposite direction was strong when, at the fourth gate he came close to her and ran his index finger down the side of her face. A pungent smell emanated from his armpits and fear gripped her. He could lock her in between one gate and the other and she'd be his prisoner. Her nerves were at breaking point. A few yards after the seventh gate brought them to a heavy metal door where a hammer hung on the wall. Marius lifted it down and knocked seven times on the door. It swung slowly open to reveal two stocky men in security uniforms each holding a gun pointed at them. Upon seeing Marius the guns were lowered and they stepped back. Marius ushered her inside. 'We're now inside the Vatican and you will do as I say without asking questions.'

Anushka prepared herself for the worst possible scenario with three men. Marius still hadn't told her why she was there. She saw sweat break out on his upper lip and his eyes glitter. He said, 'Sister Agnes who brings the Pope his meals has been taken to hospital with food poisoning. She might recover after a day or two but then she may not. In the meantime, someone has to take him his evening night-cap of warm milk. Mr Smirnov has chosen you because you have no contacts in the Vatican City. There are too many people who can't be trusted and we have to protect the new Pope from any attempt on his life.'

Anushka nodded. At first she had wondered what game he was playing. But nothing had happened to her so far and she began to relax.

'As soon as you get back, I will take you on a personal guided tour around the prison dungeons to thank you for completing your mission. I believe you will like our chamber of horrors.'

Her scalp tightened. She was in the devil's lair and he was planning pain. Or was he saying it just to scare her?

Holy Smoke

Anushka waited for Marius to give her instructions. He pointed to a tray on a narrow table next to the marble fireplace upon which sat an ornate white and gold porcelain mug with the papal crest and a matching plate with biscuits.

'This is the Pope's evening snack. In the porcelain mug there is warm milk. Be careful how you carry it.'

He pressed an intricately carved rose in the wood panelling which slid back to reveal a well-lit tunnel between the Vatican City walls.

Marius said, 'This tunnel leads into the antechamber next to the Pope's bedroom. When you come to a heavy carved-wood door with a knob, press it and the door will slide back. You will be inside the papal antechamber. Knock on the door to the Pope's bedroom and enter. Put the tray on his bedside table and leave immediately. Do not under any circumstances speak to His Holiness. When you return to this room, the guards will let you out into the *Passetto*. Then come to my office.'

Marius handed her the plastic bag. Inside was a nun's habit which he ordered her to put on.

Anushka picked up the tray and stepped into the tunnel. Patches of white fluffy efflorescence hung on the walls and brushed off onto her habit as she passed. The heat and humidity of an August night accentuated her discomfort. Fortunately, the instructions Marius had given her were precise and it wasn't long before she was inside the antechamber; an elegant room of great beauty, decorated with frescoes and tapestries. In front of a high shuttered window with crimson drapes, a magnificent renovated writing desk with two golden chairs padded with red velvet caught her attention. An idea formed in her mind. Anushka placed the tray on the desk and picked up a sheet of headed paper with the papal crest and helped herself to the Pope's pen. She started to write.

Dear Your Holiness,

I was told not to speak to you so I am writing you this letter. I'm sorry Sister Agnes is sick with food poisoning but happy to have this opportunity to serve Your Holiness. I was asked by Mr Marius to serve you milk and biscuits. I came along the Passetto from Castel Saint'Angelo into the Vatican City thanks to two security guards with guns who let us in.

I read the Holy Bible. I like the part on forgiveness but maybe I cannot forgive Boris of the Soviet Embassy for taking my virtue and enslaving it and Mr Marius who might ravish and torture me in the prison dungeon of Castel Sant'Angelo after this mission. I am also afraid he might murder me as he seems to be a bit of a psychopath. I feel privileged, in the name of international relations, to serve Your Holiness and wish you a long life. I hope to see you in Cuba one day.

Yours very sincerely,

An admirer.

Anushka put the letter in an envelope and slipped it into her inside pocket. She knocked and entered the papal bedroom. Pope Joseph sat reading in bed. He shot her a quizzical look and asked where Sister Agnes was. Anushka knew she shouldn't speak, but she couldn't ignore him. It would be bad manners. So she said, 'Mr Marius told me she's in hospital with food poisoning. Can I plump up your pillows for you?'

'Thank you, my child, and God bless you,' Pope Joseph replied quietly. As soon as he was made comfortable, he picked up the mug and took a few sips of the milk. This distraction enabled her to surreptitiously slip her letter into his bedside drawer.

Leaving as quietly as she came, she closed the chamber door behind her. In the antechamber, a large heavy paperweight sat on the Pope's writing desk. Without a second thought she ferreted it away into her pocket. It would serve her well if Marius had evil intentions. But luckily she didn't need it. When she eventually tiptoed past his office, she saw he had his head down and was sleeping.

In the antechamber of the papal apartment, Fred, Bertha and Cecilia sat on the Pope's writing table talking about Anushka having stolen the Pope's paperweight.

'I must write all this down,' said Bertha, pulling out her notepad.

'No need, I've already done it,' said Fred ignoring her stiff glare.

Cecilia raised her hands. 'I hope you two aren't going to continue arguing. This is supposed to be a peaceful place.'

Moving through the wall to the Pope's bedchamber they were in time to see him take a few gulps from a mug of milk and place it back on the bedside table. First he lay back against his pillows. Then he tried to sit up. He rolled from side to side and held his stomach, gasping. He tried to get up from the bed. Groaned. Sank back, closing his eyes.

Cecilia cried, 'Oh my God! Not now! I need to talk to him about my washing machine.'

Within seconds they were joined on the papal bed by recently deceased Cardinal Nkosi, an African, who seemed in a state of morose agitation. Cecilia objected to the cardinal's intrusion and demanded to know why he was there. 'This is a private audience,' she said icily.

Nkosi bristled. 'I have to ask Joseph if he's sorted out my last resting place. I can't live in the necropolis forever. I've been living there for three months and being tormented by two Opus Dei squatters who flagellate each other all night long.'

Fred drew himself up to his full height. 'I'd be happy to arrest them if you'd fill out a Serious Incident Report.'

'Thank you kindly but I'd rather sort it out with the Holy Father myself.'

Fred stuck out his chest and announced his role as a respected representative of Constable Ernest Barnstable, deceased, and the British Government.

'You have no jurisdiction in the Vatican State. We have our own laws and court,' said Nkosi, grinding his teeth as his face became darker.

The Holy Father stirred and raised one hand. 'Please be brief.'

Cardinal Nkosi butted in quickly. 'Thank you. Your Holiness, it's about those two from the Opus Dei—'

The Pope cut him off quickly. 'I can't deal with it now, I'm in pain.'

'I'd like to be moved somewhere else, Your Holiness. I can't sleep with the cracking of whips and you did promise you'd take up my case.'

Cecilia sympathised. 'I know what it's like having neighbours into sado-maso. What you need is a pair of earplugs.'

The Pope whispered, 'It's being sorted out. You can't expect miracles in the Vatican City.'

The cardinal turned on his heel and without so much as a 'by your leave' left for the necropolis with a poker in his hand.

The Pope's voice was barely audible. 'I have to go now—'

Fred said, 'Just one thing before you go, Your Holiness, Cecilia wants know if she can take her washing machine to Heaven. And I'd like to know why I'm white and not black.'

Cecilia said, 'Yes, I can't see myself washing my clothes by hand.' She showed the Pope her anaemic-looking nails.

Pope Joseph replied feebly, 'Send a letter up the chimney of the Sistine Chapel to Saint Peter and tell him to get rid of the Opus Dei squatters.'

Cecilia said, 'Your Holiness, Cardinal Nkosi is in the necropolis with a poker. There's likely to be a bloodbath.'

Pope Joseph fell silent and a smell of incense permeated the room.

Fred whispered to Cecilia, 'I have to send a message up the chimney about your washing machine and the Opus Dei. There's only writing paper with the papal crest and I'm a bit reluctant to use the Pope's pen.'

'He'll not need it tonight,' Cecilia said gravely, handing him the pen.

Upon reaching the Vatican stove, Fred picked up a piece of paper from the floor and scribbled his message on it. There were voting papers around and he stuffed them into the stove with small pieces of singed wood and lit the fire. It was a bit like sending a message up the chimney to Father Christmas.

In Saint Peter's Square a woman screamed and pointed to the chimney of the Sistine Chapel, out of which black smoke spiralled heavenwards to announce the death of a Pope. Unaware of the collective hysteria being shared in the square, Fred headed back to the papal apartment where Cecilia was waiting.

He said, 'I suppose I'd better put the Pope's pen back before he misses it.'

Cecilia replied, 'I'm sorry to say he's dead. I told you

earlier he wouldn't need it. You'll need to look into what was in his milk.' Fred thought Cecilia should be weeping instead of giving orders. He exchanged a glance with Bertha which said, '*Isn't she just too insensitive for words?*' and made a quick note *Suspected Murder – Pope possibly dead – possible murder weapon – mug of milk.* Fred declared he wouldn't investigate as the only way of verifying the truth was to taste what was left of the milk and he'd no intention of doing so. Bertha said she couldn't wait to get back to Witherington to be the first person to share the bad news with her friends in the graveyard and with Ernest. 'It'll be a great opportunity for Ernest to solve another murder mystery,' she said laughing out loud.

Fred visibly shrunk. 'Ernest's already stressed out and it means I'll have to sing to him again.'

Fred appealed to Bertha to save him from this torture, but all she said was, 'I couldn't give a damn about you, seeing as you said I was no spring chicken.'

She made it quite clear she was having her revenge.

News about the Pope's death reached Witherington in record time thanks to someone in the Vatican having connections with the Bishop of Rottingham. Scarlett and Roland were at the pub when there was a special announcement. A BBC journalist from Rome was saying, *Pope Joseph the First, has passed away after a short illness. The cardinals will meet again soon to cast their vote in the Sistine Chapel to elect a new Pope. This will be third conclave within as many months.*

Roland said, 'They seem to be dropping like flies. It's definitely foul play. The Vatican is the best place for a murder – no autopsy, no questions. They can do what they like. I wish I was a fly on the wall.'

Scarlett replied, 'You wouldn't last long in there with your leftist ideas.' The same journalist said, *The Vatican State confirmed there would not be an autopsy.*

Roland shrugged his shoulders. 'I knew it. There's always a cover up when they say that.'

Scarlett called in on Tallulah to give her the news. Her aunt replied she'd never liked any of the Popes anyway seeing as in the past they'd had enough illegitimate children to raise an army and were forever at war with the poor.

'So much pomp and ceremony when people are dying of starvation. I ask myself why they should be buried in the Vatican Grottoes when millions have to be content with a hole in the ground.'

Scarlett didn't see the connection between starving children and a hole in the ground. 'I see you're planning to float around in liquid nitrogen? Not many people can afford such luxury. How's *that* for privilege?'

Tallulah retreated to the kitchen in stony silence to put on the kettle.

Our Woman in Havana

The telephone rang at 7am for a wake-up call. Anushka's arm reached out to give Anton a shake but he'd already gone, leaving her a note saying he'd come by at 10am to take her to Rome airport for her trip to Madrid. After breakfast in the hotel she packed her luggage, thinking of the night with Anton in her single bed. Being a gentleman he'd insisted on sleeping on the outside while she slept against the wall. Not that they'd spent much of the night sleeping. She felt warm, exhilarated, loved. They had explored every inch of each other's bodies. No man had ever taken so much time to delve into her pleasure zones before now. Past pleasure had been rushed and sometimes not even a pleasure. But last night she was able to gorge on her senses and fulfil his, while the bed rose and fell like a ship on the sea. Perhaps it was because he was ten years older than she and probably a lot more experienced in bed. She imagined him having had beautiful starlets in his life. But it was obvious he liked her because last night, after she'd told him of her terrifying experience with Marius, he'd called Mr Smirnov who said that the man would be permanently removed so he would never bother her or anyone else ever again.

At Rome Leonardo da Vinci airport, Anton parked in a covered car park and got in the back seat with her. She gave him the paperweight and asked him to return it to the Pope's antechamber. Anton took her in his arms and kissed her and said he wanted to protect her and never let her go. She thought it was cruel destiny to find a man she loved only to have to leave him. Tears started and Anton wiped them away. He said, 'When we left the restaurant I knew you were the woman I've been searching for. I'm madly in love with you. I can't go down on my knees in here, but will you marry me?'

Anushka was speechless. Tears started again, this time happy ones. Throwing her arms around him she said a breathless 'Yes'. Everything was happening so quickly. Only yesterday she had been thinking about designer shopping down Via Frattina and lunch near the Spanish Steps but now all she could think about was Anton and a new wedding dress.

Outside the terminal they stood together as long as they could, talking about the future. Anushka walked away without looking back in case she was tempted to run to him.

The flight was delayed for more than two hours and embarkation was slow. Her thoughts went to James who would be coming to Havana before he knew it to give her away. Perhaps Pope Joseph could marry them. But no, he would never be allowed to visit Cuba unless a revolution happened inside the Vatican City. And Cuba was unlikely to permit a holy man to stir up the waters in their agnostic government-controlled society. The government was more interested in revolution than religion, she thought, remembering the Cuban Missile Crisis which had brought the world to the brink of a nuclear war in 1962.

Arriving at Madrid airport late afternoon, Anushka had had time to buy sweets and toiletries not easy to get hold of in Cuba, so Anton had told her. Her second flight of the day was also delayed. Two hours later, making her way to the embarkation gate, a man bumped into her and the contents of her shopping bag spilled out across the floor. She held back nervous tension as the man smiled and apologised profusely while helping her put the articles back in the bag. Only a few minutes had passed but she still ran to the embarkation gate, afraid of losing the flight.

Inside the aircraft, a stewardess helped her with cabin luggage and she settled comfortably and fastened her seat belt. Smirnov had bought her a first class seat. She waited until they were airborne and the seat belt sign had been switched off before opening the shopping bag to take out some chocolate. She noticed pages of a newspaper folded in four which hadn't been there before. Slowly she opened them out. On the front page, the headlines screamed in bold:

POPE JOSEPH LEAVES FOR HEAVEN

'Following the death of Pope Joseph I, the Vatican Press Office denied that missing archbishop Marius Conak has been murdered. However, an unknown source has linked his disappearance to that of Sister Agnes and bones found in the Sistine Chapel incinerator early this morning. Boris Ustinov of the Russian Embassy, a friend of the Archbishop, has been expelled for spying and is due to arrive in Moscow tomorrow.'

In the middle of the journey of our life
I found myself within a dark wood
Where the straight way was lost

Dante Alighieri
The Divine Comedy: Inferno. Canto I

SEPTEMBER 1986

Gladys gets liberated

During the first week of September, *Agriculture and Business Monthly* was distributed to every house with the morning paper. It was an important edition dealing with the planning of the community party in the streets of Witherington.

Gladys Wheeler threw aside the newspaper and picked up the magazine, hurriedly leafing through until she found the reply to the letter she'd written to Veronica. She smiled triumphantly at her little secret. Everyone in Witherington would read it but never know the anonymous writer was none other than herself, the wife of Councillor Wheeler and Roland's mother. Perhaps she'd tell Roland at some point in time.

Dear Quite dissatisfied,

In reply to your letter about the antagonistic problems between your husband and son, I suggest you send them together for psychological counselling. I'm glad you've been sexually liberated. I suggest you become more assertive. Let the dishes sit in the sink for your husband. At the restaurant, open the door yourself without waiting for the man to do it; pour your own wine; eat peas from your knife and smoke a pipe after the meal (but you may be asked to leave). Your husband may be offended about you not sleeping with him after he has bought you a meal. Stick to your guns. There's one solution – pay your way and tell him to liberate himself from everything his mother taught him about women (seeing as she was chained to the kitchen sink for years).

Regards,

Veronica.

Veronica's reply spurred Gladys to call Ignatius at the town hall.

'Councillor Ignatius Wheeler speaking.'

'Iggy, isn't it time you took me out to a restaurant? You haven't taken me in years.'

'I don't have time to talk. I'm busy with the community party and I've just received a ridiculous letter from a parishioner, recommending a bloody foreign communist for a medal for bravery,' he said, before ringing off rudely without answering her question.

Gladys made herself a cup of tea before calling a restaurant in Rottingham and booking a table for two. A sense of liberated urgency overtook her. Striding to the High Street, she entered a shop selling things for smokers and bought herself a pretty pipe and a packet of tobacco.

Ignatius returned after work, his nose twitching the moment he entered the house.

'Has Roland been here? I can smell tobacco smoke.'

'Our son doesn't smoke.'

'Then who else has been here? Have you been messing around with someone while I've been out?'

'It was me smoking a pipe and I've booked a table for two at a restaurant for 7pm.'

Ignatius asked her if she'd taken leave of her senses and, in the absence of dinner on the stove, left for the pub. Instead of being upset, Gladys donned her coat and followed him to the pub to put the pressure on and symbolically turn the thumbscrews. She would drag him to the restaurant whether he liked it or not.

'I've made an appointment for you with Dr Maynard,' she said ordering herself a drink at the bar and sitting down opposite Ignatius.

'The shrink?' he boomed, spluttering into his beer.

'Yes, he's going to help you with a bonding problem you have with your son,' she said, not daring to mention Roland's name in case he ran for the loo.

Un-shaven legs incident

At breakfast Tallulah made a list of personal needs to be addressed before the community party – a facial to smooth away the wrinkles; a trip to the hairdressers to tame the wiry grey hairs at her temples; and a quick shave of what hairs were left on her legs.

Next on the list were the names of men who could possibly accompany her to the party. She proceeded to cross off two who were desperate to get married, one who would cling like glue to any woman and another whose bossy disposition was at odds with hers. She crossed off wimpy James. As a last resort she phoned despotic Stanley.

He told her he was too tired to talk and could think of nothing worse than going to a community party, apart from falling into a silage pit. 'I can't anyway, I'm going on mission to Ouagadougou.'

'You don't even know where it is. I seem to remember you were useless at geography. You had one of our agents hanging around in Kazakhstan instead of Kyrgyzstan for a month clocking up expenses,' Tallulah reminded him.

'It wasn't my fault. He didn't have an exit visa and they wouldn't let him out.'

She asked him what he was going to do in Ouagadougou.

'I'm tracking down a spy who's setting up a raspberry growing project there and we think he's planting poppy seeds.'

'Raspberries don't do well in the heat. Do you want to escort me to the community party or not?'

'I can't dance, I've got a couple of cracked ribs.'

'Then how are you getting to Ouagadougou? You have to have a good memory to be a liar.'

Stanley objected to her slighting him and said so and added he'd fancied her when they were first married but now his libido was on the wane. She thought he was just being difficult.

Tallulah replaced the receiver and crossed him off the list. Swallowing her pride, she called James and asked him to come on over to the house to talk things over.

He said, 'Is it another dummy run?'

'No, I need your opinion on something.'

Turning up in crumpled shirt and trousers, James apologised for looking like a tramp. 'Anushka has left and I've got no one to iron my shirts,' he said dejectedly. Tallulah sympathised and offered him a cup of tea. They made small talk about the launderette and how much he missed Anushka.

'What's happening with the "Serge" project?' she asked.

'I scrapped it.'

'Good. I just have to go upstairs. I'll be down in a minute.'

In the bedroom, with memories of Paris going through her head, Tallulah slid into a smokey-grey silk dress. Forty years on it was a little tight but she managed to squeeze into it. Standing on a chair, she pulled down a box from the top of the wardrobe and took out a purple ostrich-feather boa. She slunk down the staircase and walked into the sitting room, posing with one hand on her hip, sure that James would remember their passionate time in Paris.

'What do you think?'

She waited for James to say, 'You look beautiful,' as he'd done when he'd seen the dress for the first time.

His eyes moved from head to toe. 'Do you want my honest opinion?'

'Yes, of course I do.'

'Tallulah, you're no spring chicken. You look like mutton dressed as lamb.'

She screamed and ran into the kitchen, shouting, 'Where's the meat cleaver?'

James said, 'Stop overacting. I abandoned you in Paris because you never shaved your legs.'

A wail came from the kitchen. James heard the meat cleaver come down on the bread board. She shouted, 'How do you know I had hairs on my legs when your head never went anywhere near *down there*.'

James ran for the door and slammed it behind him. He shouted through the letter box, 'Sorry, I didn't mean it. See you at the party.'

The starving hordes

September turned out to be cool and dry with no sign of rain. Fortunately, the sun shone on the day they had all been waiting months for – the Witherington community party.

By 5pm, food stalls had been set up on the pavement on either side of the High Street and in an eating area in the empty car park next to the town hall. Above the tables, hundreds of small triangular flags hung between lamp posts advertising the patronage of the *Rottingham Lions Club*. There was booze and plenty of it on tables manned by their wives. The children were already starving. They couldn't wait five minutes and didn't care to hear Councillor Wheeler's opening speech standing on the town hall balcony next to the Union Jack. Little fingers ferreted away buns from the tables. The rest of the attendees were desperate to get at the food, not having eaten and then only frugally, since lunchtime. As tempers frayed, Councillor Wheeler spouted a welcome from the balcony, hands on hips and chin stuck out arrogantly, whereby a man in the crowd shouted, 'Bloody 'ell, 'e looks like Mussolini.'

After the speech, a local band began to play a medley of 1960s music. While the community was tucking into food, Bertha, Norman, Fred, Porkchop, Cecilia and Ernest sat on the village green behind the town hall listening to the music. A little later, the band struck up a waltz and Norman took his wife's hand. 'I've taught you how to dance the waltz, now you can put it into practice.'

Bertha, radiant in her emerald green satin dress, beamed

as Norman took her in his arms and led her into a one-two-three, one-two-three rhythm. Bertha soon got the hang of it while Ernest, Fred and Cecilia looked on admiringly.

Cecilia sighed. 'It brings back memories of when I used to dance with James. I'd love to dance again but I haven't got my foot back yet.' She looked at Ernest accusingly.

'You don't need your foot to do this.' Ernest grabbed her hand and lifted her off the ground, whirling her into a waltz. Cecilia shrieked happily and said she didn't care if he found her foot or not, she was quite happy to levitate with him.

Fred looked on enviously, wondering if he'd ever dance with Ethel again. The waltz ended and another started. Fred said to Porkchop, 'We may as well join in.'

'I think I'll sit this one out,' replied Porkchop.

Cecilia thanked Ernest for dancing with her and grabbed Fred's wings. 'Now it's your turn,' she said, placing one of his wings around her waist.

A sudden, strong gust of wind carried them up in the air, over the rooftops towards the town hall where they sat on the roof chatting and enjoying the band's music.

Ernest left Bertha and Norman still dancing. It seemed they had made their peace. His mission as peacekeeper had been satisfying but he was glad it was over. 'Come on, Porkchop, let's go and join Fred and Cecilia,' he said making for the town hall roof.

The four of them sat on the roof chatting. Suddenly Fred jumped up and pointed to Tallulah picking up two drinks from a stall. She was being followed by a big dark-skinned man in a white caftan.

Revolutionary recipes

As neither James nor Stanley had turned up at the house to escort her to the party, Tallulah had accepted a lift into Witherington from a friend, knowing someone would take her home. Admiring the tables laden with food down both sides of the High Street, she stopped to pick up an aperitif. Someone tapped her shoulder. Expecting it to be James, she turned round to see Santeros towering over her.

'Mrs Millstone, such a beautiful woman. I see you have nice big purple chicken feathers on your shoulders.'

'Actually it's an ostrich boa.'

He looked perplexed. She explained in language which nice British ladies use when talking to foreigners. 'An ostrich is like a giant chicken with a long neck.'

His eyes shone and he touched it gently. 'Such a beautiful colour. I want giant chicken. Perhaps we get married and shag?'

She excused herself to go urgently to the ladies' toilet, where she fanned herself with a napkin. Waiting a few minutes she went outside but there was no sign of Santeros. What seemed to be a large over-ripe tomato waved at her – Florence, dressed in red chiffon swept towards her leading a white long-haired chihuahua whose drooping ears said it didn't like parties. A red collar studded with fake diamonds was no compensation for having to suffer crowds. Florence gushed, 'I'm so looking forward to hearing Veronica speak. I just loved her article about coitus.'

'I thought you didn't like it? You made a song and dance of it in Scarlett's office.'

'I never realised thirty million people worldwide aren't getting proper sex,' she whispered.

Tallulah was saved from further coitus conversation by the dog who lifted its leg and was about to pee on the hem of her dress, thereby spurring Florence to grab him and hurry away.

Having escaped Santeros and Florence, Tallulah proceeded to look for an ally. She saw Mr Kim waving at her from behind a table stacked with *Revolutionary Recipes*. A man she recognised from Rottingham Library was browsing through one.

'How much?' the Librarian asked, looking with interest at the picture of terrapin-in-the-hole.

Mr Kim pointed to the terrapins and said, 'Do you like my book?'

'Yes I think it's brilliant. Actually I'm used to eating toad-in-the-hole and have never tried terrapins. I never knew you North Koreans ate them with Yorkshire pudding.'

Mr Kim didn't want to put a foot wrong seeing as he'd an interested buyer. 'We like patriotic dishes.' He proudly quoted the delicious cold noodles and fire meat – barbecued marinated beef Bulgogi.

The Librarian said, 'Well there's nothing more nationalistic or patriotic than Welsh rarebit, Yorkshire pudding and Lancashire hotpot.' He said he hoped the dogpot was a joke.

Mr Kim replied, 'I see the British like oxtail soup. Do they like ox penis?'

The Librarian shuddered. 'We don't eat dogs or penises.'

'A great pity, the Chinese love them. It is certainly a matter of taste and what one is used to. For example in other parts of Asia people eat insects and they are quite delicious.'

The Librarian pointed to the book. 'How much?'

'Two pounds to you.'

'It's daylight robbery!'

'The money will go to feed hungry orphans and lactating mothers in my country.'

'So give me five copies to give away for Christmas presents. I always donate to charity.'

The man handed over a ten pound note and left smiling, commenting on Mr Kim's love of children. The Librarian's comments about children and charity drew other people to the table like magnets and soon there was a long line of buyers. Tallulah waited until everyone had been served before congratulating Mr Kim on his excellent marketing skills.

She said, 'Before long there'll be a copy of *Revolutionary Recipes* in every home and the BBC and radio stations will be lining up to interview you.' She picked up a book and browsed through it, complimenting him on his great achievement.

He was looking proud. 'You should come to my great country one day. We have plenty of kimchi and you would like the Bulgogi or Pulgogi, whichever way you prefer to pronounce it. We have rice dishes, dumplings and many other foods. We also have a Japanese restaurant.'

'I thought you hated the Japanese, seeing as you have an anti-Japanese day every year?'

'War has nothing to do with food. Perhaps you can come next year with a diplomatic mission?'

'Perhaps I will come to Pyongyang and write a cookery book.'

He looked at her gravely. 'We do not encourage writers or journalists, however you could come as an academic, we like intelligent people.'

'And if I say I've worked for Intelligence?'

'We do not like foreign spies. You could end up in enormously big trouble and you might not make it home. During the Fatherland War we put them to death whenever we could.' He began to sing 'We Shall Hold Bayonets More Firmly'.

She shuddered. She was a dangerous *persona non grata*.

'Perhaps things will get better in the future when the North and South sort out their differences?'

'Technically speaking, even in 1986 we are still at war with South Korea.'

'But I thought there was an armistice?'

'Precisely. There was no winner.'

'The armistice was in the name of peace,' she said.

A hollow laugh came from Mr Kim's throat. Reading between the lines, she interpreted it as, *Don't be so bloody stupid and naïve, the American aggressors want to be the winners.*

'What happens to the Japanese restaurant on anti-Japanese day?' she asked.

'They take a day's holiday.'

Tallulah thought it sounded like a diplomatic approach. 'So when will you leave to go home?'

'Very soon. I am going to New York to visit my father. He works in the towering inferno where diplomats do not throw enough stones at each other in the glass house.

He meant the United Nations building.

'I'll say goodbye then.'

Mr Kim took her hand and kissed it. She was surprised when he hugged her.

'Thank you, old Mrs Tallulah, for your gracious help.' He picked up a book, opened it and signed it on the inside page. Then he pointed to the Acknowledgements.

Without the help of an old lady called Mrs Tallulah, this glorious book of recipes would not have been possible.

Tallulah thanked him and turned away before he could see tears filling her eyes. She remembered him saying about an old person in his country being respected and seen as an asset rather than a dimwit. Neither James nor Stanley had paid her a compliment to compare. On the contrary, many in Witherington considered her a *fuddy* old dimwit.

Accidental murder

The last person Tallulah expected to see was Stanley. He turned up smartly dressed in a grey suit with black tie, his pate polished. She saw his pupils were dilated and supposed he'd been brainwashing unsuspecting leftists.

'Have you been on the drugs again?' Tallulah asked.

'Just a few puffs of *Maria Warner* before I left the house.'

She led him to the drinks table. 'What's your poison?' she asked.

'A double whisky,' Stanley replied.

'What made you change your mind about coming?'

His hand slipped down her hip. 'I thought some fresh air would do me good and I still fancy you even though we're divorced.'

'If you cared for me, you'd have got my medal by now,' she said pushing away his wandering hand before it reached her backside.

'I've been too busy with the rehabilitation of spies, but we can spend the night together if you want.'

'Over my dead body,' she replied.

Stanley poured himself a whisky and followed her behind the town hall to a small circular table with chairs on the village green.

'I'm just going to get some food for us,' she said.

At the table prepared by the Mothers' Union, Tallulah picked up four meat pasties. Surreptitiously opening her handbag, she took one of Stanley's left-over cyanide pills from it and pressed one of the pills into a pasty.

Stanley told her he was there because he had nothing better to do.

'I thought I'd surprise you by turning up. And by the way you look lovely,' he said.

'So how come you didn't go to Ouagadougou and how are your cracked ribs?'

'Ouagadougou didn't materialise.'

Tallulah was about to make a snide comment when she saw Florence bearing down on their table holding the sad little dog in her arms.

'Such a lovely evening,' gushed Florence, smiling at Stanley, who, playing the part of the gentleman, began to indulge her in small talk about her dog.

Florence was lapping up the attention. 'Pepito is originally from Mexico. Pure white chihuahuas are very rare you know, aren't you, *amorcito de mama*? It means "mummy's darling" in Spanish,' she said, never missing a moment to show off her knowledge of languages.

Hearing his name, Pepito came to life and lunged towards the pasties. Tallulah slid them out of reach. Stanley picked up the plate before Tallulah had time to say a panicky 'no' and offered it to Florence. Tallulah held her breath, her eyes on the pasty with the cyanide pill in it. The one meant for Stanley. She made a grab for it but Florence, obviously thinking she was being bad mannered, grabbed it first. Then she was off in a flash to talk to her friends, brandishing the pasty like a spoil of war. She looked back at Tallulah and sneered as if to say 'I got it first.'

Tallulah's eyes followed the red dress as Florence disappeared into the crowd. A short time later a voice screamed and shouted for an ambulance for someone who had had a heart attack and an epileptic fit. Mrs Horsefield rushed into the town hall to call Rottingham hospital while a crowd gathered around Florence, waiting for the ambulance and speculating on what had happened. Someone from the Mothers' Union said, 'I was expecting it sooner or later, she's got a bad heart you know and she suffered epilepsy as a child.' The others said it was news to them. Tallulah stood impassively by watching events unfold. She turned towards Stanley and said, 'I wonder what's going to happen to little Pepito. He'll be without a mother now.'

Stanley sneered. 'I couldn't give a shit about the bloody awful little dog. All this has put me off my food.' Then he walked towards his car, leaving Tallulah wondering what she'd seen in the young man she'd married years ago. At the time he'd seemed pretty courageous.

Before Florence's body reached Rottingham hospital, word spread around the village green about her long-standing ailments. Florence had probably died of a heart attack but nobody knew for sure. She'd suffered high blood pressure but no one knew how high. It was suspected she could have suffered epilepsy as a child but no one knew her then. She often had hot flushes; and was greedy for pasties.

According to eyewitnesses, Florence choked on a pasty which made her blood pressure rise enough to give her a heart attack. She'd frothed a little at the mouth because of her epilepsy and her face had turned red because of her blood pressure and choking at the same time. The village gossips added a bit more through the bush telegraph and came to the conclusion about her death being a combination of these things and more. She also liked a bit of a tipple, they said, adding that it would all be confirmed at the autopsy.

Emergency response

It fell to Mrs Horsefield to sort the problem out. A woman had dropped dead and Councillor Wheeler was in a flap. The first thing she did was search out Scarlett to tell her to get Veronica on stage to create a diversion.

Unaware of the unfolding drama, *Veronica* was in the ladies' toilet in front of the mirror adjusting his melons and attempting to stick one set of plastic eyelashes back on with a bit of spit. He heard Scarlett shouting 'Veronica!' and rushed outside in response, leaving his make-up on a washbasin. Scarlett looked agitated. 'Quick, get on the stage and do your bit. There's an emergency. We have to distract people.'

Roland looked at the crowd and stood paralysed with fear. He suddenly wanted to be in Blackpool or Clacton. 'I'm scared. I'm not used to speaking in public. I can't get my eyelashes stuck on. There's no bloody glue on them.'

'This is an emergency. Get on the bloody stage. And remember you're a woman!' Scarlett jumped onto the stage and blew and coughed into the microphone. Her voice came across the tannoy system, on loan from the Rottingham Lions Club. 'People of Witherington, this is indeed a historic day. I want to introduce Veronica, our agony aunt who you all know. Please show your appreciation.' The crowd clapped and cheered as *Veronica* climbed onto the stage, patted her hair into place and stuck out her chest. Roland's stage fright retreated and he began to feel like a full-blown woman. Whistling broke out from the back of the crowd when he took off his high heels because they were killing him. *Veronica* ran a hand seductively down his bust to his thighs to more whistling. Someone from the back of the crowd shouted, 'Show us yer tits.' A few women hurried their children in the direction of home as cackling started to someone's comments about passing her around. A woman with a raucous voice shouted, 'She looks like a bloody tart.'

Roland couldn't believe his luck at all the attention he was getting. He started his speech in a falsetto voice. 'When Veronica's column was born it was intended to address challenges between the sexes. My column started because I wanted to challenge the mindsets of men and women. It started as a joke but now I regret I took it so lightly. I would like to make a confession.'

Scarlett, out of earshot of the microphone, hissed, 'What the fuck are you talking about?'

Roland said the joke was over and apologised for conning them. He reached into the open neck of his dress and pulled out first one cantaloupe and then the other. He held them up for the audience to see. Scarlett, seeing bankruptcy on the horizon, resisted the urge to strangle him in public. She'd wait until he got back to the office.

To an open-mouthed gathering, Roland said, 'Here are my tits,' and tossed the melons into the crowd. He peeled off Tallulah's dress, took off his wig and introduced himself. 'My name is Roland Wheeler. And I want to take this opportunity to ask my boss Scarlett to marry me.'

He pulled her to the front of the stage and went down on one knee. 'Scarlett, will you marry me?'

Being taken off guard and forgetting everything else, she muttered, 'Yes,' while the crowd cheered wildly.

Councillor Wheeler reeled and staggered and held his chest. Mrs Horsefield rushed to his side.

Gladys said, 'Stop being so dramatic, Iggy, isn't our son wonderful?'

The band struck up and started to play the wedding march. Tallulah watching from a distance commented aloud, 'Such bad manners. He could have asked me for her hand in marriage!'

A familiar voice said in her ear, 'In our day we never followed our hearts because we were tied to stupid protocol.'

She turned to see James. He said, 'I was too stupid to break it off with Cecilia and marry you. I should have had the courage to do so.'

Tallulah thought it was the first time he'd said something intelligent.

'I hope you're not going to oppose their wedding,' said James.

Upon reflection, Tallulah thought Roland might be the right man for Scarlett. He was sensitive, strong and had a good job. The only wart on the horizon was his strange phosphorescent socks.

Mrs Horsefield dabbed her eyes with a white linen handkerchief. 'Isn't it so romantic?' she said to Gladys through tears, barely able to see what was going on.

Gladys replied, 'It certainly is. It takes me back to the time Ignatius and I were in love, before Roland was born.' She turned to a pale Councillor Wheeler. 'Isn't it wonderful, Iggy? We might soon have a grandchild.'

Putting his hand to his forehead, Ignatius gazed into space and left them without a word to go to his office. Mrs Horsefield and Gladys looked at each other. They both knew he'd been under a bit of stress lately.

'I'd better go and see if he's alright,' said Mrs Horsefield. Gladys nodded. She watched as Roland took Scarlett's hand and led her on to the dance floor. She remembered when her husband, more than thirty years ago, had done the same. He'd been gentle and considerate. That was before he'd gone into politics.

Mrs Horsefield found Councillor Wheeler at his desk looking bewildered.

She said, 'You've got a fine boy there. We all underestimated him.'

Ignatius loosened his tie and told her it hadn't been easy being father to a drop-out.

'Just get out there and tell him you're proud of him,' she said.

'I don't know if I am. He's humiliated me in front of the whole community dressing up as a woman.' Ignatius didn't say he felt an ass for being taken in and fancying Veronica, his own son, in the men's toilets. He thought it better to stick to his reputation as a faithful family man.

Mrs Horsefield became insistent. 'But now he's got a good job and he's getting married. Just swallow your pride and get out there and tell him.'

Councillor Wheeler said, 'I'll do it tomorrow.'

Mrs Horsefield felt bold, having drunk three glasses of white wine.

'Ignatius, you're the one who's the idiot,' she said brazenly, having always called him Councillor Wheeler. Then she said she had to go somewhere, meaning to the toilet. A flush of embarrassment spread over her face. She'd called him by his first name in such a familiar way and prayed he'd forget it by tomorrow morning.

For quite a while after Roland's speech to the community, he and Scarlett were surrounded by well-wishers and good-natured people wanting to compliment Veronica on his magnificent strip show. No one seemed to mind Roland being barefoot and wearing women's underwear and make-up. He whispered in Scarlett's ear, 'Let's go home, my bloody toes are being trodden on,' to which she replied, 'Are you kidding? You're famous now. It's good publicity.'

He grabbed her by the hand, dragging her behind him. 'Get in the bloody car, we're going home.' Enough was enough. Perhaps if his bare toes hadn't been stepped on so many times, he mightn't have been so intolerant. As it was, they looked like raw sausages.

Back at Roland's room, Scarlett walked over to his tree and angrily snatched a parrot from an overhead branch. 'We're missing all the dancing,' she said petulantly.

Roland grabbed the parrot and said, 'It took me four days to make that bloody bird.'

Then he stomped to the bathroom to remove his remaining false eyelash. She heard a groan of pain. She took two wads of cotton wool from the bathroom cabinet, dampened them under running water and pressed them over his lids. All Roland heard was the tinkle of a mountain stream and the vision of a beautiful woman who smelt like a rainforest, handing him an olive branch. He stripped off his vest, kissed her and told her how much he loved her, notwithstanding her moods and her having carved up his meditation tree. Tarzan wanted to know when Jane had first fancied him.

'When you pulled me into your bathrobe,' she said, taking off her dress.

'Why didn't you say so?'

'I was your boss and you're a few years younger than me.'

'But it didn't stop you getting into the sack.'

'I love you, Roland.'

'Why didn't you tell me before?'

'I was scared.'

'I suppose I'd better resign now that the whole of Witherington knows I'm Veronica and will no doubt brand me a liar.'

'Not again!' said Scarlett, laughing and taking off the rest of her clothes.

Burn-out

Leaving Bertha and Norman dancing on the village green, Ernest, Cecilia, Fred and Porkchop drifted over the trees and followed Santeros to his second-hand station wagon. Revving the engine, Santeros sped off around the back streets heading out of town. At the roundabout he turned towards Bluebell Vicarage, passed the farm and drove straight into Tallulah's drive. Getting out of the car he peered into the chicken-run. There were three chickens huddled on a perch. Swearing and muttering he proceeded to search the back garden, shining his torch into every nook and cranny, looking for a giant purple chicken.

Fred's crest stood on end as he watched Santeros enter the henhouse and grab Ethel and Ms Prim by their legs. The two hens squawked and flapped their wings in fear before they were bundled into a cardboard box in the back of the station wagon which quickly reversed and sped off.

With a surge of adrenaline, Fred rushed forward, flapping after the car.

Ernest called him back, shouting, 'There's nothing you can do right now.'

Fred protested and felt the blood rush to his head. Then he passed out. Cecilia explained it away by likening Fred's black-out to a hairdryer that's been on top heat for too long – it stops working for a while until it cools down. 'I'm taking him home and putting him to bed. He's burnt himself out,' said Cecilia, in a motherly fashion, picking him up and speeding away.

Ernest turned to Porkchop. 'Do you know where the farmhouse is?'

'No, but we can easily spot it from the air. You can sit on my back and I'll take you there.'

'As long as you land gently,' Ernest said, making for Tallulah's shed to look for a piece of rope which he tied around Porkchop's middle to hang on to in case of turbulence. 'And no playing loop-the-loop. I don't want to have to go searching the countryside for my helmet.'

Porkchop lifted off gently, while Ernest held on tightly to the rope. 'It reminds me of when I went up in a hot air balloon in Tuscany,' Ernest imparted as they flew over the treetops.

There was no sign of the car. 'Try the farmhouse down there.' shouted Ernest above the sound of the wind. But it wasn't the place they were looking for. 'There's no sign of a car, let's try the next one.'

At the next farmhouse, dipping closer, the car came into view in a yard. Porkchop began his descent and landed in a grassy field with a jolt, throwing Ernest onto the ground. Complaining profusely, he brushed down his police uniform, retrieved his helmet and floated over the hedge towards the farmhouse.

Two ghostly white hens sat on wide wooden gate. The first one said, 'Constable Barnstable, you took your time getting here! We'd still be alive if you hadn't been faffing around. You'd better hurry up and get in there before Gottfried gets the chop.'

'Am I speaking to Ethel and Ms Prim?' Ernest asked. The second hen said he certainly was and if Gottfried got the chop, she couldn't care less as he'd never given her a second look.

Ernest said, 'You must be Ms Prim.'

'Yes and still intact,' she said proudly. Ernest suggested the two hens leave as soon as possible for the graveyard to comfort Fred, who would be delighted to see them.

Ernest explained his plan. Porkchop was to stay outside in the yard to block the exit and wait while he slipped through the walls to look for Gottfried.

The Berlin Wall

James thought it would have been better had the Council illuminated the community park a bit better. As it was, he could barely see what Tallulah was drinking, although he knew how many glasses of whatever it was she'd had, having counted them each time she'd excused herself for a refill.

To his question of what she was drinking, she said, 'Red wine of course, what else could it be? Are you counting? You're not a control freak are you? In any case, you've had quite a few yourself.'

'I suppose I have,' James replied, a little embarrassed.

The band stopped playing at midnight. Merriment retreated. Silence stimulated an urge to talk.

'I feel a bit sorry for Florence,' Tallulah said, sitting forward, her head almost touching the table.

'You told me you didn't like her.'

'Little Pepito has no one to look after him now.'

'We don't know she's definitely dead. And you hated little Pepito.'

'I did, but now he's an orphan. Perhaps I should adopt him.'

James grabbed her arm and pulled her to her feet. 'Time to go home, you're drunk.'

She resisted and tried to sit down again. 'I walked here. I don't know how to get back.'

'I'll take you,' he said.

James helped her into the passenger seat. Fortunately it was late and there were no cops around to breathalyse him.

'You know you shouldn't drink and drive. We could have an accident,' she slurred.

He ignored her comment and drove her to the Wailing Willows Hotel.

'I thought you were taking me home?'

'I wouldn't want you to be alone tonight after drinking so much wine. You might fall up the stairs.'

'I'm not sleeping with you, James.'

'Don't worry, I won't force you to do anything.'

She let him lead her through the front door, down the corridor and into the lounge. It was time for a cup of tea. Tallulah stretched out on the settee while James disappeared to put on the kettle.

He shouted from the kitchen, 'Tally, if you want you can sleep in my bed, while I sleep on the settee.'

'Don't be silly, James, I won't hear of it. There's enough room in the bed for both of us. We can put some pillows down the middle.'

He nodded and went to hunt for three pillows, which he found in the bed-linen cupboard and took to the bedroom.

'Talk about the Berlin Wall,' he said with a laugh, returning to the lounge.

In the end, they gave the cup of tea a miss in case it kept them awake all night.

'It's got tannin in it,' she said, pushing away the cup.

James decided he'd had enough and steered her into the bedroom, explaining where everything was and, in the event of the en-suite being occupied during the night, how to get to the second bathroom in the corridor. Pulling out a pair of clean pyjamas from a drawer, he toddled down the corridor to the second toilet carrying towel and toiletries.

Returning to the bedroom after necessary ablutions, he found Tallulah asleep between the sheets, her clothes strewn across the chair. He took off his pyjamas, slid in beside her and demolished the Berlin Wall.

Headless Hannah

Moving into the basement at Stanley's farmhouse, the first thing Ernest noticed was an altar against one wall with a sheet hanging from the ceiling behind it. The sheet was painted with voodoo scenes of chickens being decapitated. In the centre of the altar sat a human head with dark skin stretched over the cheekbones and a mess of wiry ginger hair. A plaque on the wall read: *Hannah, dearly loved wife of her husband.* So this was where Headless Hannah's head had ended up. Her husband had hidden it in the farmhouse.

The eyes suddenly opened.

'My name's Hannah and I was decapitated by my husband with an axe,' she told Ernest.

Ernest was a little taken aback as he hadn't expected a talking head. 'Are you willing to repeat that in a court of law?'

'I certainly am. But I'll only do it if you start an investigation to find my body.'

The thought of another investigation didn't appeal to him. 'I'll inform the police,' he said diplomatically.

The man they'd seen following Tallulah came into the basement. His white caftan had the name *Santeros* embroidered on the breast pocket. Clenched between his back molars was an intricately carved white pipe emanating sweet tobacco and his pupils were dilated. In a corner huddled in a cage awaiting his fate was Gottfried. Moving across the room, Ernest spoke to Santeros who seemed to be in a semi-trance. 'I want to talk to you about kidnapping, murder and mutilation,' Ernest said.

Santeros said, 'Who the hell are *you*?'

'I'm Gottfried's guardian angel and I've come to take him home.'

Santeros shuffled from one leg to the other before announcing he'd spent a lot of time fattening up Gottfried so he could have decent feathers for a hat he was making.

'My name is Constable Ernest Barnstable and I hereby accuse you of committing a crime – animal cruelty. In the United Kingdom it is against the law to cause suffering to animals.'

Santeros gave a cackling laugh and mentioned fox hunting, dropping lobsters into boiling water and prawns onto hot plates. He added to the list badger baiting, cock fighting, bad slaughter practices and abandoned cats and dogs.

Ernest silently admitted it did rather sound like animal cruelty. He said, 'I know you were in the Wailing Willows Hotel on the night Cecilia Willows fell from the window. I also know you cut off her foot with the knife on your altar. It has the Wailing Willows' crest on it. I demand to know what you did with her foot and I warn you – anything you say will be taken down and used in evidence against you in a court of law.'

Santeros said gravely, 'You have no jurisdiction here. I'll put *you* on trial for disturbance of *my* peace. Can you wait two seconds while I call the Judge?'

He shuffled to the nearest wall and knocked three times. A rumbling came from the other side and a man in a yellow-and-black checked shirt with burning coals in his hair, slid through the wall holding an axe and Cecilia's skeleton foot, the bones of which, neatly tied together, rattled as he walked.

Hannah's head turned from side to side. 'That's my husband and he's not a judge, he's a butcher. And he's got bad breath.'

The man lumbered towards Ernest brandishing an axe.

Headless Hannah shouted, 'Bloody hell, Constable, he's going to chop off *your* head as well. Go for his bloody legs.' Ernest took handcuffs from his back pocket. The man pulled a burning coal from his hair and threw it forcefully at Ernest. It would be a matter of seconds before another might hit him, sending his police uniform, hair and eyebrows up in flames. Drastic action was needed.

Ernest boomed out, 'I order you to raise your hands and drop Cecilia Willows' foot.'

Hannah's husband said the only thing he was going to do was to tear Ernest limb from limb. Fearing for his life, Ernest dodged him and grabbed two chicken bones from the altar, hoping they didn't belong to Ethel or Ms Prim. Holding them together, he made the sign of the cross in front of him. The man came closer, howled in pain at the chicken-bone crucifix and dropped Cecilia's foot on the ground. Ernest took the opportunity to handcuff the axe-man's bony legs together while Hannah's head whooped and shrieked with joy.

Santeros came out of his trance. Ernest said, 'You're under arrest for instigation to murder—' He didn't manage to finish the sentence as Santeros took to his heels and ran out of the room, his white robes flapping behind him, up the stairs and out into the night.

In the basement, Gottfried saw the cage door open as if by magic and felt someone lift him and carry him outside the house. A gruff authoritative voice whispered in his ear, 'Go back to the henhouse and keep Virgin company.' Gottfried needed no further encouragement. He couldn't wait to get home. Outside in the darkness, Ernest could hear someone running and panting and the sound of Porkchop's trotters in hot pursuit. Then a howling scream and silence. He ran behind the farmhouse and into the field looking for Porkchop. There was a full moon, which highlighted his pink body. Santeros was squashed flat, his robe in tatters and imprints of trotters down his legs. Ernest turned him over and saw he was well and truly dead.

Porkchop said, 'It was an accident. He tripped over a rock and I tripped over him.'

'Are you telling the truth? It wasn't revenge was it?'

'Of course not, I didn't have anything against him.'

'I'll have to interrogate you.'

'I think you're being a bit unfair, Ernest. You can't go around suspecting all your friends of being liars.' He said he was offended.

Ernest took out his notepad. 'I'm a police officer and I don't have friends when it comes to murder.'

He was surprised when Porkchop told him he could find his own way home and trotted towards a flat part of the field for take-off. Tonight was the first time Ernest had found himself alone in a situation of real danger. He had to admit he felt a teeny-weeny bit scared. Hurrying towards the gate, he felt a tap on his shoulder.

Turning around, Ernest saw the ghost of Santeros towering over him like a huge vulture. He didn't have his handcuffs as they were on the axe-man's ankles, but he knew what to do. Ernest grabbed an ankle and gave a sharp tug. Santeros tottered and fell to the ground with the force of a building being demolished by dynamite. He lay spread-eagled and groaning and holding his head.

'Now get up and march,' Ernest ordered, pointing in the direction of the door.

Once inside the basement, Ernest pushed Santeros into a corner and made sure he was out of reach of the axe-man. Santeros held up his arms across his face as Ernest picked up a knife from the altar and advanced on him. He needn't have worried, the knife was used to cut off strips from his caftan to bind his wrists and ankles.

He heard Hannah laugh, 'That's two jailbirds with one stone. You should roast them for dinner.' Her head rocked from side to side as she began to croon, 'I lost my head in San Francisco.'

The axeman retorted, 'You've never been there.'

'You wouldn't take me. I wanted some flowers in my hair.'

'You'd already been dead ten years by the time flower power was in fashion.'

'That's no excuse.' She continued crooning, 'And those little cable cars shot quickly to the stars.'

'You've got the words wrong.'

'No I haven't.'

'Yes you have.'

Ernest could see the axe-man's face redden as he was about to unleash his violent temper. Picking up the axe from the floor, Ernest quickly threw it into the cage in the corner, previously Gottfried's prison. Hannah rattled off a stream of abuse at Santeros and her husband which turned into a marathon nagging session. Ernest left them to their fate, knowing that an even worse one was about to descend upon them. Their time had come.

Floating down the lane towards home, Ernest saw a black carriage pass in front of the full moon. It was drawn by six laughing, brown and black spotted, snarling hyenas. Beasts from the Underworld. Greedy. Gluttonous. Powerful. Jaws able to crush a skull. Or so he'd heard. Whipping them to a frenzy was a fiend in a fiery cloak. Ernest glided quickly away as the carriage landed in front of the door to the basement. In the dark he could hear screams and Hannah laughing uncontrollably.

Dancing in the moonlight

Cecilia returned to the graveyard with Fred and laid his seemingly lifeless body on the grass. His heart was beating but he was out cold. She shook him gently. Fred was enjoying being fussed over and pretended to be dead. He heard her say, 'Come on, Fred, wake up.' He felt her open his beak and breathe her breath down his throat then shout, 'Come on, you goddamn bird, wake up.'

He opened his eyes and struggled free. 'I'm not a bird—' he started to say.

Cecilia grabbed him and held him close to her chest. She was crying, 'Oh Fred, I thought you were dead.'

'I can't die twice. Please let me down, your tears are wetting my feathers. And the tulle of your ballet dress is sticking into my chest.' He felt her place him gently on the grass.

'I hope you realise I resurrected you,' she said.

'I wasn't dead, I was just pretending.' She said she felt like slapping him. Fred told her to dry her eyes and stop being so dramatic. 'But thank you anyway for your concern.'

Cecilia started bawling, 'Don't ever do that to me again, you gave me a fright.'

'Does it mean you like me?' In response she picked him up and planted a kiss on his beak. There followed a conversation during which they talked about life on earth.

Fred said, 'Actually, I prefer to be dead. At least I'm free and not confined to a chicken-run.'

'I feel free too and I don't have to cook and clean and stay in the house. I can do what I want with only you and Ernest to bother me.'

'I'll try not to bother you in future,' replied Fred, crossing his heart.

'And I'll try not to bother you either. By the way, your harem, Ethel and Ms Prim, will be arriving very soon.'

Fred whooped and jumped up and down and turned around, spinning faster and faster until he felt dizzy and fell over. Cecilia watched, impressed. 'Well, I do believe you've passed the whirling test. You're whirling very well. Just don't go materialising in front of Tallulah. You'll scare her to death and end up in Hell. And Ernest won't be pleased.'

Fred thanked her for her advice and asked her to dance with him the way they'd danced at the party.

'Whenever you want,' she replied, grabbing his wings and laughing.

'Just remember one-two-three, one-two-three and turn,' said Fred as she whirled him around the graveyard in perfect time, humming a waltz as they danced up and over the church steeple in the moonlight.

'Life was never like this,' said Fred. Cecilia nodded in agreement saying that now she could dance and fly, even the sky was no limit.

'We could reach the moon,' said Fred as they whirled higher.

She laughed, telling him to keep his feet on the ground and think of Ethel.

The morning after

James awoke at around 6am. He wanted to surprise Tallulah with a cup of tea in bed. He felt like bursting into song but it was a bit too early. After making the tea, he carried it to the bedroom and woke her up gently. She smiled and stretched. Her face, smooth and relaxed, glowed youthfully. The wrinkles seemed to have disappeared overnight.

'What time is it?' she asked.

'Seven o'clock.'

'You look much younger this morning, James. Just like you did in Paris. In fact last night we were young all over again.'

James beamed. 'Well, I have to admit, when I made love to you, I only saw your beauty and how you were all those many years ago. You are lovely you know.'

Tallulah laughed. 'In other words, you were fantasizing about me being a young thing.'

He felt his face redden. 'I don't want to give you the wrong impression. I respect you and I'd ask you to marry me if I was better off but the hotel's going downhill.'

She sympathised. 'That's the trouble with old buildings. They're high maintenance. Bluebell Vicarage is too big for me and I'll probably give it to Scarlett and Roland as a wedding present. And talking about marriage, I wouldn't mind marrying you.'

'Would you really want to live in a run-down hotel?'

She said, 'I have quite a nest egg. We could convert it into a rest home or invent other money-making schemes to help maintain the place. We could hold writers' workshops and ask

Roland to facilitate them. Or Marigold could hold seances and meditation classes to connect with the dead.'

He told her he liked the idea. Her next question disturbed him.

'James, would you like to share my cryonics canister?'

'I'm not intending to die just yet.'

'We can still be together in ninety years' time—'

'All right then, as long as I can spend ninety years in the nude with you,' he joked.

She laughed coquettishly. 'You have to get your act together, James. I don't want the project turning into a white elephant and we'll have to get married first.'

James chortled. 'Of course we have to get married first, otherwise what would people think about us sharing a canister in the nude?'

'I'm not moving in here until we're married.'

'Fine, but can we still have fun now and then?'

'Why not?'

After their romp last night, he felt different – more assertive, courageous and handsome. Tallulah reflected that his body wasn't so bad and she couldn't see it in the dark anyway. Before he'd kissed her, he'd cleaned his teeth and washed his armpits and the bits below. And no mention had been made about her legs, which in any case had been shaved before she left her house.

After changing into his clothes, James strode to the kitchen to prepare breakfast. From now on there would be no slouching or shuffling along in his slippers. Over a breakfast of eggs, bacon and the works, they talked about the future.

'Do you still want to marry me?' James asked.

'Well, it's only forty years late, but yes, I would.'

They held hands and kissed briefly. Tallulah said, 'Sorry, but I have to get back home and feed the chickens, they must be starving.'

'I'll drive you home,' said James, feeling on top of the world.

At Bluebell Vicarage, Tallulah put the kettle on and brought out the biscuits. While the tea brewed, she unlocked the back door. 'I'm just going to feed the chickens,' she called brightly. 'I'll be back in a minute.'

James was stirring the tea in the pot when he heard Tallulah scream. Before he'd time to get to the back door, she appeared and stood in the doorway, her face ashen. She spoke with a breathless staccato voice. 'There's only Virgin and Gottfried in the chicken-run. The others have disappeared. I don't understand it. Gottfried's been missing for ages. How did he get back in and where are the others?'

James took her arm and led her to a chair. 'Don't worry. At our age, we sometimes forget things like closing gates. They're probably running around the countryside with their feathered friends.' James hoped so. The last thing he wanted was chickens running around the hotel after they were married.

Veronica's resignation

Mrs Horsefield came unannounced to *Agriculture and Business Monthly* to talk to Scarlett. 'I've been told Veronica's resigning,' she said, asking why.

'Speak to the man himself about it.' Scarlett replied offhandedly, pointing to Roland who had his head down in documents partly covered by his long hair. Mrs Horsefield shuddered. As much as she'd despised him in the past, she now had to make amends in the name of peace for all, otherwise her life in the office wouldn't be worth living.

She said stiffly, 'Roland, we all underestimated you.'

Roland continued writing. 'Let's forget it. It's in the past, I've given my notice in.'

Scarlett stepped in to explain. 'He hasn't exactly given in his notice. He's just changing places with Serge for the moment. Serge won't be coming back.'

Mrs Horsefield said, 'I'm so sorry to hear it. So many disasters in our lives. And poor Florence too.' She paused for a decent length of time as people do when faced with death and need to get on with business. 'I'm sure the community would like Roland to continue being Veronica.'

Roland said he had to put her right about the mutual animosity between himself and his father, who would block him at every turn.

She said, 'Tomorrow we have a council meeting and I can slip it onto the agenda so a vote can be taken on it. I'm sure the other councillors will be on your side.'

'Forget it, everyone thinks I'm a liar. I'm hardly a good advertisement to preach love and harmony.'

The following morning in his office, Councillor Willows looked at the addition to the agenda which read, 'Veronica's dismissal'.

'What the hell is this?' he asked Mrs Horsefield.

'Your son has decided to give in his notice. He's thrown in the towel.'

Ignatius sprang out of his chair and banged his fist on the desk. 'My own flesh and blood throwing in the towel? I don't believe it. I won't allow a son of mine to give up so easily. He's getting married soon.' He picked up the phone and called Roland's direct number at the office.

'Roland, what's this I hear about you giving in your notice?'

'Dad, I conned you and the community.'

'You said it was a joke, so let it be.'

Their conversation was brief. Both felt a bit embarrassed. Emotions were not something they were used to sharing.

'Your mum and I want to invite you and Scarlett for lunch. We can talk about it then.'

Roland said, 'Thanks, Dad. See you soon.'

Veronica's dismissal was scrapped from the agenda.

Seeing as Ignatius had always complained about her putting her freezing cold feet on his legs in bed, Gladys decided to be nice and wear a pair of bedsocks. Cuddling up, she told him she loved him. When he asked her if she was on a high or had a hormonal problem, she took off her nightdress and threw it across the room where it missed the chair. She didn't get up and put it where it belonged. She was tired of being tidy. The house hadn't looked lived-in since Roland moved out.

'Iggy, I can't wait to see Roland and Scarlett. We've got a daughter as well now. There'll soon be the pitter-patter of tiny feet.'

Ignatius cringed. He knew the pitter-patter of tiny feet would soon turn to a clomp-clomp of hob-nail boots, but decided to count his blessings. Looking on the bright side, he had a son to 'bond' with and a soon-to-be daughter-in-law and maybe eventually a grandson. His secretary was a bit rebellious but worth her weight in gold. And his wife loved him, at least for the moment. He shouldn't complain. Last night was one of the rare times in the past ten years he'd seen her naked.

The prodigal son returns

Gladys sensed her husband was a bit tense today. He looked older. She desperately wanted him to be in a good mood for Roland and Scarlett's engagement lunch.

'I'm sure Scarlett's a nice girl. She'll make a lovely wife for Roland,' she said as Ignatius looked at her from below dark eyebrows.

'It's not her I'm worried about. It's her mad aunt. She's always causing trouble.'

'She's just a nice harmless old lady who tends her vegetable patch and keeps down the slugs.'

'You're talking rubbish as usual,' Ignatius said in a tone he used before breakfast or lunch or when his blood sugar was low.

'By the way, I've invited your assistant Mrs Horsefield.'

'What for?'

'Well, she was the one who brought the family together.'

'You shouldn't have invited her. The working class should mix with their own kind. We can't start changing society's rules.'

'If it weren't for the working class you wouldn't be where you are. You didn't think they were the pits when you took their votes and became *Councillor* Wheeler.'

Over the years, Gladys had learned to read doorbell rings. At a sharp business-like ring, she quickly removed her apron and threw it on the draining board.

'It's sure to be Mrs Horsefield,' she called. Ignatius shot up the stairs and locked himself in the bathroom to prepare a welcome speech for the unwelcome.

Mrs Horsefield had gone to great lengths to look elegant in an electric blue jersey dress and a black wool stole. Her usually unruly blonde hair had been to the hairdressers along with her eyebrows, which had been trimmed. Gladys welcomed her and led her to the photos carpeting the coffee table. 'The others will be here soon. Roland's coming home at last thanks to you. It's been nearly three years since Ignatius kicked him out of the house.'

It wasn't long before Roland and Scarlett arrived. Theirs was an insistent loud ring announcing 'We're here, hurry up and open the door'. Gladys hugged them both warmly and led them to join Mrs Horsefield on the settee to look at photos of Roland when he was a baby.

'Your dad's in the bathroom getting ready. He'll be down in a minute,' she told Roland.

They heard knuckles rap the door several times.

Scarlett jumped up and rolled her eyes. 'Aunt Tallulah always has to do things differently.'

In the meantime, Ignatius leaned with both hands on the washbasin and peered into the mirror talking to himself and mentally preparing a speech about the prodigal son returning home.

Gladys shouted up the stairs, 'The guests have arrived!'

He combed his hair and emerged from his safe haven, walking heavily down the stairs trying to remember what he was going to say. Luckily the assembled were poring over photos on the coffee table. He coughed and addressed them. 'Welcome to our house.' He couldn't remember the rest which was something about forgiving the wayward. When he embraced Roland, they all clapped.

Gladys felt the tears start. 'I'm just going to the kitchen to finish the lunch. It'll be ready in a jiffy. You can take your places at the table.' She didn't want them to see her cry. Ignatius would think she was being silly, although she told herself she no longer cared about what he might think. She wanted to be liberated from the kitchen sink.

The dining room table had been set with best china and cutlery Gladys only brought out on special occasions. There were murmurs of admiration as they took their places. Sitting on each plate was a prawn cocktail.

Tallulah was the first to speak. 'It's a long time since I've seen such finery in someone else's house.'

Scarlett and Roland looked at one another as if to say 'does she think she's the only one with finery?'

Ignatius brought out a bottle of champagne and filled the crystal champagne flutes. Gladys joined them. She'd been waiting for this moment all her life. Her little Roland was going to get married.

Ignatius raised his glass and looked at Scarlett and Roland. His memory suddenly failed him. He couldn't remember his lines. He said the first thing that came into his head. 'Congratulations to the happy couple and welcome to our house.'

After the hugs, kisses, clapping, congratulations and happy tears, Gladys brought in roast lamb with mint sauce, roast potatoes and peas, while Ignatius served red wine. Compliments flowed about the food and it seemed natural to talk about the wedding catering and how many guests would be invited.

After the main meal and wine, Gladys brought in the sweet – chocolate pudding with custard. Another bottle of champagne was produced and they toasted again and tucked into the pudding.

Mrs Horsefield dabbed at her eyes. 'It's all so romantic,' she said.

Tallulah said, 'I feel a bit tiddly but we have to celebrate another happy event. Ignatius, could you kindly pour me a little more champagne.' She lifted her flute towards him.

Scarlett and Roland exchanged glances and waited for Tallulah's bombshell.

'I'm going to marry James,' she announced.

For pure impact she couldn't have chosen a better moment. Spoons stopped halfway to mouths. Champagne flutes hovered. Hands trembled. Gladys dropped hers by accident. Ignatius thought of going to the pub – his speech in the bathroom hadn't prepared him for such an emergency as two weddings at once.

Scarlett broke the shocked silence. 'Come on, I'll take you home, you've had too much to drink.'

But Tallulah wouldn't hear of it. 'I'm not drunk and I didn't invent it. I really am getting married. I never told you I was supposed to marry James forty years ago before he jilted me for Cecilia, did I? We're just tying the knot a bit late.'

Ignatius hadn't foreseen a drama unfolding in his house nor wanted to hear further embarrassing confessions. He did the only thing possible. He poured himself another glass and raised it in toast. 'Congratulations to the second happy couple and welcome to our house.'

They raised their glasses and toasted Tallulah and James.

Scarlett whispered to Roland, 'Let's get out of here and take her home before she asks if we can have a double wedding.'

Roland whispered back, 'Lock her in the basement and throw away the key.'

Tallulah sang in the car all the way home. After dropping her off and making sure she had her key on the inside of the door, Scarlett and Roland left her there.

Locking the front door, Tallulah retired to the living

room and sank into an armchair. She poured herself a gin and tonic to give her some inspiration to write 'The Plan' to remove Stanley before he could harass her further and ruin her future with James. Two gin and tonics later, she tore it up and fell asleep.

Holy ghosts

Two coffins lay side by side in Saint Peter's Basilica. In the first lay Pope Joseph I, in the second, Cardinal Desi Nkosi. It had taken some doing and taken up a lot of his time, but eventually Joseph had wrung a promise from his confessor to have Nkosi and himself buried side by side in the Vatican Grottoes.

'If it weren't for you, Joseph, I'd still be hanging around the necropolis with the Opus Dei,' Nkosi said, thanking him for helping to sort out his last resting place. Pope Joseph, his head comfortable on his pillow in the coffin, smiled smugly. 'Before my death, I trod on a few toes by promoting you, but it was worth it, even though it cost me my life. There were a few devils opposed to you because of your work in South Africa. You did well to speak out about the massacres and Apartheid. If it's of any comfort the United States is now discussing the Comprehensive Anti-Apartheid Act.'

Nkosi said, 'Such a pity I dropped dead so soon. There hasn't been an African Pope since the year 496. We've been waiting almost two thousand years.'

'My goodness, have we? How time flies.'

'Just one question, Joseph. When we get to the Pearly Gates will black people be divided from the whites?'

'Certainly not. We're all equal in the eyes of God.'

'In my country blacks are divided from whites even on the buses. We've been forced into segregated neighbourhoods and punished by law for mixed marriages.'

Pope Joseph said, 'I know. Look on the bright side. Your

death has set off a series of events which has shocked the international community and it's just a matter of time before Apartheid comes to an end. I predict it'll happen in 1990. That's in four years time. I know it's no comfort, but your death, though painful for many, has served a purpose, similar to our Lord's sacrifice for humanity.'

'Does it mean I'll be made a saint? Not because I want any privileges, you know I'm against them, but it's just a matter of principle.'

'You have to get a couple of miracles attributed to you first,' said Joseph.

Nkosi replied he'd survived the College of Cardinals, which was in itself a miracle. And that having to lay in State for twenty days should get them both a sainthood.

Joseph laughed. 'We won't be lying here for twenty days. Very soon we're going to escape and take the Pearly Gates Express train. Now sleep.'

Nkosi closed his eyes and slept the sleep of the dead. He was flying over the Zululand savannah where the animals ran free but where his people were in chains. He looked in awe at the sunset and the dream changed. He was riding in a bus full of people of different colours. There was no Apartheid sign dividing blacks from whites. Everyone smiled and prayed together as one.

The last goodbye

James opened the letter Anushka had sent him from Cuba. His heart quickened, hoping he could eventually visit her and perhaps give her away at her wedding, if she ever found a husband. She hadn't been lucky so far what with Serge deserting her.

Havana, Cuba, September 1986

Dear James,

I am thinking of you and your kindness. My job in Havana is full of embassy parties and soon I will visit raspberry projects in Pinar del Rio province (but the location is secret as the raspberries are only for the privileged and the foreigners), I will also visit the beach at Maria La Gorda and Cape San Antonio in the national park of Guanahacabibes Peninsular where there are vultures, iguanas and beautiful log cabins on a deserted tropical beach.

The abandoned dogs in Cuba are in a terrible state with no fur with so much scratching from having fleas. I have some good news for you. I will get married in the second week of December after the hurricane season. I will ask a nice diplomat to send an invitation for you. You will be my father and walk me down the aisle. I will get married to Anton, who I met in Rome, as we are in love. I will get him a job as a driver at one of the embassies. Please bring anti-flea powder which I will give to the vet for the dogs. I am very happy here as I am finally a liberated woman. I have to go now as there is a party in the streets of Havana to celebrate the Carnival.

Very much love to my adopted father.

Anushka.

James put Anushka's letter in his bedside drawer. It seemed she was having a good time. How exciting, he would soon book a plane ticket. It worried him how Tallulah would react to his trip. Would she object? Or want to come with him? And how would he tell Cecilia he was going to marry Tallulah? He hoped she would visit him tonight so he could tell her.

Thoughts of Cecilia assailed him as he got into bed. Much later she arrived, fortunately without her feather duster. He waited for her to start vacuuming his bedroom and flushing the toilet, but she didn't. She didn't sit on his chest either, she just sat by his side.

'I know you didn't push me from the window,' she said. He knew it was a half-apology.

'Never mind, we all make mistakes,' he replied.

Her fingers touched the dust on the bedside table and flicked it off. 'I'm sorry I tormented you all those years with the housework.'

'You always were headstrong, Cecilia. But even though I was angry with you I swear I would never have pushed you from the window. You were my princess.'

She started to sniffle. 'I'm not coming back to see you. I'm starting out on my trip to Heaven.'

He was happy and sad at the same time. It was their last goodbye. He took the bull by the horns. 'I'm going to marry Tallulah,' he said sorrowfully, knowing she'd be hurt.

Instead, she placed a kiss on his cheek. 'Have a good life with her,' she said in a resigned kind of tone.

Then she swirled upwards and was gone, leaving a smell of mothballs behind her and a cloud of dust heading up his nostrils.

Rumbles of dissent

The time had finally arrived. As had been promised in March, the Pearly Gates Express was on its way. It was the end of September and almost dawn in the waiting room of Witherington station. Ernest, Fred, Porkchop, Bertha and Norman listened to Cecilia telling them she'd said goodbye to James forever. 'He's going to marry Tallulah,' she wailed.

Fred looked perplexed. 'So what's the problem? You're leaving for Purgatory.'

'I'm too upset to answer questions.'

Ernest imagined it was jealousy speaking. He said gruffly, 'What about your death? Can I write it off as case closed?'

Cecilia showed him her stump. 'Certainly not. What I want to know is – when am I going to get my foot back? I can't hobble around forever.'

'I promise you'll get it back once we're on the train. It's only bones now, but as soon as you step onto the train you'll find a new foot on the end of your stump, then you can dance whenever you want.'

Cecilia's face lit up then darkened. 'What about Santeros? Can I be sure he won't be after my other foot?'

Ernest's reply was blunt. 'He's dead and in Hell with headless-Hannah's husband. They were dragged away by the devil's evil hyenas.'

Cecilia said, 'I object. It's politically incorrect to call animals evil.'

'Hear, hear,' said Fred, saying they'd probably make good pets if treated properly.

Ernest begged to differ. 'You can't domesticate wild animals and you wouldn't want one of those prowling around your sleeping quarters.'

Cecilia chipped in, 'That may be the case, but I once saw a man on the television being kissed on the cheek by an hyena and they were wandering around a village in Africa and being fed, which means they're not all bad. They're mammals and need love and attention.'

Seeing as she always had to have the last word, Ernest said nothing but to his chagrin, Fred picked up where she'd left off. 'What I object to is the idea of black horses pulling the devil's carriage. I've never known a horse be so evil as to be sent to Hell. On the contrary, some of their owners deserve to be sent there.' He ruffled his feathers as a sign of protest. Ernest foresaw a rough time on the train. 'Look, can we get back to reality? I don't want any trouble from the pair of you when we get to the Pearly Gates. You have to toe the line.'

Cecilia stuck out her stump again for all to see. 'I can't toe the line if mine are missing.'

At that point Ernest pulled rank. 'One more word from you and I'll put you in isolation for a month.'

Cecilia's voice rose a tone. 'Constable Ernest Barnstable, you're a tyrant and you can't gag *me*.'

Fred looked at Ernest's face, getting redder by the minute and said, 'If you want I can sing you a song, Ernest?'

Ernest said, 'How about if I sing *you* a song called, *I want to wring your neck*?'

'I don't know that one. How about *I've lost my cool*?' Fred said, smirking and exchanging a rallying glance with Cecilia. Ernest fought down his anger and hoped the train would arrive before he lost his reasoning and committed yet another sin.

He looked at his watch. The train was late. Anxious to avoid further discussions he decided to speak about the

Seven Terraces of Deadly Sins and allocate them their terrace of punishment. He read from his notes:

Pride – Valley of odd shoes and lost socks – Bertha, Cecilia, Ethel and Ms Prim.

Envy – Swamp of bile-green boiled cabbages – Cecilia, Ethel and Ms Prim.

Wrath – Cliff of Scottish Whirling Dervishes – Bertha and Cecilia.

Sloth – Stream of snapping turtles under treadmills – Fred and Norman.

Greed – Coal mine of fool's gold – vacant.

Gluttony – Cesspit of fermented prunes – Porkchop only.

Lust – Field of raw garlic and onions – Cecilia, Fred and Norman.

Before Ernest could open his mouth further, there was a rumbling of dissent. Cecilia objected to being subjected to four terraces as she hated odd shoes and never wore socks and wouldn't be seen dead eating boiled cabbages or raw garlic and onions. As for whirling on a cliff, she didn't want to fall to her death or have the Whirling Scottish Dervishes see her knickers. Bertha said she also hated odd shoes and was worried for her bunions. Norman and Fred, who were due for the terraces of Sloth and Lust, both agreed they hated bad breath from garlic and onions, which would keep any nice women away and opted for the stream of snapping turtles and treadmills. Ethel, although she loved Fred, didn't want to run behind him on a treadmill as it was demeaning. The biggest complaint came from Porkchop who felt he was being discriminated against over his weight, which was hereditary. He objected to being called a glutton and wanted to join Fred and Norman on the treadmill. Ethel then changed her mind and said she wanted to run on it too with Fred, until he started squawking because four of them on the treadmill running at different speeds would cause them all to fall off into the stream of snapping turtles. Ms Prim complained she was getting a headache and Ernest admitted he was getting one too.

Cecilia asked Ernest how many days they would purge in Purgatory.

'One month.'

'Over my dead body. It's far too long and I don't want the whirling skirt to show my bloomers to all and sundry for thirty days,' Cecilia said, hopping around on her stump as if it was a pogo stick.

Ernest said, 'How about two weeks?'

She shook her head. 'Unless you can come up with something better, you're going to have a strike on your hands.' The others nodded and Ernest foresaw a full-blown rebellion on the train.

'As a special concession, but only because I myself have decided, I'll give you all only one week in Purgatory.'

They nodded in agreement and Ernest congratulated himself for his peacemaking skills. Hearing a cock crowing – no doubt it was Gottfried – Cecilia hobbled out onto the platform and pointed along the track as the Pearly Gates Express approached. 'I can see people hanging out of the windows and waving,' she yelled excitedly.

The ghostly Pearly Gates Express steamed into the Witherington Railway Station. Stately and grand, it looked a bit like the Orient Express. The seven carriages, with forty-nine seats in each, were not altogether full, in fact the first one was almost empty. A sign on the window read *Reserved for Security Officer and Gatekeeper of Purgatory ad interim and entourage.* Ernest beamed, stuck out his chest proudly and invited them to alight. As Ernest had promised, Cecilia's foot miraculously soldered to her stump as soon as she entered the carriage.

Whirling around, she danced up and down the aisle on her new-found foot. With a shriek of delight, Fred ran to the back of the carriage where Ethel and Ms Prim were sitting with the graveyard crowd. Ernest looked around and checked names on his list. 'Florence and Mrs Sarehole-Reape are missing,' he said, wondering where they could be. Heads turned to see the two women running along the platform waving their arms. Too late. A man on the list was also missing.

Ernest said, 'Has anyone seen Serge Gallo? He was run down on the Isle of Wight by a black removals van.'

No one had seen Serge and Ernest wrote next to his name *Absent Without Leave. Destined for the Terraces of Sloth and Lust* and ticked the names of the two popes as being present. With a shudder, the train pulled out of the station. The Pearly Gates Express rose above the houses and treetops on its way to a new location, somewhere in a big unknown space they imagined would be Heaven. The trip was just long enough for Cecilia to dance a waltz with Norman and for Fred to swing Ethel around backwards in a fox trot down the aisle before the train came to a halt.

The Pearly Gates Railway Station looked suspiciously like the one in Witherington – two tracks, two platforms in the middle of a cow field. Except with differences – there were no cows or other wildlife and no rain-clouds in the incredibly blue sky. Disembarking they looked around in wonder. In the distance beyond the gates were white-painted Nissen huts as far as the horizon.

Fred said, 'Just look at those huts. They must be left over from the Second World War.'

'Is this an army camp?' Cecilia asked Ernest.

He pointed to a sign on the Pearly Gates which read, 'Welcome to Paradise'.

Cecilia said, 'It looks more like Hell to me.'

Life of hell inside the Pearly Gates

A man in a long white robe with white spiky hair and beard introduced himself as Saint Peter and presented his deputy Napoleon who stood to attention in full uniform and bicorn hat.

'Welcome to the purge, sorry I meant Purgatory.' Saint Peter laughed at his own joke and took a playful swipe at Napoleon's hat. He pointed at the Pearly Gates which had no pearls and were tall planks of wood painted white and partially covered by 'forbidden' notices. 'The gates have been made by our carpenter. We don't have pollution up here so everything stays white. Let me lead you all through.'

Like the Pied Piper of Hamelin, Saint Peter skipped through the gates with Ernest and about two hundred people. 'I'm skipping the light fandango, which I invented myself. We like to encourage creativity here, but every initiative has to be first authorised by the Pearly Gates Censors and the Security Officer.'

Cecilia whispered to Fred, 'He's not at all how I imagined Saint Peter to be.'

Ernest said, 'Pope Joseph and Pope Nkosi should be sent directly to Heaven. There's no need to put them with the others going to Purgatory.'

Saint Peter smiled. 'They will be taken care of.'

They were led towards a large hut. Saint Peter said, 'This is our Reception and Security office and here are our assistant security officers.' He indicated two heavies with squashed boxer-like noses and said to Ernest, 'As the new Pearly Gates Security Officer, you will be supervising them.'

The one with the biggest nose pointed to Fred and Porkchop. 'Chickens and pigs aren't allowed in.' He thumped his left palm with his right fist.

Fred stuck out his neck. 'First of all I'm not a chicken, I'm a cockerel and I want to make a complaint. I was black and now I'm white,' he protested.

Cecilia sided with Fred. 'This is discrimination. Animals should be allowed into Heaven.' She quoted from the scriptures about the fowl of the earth and the galloping horses.

The man looked at her blankly and walked away saying, 'I've got a carriage full of politicians to sort out, I don't have time for nonsense.'

Cecilia called after him, 'Just send them all to hell.'

Pope Joseph whispered to Saint Peter, 'Look, my son, if it weren't for animals, our earth would be barren, as they supply fertilizer. And they do it free of charge. So if you want eggs for breakfast, I suggest you let them in. They're free from worms.'

Saint Peter hesitated. 'I'll have to ask the boss upstairs.'

Cardinal Nkosi chipped in, 'Use your initiative, old man. When you come to the negotiating table you have to bring solutions, not problems. I'm sure God wouldn't want to be seen discriminating against animals.'

In the end, Saint Peter let them stay, being short of patience and no time to talk to God.

Fred looked around. 'What a weird place. There aren't any pearls on the gates, just lots of pieces of paper pinned to posts, telling us what we can and can't do.'

Napoleon and the heavies handed out flyers with 'Rules and Regulations' printed on them:

FORBIDDEN: Swearing and insulting behaviour; fighting, including kicking and chasing; whispering in groups; political activism; rebellion; jumping on beds and pillow-fighting; bringing coloured paint inside the Pearly Gates (the only authorised person is our carpenter). Absolutely forbidden are: cosmetics and mod cons such as washing machines.

Cecilia's mouth opened like a chasm and she screamed, 'I want my washing machine. I can't possibly wash my clothes by hand.'

Saint Peter's eyes blazed as they met hers and everyone could see he was on a short fuse. 'Good lady, you can have your washing machine as long as you go back to earth and load it onto the Pearly Gates Express yourself.'

Cecilia told him she'd never had to lift anything in her life and it was far too heavy for her.

His reply was, 'We have a laundry where we send troublemakers to trample clothes with their feet. If you prefer, I can arrange for you to work there instead of going to the terraces.'

Cecilia whirled and screamed, 'I'm not working in a sweat shop and I'm not touching anyone's dirty smalls.'

Saint Peter turned his back on her and signalled to Ernest to sort her out. Ernest put a friendly hand on her arm. 'Please be reasonable, Cecilia. There's no one to bring your washing machine here and you'll get clean, white clothes whenever you wish. If I were you I'd stop making a fuss. If you continue, I'll make you swim in the stream of snapping turtles.' She replied she didn't want her toes snapped off as she wanted to dance with Norman.

'Is it settled then?'

'I suppose so.'

'Are you satisfied and happy without your washing machine and your clothes being washed in the communal laundry?'

She didn't reply and Ernest took it for a 'yes'. He walked away leaving her complaining to Fred and angrily questioning Saint Peter's authority.

As they all trundled past reception, an unexpected blast of a trumpet brought them to a halt.

Saint Peter shouted, 'Silence!' and gave a welcome speech about being delighted to be their host. He ended it by saying, 'Please read the rules and regulations pinned on the notice board by the reception. Regarding accommodation, fourteen Nissen huts are divided between male and female. I assume there are around two hundred of you here so hopefully there should be enough otherwise you'll have to build a few yourselves. Each of these barracks has around forty-nine beds, side by side with a laundry basket in between where you will find your white robe. It is forbidden to wear jewellery, therefore any pieces should be given to my security officers to put in the safe. The week will proceed as follows:

4am. Trumpet call and bed-making supervised by Napoleon.

4.30am. Barrack inspections by the Salvation Army – you should stand to attention by your bed for this.

5am. Morning prayers and confessions with Saint Peter – myself.

6am. The long march forward to the seven terraces of punishment with the security team. Sheets and robes will be sent to the communal laundry every Saturday and any subversive activities are punishable by a day listening to sermons by the security team.'

Saint Peter went on to talk about the absence of toilets, 'motions' and 'evacuations' were no longer needed as there was no food for their bodies to process and in any case there was no toilet paper either. They would never again need to go to the toilet.

Someone shouted, 'Thank God we don't have to shovel shit.' Saint Peter glared and motioned to the man with the biggest squashed nose who carted the heckler away.

Saint Peter shouted above the murmur, 'There'll be no bad language here and anyone caught doing so will have their mouth washed with carbolic soap.'

Cecilia began to hyperventilate. She threw her arms into the air, screamed and faked a faint. Attention moved from Saint Peter to Cecilia. Strangely enough, her ballet dress was down over her legs and her bloomers were well covered. Ernest whispered in her ear. 'Get up immediately or I'll tell everyone you're putting it on.' Cecilia opened her eyes slowly, swept a hand across her brow and lifted her arms to be helped up off the ground. Saint Peter said he hoped she was alright before continuing his speech.

'Tomorrow morning you will all visit the Terraces of Purgatory, except for the two popes who will be temporarily accommodated in one of our cells for their safety. You can find the definitions of the seven terraces on the table outside reception alongside the complaints forms. Please disperse quietly in single file.'

Fred had a headache. It had been a long day, he was tired and he didn't know where he was going to sleep. He felt tears start. Then his nerves snapped and he screamed, 'Why am I white? I want to be black again.'

Saint Peter called on Ernest to shut him up in case he started a riot. Ernest nodded and felt his patience fading.

Ernest took Fred and Cecilia aside. Grabbing Fred by the throat and Cecilia by the arm, he pulled them inside reception and into his office. 'You can sleep on the floor tonight and I'll be here in the morning to take your complaints.'

Fred and Cecilia glanced at each other and grimaced. They foresaw a life of hell with Ernest and Saint Peter.

After Ernest had left, Cecilia took Fred's wing and pulled him under the desk. She whispered, 'Did you see the plaque over the Reception hut?'

'No, what did it say?'

'Dedicated to George Orwell's revolutionary book.'

'Which one? *The Road to Wigan Pier*? Or *Nineteen Eighty-Four*?' Fred asked.

'Well it definitely wasn't *Wigan Pier*.'

'*Nineteen Eighty-Four*? I don't see the connection with this place.'

'Fred, stop being a dumb cluck. Don't you understand? Saint Peter is Big Brother and he's evil!'

Big brother

Entering his office the following morning, Ernest found Fred and Cecilia crouched beneath his desk. 'By the powers invested in me as Security Officer—'

Before he'd finished the sentence, Cecilia scrambled out, protesting she was about to have a nervous breakdown with all the spying going on. She then burst into a flood of tears which threatened to run down the front of her white ballet dress. Ernest handed her his handkerchief – the one upon which Bertha had blown her nose.

'I'll never get used to sleeping in barracks,' she sniffed.

'You have to be flexible. I'm sure you'll make some nice friends. We encourage community spirit and you'll get used to it. There'll be a "Love thy neighbour" policy and a party every Saturday night.'

Fred said, 'It doesn't sound too bad. There's a dance this Saturday and I'd like to take Ethel.'

Cecilia howled, 'I've no one to dance with. I feel lonely.'

'What about Norman?' Ernest asked.

'He'll be dancing with Bertha.'

Ernest said, 'Perhaps you need to reflect on your bad behaviour and your attitude about the grass being greener on the other side. Tomorrow I'm sending you back to earth to rest and meditate. There are two conditions – you will come back in one month's time and you will not visit James.'

Cecilia looked pleased.

Fred said, 'She thinks Saint Peter is Big Brother.'

Ernest guffawed and said he'd never heard anything so

ridiculous. 'Saint Peter is not Big Brother – he's everyone' brother. There has to be discipline here with so many people with different ideas. We can't have anarchy reigning.'

Cecilia replied, 'It seems to me as if we've landed in a lunatic asylum and I don't believe Saint Peter is who he says he is. I think he's a fake.'

The constable looked about to blow a fuse.

Fred intervened. 'I think Cecilia's right. Saint Peter is an imposter,' Fred mentioned the two popes being held in a cell as if they were prisoners.

Ernest left, slamming the door behind him, the seeds of doubt beginning to flourish in his mind. Saint Peter was acting a little strange and it was time to investigate.

Cecilia turned to Fred. 'I think you'll have to sing to Ernest again, he looked a bit stressed.'

'I don't think so. Ernest is on the warpath.'

'And due for the Terrace of *Wrath*?' Cecilia asked smirking spitefully.

'Probably. But I doubt it. There's going to be a big shake-up in this place.'

Cecilia grabbed Fred and whirled him around the room. 'I'm going to earth for a month,' she said with a sing-song voice, ignoring Fred's protests about leaving him to a possible full-scale holy showdown.

She stopped whirling and dumped Fred on Ernest's desk, then threw her arms in the air and shouted. 'I'm going to see James.'

Fred paled. Constable Ernest Barnstable's authority was being trampled on. 'Ernest said you shouldn't. He's going to marry Tallulah.'

'Then in the meantime, I'll just pop in to do a bit of dusting.'

The next morning, Fred and Ernest accompanied Cecilia to the station and waved her off. Fred kept quiet about her intention to visit James as he was sure Ernest had enough on his plate with the investigation and the sudden overnight disappearance of the two popes, Saint Peter and the two heavies.

Hours later, Ernest told Fred what he had learned so far – when the real Saint Peter had taken a sabbatical to visit his old haunts at the Vatican City, three communist infiltrators had taken over inside the Pearly Gates – the two heavies and the man posing as Saint Peter.

Ernest said, 'They have now been arrested and sent to where they belong. Had it not been for Cecilia putting doubts in my mind, the imposter and his cronies would have sent the two popes down to Hell – to the *inferno*. Perhaps I'll call Cecilia back after a week, she deserves to be with us.'

Ernest's thoughts then turned to his Serious Incident Reports and the conclusions of investigations. He sought out Bertha and asked her to set up a seance at the Rottingham Police Station with Marigold. Bertha said she would be delighted to visit her previous house to see who was lying in state in the viewing room and was curious to know how many people had died since Norman. Her comment didn't shock Ernest, who was used to the human trait of morbid interest. The village gossips enjoyed feeding on macabre information and disseminating it. Such information was powerful, precious, and stimulated a cathartic urge to rush to the telephone to be the first to share it with the whole community.

The final seance

Marigold sat at a small oblong table in the filing room of the Rottingham Police Station with three policemen and a policewoman who, according to town gossip, had once been Constable Barnstable's girlfriend. Her name in those days was Barbara, Babs for short.

Before the police had agreed to meet with Marigold, she'd had to guarantee confidentiality, as they weren't keen to let the public know they were dabbling in the paranormal.

The seance began and Marigold asked them to link hands. She told them not to break the circle. Closing her eyes, she focused on Ernest. Bertha was watching.

'Is there anybody there? Are you there, Ernest?' Marigold felt a hand touch her shoulder gently.

'Ernest is here. He wants to talk about his investigations into the flasher in the park and the death of Cecilia Willows and the new pope.'

Bertha noticed a flicker of interest in their eyes as they glanced at one another.

Marigold cocked her head to one side. She nodded and continued.

'He's telling me Pope Joseph was poisoned. The proof is in a letter in his bedside table, incriminating Archbishop Marius Conak and two Vatican guards. But it'll be hard to prove as the archbishop is dead.'

The youngest policeman said. 'I don't believe it. Who would want to poison the Pope?' The policewoman glared at him and he retreated into silence.

Marigold continued. 'Regarding the flasher in the park, Ernest urges you to detain the plumber's assistant for questioning.'

Marigold nodded again. 'Ernest is telling me Cecilia Willows wasn't murdered by her husband James. Her foot was severed post mortem by a Cuban exile called Santeros who wanted it for voodoo rites during a mind-control session. The proof is in the basement of Stanley Butterworth's farmhouse. There's a knife with Cecilia's blood on it and the man's fingerprints. Santeros was accidentally trampled to death by a pig and his body is in a field behind the house. In the farmhouse basement, there's a well-preserved head belonging to a woman of the fifties murdered by her husband. The head should be returned to her relatives for burial.'

The eldest police officer asked permission to break the circle.

'It all sounds a bit far-fetched to me. I want to check this out. I hope you're not wasting police time,' he said stiffly.

Marigold promised she wasn't and the three policemen left to check out the farmhouse.

The policewoman said, 'As soon as they get back with some proof, I'll pass on the information.'

Marigold added some information she didn't want to speak about in front of the others.

'Ernest asks if you can please visit his mum and tell her he's fine and misses her and will soon see his dad. If she doesn't believe you, tell her there's a box on top of the wardrobe with the Bible she gave him on his eighth birthday and a letter from you about the kiss in the woods on your sixteenth birthday.'

The policewoman's voice shook with emotion when she said, 'I'll be delighted to visit his mum. She's sure to remember me. Tell Ernest he's sorely missed.'

Marigold left the police station with Bertha, both happy with the outcome of the seance.

Bertha said, 'I can't wait to tell Ernest about his paramour and the loving look on her face each time his name was mentioned.'

Marigold said, 'Let's go to the pub. I need a drink. Talking to Ernest has worn me out.'

Bertha nodded. 'You can have one on me. I'd love to have a beer, but can you imagine the reaction if people see a glass of booze hovering in thin air over a table.

Marigold gave a hearty laugh. 'Thanks, Bertha. In that case, I think I'll have a double cognac and you can watch me drink it.'

'No problem. I don't want to go back to Ernest with alcohol on my breath. He's a devil to cope with. A right nosy parker. Talk about snooping around—'

Marigold felt a tap on her shoulder. A voice whispered in her ear.

'This is Ernest speaking. Tell Bertha I can hear every word she says.'

Closure

At the end of the Sunday service, Reverend Pontius Pottering watched his flock file out of the church. Today he had blessed the Witherington deceased, all by name, and had talked about Constable Ernest Barnstable and his contribution to the community and briefly mentioned Florence of the Mothers' Union, sadly missed in the pew near the back of the church. He had blessed Porkchop at Farmer Wormsley's request to help give closure to his wife's grief upon receiving him back home stuffed on a pedestal. He'd assured Farmer Wormsley that, yes, Porkchop would also be allowed into Heaven and was in a better place with angels and the Lord.

After everyone had gone, he saw a lone figure sitting in the second row pew with her head bowed. He thought at first it was someone praying until he heard a sob. Mrs Barnstable, Ernest's mother, dabbed at her eyes with a white handkerchief and blew her nose quietly. He sat down beside her and took her hand.

She said, 'I miss Ernest. I can feel him in the house. When the wind blows through the curtains I imagine he's come in to see me. But I can't see or touch him.'

Reverend Pottering felt her pain. If he hadn't been wearing his robes, if he'd been a friend, he would have embraced her and comforted her the way friends do. But all he could offer were words he'd learnt which were supposed to give comfort to the grieving, but were always inadequate.

He said, 'Ernest is watching over you. He was a good son, so be proud and rejoice in his life and not in his passing.'

'It's not easy,' she replied.

They sat together for a while discussing Ernest's police work, his achievements and his love of God and the family. She talked to him about his father and Lovey. After a while she put away her handkerchief and smiled.

'Thank you, I feel better now. I didn't have anyone else to talk to about this.'

'You're welcome to come and talk to me at any time. How about if we continue our conversation in the Bull and Bullocks? I could offer you a gin and tonic perhaps? They call it mothers' ruin but I think it might give you a lift.'

She laughed. 'I thought you said the pub was the devil's lair where drunkards abide?'

'Well it is but quite a few of my flock are in there and I think we should join them.'

'Is it your intention to save their souls?'

'Good heavens no. I'm off duty and not averse to a tipple of sherry or port now and then.'

She said, 'Ernest used to bring out a bottle of port on special occasions like Christmas or my birthday.'

'Then let's go and have a drink to celebrate the life of your loving son. Just give me time to change. I can't go into the pub looking like this.'

Mrs Barnstable raised her eyebrows and with a twinkle in her eyes said, 'Who would ever think of you getting up to mischief once you're off duty.'

'Behind my robes, I'm just like everyone else.'

'Perhaps not everyone.'

'Most people.'

'Yes, there are many good people in Witherington. The church was full at Ernest's funeral.'

'Indeed it was. You have to reach out to those people and share your grief. But not for too long. You have to come to terms with it.'

'I'll give it a go.'

Reverend Pottering retreated into a back room and emerged five minutes later looking younger in jeans and white shirt. He bowed slightly and with the flat of his hand indicated the door.

He said, 'Let's go to the devil's lair. Perhaps we could have two glasses each of port. One glass to toast Ernest and other to celebrate your past birthday.'

She laughed again. 'Are you trying to lead me off the right path into the dark wood?'

It was his turn to laugh.

'I see you're conversant with Dante Alighieri's *Divine Comedy*.'

'Sort of. I haven't read it all yet. Ernest bought it for me last Christmas. I've read *Paradise* which I liked but I gave *Hell* a miss. And I'm just starting on *Purgatory*.

Acknowledgements

Several people gave up their precious time to give feedback during the preparation of this book and thanks are due to Stella Spargo, Nicola Dado', Stephanie Lopez, the amazing Josephine Gonzalez, Lynne Polidori, Di Harris and Kathryn Alessandrini. My whole family deserve a special mention for their moral support. I'd also like to thank the professionals – proofreader Helen Baggott and cover designer/formatter Jane Dixon-Smith.

About the Author

Sienna Riddle was brought up in Yorkshire in the 1950's under strict parental control and censorship. Thanks to this, she sailed through childhood blissfully unaware that her parents, the community and national authorities were preparing for an impending nuclear attack while she was in the school library reading fairytales. It was probably this monumental charade that inspired some of *Seven Months of Unruly Sinners*.

Sienna put pen to paper at an early age, fuelled by a love of adventure books and an interest in pirates, secret passages, graveyards and courageous intrepid explorers on camels.

At the end of the 1960s, after uninteresting white-collar jobs, she hitch-hiked to Spain on the £50 government currency limit and worked in a pub cooking eggs and fries for the tourists until the money ran out. On the way, she sang in a nightclub in Paris and danced flamenco (after a crash course at a night school in London).

Sienna married, had two children, moved to Italy with the family and worked for United Nations agencies. Her job in Rome took her to Iraq, Cyprus, Jordan and North Korea. She sings well in English and Italian and rather badly in North Korean.

Website: www.siennariddle.com
Twitter: @siennariddle1

Made in the USA
Middletown, DE
09 November 2019

78304168R00274